Blood Creek

Mingo Chronicles: Book One

Kimberly Collins

Blue Mingo Press

Copyright © 2019 Kimberly Collins. All rights reserved. No part of this book may be reproduced, stored in a retrieval system or transmitted in any form or by any means without the prior written consent of the publishers, except by a reviewer who may quote brief passages in a review to be printed in a newspaper, magazine, blog, or journal.

Requests for permission should be sent to the author.
Kimberly Collins
www.bluemingopress.com

This is a work of fiction. Names, characters, businesses, places, events, and incidents are either the products of the author's imagination or used in a fictitious manner. Any resemblance to actual persons, living or dead, or actual events is coincidental.

PUBLISHED BY BLUE MINGO PRESS

ISBNs
Print: 978-0-9904208-2-8
Digital: 978-0-9904208-3-5

We will kill for each other, if we must.

Bone to bone, dust to dust.

For Katherine (missing you every day)

Teensy ♥ Taffy

Author's Note

Blood Creek and other books of Mingo Chronicles are works of historical fiction inspired by the southern West Virginia mine wars. Given the historical significance of these events, I have depicted them as accurately as possible, while still weaving my characters and their lives throughout. I took the details of these events from various sources, including West Virginia historical documents and newspaper and magazine articles.

I hope to break through today's stereotypes and shine a more accurate light on the people of Appalachia and the coal miners—their grit, determination, and fighting spirit.

Coal has been given a dirty name, but I would like for you to take a step back from what coal is today and see it through the eyes of the 1912 coal miner. Our nation's industry was ignited by coal. It provided electricity, forged steel, and powered ships. Coal was king, and every greedy man in the land wanted a piece of the pie. And they were willing to kill for it, enslave the workers to extract it, and lie about their dirty deeds. Greed ran from Wall Street through Washington, D.C., and down into the West Virginia coal fields. The battle was fought hard all the way down the line. But at the end of that line—in the hollers of Appalachia—is where the battle became a matter of life and death.

Make no mistake: there was greed on both sides of the battle line. When the stakes are high, people want control, money, fame, and prestige.

Regardless of your stance on coal or organized labor, this story is about the workers. The people. Appalachia. It is a story about a place—remote, beautiful, wild, wonderful, and full of extractable minerals. It is a story about people who were robbed of their land, their constitutional rights, their liberty, their freedom, and their dignity. The coal miners of the early 1900s—and their fight for a better, safer working environment and a living wage—were very real. We should all be thankful for their valiant pursuit of the workers' rights we take for granted today.

The real events

The major events depicted and listed here are real:
- Tom and Ellie's relationship
- The Bull Moose Special
- The Bullpen
- Prison Riot
- Evictions
- Gatling Gun
- Mother Jones's speech (excerpts from her speech in Charleston, 15 August 1912)
- The tent colony at Holly Grove
- Martial Law

The main characters and the real deal

As with any work of historical fiction, some of the characters are real people who are central to the story and the events depicted. Others are creations of my imagination.

<u>Ellie Chafin</u>

Ellie was a real person; however, the details I was able to gather on her were scant. She was married to Tom Chafin, and the events between the two of them depicted here are 99 percent the real story. My one diversion is that Ellie and Tom had one child, a boy. (My story does not include a boy.) From all accounts, Ellie was a stunning, raven-haired beauty who could talk any man into giving her anything. I have taken a few liberties with her story. Starting in Part II of *Blood Creek*, Ellie's story is complete fiction. Don't worry: she returns to her real story (mostly) in the next installment of Mingo Chronicles: *The Massacre*.

<u>Tom Chafin</u>

All events depicted about Tom are real and taken from family history as relayed to me by Tom's grandsons, Tommy Copley, Alvin Harmon, and Sam Harmon, and Tom's great-grandson, Thomas Copley (Tommy's son). Tom was the nephew of Devil Anse and Vicey Hatfield. Devil Anse gave him the moniker, Black Dog. Tom is fondly remembered as Poppy Tom and, from what I have heard, was quite a man. He was kind, generous, and wise. And he really did make some of the best moonshine this side of heaven.

Side notes:
1. Alvin and Thomas are my brothers-in-law (my sisters married cousins)—even though Alvin and my sister divorced years ago, Alvin will always be my brother.
2. The cover photo is one I took of my niece, Natalie Harmon Caple-Shaw, in the Tug River. Natalie is Alvin's daughter and Tom's great-granddaughter.

<u>Walter Musick</u>

He was the police chief of Matewan. The events depicted in *Blood Creek* are as close to the real story as possible.

Remine Hoskins
He was the mayor of Matewan. The events depicted in *Blood Creek* are as close to the real story as possible.

> *Side note:*
> There is some debate over who was Ellie's lover—the police chief or the mayor. For the sake of the story, the police chief made a better character. Also, the majority of historical data and newspaper accounts of the events indicate the police chief.

Deannie
She is fictional and named after my mother.

Polly and Jolene
They are fictional and inspired by my mother, her sisters, and pretty much all the warrior women of the Dingess clan.

Jake, Deacon, and Sammy
Unfortunately, they are all fictional, but they are inspired by a few men I'd like to fall in love with. Can we combine them all into one?

Aunt Ella
She was my mother's aunt. She moved to San Antonio as a young woman as a result of the family not liking her "witchy" ways. The family history is that she had a crystal ball and read tarot cards. The real Ella did not run off to San Antonio until the early '50s. For the sake of the story, I have her moving much earlier.

Granny Cline
She is kind of real, but mostly inspired by my mother's grandmother.

John Havers
He is fictional and not even inspired by anyone I know—I don't hang out with men like John Havers.

The Baldwin-Felts Detective Agency
They were real and played a pivotal role in the early years of the coal industry and the labor union. They were paid by the coal operators to enforce public law.

Tom Felts
He was the "Felts" of the Baldwin-Felts Detective Agency.

Tony Gaujot
Tony was Tom Felts's right-hand man.

Quinn Morton
Although a minor character, it is worth nothing that he was a coal baron in Kanawha County and played a significant part in the Paint Creek/Cabin Creek strike and promoted the violence.

Cesco Estepp
Although appearing in only one scene, it is worth noting that Cesco was a real person who died an unnecessary death at the hands of Baldwin-Felts and Quinn Morton.

The Baldwin-Felts Ladies
They are all creations of my imagination.

Mother Jones
Mary Harris Jones was very real and very instrumental in the early days of the United Mine Workers of America. She was referred to as the "Miners' Angel" and was a prominent organized labor representative and activist. She was pivotal in the miners' war; therefore, I have included her in the story, but not as a main character. I feared her presence would overwhelm the other characters—much as she did in real life. All events depicted with her are taken from real events—I wrapped my characters around her scenes as reasonably as possible. In her own words "I'm not a humanitarian, I'm a hell-raiser." If so, then may we all be hellraisers!

The Hotel Ruffner
It was a grand hotel in Charleston built in 1885. The hotel was demolished in 1970 and replaced with a parking lot. Ahhh . . . progress.

The Holly Grove Tent Colony
A real tent colony with thousands of families living like refugees. The living conditions and disease depicted were very real and probably thousands of times worse than I have created on the page.

Happy Reading,

—KC

Part 1

We will kill for each other, if we must.

Bone to bone, dust to dust.

1.

Late March 1911 (Matewan)

The rain pattered as soft as kitten paws against the tin roof. Tom was working a twelve-hour shift at the mine and wouldn't be home until morning. That would give her and Walter plenty of time to have their fun. She brushed her hair, changed into her worn blue dress—Walter's favorite—and waited.

Her heart beat a little faster as she thought of him—his hands wrapped in her long black hair, pulling her head back before he kissed her. His breath with the faint smell of whiskey whispering on her skin. His yearning for her consuming them both.

Ellie knew it was wrong. His wife was her friend. Her husband, a jealous man. Even violent. Ellie didn't care about any of that. She wanted Walter. He set her on fire as no other man had ever done. And she had enjoyed her share of men. Many before she'd married Tom—and a few since.

Ellie heard the wagon wheels bouncing in the darkness as Walter approached the house to stop in for a taste of her before he made his rounds for the night. She ran to the door and opened it as he stepped up on the porch. Ellie admired Walter's stark silhouette against the night sky. He came in and kissed her hard, cool rain dripping from his hat onto her warm face. He undressed her and carried her to Tom's bed, leaving her blue dress in a puddle on the floor.

Walter removed his clothes and crawled under the quilts with Ellie. "You're one hell of a woman, Ellie. I've thought of nothin' but you all day." He pulled her close and kissed her.

She pulled back and held his face in her hands. "When can we be together? Really together?"

"Soon."

"It's just a matter of time a'fore Mary and Tom figure out what's goin'on. I'm more worried 'bout Tom findin' out 'bout us than Mary."

"Why? You think I'm scared of him and his damn temper?"

"No, it's just that . . ."

"What? 'Cause he's the nephew of Devil Anse? I told you, them Hatfields don't scare me, Ellie. I love you and nothin'll keep us apart." Walter rolled over onto his back. "Why you with Tom anyway?"

"Mostly, he's just a way out of my mama's house and her anger and yellin'. He's older and kind . . . and a safe place to be."

Ellie wasn't sure she had ever really been in love with Tom—he certainly wasn't the kind of man she needed any longer or wanted for that matter. She was only seventeen when they married five years earlier. She had been happy with Tom when they first got married, but the relationship had slowly deteriorated. He rarely even shared her bed anymore. Hell, they barely spoke these days. Leaving him was the obvious solution, but it wasn't that easy for a woman to divorce her husband for no better reason than she's just unhappy. Ellie only knew one woman who had divorced her husband, and the entire county had shunned her. If she did divorce Tom, they would have to leave West Virginia.

Ellie shifted to face Walter. "I wanna be with you. Why can't we up and leave? We could go out west. We could go anywhere."

"Baby, I'm the police chief of Matewan. I can't be runnin' off. We need to give it a little bit more time and sort it out. Besides, right now I just wanna make love to you."

Walter got dressed, put on his badge, and strapped his gun on his hip. He kissed Ellie goodbye and stepped outside. The rain picked up as his wagon rattled down the dark holler, a muddy path he knew well.

Ellie was worth any risk he was taking. He was pretty certain Mary had no clue where he went most every night before he started his rounds. She had no clue about most things. Mary's dishwater hair and watery blue eyes were no match for Ellie's dark beauty. Those black eyes could cut through anyone—man or woman. Besides, Mary rarely wanted him in her bed anymore, and if she did, it was a wifely duty. She played dead most of the time and made him feel he was taking something he had no right to. She was a good woman, but her bed was wrapped in a lingering coldness, and he'd grown weary of it.

But Ellie—Ellie was every man's dream. That woman made a man feel alive. She had a way of driving him out of his mind with a simple kiss. He was taking a chance fooling around with Tom Chafin's wife, but he didn't care. As the chief of police, Walter doubted even Tom Chafin wanted to mess with him. He wanted to be with Ellie, and nothing was going to stand in his way.

Ellie wrapped her thin robe around her warm, naked body and turned out the lamp in the kitchen window. She tiptoed across the cold floor back to the bedroom. She closed the door, thinking she could somehow keep their love hovering between the four walls. Walter had stoked the fire before he left, and it now burned brightly in the tiny room. She stood by the hearth, warming her hands and feet. The flames from the candles flickered and danced in the darkness, casting shadows on the ceiling. The bed was now a tangled mess of quilts from the few stolen moments she and Walter had enjoyed. She blew out the candles and crawled under the heap. His smell lingered on her pillow, her skin, her hair. She had fallen in love with him.

You can't help who you love, can you?

Ellie couldn't. This thing between them was a force she couldn't resist.

She would leave Tom. She had to. He was too jealous. She'd been unfaithful to Tom from the beginning. That was just the way it was. It was just the way *she* was. She realized early in life she could have any man she wanted. So why remain with someone she didn't love or desire. Yes, it was time to leave Tom.

2.

The shift was over, and the last load of workers made its way to the surface. Bessie and Mable, the mules, pulled the team in the bucket along the rails up to the face of the mine and fresh air. Tom Chafin was on the last load. He was covered in black dust from crawling around in muck all night extracting as much coal as one man could. He hated working this new section. His back ached, his knees ached, he was cold and hungry. The coal was too low—fifty-three inches at its lowest and eighty-two at its highest. The mine operators didn't care how low the seam of coal was or the dangers the men faced every day; they were concerned only about getting every last black rock out of that mountain.

Tom's lungs felt heavy with coal dust. Most of the men who'd been working in the mines for years coughed and hacked their way through every shift. They'd stop and spit up black liquid every few minutes. The black lung had crippled or killed more hard-working men than Tom could count.

For Tom, the night shift was proving to be more of a personal problem than a sleep problem. The thought of Ellie spending her evenings with another man tortured him. Walter

Musick, the Matewan Police Chief, was the current affair. There had been many others, starting less than a year after they'd wed. This one was different. Ellie was different. She barely tried to hide the fact she was sleeping with Musick.

Carrying his pick and lunch bucket, Tom shuffled along with the other miners to check out at the office, which was little more than a shack with a coal stove and coffee. Not good coffee, but hot. A few yards beyond the office was his ride home—an old logging wagon converted to haul people instead of timber. Its worn, muddy benches on either side were packed tightly with weary miners. The wagon rattled away from the mine and dropped off most of its passengers in the mining camp right outside the gates. Then it continued down the road toward Red Jacket and on into Matewan.

Tom was one of a few miners who didn't live in the mining camp. He and Ellie lived on land his family had owned for as long as Tom could remember. He'd work for the sons of bitches, but he'd be damned if he would live in one of the shacks they called houses.

The men were dirty and tired. Their faces black from coal dust, only the whites of their eyes showing clearly. Some of them weren't even men yet. The Johnson boys were only fourteen and fifteen. The younger kids—those under twelve—were mostly breaker boys who separated the impurities out of the coal. Even that work was a man's work, not fit for a kid. Most of them had to work to keep food on the table at home. If their daddy was hurt and couldn't work, they had no choice. The youngest boy on the wagon, eleven, worked one day inside the mines, and his mama threw a fit; they pulled him out. Shame for the fella—the others made fun of him, called him a "little mama's boy." Tom figured the kid would live with that for a long time. Working underground, crawling around in low coal for twelve to fourteen hours a day wasn't for the faint of heart. It took a real man to return to the mines day after day, year after year, eking out a living digging into the pits of hell to bring out a lump of coal.

Mutterings of a strike had been going around for some time. Tom tried not to get too involved in the politics of it. It was a job, pretty much like any other. He'd worked for his uncle Devil Anse in the timbering business most of his life. The past few years had been rough; everybody and his brother was trying to get in on the lucrative timber trade, and the onslaught flooded the market. Then demand dried up. That's when he decided to get a job in the coal mines, which were booming. The timber business was starting to come back, and he hoped to return to it before year's end. He liked working outside in the daylight. Crawling around on his hands and knees in the dark was no way for a man to spend his life.

Winter had held onto most of her misery for the end of March. The cold rain fell hard, and spring looked like she might never show up. The mountains were barren and bleak rising on either side of the narrow road. The wagon jerked to a stop. One of the men had fallen asleep and bumped his head on the hard wagon floor. "Damn, Bobby, you'd think you'd know how to handle this thing by now!"

Bobby yelled back with a few expletives, and Tom jumped off the wagon, his boots sinking two inches in the thick mud.

Through the steady rain, Tom walked up the holler to his house, and Ellie. It was almost morning. The sky was still dark, and the road darker. The mountains loomed even higher here. The trees covered the well-worn path, their barren branches providing a momentary shelter from the rain. Ellie was still sleeping in the dark, quiet cabin. In the beginning, she was up early cooking breakfast and being a wife. Now? She slept in most every morning. Breakfast was something he typically cooked for himself. She used to sit on the porch in the warm months and play her mandolin and sing for him. He supposed she played and sang for that bastard Musick now.

Tom grabbed the bucket off the porch and headed to the well at the side of the house. Back on the porch, he sat on the steps and removed his boots. Daylight streaked the morning sky and highlighted the tracks where Musick's wagon had been and the pile of manure his horse had deposited in the yard.

Tom stripped down and shook out his work clothes. He hung them on the back of a chair, where he would pull them on again before returning to the mine that evening. Using the soap he'd left there yesterday, he washed himself. Ellie used to like to wash him when he came home from work. She said she liked the way his muscles moved under his skin. The way his body responded to her touch. The way he towered over her and completely enveloped her in his arms. That was another lifetime and two different people. A different Ellie.

Chilled and naked, Tom entered the cabin. The inside was dark and not much warmer than outside. He placed several logs and some kindling in the fireplace and lit a match. The dancing flames warmed the small room. The rain picked up again and pelted the tin roof. He slid into a pair of long johns he saved for sleeping and took a bottle of whiskey and a cup from the cupboard. He poured himself a shot. Then another. And another.

The thought of Ellie, his beautiful Ellie, with Walter Musick made him sick to his stomach. Then it turned to an all-consuming rage. He hated her for what she was doing to him. What she had been doing from the beginning. He was the laughing stock of the whole damn county. He hated her, and he loved her. Damn it, he wanted her. He wanted to walk right into that bedroom and take her. She was his. But he knew Musick had been there. In his bed. With his wife. He could smell the bastard and his cheap-ass cigars. He didn't go into the bedroom for fear of breaking his beautiful Ellie's lovely, elegant neck. Yeah, if he went in there, he would break her fucking neck. So, he would stay seated at the kitchen table and have another shot of whiskey. Then he would make breakfast, eat, and crawl into the loft and sleep . . . as he did every morning.

Tom knew this would come to an ugly end.

3.

20 April 1911

Ellie struggled with the basket of wet laundry and made her way out to the side of the cabin. Early April had brought nothing but rain. It seemed as if spring had gotten washed away or lost on its way to the mountains. With May only a few weeks away, Spring had finally peeked down over the mountain tops, bringing sunshine, crocuses, birds, and bunnies. The stench of smoke and coal had lingered on her dresses all winter from drying by the fireplace. Ellie longed for the crisp smell of sunshine on her clothes and linens. She had risen early to do the wash and get everything hung on the line so there would be plenty of time to dry before the sun went down. A new beginning floated in on the crisp breeze.

Ellie hummed an old Irish song her Granny Cline had taught her. She released the pole holding up the clothesline and sorted through the basket of wet laundry. When she picked up the dress that was Walter's favorite, she instinctively reached for her belly.

She couldn't wait to tell him she was pregnant. He would surely leave Mary when he found out his baby was growing inside her. As best she could estimate, she was about three months along.

She had pinned the last of Tom's things when she heard a wagon and someone calling her name. She peeked through the clothes. Walter's wife was making her way up the holler.

"Mary? What brings you out this way so early?" Ellie asked.

Mary stopped the wagon. "I'm sorry to drop in on ye like this. I needed to talk for a spell. And since we been friends since school, I thought you'd be 'bout the best person I could talk to."

"Is ever'thang all right? You look mighty pale. Come on down from that wagon and sit a spell."

Mary got down off the wagon and sat on the porch steps. "Oh, Ellie. Ever'thang's a mess." She removed her bonnet and smoothed down her unruly hair. "I think Walter may be cheatin' on me. I ain't sure, and I ain't got no proof or even an idea who it might be, but ... a woman knows. A wife knows when her man's messin' 'round."

"Why you think he's cheatin'?" Ellie continued to hang up the remaining items—her own undergarments—taking her time to keep her shaking hands busy.

"Well, like I said, I ain't got no proof, other than he leaves earlier and earlier for his evenin' rounds. He seems distant and cold. Not like his self, I s'pose."

"Well, bein' the police chief's prob'ly a job that keeps his mind occupied, don't ya think? It prob'ly ain't nothin'." Ellie stared hard at the wet clothes stirring in the breeze.

"Oh, Ellie, you know how men are. They can't seem to keep it in their britches. Always lookin' for somethin' new. Somethin' differ'nt."

Ellie adjusted the linens and straightened out a few items on the line, including her worn blue dress. "Well, that's right. Men cheat. All of 'em. What're we s'posed to do? I guess we just gotta accept it."

"That's all well and good, but they's more to it." Mary placed her hands on her stomach. "I'm pregnant, Ellie."

Ellie swung around and looked Mary square in the eye. "You sure? How far along?"

"I'm thinkin' a little more than three months."

Ellie was certain she was hearing wrong or Mary had no clue when her last flow was. Ellie had been seeing Walter since right after Thanksgiving, and he had sworn to her he hadn't touched Mary since right after their first time together.

That lousy, lyin' son of a bitch.

Ellie left the clothesline and walked toward the porch. She sat down on the top step beside Mary. "I can't believe he'd cheat on you. And you pregnant! Have you told him?"

"No. Not yet. I'm gonna tell him soon, though. Do you think I should confront him 'bout the other woman when I tell him?"

Ellie wanted to tell him about her baby first. She needed to calm Mary down. "No, Mary. Let's think 'bout this a'fore you go doin' somethin' that completely runs him off. Men are strange creatures, and you need to treat 'em as such." Ellie took Mary by the shoulders and turned her so they were face to face. "If you go askin' him 'bout this other woman and tell him you're with child you might run him straight to her— 'specially if he cares for this other woman."

Mary began to cry. "Do you really think he loves her?"

Ellie reinforced her grip on Mary's shoulders and gave her a little shake. "Look at me, Mary. Look at me! Stop cryin' and pull yourself together. Men are all sons of bitches. Ever' last damn one of 'em, so don't go thinkin' your'n is somethin' special. He can do one of two things—he'll act like all is well and then keep cheatin' on you while you're at home takin' care of his baby, or he'll leave you and your baby high and dry for this other woman."

"What am I s'posed to do?"

"First, we need to find out who this other woman is and then deal with her. Once she knows you're with child, she'll prob'ly break it off with him. Then you and him can start over."

"You really think so? You think that'll work?"

"I do. I really do."

Mary laid her head on Ellie's shoulder and cried for a good ten minutes.

4.

23 April 1911

Ellie slid into a dark place after Mary's visit. It had been three days, and Ellie wouldn't see Walter until Tuesday night. Tom had left early to help his brother repair his barn. A bad storm had knocked a tree onto the roof the previous night, and he needed to fix it quickly before the rain returned. After Tom left she had tried to sleep, but sleep wouldn't come. She tossed and turned for over an hour; around ten, she decided to get up and bathe. She pulled the tub in front of the fireplace and started a fire. She took the water pail and headed to the well.

Five buckets later, she sat at the edge of the porch to rest. The sun peeked over the mountain and warmed her face. The yard was full of birds. She spotted two robins chasing each other in and out of the dogwood trees. She rubbed her stomach and thought about the little life growing inside her. Would she be happy with Walter and a baby? She loved him something fierce and knew they could make this work somehow.

She picked up the pail and started inside. A sparrow swooped past her head and into the cabin. She dropped the pail, and water splashed onto the wood floor. "You little bastard. Get out of here." Ellie grabbed the broom and chased the bird around the room, trying to shoo it out the door. "Go! Get out of here." The bird flew up to the loft and slipped into a corner. "Damn you! You gotta come outa there sometime. And I'll be waitin' right here with this broom."

She warmed the last of the water and dumped it into the tub, never taking her eyes off the loft for too long. She pinned up her hair and slipped off her dress and underthings. She slid into the water and closed her eyes. Her eyes flew open when she remembered the omen her Granny Cline had told them—anytime a bird flies into your house, it's an omen of death.

After her bath, Ellie dried herself in front of the fading fire and got dressed. She grabbed her broom and started toward the loft and the sparrow when she heard a soft knock at the door.

"Mary? What're you doin' here on a Sunday mornin'? I'd a thought you'd be in church."

"I figured I'd skip church today. Sometimes I simply don't wanna go to church, Ellie. You don't go all too often, and it don't seem to have hurt you none. Besides, I couldn't bring myself to be around people today. I thought we could go to Matewan and enjoy this beautiful day. My brother's waitin' out at the road with the wagon. He said he'd take us. Please, Ellie. I need some time out of the house, and it's such a pretty day."

"Well, I s'pose that'd be a right nice way to spend the day. Let me get my bonnet and shawl." She turned to get her things, but an old, familiar tug in her gut told her not to go with Mary. It made her a little dizzy it was so unexpected. She had learned early in life, when she wanted to and if she focused on it, she could see people's motives and almost know what they were thinking. Her aunt Ella, whom she was named after, called it "The Knowing." Ellie, like her aunt, somehow knew what people wanted and when they were lying. Ellie had used this knowledge to manipulate and get her way most of her life.

The Knowing had been silent where Walter's lies were concerned. Why? What was different? Had she lost her ability to see into people's hearts? Or had she simply not wanted to see his lies?

Her Aunt Ella had told her The Knowing would only get stronger as she got older, but she had to pay attention to it. She had to nurture it. She told Ellie to sit still and let The Knowing speak to her; she couldn't go running headlong into a situation without listening first. She certainly hadn't stopped for one second to *listen* to Walter's reasons. She jumped blindly and never stopped long enough for The Knowing to rise within her. And the baby. Maybe the baby had everything all confused inside her.

She did think it quite odd for Mary to show up with her brother to take them to town. Maybe it was the bird hiding in the loft and the omen. Maybe being pregnant made her feel dizzy and outa sorts. She was bored and wanted to get out of the holler and enjoy the beautiful day, so she tied her bonnet and ignored The Knowing. Anything was better than wallowing in her gloom chasing a bird around the cabin.

Ellie and Mary walked out of the holler and climbed up on the wagon with Mary's brother.

"Ellie, how's Jolene doin'?" Mary asked. "I ain't seen her in a coon's age."

Ellie didn't really want to talk about her sister but figured it would be a better conversation than talking about Walter. "She's doin' fine, I s'pose. She's livin' up at Paint Creek."

"She and Deacon got any young'ns yet?"

"No. I know she wants to have whole bunch of kids, but not yet." Ellie said.

"I saw your cousin Polly last Sunday at church. She sure looks good. Shame 'bout her baby girl. That musta been real hard on her. I remember when we's little and you and Jolene would follow me and Polly 'round. We sure had some good times playin' together. I'm glad we're still friends, Ellie." Mary took Ellie's hand in hers.

"Me, too." Ellie felt a jolt when Mary took her hand. She wasn't sure if it was The Knowing or her own guilty conscience. She removed her hand from Mary's under the pretense of tightening her bonnet.

Mary's brother dropped them off at the train depot and continued to the feed store. Mary and Ellie window shopped at the dressmaker and the dry goods store. Ellie could no longer ignore that Mary was up to no good—she just wasn't sure what exactly she had planned. They chatted about the new styles shown in the local newspaper the day before. They caught up on the gossip. As they walked, Ellie realized they were heading toward the city jail. When they approached the jail, Mary took her arm and pulled her toward the building.

"Oh, no, Mary. I don't wanna go inside." The Knowing punched her gut again.

"Come on, Ellie. Just for a minute. Just to say hello."

Reluctantly, Ellie went along. Once inside, The Knowing screamed at her to listen and flee. She couldn't deny it now. She'd been set up. Mary's brother was there waiting for them.

"What the hell is this?" Ellie jerked her arm away from Mary's grasp.

"Deputy, I want this woman arrested for adultery with my husband and abusin' the sanctity of my home."

The deputy on duty stuffed his cheek full of tobacco and listened to Mary's demands. "Now, Mrs. Musick, we can't go 'round 'restin' ever' purdy woman in town for adultery. Ye got'ny proof?" The deputy leaned over and aimed his mouth at the spittoon on the floor beside his desk.

"What kinda proof you need?" Mary's brother asked.

"Well, first off, witnesses? A confession? Somethin'. Anythang'll do." He spit again.

Mary stepped up to the desk. "No, I ain't got no witnesses. *I* know it's true. *You* know it's true. You *all* know it's true." She pointed at the others who had gathered to watch the spectacle.

"Mary, why're you doin' this? What's wrong with you? Why're you lyin' on me like this?" Ellie quietly cursed her pregnancy emotions when the tears came. She was nervous and sad and felt betrayed on all sides.

"Now, Mrs. Chafin, try to calm down a bit. It ain't that bad." The deputy turned to Mary. "Mrs. Musick, you know we can't 'rest this lady 'cause you're jealous of her."

Mary's brother was leaning against the wall near the door. He stepped forward. "I'm a witness."

"You're a filthy liar's what you are!" Ellie was in shock. She barely knew him, and unless he had been hiding up on the ridge or under her bed, he had not witnessed anything.

The deputy spit once again. "What? Whad'ye say? A witness? You're tellin' me you witnessed this woman here in the act of adultery with Chief Musick?"

"Yep. I sure did." Mary's brother shuffled his feet and looked at Mary.

"Boy, you know what you're sayin'?"

"This is utter nonsense, and I won't stand here and be humiliated by these crazy people." Ellie's voice shook, more with fear than anger.

Mary placed her gloved hands on the desk and leaned over to be eye level with the deputy. "This woman is an adulterous whore, and you *will* arrest her for attemptin' to steal my husband and destroy my home. We's good, God-fearin' people, and the law's s'posed to protect people like us. Not women like that." She pointed back at Ellie.

Ellie couldn't believe Mary had out-smarted her. Why had she not listened to her gut? Normally, she would have seen this scheme from a mile away. Ellie's anger at Walter for lying to her had blinded her to Mary's cunning scheme. Well, it didn't matter. The deputy didn't believe Mary, and they couldn't arrest her simply because Mary wanted them to. "This is plain crazy talk, Mary, and nothin' else. You've obviously lost your mind. You *and* your crazy brother." Ellie pushed past Mary's brother and stormed out of the jail.

Ellie had made it to the edge of town when a deputy pulled up in a wagon and offered to take her home. She reckoned he was doing it only because he knew Walter would be furious with him when he found out they let her walk the five miles home. Without saying a word, she let him help her onto the wagon.

When they rounded the curve in North Matewan, the deputy stopped the wagon. "What we stoppin' for? You change your mind?" She started to climb down.

"No, ma'am. The Chief wanted me to wait here for him. He'll take you on home."

A few minutes later, Walter rounded the curve, and she got on the wagon with him. "What the hell's wrong with that crazy wife of your'n?"

"I'm sorry 'bout what happened. I had no idea what she'd been up to. She's been actin' crazy for a few days, but I didn't think she was capable of this."

"Well, I guess you don't know ever'thang. Has she told Tom?"

"I don't know. I don't know when she would'a. I'm sure word'll spread through town pretty darned fast after what she pulled today. I'm real sorry, Ellie. We'll sort this out. I promise."

They rode the rest of the way in silence. How could she tell him about the baby? The babies? Should she tell him about Mary's baby? Or let him figure it out on his own?

Walter brought the horses to a stop at the bottom of the road. The sun was sinking beyond the mountaintop. Tom would be home soon. She needed to tell Walter now that she was carrying his baby. Otherwise she might not get an opportunity before Mary got to him. This wasn't the way she wanted to tell him. She wanted to tell him after they had made love, when they had time to talk about it and decide what they would do.

"Walter, Mary's the least of our troubles." She held her bonnet in her hands and stared straight ahead. "I'm carryin' your baby. I'm 'bout three months along as far as I can tell." She looked over at him and waited for a response.

"A baby? Damn, Ellie." He wrapped and unwrapped the reins around his hands. "How you know it's mine and not Tom's?"

"Are you serious? You know that man ain't spent a night in my bed since a'fore Christmas. How can you even think somethin' like that?" Ellie was a great liar; it was the other side of The Knowing—she had learned early on how to lie by watching what others did that got them caught. Tom hadn't been in her bed since early February and only once in January. It didn't matter; she *knew* this baby belonged to Walter.

"It ... it's just I wanna make sure, that's all Ellie. You know I love you."

"Well, accusin' me of lyin' sure ain't no way to show your love." The tears came again, and she started to get down from the wagon. Walter grabbed her arm.

"Don't go. Not like this. I ain't accusin' you of nothin'. I don't wanna share you with that man—or any man, Ellie. If that baby *is* mine—and I believe it is—well, then we need to get on with this and sort out what we need to do."

"What's that mean? You're gonna leave Mary? Right away? A'fore I start showin' and the whole county starts talkin' 'bout me and callin' my baby a bastard? You sure seem to want to sort out a lot of things, but never get 'round to any of it."

"I'll go home and talk to Mary. Let her know she went too far today. You better get on in a'fore Tom gets home." Ellie turned to get down, and Walter took her hand. "Ellie, we should prob'ly not press our luck with this thing. Let's give this mess some time to die down. Tom'll more'n likely hear 'bout what Mary did to you today, and then he'll be lookin' for me to show up here. I'll be by in a week or so when things quiet down a bit."

"I ain't none too pleased 'bout not seein' you, but I guess you're right." Ellie got down off the wagon and started up the road to her house. She turned back toward him. "Walter Musick, don't you leave me sittin' here in this damn holler waitin' on you. You know I'll come to your house. I don't give a damn 'bout Mary or Tom. I'll come find you."

"Ellie, I do love you, and this'll all work out the way it's s'posed to. Trust me."

Walter left Ellie's and took his time getting home to Mary. He didn't know what to expect when he arrived. She was probably crying and would insist he break it off with Ellie. He wouldn't. He couldn't. Ellie was a consuming fire he couldn't extinguish. She was an obsession. An addiction. She was like opium, and he would never be able to escape her inviting embrace.

He needed to figure out what to do about Mary. Mary was a good woman. Divorcing her would destroy her. Running off with Ellie wasn't going to work. He was the chief of police and had a future here in county politics, and Mary and her family were part of that plan. Ellie's being with child sure complicated things. He'd have to stop sleeping with Mary. Last thing he needed was for her to be pregnant, too.

If he timed it right, he would get home before supper. He was hungry and hoped Mary had at least cooked her typical Sunday meal. She knew her duties as his wife and performed them well.

Their house was situated on the lower end of Matewan on Main Street. The place had belonged to Mary's grandparents, and when they passed away he and Mary moved in. The two-story, white house with its wraparound porch was the perfect home for the Matewan Chief of Police, an up-and-coming politician. The place commanded respect and set him apart from most of the townspeople. He had big plans for himself and needed to clean up this mess with Ellie and her baby. There had to be another way. An easier way.

Under the last rays of sunlight streaking through the April sky, he pulled the wagon around to the back of the house. He stepped through the back door and was surprised to not smell bread baking.

"Mary! Where ya at?"

"I'm in here."

Walter removed his gun belt and hat and laid them on the table. He continued through the kitchen into the room at the front of the house, which served as a parlor of sorts, where they received visitors and entertained. It was by far the largest room and the best decorated. Mary rarely sat in it. She was typically in the kitchen or her sewing room. "Why you in here? You expectin' comp'ny? And why ain't you cooked dinner?"

Mary looked up at him from her chair. "Have a seat, Walter."

He sat down in the chair opposite her. They sat facing each other in front of the large window that looked out on

Main Street. Mary had been crying. She looked worn and tired. Walter knew her well enough to know Mary probably felt guilty about what she had done with Ellie, and he felt bad for her. She'd overstepped her bounds, and he needed to tell her so.

"Walter, they's somethin' I need to tell you."

"Is it 'bout Ellie at the jail today? I know. You went too far, Mary."

"No. It ain't that. It's somethin' much more import'nt than *Ellie*. It's 'bout *us*." Mary sat straighter in her chair and wiped her eyes.

"Well, what is it?"

She took a deep breath. "We're gonna have a baby, Walter. I'm with child."

Walter leaned forward. Certainly, he was hearing things. How could she be with child too? "What?"

"Yes, you heard me correctly. I'm with child. I figure 'bout three months along."

"Now, Mary, if you think lyin' to me 'bout bein' with child's gonna make the stunt you pulled today go away, it ain't gonna work."

Mary sat forward in her chair. "Why would I *lie* to you 'bout a *baby*? Is that the kind of woman you think I am? You obviously have me confused with that tramp you've been cheatin' with."

"Calm down, Mary. Don't go gettin' all upset. If you're with child, you can't be screamin' and scarin' the little thing."

"*If* I'm with child? You are one sorry son of a bitch, Walter Musick." Mary got up and went upstairs to the bedroom and locked the door.

"Well, fuck." Walter sat for a long time looking out the window at Main Street.

5.

Tom finished up early at his brother's house. He stopped at his favorite fishing hole on the Tug. He preferred sitting alone on the sandy river bank and enjoying the sunny day to being cooped up in his own house with a woman who loved another man.

Thoughts of Ellie invaded even his favorite fishing hole. The first time he'd brought her fishing with him, the fish weren't biting. After an hour of not catching any fish, she got bored and slipped out of her dress and walked into the river. She looked over her shoulder with a smile, "You comin' in or not?" He stripped down and joined her. They'd spent the rest of the afternoon swimming and making love on the river bank.

He loved Ellie. Tom knew he was a good husband, and their marriage started out solid. Ellie sure wasn't shy in the bedroom, and they hadn't been able to get enough of each other. They'd planned their future together; they talked about having children, maybe moving out west. Six months in, Ellie changed overnight. Being ten years older, Tom wrote it off as her age. He'd decided to be patient with her. When she stopped wanting him to sleep in her bed, he had taken to sleeping in the loft. Soon after, she was distant and gone most days when he got home from work. Then the rumors started about her being with other men, mostly young boys her age.

He had heard about her reputation before they'd even met. He hadn't expected her to be a virgin when they got married; he didn't care about any of that. She was about the most beautiful thing he had ever laid his eyes on. He wanted to love her and care for her and make her happy. Tom realized now a woman like Ellie can't be happy—no matter what she has or who she's with. A woman like her will always reach for the thing just beyond her grasp. The current thing happened to be the chief of police.

Tom sat on the river bank for a few hours, torn about what to do. He was a laughing stock in his home town. Hell, even his own home. Divorce wasn't an option he liked; it appeared to be the only thing he could do. He didn't want to humiliate Ellie and have her branded an adulteress—a whore—but she hadn't left him with much of a choice. He couldn't go on like this.

Tom packed his fishing gear and the few fish he'd caught and headed home, uncertain of how well Ellie would receive his return. He approached the holler and led his horse up to the dark cabin, the sun having long disappeared behind the mountain. The blooming trees created a tunnel over the narrow path, blocking the last of the sky's light. If he didn't know better, he would think Ellie was gone. He knew she was there, in her bedroom, not caring whether he came home or not.

He carried in a bundle of firewood and started a fire. Ellie's sobs drifted from the bedroom. He knocked gently on the door. "Ellie, you a'right in there?"

"Go away, Tom. I'm fine."

"Why you cryin'?"

"Leave me be."

Tom made dinner for himself and crawled up into the loft. He figured Walter had ended things with Ellie. Other than that, she had no reason to be crying in her bed. She was hurting, and Walter had caused it. Serves her right. A whore gets what's coming to her eventually.

Ellie marked the day on her calendar—Sunday, April 23. She didn't expect to see Walter for another week, maybe two. She would give him two weeks. She'd be damned if she would sit and wait on any man to decide if he wanted her and her child. She assumed Mary had told him she was pregnant as well. Ellie was prepared to go into town and find him when the time came, just as he had come to her that first night a mere five months ago.

When Mary had insisted on introducing Ellie to her husband, Ellie had no idea what to expect, but she certainly didn't expect Walter. Ellie assumed Mary's husband would be like Mary—bland and boring. Ellie knew he was smitten with her from the instant she looked into his eyes. The Knowing had spoken loud and clear on that. Ellie should have listened to what else it had to say—before jumping into the current.

Two nights later, he showed up at her cabin, not a full hour since Tom had left for the coal mine. She didn't need to pretend to be surprised. She had known he would show up—eventually. There was no need for small talk, no need to explain why he was there—they both knew. They both wanted it. Each needing the other. Their lovemaking had been like a torrent of pleasure and pain washing away everything she had ever thought she wanted or needed in a man. It left her with a single focus—Walter Musick.

Ellie brushed her hair and let the tears flow. The bed in the loft creaked under Tom's weight as he settled in for the night. She hadn't set out to hurt him, but she certainly had never been in love with him. Over the years, what little bit of love she did have for him crawled away. Tom was a good man. A good provider and a hard worker. He loved her and would do anything for her. None of that mattered; the only man she wanted right now was Walter Musick, and she would have him at any cost.

6.

26 April 1911

Tom was up on the small ridge at the front of the holler clearing some trees when he saw them coming—Walter, Mayor Hoskins, and a couple of deputies. Knowing this wasn't a friendly visit, Tom stealthily made his way back to the cabin. He slipped inside and loaded his .45 Peacemaker and shotgun.

He walked outside to the well and washed his face and hands. "Why're you washin' up? You done with your chores already?" Ellie asked, hanging a shirt on the line.

"We's got comp'ny comin'. You's best get inside. This might not end well."

"Who? What're you talkin' 'bout, Tom?"

"Your lover's makin' his way up the road with the mayor and a couple of deputies. I s'pose they's comin' to arrest me. Or kill me."

Ellie stood looking at him. "Kill you? My *lover*? What on earth you talkin' 'bout?".

"Woman, I said you's best be gettin' inside. *Now!* This ain't no time to be playin' the fool. Best as I can tell, they's gonna be shots fired. Now get your ass in the house. I ain't tellin' ye again."

He was serious. She had never seen him like this. He was typically soft spoken and gentle with her. He was in fight mode and demanding she do what he said. She needed to move. *Now*! She grabbed the laundry basket and ran inside.

She dropped the wash and stood inside the door. Walter and Mayor Hoskins approached. Walter was in front. He was so handsome sitting high upon his horse. In charge. Confident and so cocksure of himself. That was what she found so captivating and irresistible. When she'd met Tom, she saw these same qualities in him. The years had changed him, and he wasn't so sure of himself anymore. Or was he?

Tom stood on the front porch with his arms down by his side—not moving and certainly not afraid. She hadn't really looked at him in so long she'd forgotten how big he was. Wasn't he afraid? Wasn't he concerned? He stood there, calm and certain. He had a mean look on his face, and his eyes were icy blue and deadly. This was the warrior blood boiling up—that thing Tom kept quietly tucked beneath the surface. This was the man Devil Anse called Black Dog. This was the man with the reputation Ellie had heard about but rarely saw—the man others feared.

"Tom, now we don't want no trouble." Walter said.

"Where's your deputies? You leave 'em at the mouth of the holler so they ain't no witnesses to what you're a-doin'?"

"I figured they wasn't no need for 'em to come up here." Walter dismounted. "We got a warrant for your arrest, Tom. Now you can come peacefully, or we can take you by force."

The mayor stayed in his saddle, looking like he might turn and run at any moment.

"A warrant? For what? You arrestin' me 'cause you been fuckin' my wife?" Tom never moved. "Seems to me you's the one oughta be arrested."

"Now, Tom, calm down," Mayor Hoskins said. "Walter's right. We don't want no trouble."

Walter dismounted his horse and approached the porch slowly as if trying to capture a wild dog. His hand hovered over the butt of his gun.

Tom never took his eyes off Walter. "Mayor Hoskins, I ain't sure how you got roped into this mess—unless you're one of my darlin' wife's many lovers, too. As far as I can see, you best be leavin' a'fore you get yourself hurt."

The mayor chuckled. He pulled out his tobacco and rolled a cigarette.

Walter took another step closer to the porch. "Tom, I got the warrant right here in my pocket." Walter patted a piece of paper in his shirt pocket. "Now come on down off the porch and put your hands where we can see 'em."

Ellie wondered what the warrant was for; Tom hadn't done anything wrong. Perhaps Walter had made up some crime to accuse Tom of so they could be together.

Walter moved closer toward Tom, uncertain of his next step—a crazy man hell bent on arresting Tom. Beads of sweat covered Walter's brow, and he suddenly looked small and insignificant—cowardly and scared.

Tom stood still. Solid as a mountain. Never wavering.

Sitting securely in his saddle, the mayor yelled, "Walter, we need to get this over with. Go on and get Chafin. Or kill him. We's wastin' time here." He continued to roll his cigarette.

Kill him? Ellie couldn't understand why they would want to kill Tom. She froze to her spot inside the door. Before Ellie could move and tell them to leave, Tom pulled his .45 and shot Walter twice in the chest.

Ellie had no idea Tom was even holding his gun in his hand, hidden in the fold of his pants. Everything happened in slow motion. The mayor dropped his half-rolled cigarette, sending tobacco flying across his horse's mane. He pulled his gun, and Tom fired again hitting the mayor in the chest. He tumbled from his horse and hit the ground a few feet from Walter.

Ellie ran to Walter's side. She heard herself screaming as though it was coming from the trees and not her own throat. She dropped down beside him. "Nooooo ... noooo ... wake up! Look at me, Walter! Walter? Walter Musick, don't you die on me, damn it. Look at me." She slapped his face. "Open ... open your eyes. Walter? Noooooo. No!"

Ellie cradled Walter's head in her lap, rocking back and forth. The tears skewed her vision, and Walter's face became a watercolor of blood, tears, and dirt. She leaned over and whispered, "Please wake up. Please. Don't die on me. Not like this. Please wake up."

A shadow covered Walter, and Ellie looked up to see Tom standing over them, with his gun still in his hand.

"Look what you've done. *Look what you've done*! You son of a bitch. You killed the only man I ever loved. He's dead!"

"I reckon you're right, Ellie. I killed the son of a bitch. Prob'ly Mayor Hoskins, too, and I got two bullets left."

"I guess you wanna shoot me, too? Tom, don't. I'm beggin' you, don't shoot me."

"What makes you think I wanna shoot you, Ellie?"

"I know you hate me. I know you do. Shootin' me won't change nothin', Tom."

"Well, it would save me from divorcin' your sorry ass, I s'pose. Might even bring me a little bit of satisfaction to watch you bleed to death here next to your married lover."

"Tom, please. I'm beggin' you. I know you hate me and want me dead, but I'm . . . I'm with child. Think 'bout this little baby livin' inside me. You don't want to murder an innocent babe, do you?"

"Well, ya don't say? A *baby*? You're carryin' the son of a bitch's baby? Well, if that ain't some shit, Ellie. Hmmm. How you know it ain't mine?"

He stood looking down at her with a mixture of disgust and pity on his face. He spat on the ground next to Walter's head. Ellie jerked to the side to avoid it hitting her in the face.

7.

Tom figured the deputies were waiting at the bottom of the road for their hero to come riding out victorious. It would be a matter of minutes before they started up the holler. He was sure they heard the shots ringing out and probably assumed it was him who had been on the receiving end. They were certainly in for a surprise when they found their hero and the mayor dead.

He grabbed his coat and put what food he could in an empty flour sack. He strapped his Peacemaker on his hip and slung his rifle over his shoulder. He put all the ammunition he had for both guns in the flour sack with the food and took off up the holler. He planned to cross the mountain, make his way down to Newtown to get a horse from his brother, and then high-tail it out of there to Devil Anse's house at Island Creek. He figured he'd be half-way up the mountain by the time the deputies figured out he was gone.

Tom didn't necessarily feel bad about killing Walter. Hell, he'd thought about killing him ever since he found out the son of a bitch was spending time in *his* bed with *his* wife. He did kinda regret shooting Mayor Hoskins. Why had the mayor gotten involved? Far as Tom could tell, Walter was too much of a coward to come alone. Tom couldn't stand a cowardly man, and he knew plenty of them.

The one thing that *did* piss him off was Ellie being pregnant with Musick's baby, and it probably was Musick's baby. Ellie had allowed Tom in her bed only a handful of times in the past few months. It didn't make him mad enough to shoot her, but he did want to snap her beautiful neck.

Whores. A man just can't trust 'em.

8.

Ellie's mother entered the tiny cabin and instantly sucked every drop of air out of the place. Ellie stayed on her bed, not moving. Her mother stood over her, and Ellie's brother, Franky, stood in the doorway.

"Well, this is just one more ugly mess you've made, Ella! What the hell's wrong with you, girl? Sleepin' with a married man? Your friend's husband? How dare you? You're a disgrace a'fore God almighty. I'm ashamed to call you my child. You've managed to ruin a lot of lives today."

The deputies had finally given up trying to get Ellie to tell them where Tom had gone. She simply didn't know. Nor did she care. To hell, she hoped. They stayed with her until her mother and brother arrived.

Ellie remained curled up on her side and sank as far into the bed as she could. She barely breathed and didn't dare move to look at her mother's face. She stared at the floor. Her mother's dusty shoes peeked out from under her black dress. The dress looked as though it hadn't been washed in a good two months, and if Ellie knew her mother, it hadn't.

She had been wearing her widow's uniform for the past six years—ever since Ellie's daddy had been killed in a poker game gone bad. He was at the Blue Goose Saloon playing cards, and Danny Hamby caught him cheating. They had words. Danny pulled his pistol and shot her daddy in the face. Her father had been drunk on moonshine or Danny would never have gotten a shot off. That day, Ellie's whole world had tipped upside down.

She had been her father's favorite, and her mother hated her for it because her mother hated her father. For as long as Ellie could remember, her mother was a bitter old hag. When Ellie's father died, she actually became even nastier and dumped her anger out at the world—mostly her children—under the guise of religion and doing God's will. As the oldest and their father's favorite, Ellie took the brunt of their mother's rage. Ellie tried to protect Jolene and Franky and stood up to their crazy mother more often than not. But not today. Ellie didn't have the strength to withstand her mother's judgment and rage.

Franky shifted nervously at the door. Ellie was certain he wanted to bolt, but he knew he'd face their mother's wrath if he did.

"What've you got to say for yourself, Ella? You need to fall to your knees and beg God to forgive you. *You* are a whore, and the likes of you will go straight to hell." Her mother paced the tiny room.

The temperature was suddenly unbearable for Ellie, and her stomach roiled. The baby. She had forgotten about the baby. She did pray at that moment. Prayed her mother didn't know.

"What kinda girl did I raise? You weren't raised to be like this, Ella. You were raised to be a good, God-fearin' woman. Instead you chose the ways of Satan. Tom's a good man. Too good for the likes of you."

Despite the increased temperature in the room, Ellie pulled the quilt tighter to shield her from her mother's anger. When they were little, she, Franky, and Jolene would hide in the woodshed or under the bed; usually they ran to the river bank. Anything to get away from the hateful woman they called Mommy.

Her mother moved to the side of the bed. Leaning over, she grabbed Ellie's face, forcing her to look at her. The old woman's calloused hands cut into Ellie's soft skin. "Look at me, you whore. *Look* at me!" She jerked Ellie's head toward her.

Ellie met her mother's black eyes. The lines on her face had gotten deeper the past two years, and her mouth still held its perpetual frown. Her dull gray hair was pulled back into its usual tight knot. She wasn't as heavy as Ellie remembered. But still as big and as scary. She was taller than Ellie and still stronger in every way. She scared Ellie with her judgment, her anger, and her hatred.

"Look at you. You got that man's blood on your face and hands. Your clothes are soaked in his innocent blood. Girl, *you* killed those men today as sure as if you had pulled the trigger yourself. And don't you ever forget it. I'm done with you, Ella. Done." She held Ellie's jaw tight. "Don't ever darken my door again. Don't speak my name. When people ask whose child you are, don't convict me of that crime. May God forgive me for bringin' you into this world." She released Ellie's face, pushed her back, and stomped out of the cabin.

Franky quickly gave Ellie a kiss on the cheek. "I love you, Ellie. I'll be back as soon as I can." He ran after his mother.

They were barely out of sight when Ellie ran outside and threw up over the edge of the porch. Her mother still had the power to shake her and scare the hell out of her. She threw up two more times. Leaning back against the post, she wiped her mouth on her sleeve and pushed her hair out of her face. She looked at the place where Walter's body had fallen. His blood had soaked into the ground and left a stain. Only hours ago, his last breath was taken twenty feet from her front door.

Ellie looked at her hands. Her mother was right; she had blood all over them, her dress, her face. She drew a bucket of water from the well and used Tom's soap to wash the red away. The old hymn flooded into her mind. *"What can wash away my sin? ... nothing but the blood of Jesus."* Maybe God *had* cursed her. Maybe even the blood of Jesus couldn't wash away her sins.

No, she was innocent in this. Tom did this. *Not her.* She stripped her dress off and threw it into the yard. She would burn it later.

At dusk, Tom devised a makeshift bed in the mouth of a cave on the downward slope of the mountain and braced himself against the chill of the night air. He would get up before daylight and get the hell out of Mingo County.

He made himself as comfortable as he could. He made a small fire and ate a little of the food from his flour sack. He needed to get to Devil Anse and figure out his next move. Devil Anse Hatfield had been more than an uncle to him. He had raised Tom from the time he was eight years old. He loved the old man. Even before the feud, Devil Anse had a reputation of being a mean man, and he could be if you crossed him. To Tom, his uncle was a gentle but firm man. He loved his family, and he would go to any measure to protect them.

Tom thought of his own father, dead these past two years. Simply too poor to raise Tom themselves, his parents had sent him to live with Anse and Vicey. At first, Tom felt betrayed by the only people he loved. The day Anse sent for Tom, he entered his uncle's house feeling shame and resentment. It didn't take long for him to realize he had gotten the better deal. Anse and Vicey treated him as their own. He had a warm bed and plenty of food. They expected him to work hard, and he did. Anse quickly made him his messenger and sent him out daily to his men. The feud hadn't been over all that long, and some people were still after his head. Anse kept guards on and around the property to protect his family and keep any poachers away from his timbering business.

Anse taught Tom how to make the best moonshine this side of heaven. Smooth and clear. Tom was pissed he had to leave his still. His brothers would go dismantle it as soon as it was safe to do so.

He drifted off to sleep as the last flames of his fire flickered out.

Ellie was alone and afraid. Afraid Walter's or the mayor's family would come after her. Or Mary and her crazy-ass brother. Even before the sun disappeared behind the mountain, she bolted the door to the cabin and loaded the two guns Tom had left behind. She started a fire in the bedroom fireplace and decided to leave the lanterns lit for as long as they would burn. She tucked the pistol under her pillow and placed the shotgun beside her under the quilt. For once, she was glad Tom hadn't put a window in the bedroom as she had wanted.

A shotgun blast went off in her head and she awoke with a start in the wee hours of the morning. She felt for her guns and listened. Nothing. Quietness. It must have been a dream. She wanted it all to be a dream. She lay there in the stillness. The fire and lanterns had burned out long ago, and the black silence crawled up her skin, threatening to suffocate her. This was the worst part, being alone. Alone in the bed she had been sharing with Walter almost every night for the past five months. She pulled the quilt around her neck and curled up into the tiniest ball possible. She buried her face in the pillows and breathed deeply. His scent still lingered—a mixture of whiskey and tobacco. Tears flooded her eyes. She wasn't sure where the tears kept coming from or when they would stop.

9.

At sunrise, Ellie swung her feet over the side of the bed and placed them on the cold floor. The grit left behind from her mother's shoes dug into her bare feet. She made a mental note to clean it up. She didn't want any residue of her mother lingering and conjuring her hate. She left the door bolted and put the pistol in her pocket.

Every few minutes she looked out the window, the same window she had watched for Walter for the past five months. He was never coming back. All she had left was the bloodstained dirt in her front yard. She added this to her list of things to clean up—as soon as she felt brave enough to open the door.

She cleaned the cabin from top to bottom, starting with the floor in her bedroom. It was nearly noon when she stopped. There was nothing left inside to clean or tidy. She looked out the window again, searching the road for traces of anyone who might mean her harm. She tentatively slid the bolt and barely cracked the door. She held her breath and stood still, listening for anyone who may be approaching. Nothing. Only a few birds singing a spring melody. She thought about the sparrow that had taken up residence in the loft the Sunday before Tom shot Walter and the mayor. Granny Cline's omen had been real.

She opened the door a bit more and stuck her head out. Still nothing. She pushed the door open the entire way and filled her lungs with fresh air. The warm sun beckoned her out and assured her she had nothing to fear. If they came for her, they came. She stepped out on the porch. Her hand went to her pocket for reassurance the pistol was still there.

She picked up her bloody dress from the yard and threw it on the spot where Walter had died. Tears filled her eyes. "No! I will not cry another tear over this man. He lied to me and left me in this terrible situation. Damn you, Walter. Damn you!" She threw the dress on the blood stain and burned it. When the dress was reduced to ashes, she raked it all away and covered the darkened soil with fresh dirt from the garden.

She packed a lunch and both guns and took off for the ridge where Tom had seen Walter approaching. From there she would be able to see anyone coming up the road. She would spend most of the day up there if need be.

The animals needed tending to, but she didn't have it in her to deal with it today. She spread her quilt on the ground and placed her lunch and guns there. She looked over the ridge but didn't see or hear anything.

The baby had certainly increased her appetite; she was hungrier than she had been in weeks. After eating her lunch, she removed her bonnet, unpinned her hair, and stretched out. A gentle breeze scuttled across the ground.

Her mind rewound back through the years, attempting to trace her steps that brought her here, to this moment, to this mess. She had always thought she would have a better life. When she met Tom, she thought he was the one who would give her that better life. In his way, he had. At least he had tried. As the years wore on with Tom, she knew he would never make her happy or be able to give her all she wanted. Tom wanted a quiet life with a wife who cooked, cleaned, and had babies. She would never be that woman. She always wanted more than she had. Would it ever be enough?

She couldn't imagine how her sister Jolene could possibly be happy with Deacon. They had nothing. They lived in a coal camp in company housing with no chance of ever having anything better. Ellie missed her sister and her cousin Polly. Polly was four years older than Ellie, and Jolene was one year younger. Polly had always been more of a big sister than a cousin. Their houses had been a mile apart their entire lives. If Ellie and Jolene weren't at Polly's house, she was at their house. Mostly, they were at their Granny Cline's, who lived right in the middle, and the three girls had beat a well-worn path to her home.

Granny Cline was beautiful and wise. She also had a short-fuse temper, a mixture of her Irish and Cherokee roots. She taught the girls about herbs, gardening, quilting, midwifery, and Irish and Cherokee traditions and languages. She had even helped the girls develop their own written language of half-Celtic, half-Cherokee, coupled with symbols and drawings. It kept Ellie and Jolene's mother from knowing what they were doing. Their world was never the same after their Granny Cline passed away five years earlier. She was their rock and the center of their world.

Ellie drifted off to sleep thinking about Jolene and Polly. She was startled awake and sat up in a panic. She heard voices and a wagon. She grabbed the shotgun and peered over the edge of the ridge. A wagon was coming around the bend. Surely, she was seeing things. It was Jolene, Polly, and Polly's husband, Jake. She had never been happier to see anyone in her entire life.

She grabbed the guns and ran down to the cabin.

"Oh, my goodness! I'm so happy to see y'all." Ellie couldn't stop the tears.

Polly and Jolene hopped down from the wagon and ran to her. The three of them held each other and cried.

Jake grabbed a basket from the back of the wagon and handed it to Polly. "Polly, if you don't need me here, I'm gonna go on into town. I think you'ns are safe enough here for a couple of days. Y'all have a gun or two. Remember, shoot first, ask questions later."

"Come on, ladies, I've got some good stuff in this basket. Fried chicken, bread, and apple pie. As Granny Cline always said, pie makes ever'thang better," Polly said.

They walked back up to the ridge and sat on the quilt. Ellie was surprised she could eat again so soon after lunch, but Polly's fried chicken was not to be ignored.

"I can't believe y'all came. I'm so happy to see you."

"How are you, Ellie? It must've been terrible. Did you really see the whole thing?" Polly asked.

"Yes, I was standin' inside the door. I can't figure out for the life of me what they's gonna arrest Tom for. He hadn't done nothin'. You know Tom—he's a good man. He never hurt nobody."

"Where's Tom now?" Jolene asked.

"I've no clue. I s'pose he went to Island Creek to be with Anse. He'll be safe there. Or they'll manage to get him off someplace that is safe."

"Are you gonna be all right here by yourself, Ellie?" Jolene asked.

"I ain't sure. Last night was kinda rough. I was scared. Not knowin' who might come for me and blame me for what happened. Mama came yesterday with Franky. I guess if I can survive that I can handle anybody that comes up the road."

"Mama came *here* to see you? Why? We know she wasn't offerin' comfort or any words of wisdom."

Ellie took another chicken wing. "She was her same old mean, nasty self. She was so angry. I'm surprised she didn't hit me. She blamed me for ever'thang and called me a whore and Satan's spawn—same as always. Told me to never darken her door again."

"Poor Franky. I don't know how he stays with her or why. Truth be told, she was never as mean to him as she was to you or me. Especially you. You took the brunt of her wrath and protected us from many of her beatin's," Jolene said.

"Well, I don't have to worry 'bout her comin' back."

Jolene put her hand on Ellie's shoulder. "Ellie, you should leave here. Get what you can carry in your wagon and go. They ain't nothin' for you here no more and nothin' holdin' you back."

Ellie wasn't sure what to make of Jolene making the trip from Paint Creek to be here with her. She hoped this meant they could put the past behind them and move on. She didn't want to discuss it today and hoped Jolene didn't bring it up. Whatever her reasons for coming, Ellie was glad she did.

"Well, I can't rightly do that for a bit." Ellie squirmed and didn't make eye contact with Jolene or Polly.

"Why? What on earth could be keepin' you here?" Polly asked.

Ellie looked at Polly and then Jolene.

"No! A baby? You're with child? I thought you's glowin'," Polly said.

"You're gonna have a baby, Ellie?" Jolene was in disbelief.

Tears spilled from Ellie's cheeks, and she nodded her head yes. They both held her and tried to comfort her.

"I hate to be the one to ask this, but who's the daddy, Ellie? Walter or Tom?" Jolene asked.

"*Walter!* Of course." Ellie snapped.

"Does Tom know?" Polly asked.

"Yes."

"Oh, Ellie. Oh, sweet, Ellie." Polly held her close.

The next morning, Jolene and Ellie set the table for breakfast. Polly pulled the biscuits out of the oven and turned them out onto the plate. "You girls want gravy with these biscuits?"

"Of course we want gravy!" Ellie said. "I'll fetch us some fresh eggs."

Jolene waited until Ellie was outside. "Polly, what on earth is Ellie gonna do with a baby?"

"This is a horrible situation, Jolene, but God works in mysterious ways."

"As much as I want to believe this baby'll make things different, I ain't so sure it's gonna make her any less selfish." Jolene placed a plate of bacon on the table.

"I know you're still mad at Ellie for what she did to you, Jolene."

"I ain't mad at her no more. But I don't know if I'll ever be able to trust her again."

"Give it some time. Maybe a baby'll change Ellie." Polly continued stirring the gravy.

"It's just unfair that she can so carelessly get pregnant—and not even be sure who the daddy is—and I've been tryin' for years ..." Jolene turned back to the frying potatoes when Ellie stepped up on the porch. They finished preparing their morning feast and sat down to eat.

"What're you gonna do for money, Ellie?" Polly asked. "You're welcome to stay with us as long as you need to. If you want your own place, you'll eventually need some money."

"Tom's moonshine's the only thang I got worth sellin'. He makes some of the best moonshine in Appalachia. He's had folks comin' from as far away as Ohio to buy it for years. I think we oughta get what he has left and hide it at your place, Polly. I'm skeered if we leave it here it's a matter of time a'fore some fool decides to come lookin' for it."

"How much moonshine you think he's got stored up?" Jolene piled potatoes on her plate and reached for a biscuit.

"They's thirty gallons already bottled up in quart jars. Another twenty or so in the barrel—he was gonna get more Mason jars this week. He had some fellers come by last month and ask for fifteen gallons for a saloon they have in

Ohio. The other fifteen, plus what's in the barrel, he planned to sell to locals."

Polly crumbled up a biscuit and poured gravy over it. "When are those saloon men s'posed to show up?" she asked.

"This week. Tom already put those under the porch. He never let anybody go up to the still with him. Other'n me."

"Polly, pass me the gravy." Jolene said. "Well, I can take a few gallons back with me to Paint Creek. Those boys are always wantin' some good Mingo County moonshine."

"That should be worth a pretty penny if we can sell it." Polly said.

"Well, I reckon we oughta get those jars and get it ready to go," Jolene said as she buttered the last biscuit.

They cleaned up the breakfast dishes and went to the barn to tend to the animals. Ellie gathered the remaining eggs, Polly fed the hog, and Jolene fed the chickens. They sat down on the porch to rest when all the chores were completed.

"I've been thinkin', girls. We shouldn't send normal letters to discuss any of this business 'bout Tom, the moonshine, or anythang really," Polly said. "We need to use our secret language we came up with as kids."

"You're prob'ly right," Ellie agreed.

"I hadn't thought of that language in years," Jolene chuckled.

"Do you remember how to use it?" Polly asked.

"Yes, some things never leave you," Jolene said. "What'd we call it?"

"River Talk, 'cause we's always on that danged river bank," Ellie said.

"I'll have to practice drawin' all those signs and symbols Granny Cline taught us. Instead of our signatures, we signed our letters and notes with Celtic symbols. Ellie signed with a Celtic cross, Jolene you signed with a Celtic heart, and I signed with a Celtic knot," Polly said.

10.

Tom descended the mountain into Newtown to his brother's house.

He'd spent the better part of his days in torment over Ellie. He'd been fool enough to imagine she would grow out of her wild ways. He was old and wise enough to know better. He'd been mesmerized by her beauty for certain, but it was more than her appearance. That woman had a magic about her that was hard to resist. It was just how Ellie was. She got inside a man's head as well as his heart. And his pants. Hell, he couldn't blame Musick for being trapped in her web. He did blame him for being fool enough to think he could get away with it.

He waited until dark to approach his brother's cabin and then slid around the barn and stepped up on the back porch. The door creaked open.

"I's expectin' ye to show up yesterd'y. What took ye so long?" Alvin whispered.

"I figured they'd been here by now lookin' for me. I wanted to make sure I wasn't walkin' into an ambush."

"They come and gone that first day. Hell, Tom, them fools ain't got enough smarts 'bout 'em to stay a step ahead a ye." His brother chuckled. "Come out to the barn. I got you a passel of stuff you're gonna need."

His brother provided a horse, food, a pistol, more ammo, and a quart of moonshine.

"I figure they'll be lookin' for me at Anse's next—iffin' they got the guts to go to his house. Get word to Anse that I'll be makin' my way over to the cabin on Tank Mountain. I figure it'll take me a day or two. I'll be there waitin', and he can send for me when he thinks it's safe."

"Whatta 'bout Ellie? What'cha gonna do 'bout her? You want us to throw her outa the cabin?"

"Nahhh. Not yet, anyways. Let some of this die down first and then we'll see what we need to do."

"Those bastards deserved what they got, Tom. Ellie deserves the same."

"Musick got what he deserved. I ain't sure what the hell the mayor was doin' there. Prob'ly owed Musick a favor. Who the hell knows?"

Tom meandered through the mountains for two days to throw off any would-be vigilantes. The cabin at Tank Mountain had been used by Anse for a hideout during the feud. It was small and built into the slope—more a cave with a door than an actual cabin. He took a gun and the moonshine and climbed to the peak, the highest point in Mingo County. From the top, you could see Virginia,

Kentucky, and West Virginia. He sat on a rock bluff and watched the sun sink into Kentucky. It changed the mountains from green to red to blue to purple. And Tom plotted his next move.

11.

4 May 1911

Ellie left her wagon in a grove of trees on the banks of Mate Creek and walked nearly a mile to the First Baptist Church of Matewan. She stood across the road from the church behind a tree. The mourners arrived—some on wagons, some on horses, some on foot. Dressed in all black, Mary arrived on a wagon with her brother and mother. Mary looked as plain and dumpy as the day she tried to have Ellie thrown in jail for adultery.

Mary wasn't far enough along for the baby to be showing; Ellie doubted she was even pregnant. The mourners filed into the tiny church. The windows had been lifted and the songs and the prayers floated on the cool spring breeze. Ellie wanted more than anything to go inside and kiss Walter's face one last time. Instead she waited across the road from the church, more like a thief than the lover of the man who lay dead inside.

Ellie slumped down to her knees behind the tree when the pallbearers appeared at the door and carried Walter's casket down the steps to the wagon. She placed her hands over her mouth to stifle her sobbing. The realization that he was gone forever was a heavy stone tied around her heart.

Mary walked out behind the coffin, wailing that her husband was dead. The breeze carried Mary's voice across the road and up to Ellie's hiding spot. "Why? Why is *my* husband dead? The father of this little baby? Why is *he* dead? *She* should be dead. That tramp, Ellie, should be dead."

Mary's mother and brother held her and comforted her.

"Why should *I* be dead, you silly woman? What did *I* do?" Ellie whispered. "I loved that man more than you will ever be able to love anythang." It wasn't her fault, and she would not take the blame for this. Tom did this, not her.

She sat behind the tree until the mourners departed for the cemetery. Then she trudged home, crying harder with each step.

12.

<u>26 June 1911</u>

"Tom, Anse says you's facin' at least two to five years in the state penitentiary." Alvin said.

Tom had spent the last couple of months on the run, holed up in various hideouts Anse kept guarded in the mountains of West Virginia. He roamed from Mingo County to Logan County and then on into Lincoln County for a bit. His plan had been to let the dust settle and then make his way out west. Anse cautioned him on the risks of living the rest of his life as a fugitive and convinced him to linger in the area until they could figure out a solution. Anse knew everyone in Mingo and Logan County, and a lot of people owed him favors. So Tom had returned to Tank Mountain to get word from his brother.

"Well, damn. He can't do nothin'?" Tom asked.

"They wanted to give ye *ten* years. Anse called in a few favors people owed him."

"I reckon considerin' I murdered two men—the police chief and mayor, no less—a few years ain't too bad a punishment."

"Tom, you need to know, Musick's brothers and some of the mayor's people been threatenin' all of us. Now, we can fight as long as it takes, but I don't see this stoppin' anytime soon. This could blow up into another damn feud. Ain't none of us want that."

"No, we don't need no more killin'. They's been enough bloodshed for ten lifetimes."

"This mess of your'n is over a damn whore. What're you a gonna do 'bout Ellie, Tom? She shouldn't be allowed to stay in the cabin. That's our cabin. That farm's been in our family for generations. Ain't right that Ellie caused all this shit and gets to keep livin' there like she has some right to it."

"I hear ya. But she's gonna have a baby."

"You ain't fool enough to think that baby's your'n, are ye?"

"I ain't rightly sure. It could be. But I ain't ready to kick her and the baby outa the cabin 'til I know or have a better feelin' 'bout it. Right now, I need to get to Anse's and turn myself in. Ellie can wait for a bit."

Tom didn't want to think about Ellie. Even though she was the cause of his current misery, some part of him still loved her. A man didn't stop loving a woman like Ellie overnight.

The one thing Tom was certain of was that he didn't want any more violence. This was his mess, and he needed to do the right thing—turn himself in.

Ellie had been in the garden since sun up and was bone tired. A storm was brewing, and she wanted to gather as many vegetables as possible before the rain came. Her small crop was coming in faster than she could eat it.

Polly had sent news to Ellie that Tom was going to turn himself in. Ellie had no idea how soon a trial would be, but she planned to stay in the cabin regardless of Tom's fate. Seeing the place where Walter had died everyday was a punch in the heart, but she had nowhere else to go. Other than staying put and having the baby, she didn't really have a plan for her future. She needed to get through the next few months and then decide what she would do.

The tomatoes were ripe for picking, and she planned to start canning in the coming weeks. She picked a tomato and leaned over and breathed in the scent of the vine; it took her back to a happier time and place with her Granny Cline.

She walked barefoot between the rows of vegetables, picking the ones that were ready. Granny Cline had always gathered the tomatoes, peppers, and other small things while barefoot. Said she liked feeling grounded to the earth, a part of God's creation. The rich black soil was warm and soft, providing comfort to Ellie's swollen feet.

The wind kicked up, and the dark clouds gathered in the corner of the mountain. Ellie picked up the overflowing basket of tomatoes and peppers and wearily walked to the side of the porch to rest. This was work Tom normally helped with, but she was forced to take care of everything on her own if she wanted to eat. Polly had sent her farm hand

and her boys up to help with the animals and more strenuous chores. Still, it was a lot of work Ellie wasn't accustomed to doing alone. She hadn't realized how much Tom did to make her life comfortable.

Hoofbeats coming up the holler startled Ellie. Not knowing what or whom to expect, she kept a shotgun close at all times. She scrambled up and grabbed it. She was surprised to see Tom's brothers riding toward the cabin. She leaned the gun against the porch railing, never moving too far out of reach. Even though she didn't think Tom's brothers would hurt her, she was cautious.

"Ellie, how ya doin'?" Tom's younger brother, Jesse, shifted in his saddle.

She stood with her hands on her hips. "What y'all want?" Thunder grumbled on the other side of the mountain, announcing the storm it held.

Both brothers slid off their horses; Alvin tried to explain things to her. "Ellie, with Tom goin' to prison we's gotta sell the cabin and all the land. Tom was helpin' Mommy what little he could, and now that she ain't got his help, well, we gotta sell this place."

"Sell it? You'ns are gonna sell my land out from under me? Where exactly am I s'posed to go? I gotta baby on the way. *Tom's* baby. Did you'ns forget that or you just don't care?"

"Now, Ellie, it ain't like that." Alvin took a step away from her toward his horse.

"Oh? Then tell me what it's like? What exactly you think'll happen to me and this little baby?" Ellie paced back and forth in front of the porch.

"You'ns can go live with your mommy."

Ellie grabbed the gun, came around the side of the porch, and firmly planted her dirt-covered feet. "Have you talked to Tom 'bout this? Does he even know you're doin' this to me?"

Alvin took a few more steps back. "Now, Ellie, don't go gettin' all upset over nothin'. I'm just lettin' you know. It'll prob'ly take place in the next month or sooner. Put the gun down. They ain't no reason to be aimin' that thang at us. We's family, after all."

"Get out. Get off my property, you rottin' pieces of shit." She stood defiantly in the yard, holding the shotgun in both hands.

They remounted their horses and turned to leave. "You's got another month, Ellie," Jesse yelled over his shoulder as they rode away.

Ellie stood holding the shotgun until they were gone and then returned to her spot on the porch. Lightning lit up the darkening sky. Seconds later, thunder cracked. She jerked her head up at the first drops of rain. She kept her face towards the sky, letting the rain soak her. The smell of the rain, the dirt, the tomatoes, rose like a balm to her weary soul. She wanted to cry, felt she should cry, but she had cried enough. Right now, she just needed to *be*. The rain fell harder, washing the dirt from her toes and her basket of tomatoes and peppers. She sat still and let it soak her through . . .

What can wash away my sin? Nothin' but the blood of Jesus.

13.

<u>Early July 1911</u>

The unbearable July heat arrived with no gradual slip from spring to summer. The heat was oppressive, and the only escape on days like this was the Tug River. Ellie was miserable. The baby kicked hard to let Ellie know the misery was mutual. She looked down at her expanding belly and rubbed the spot below her ribs. What was she going to do with a baby? She had no business with a child. The only reason she had wanted it to begin with was Walter. But he was gone. She couldn't raise a baby by herself, and she didn't want to. She didn't want to do anything.

Ever since Tom's brothers had delivered her eviction notice, a hopelessness dropped into her heart that Ellie hadn't known was possible. It was a darkness that filled the air around her and seeped in through all the cracks in her life—and there were plenty. No matter how sunny, bright, and beautiful the day was, her world was as dark and dreary as the blackest coal mine.

Living wasn't a priority any longer. She packed a lunch, hopped on the wagon, and headed to the river to cool off.

She took the picnic basket and her quilt and walked down the narrow path. The walk down to the river seemed longer than usual; the baby pressed into her ribs, and breathing was a chore. She stopped a few times to rest her legs and work out the cramps. At first the cramps had crawled from her feet and up her calves when she slept. Now her legs cramped during the day if she stood on them too long.

She arrived at her usual spot on the river bank, the spot she and Tom used to come to during their first summer of marriage. She spread out her quilt on the sandy river bank; across the water was a rock bluff she and Tom used to swim out to. That all felt like ten lifetimes ago. How did her life end up like this? This was not in the plans. This was a living nightmare. Living? She wasn't living. She was quietly stepping through each breath with no promise of the next one. What was the point of continuing?

She sat for a long time watching the river gently flow away from her, listening to its gentle caresses against the rocks and shore. Where was it going? Could she go with it? Was there something better at its end?

She slipped off her shoes and entered the river. The water was cool against her skin, and her thin cotton dress billowed on the surface. She floated on her back and let the river move her farther out, taking her wherever it chose. Sunshine dripped through the trees and danced across her face. She closed her eyes, and the river embraced her body, gently caressing her warm skin. She wanted it to engulf her—take her completely. She lay still. Waiting. Waiting for the river to make her its own. To end her pain. The current grew stronger, and she willingly gave herself and Walter's child over to the Tug.

She opened her eyes and saw four black buzzards at the top of the mountain circling against the clear blue sky. She wondered what was dead, wondered if the buzzards would circle her dead body and feast on her flesh. Or would her body stay buried in the depths of the Tug River—never to be seen again? The buzzards moved slowly, rhythmically, waiting for the precise moment to descend on the dead or dying thing they had claimed. Ellie closed her eyes again and floated downstream. She hummed the song that had been stuck in her head since she'd washed Walter's blood from her hands and face.

What can wash away my sin . . .

She hummed, and she floated.

The baby kicked. Hard! Then kicked again. Ellie's eyes flew open. She had no idea how long she had been floating. Had she fallen asleep? The river licked at her face. The baby kicked under her ribs harder than ever. She could barely breathe. She wanted to die. The baby wanted to live. The baby wanted to be everything Ellie would never be. Could never be.

Two iron wills struggling against each other. Her scream echoed down the river as she gave in to the baby's demands. Still on her back, she tried to turn her body toward the shore. She had moved into the main channel, and the current was swift. She rolled over onto her belly and swam for shore. The baby kicked harder. A cramp grabbed her right foot and shot up her calf. She screamed, rolled over onto her back, and pulled her legs up to her chest. The cramp was agonizing, and the river tugged her under. The cramp held onto her leg, and the river wrapped around her. The baby kicked harder.

Her face broke the surface, and she gasped for air. She looked up at the sky. The buzzards were gone, and the sun was sinking behind the mountain. A few minutes earlier she had been ready to die, and now she was fighting for her life. For the baby's life.

She held onto her cramped foot with one hand and used her other hand to paddle her way toward the shore. The cramp finally eased up, but Ellie was afraid it would return with the first kick of her leg. She stayed on her back and used her arms to make her way to a rock jutting out of the river. She clung to it until she felt rested enough to attempt swimming again.

The river had never felt so wide, so deep, so treacherous. She stretched out her legs to see if she could touch the bottom. Her toes barely moved across the soft sand. She had one small, mild rapid to swim through to get to shore and begin the long walk back to the quilt and the lunch she had abandoned earlier. She turned on her back and pushed off the rock with her feet. She swam strong, focusing only on moving. The tiny life inside her belly was hellbent on living.

14.

<u>17 July 1911 (Mingo County Jail)</u>

Tom realized he would be halfway to California by now if he hadn't surrendered. Being on the run for the rest of his life didn't appeal to him too much—neither did five years in the state pen. He knew Musick's and Hoskins' families would eventually have found him and killed him or killed his brothers. He'd made the right decision to pay the price for what he'd done. So here he sat in the Mingo County jail awaiting his trial.

His attorney thought five years would be the maximum he would get. Anse was friends with the judge and had pulled some strings. Apparently, the judge wasn't a friend of the Matewan mayor or his chief of police. This worked in Tom's favor, as well.

Five years in the state pen. Could he do it? What would life be like when he got out? He had instructed his brothers to kick Ellie out of the cabin. She was cunning and would do everything she could to keep it. He was betting on her whoring ways being less alluring now that she had a growing belly. He wondered if the baby was his. He figured he wouldn't know until he saw it. Even then, he might not be certain.

"Chafin? Get up. You got a visitor."

Tom rolled off his cot and waited for the guard to open his cell. The cell block was hot, and the air was still and thick. The few windows they did have were too small and narrow to let in even a hint of a breeze. The guard wiped the sweat from his brow and took the giant ring of keys from his belt. The keys banged against the cell doors and echoed down the hall. He opened the cell door and led Tom to the visitors' room. Ellie's black eyes met his with an icy glare. Tom didn't try to hide his surprise at seeing her.

"Well, well. Look what the cat dragged in." He sat across from her. "What brings you to town, Ellie?" The guard closed the door and waited outside. The room was hot, but the window was bigger than those in the cell block, and a slight breeze ruffled in.

"Tom, your brothers came to pay me a visit last week and said they's sellin' the cabin? Is that true? Did you know 'bout this?"

"Yep. I sure did." He leaned back in his chair and placed his intertwined hands behind his head.

"How can you let them do this to me? That's my cabin as much as your'n."

"How you figure?"

"I *am* still your wife, Tom Chafin."

"Well, I guess we'll be needin' to change that, won't we?"

"What are you talkin' 'bout? You can't divorce me while I'm pregnant and let this baby be born a bastard. At least have the decency to wait till the baby's born."

Tom leaned across the table. "Well, sweetheart, as far as I can tell, that baby's a bastard either way." The words felt heavy on his tongue. He wasn't sure about the baby. One thing he was sure of was Ellie using the baby to manipulate him to get her way.

"Go to hell, Tom." Ellie took her handkerchief and wiped the back of her neck. "How are you gonna divorce me? You got too much goin' on with your trial for murder. Remember? You murdered the only man I ever loved."

"Well, ya know, maybe you're right, Ellie. Maybe I should wait 'til I'm outa prison to divorce your sorry ass. That way you can't marry some other poor fool. I feel like it's my civic duty to save my fellow man from the likes of you."

"I'm not waiting five years to be rid of you! After this baby's born, I'll divorce you while you're in prison."

Tom laughed. "Well, ya see, Ellie, my lawyer tells me I can delay any divorce proceedin's till I'm out. So you go right ahead with your divorce plans."

"You're a son of a bitch, Tom Chafin."

Tom leaned in closer until he was a few inches from Ellie's face. "Sweetheart, you started this mess. Not me."

"I hate the day I ever married you. *Hate it.*"

Ellie stood up, her swollen belly showing under her thin dress. "Well, ain't that a sad sight, indeed? Look at you, all swollen with your dead lover's baby."

"Go to hell." She turned to leave.

Tom sat at the table and watched her walk to the door. "Oh, Ellie, I'd be gettin' outa the cabin if I's you. My brothers are comin' back next week to kick your sweet little ass out." He snickered as she slammed the door shut behind her.

The guard escorted Tom back to his cell. He stretched out on his cot and lit a cigarette.

Damned if Ellie wasn't beautiful even with a bastard baby in her belly, but he felt nothing for her except disgust. It was a good thing there was a guard close by during her visit because he knew he would have wrung her long, lovely neck.

He ground out his cigarette on the wall, rolled over, and went to sleep.

15.

<u>28 July 1911 (Matewan)</u>

Ellie didn't want to risk being seen by anyone, so she decided to climb up the backside of the hill to Walter's grave. She walked slowly through the trees, graves, and headstones. The day was warm, with the scent of rain in the air. The wind picked up and blew strands of her hair loose. She stopped under a dogwood tree to catch her breath and wipe the sweat from her brow before she climbed the last section of the hill.

She stopped short of the grave. The dirt, not quite settled, was covered with dying flowers.

Ellie slumped to her knees by Walter's headstone. She buried her face in her hands and wept for him, for the baby, for herself. The wind carried the faint sound of footsteps coming up the hill.

A shadow fell over Ellie. She looked up, stunned to see Mary clothed in black from head to toe, looking miserable. Her belly was huge and round underneath her black frock. She must have gained ninety pounds as far as Ellie could tell from looking at her fat face. According to Mary's account of her pregnancy, Ellie calculated they must be within weeks of a due date, but Mary looked much bigger. Ellie couldn't stop staring.

Ellie scurried to her feet, using Walter's headstone for support.

Mary looked at Ellie's growing belly. "It's true? I heard rumors but didn't dare believe 'em. You're pregnant? With Walter's baby?" Mary's breath caught in her throat. "Answer me!"

"Yes, it's Walter's baby."

"I feel sorry for that poor child havin' you for a mother. You couldn't handle bein' strapped with a husband, let alone a baby. You're a horrible friend and a miserable person, Ellie."

"Mary, I don't wanna fuss with you. I didn't think anybody would be here today. I didn't mean no disrespect. I'll be leavin' now."

"You disrespected me months ago, Ellie, when you decided to sleep with my husband. Why feel bad 'bout it now? Because of you, I lost my husband, a friend, and worst of all—my dignity—in one thin slice."

"Mary, what's done is done. Tom killed Walter—not me."

"Is that what you think? You tramp, *you* killed Walter. Tom's just an innocent victim like me. He might have pulled the trigger, but you're the reason *my* husband is dead. And this baby in my belly will remind me of what you've done every single day for the rest of my life."

Mary's words ripped through Ellie, exposing the truth of what she and Walter had done. She leaned against Walter's headstone and wiped the tears from her face. Thunder grumbled in the distance, and Ellie wanted to get off the hill and away from Mary.

"Leave." Mary held her burgeoning stomach. "Leave now a'fore I throw your lyin' ass off this hill."

The baby kicked Ellie hard and jarred her back to the moment. She would not let this woman speak to her this way. She brushed the leaves from her dress and straightened her bonnet.

"You can think what you want, you dried-up old biddy. *That* man," Ellie pointed to Walter's grave, "loved *me*. He made love to *me* every night—not you. He slept in *my* bed, not your'n. So don't you lecture me on Walter. I loved him more than you were ever capable of. I don't know what you did to trick him into sleepin' with you so you could get pregnant, but he was in my bed because he wanted to be. *I* was the one he loved, not you. And don't you ever forget it."

Ellie pushed past Mary and started down the backside of the hill as the first drops of rain fell on her face.

16.

3 August 1911 (Lynn – close to Matewan)

The seat was hard as stone, and every jostle sent the baby bumping into Ellie's bladder. Franky had already stopped the wagon four times so she could pee. At this rate, they would never get to Polly's. With Walter dead and Tom in jail, Ellie was alone with nowhere to go. No one to turn to. She could have had her pick of men if she weren't pregnant. Up until this last month, most people couldn't even tell; she looked a little heavier, but certainly not with child. Polly was the only person she knew who would take her in. So here she was on the wagon with her brother Franky on her way to Lynn. The trip was taking longer than she remembered. A soft drizzle fell when they came around the bend at Blackberry City. Ellie's back felt as though it would snap in two. Her stomach was tight as a drum and ready to burst open if she breathed too deeply. She had another two months to go; Ellie wondered if the baby had other plans and was ready to make its entrance into this cruel world.

When Polly had found out Tom's brothers were kicking Ellie out, she had insisted Ellie come stay with her. Ellie knew

Polly would never turn away her cousin, whom she had once vowed to love and protect until their dying day. Of course, she'd made that vow when they were kids playing on the river bank. Back then, Ellie had decided they needed to be blood sisters, along with Jolene. She stole a knife from Polly's daddy's work bench, and they headed down to the water. They cut their fingers, tied their wrists together with a dirty bandana, and took the pledge. Polly wrote the vows:

Sisters until the end—to protect, love, defend.
No man or child shall come between. On each other, we will lean.
We will kill for each other if we must. Bone to bone, dust to dust.
Toward each other we will bend. Sisters until the end.

Sisters until the end. The end of what? The wagon lurched toward Lynn and an uncertain future.

The last time Ellie had visited Polly, the house was just a dream. Now it was a real home. Two stories, four fireplaces, a porch that wrapped all the way around. It was a far cry from the three-room cabin she and Tom had lived in.

Ellie gingerly climbed down from the wagon with her brother's help. The door behind her opened and footsteps hurried along the porch through the rain. "Ellie? Ellie, my goodness. Look at you. Come here." Polly wrapped a shawl and her arms around Ellie's shoulders. "My goodness, you are soaked through to the bone. Hurry up and come on in the house and we'll get you some dry clothes."

They walked arm-in-arm to the porch. Polly's two young boys stood waiting for orders. "Go help your cousin unload the wagon. Put Ellie's things in the back bedroom and then come and sit yourselves down for dinner. Hurry up, now."

Ellie wasn't sure what she expected, but it wasn't this. This enfolding of her. This love and complete acceptance.

She should have known. She looked at Polly, saying softly, "Sisters till the end?"

"Yes. Sisters till the *very* end." Polly squeezed Ellie's shoulders.

They entered the house, and Polly took Ellie to the back bedroom. The room was comfy and cozy. An iron bed hugged the far wall, and a small dresser stood next to the door. A rocking chair sat at the open window, and a gentle breeze ruffled the lace curtains. The boys brought in her meager belongings—mostly clothes, her mandolin, and the quilt she, Polly, and Jolene had made with their grandmother. They each had made a quilt the winter before their grandmother had died, and they vowed to always keep them. She had kept hers on her childhood bed until she could lovingly place it on the bed she shared with Tom on their wedding night. It was the same quilt she and Walter wrapped up in after making love on that same bed years later. The scent of Walter had long vanished, but she wanted to wrap his baby in the blanket.

She wore a Celtic cross Granny Cline had given her; it was the only piece of jewelry she owned—aside from her wedding band, which she'd left at the cabin. She had no use for it now. Ellie sat on the bed and took off her shoes and stockings. Polly unpacked Ellie's clothes and helped her change into something dry.

"I figured you wouldn't wanna deal with this bunch till mornin', so I'll bring our dinner in here and we can eat together and catch up," Polly said.

"That sounds perfect. I'm not really up to visitin' with nobody 'cept you right now." Ellie fell back into the pillows.

Polly brought two bowls of chicken and dumplings and a small plate of cornbread into the room, and they ate on the bed. Ellie ate all of hers and half of Polly's. After eating they sat and talked for hours. All the things they avoided discussing when Polly and Jolene came to visit after the murders, they freely discussed now.

"I think I did love Tom. At first, anyway. Then it got to be borin' and stiflin' in so many ways. It wasn't nothin' Tom did—I wanted somethin' different. Somethin' new and excitin'." Ellie shifted and lay on her side. Polly stretched out, facing her.

"How'd you end up with Mary's husband?"

"You know Mary. She's been 'round for as long as I can remember. I hadn't seen Mary in years and ran into her at the feed store one day last fall. She invited me to a church social. We lived up that damnable holler, and I never saw a soul, so I thought it'd be fun. That's where she introduced me to Walter. What I can't figure out is how she got a man like Walter to marry her in the first place. He said it was for the political connections her daddy has. Polly, it was truly love at first sight. I never met nobody who so completely swept me off my feet. Then he came callin' one night that very week. He knew when Tom worked and came as soon as Tom left for his shift. We never looked back after that first night."

"Ellie, ever' body's talkin' 'bout it. They's sayin' some awful things 'bout you. And Walter."

"Well, they can say all the nasty things they wanna. I know the truth. He loved me. And I loved him. And now I have his baby in my belly." She rubbed her stomach. "Polly, what on earth am I gonna do with a baby?"

"Well, you'll stay here as long as you want. We'll raise her together."

"Her? You think it's a girl?"

"You're carryin' real high. It has to be a girl. If you want, we can try the ring?"

"Yes. Let's do it." Polly left the bedroom and returned within a few minutes with a ball of twine and scissors. She cut off a twelve-inch piece of the twine, removed her wedding band, slipped the twine through the ring, and knotted the ends together.

Their Granny Cline had been a midwife and taught them how to tell if a baby was a boy or girl. They had watched their granny perform this on many women over the years, and she had never been wrong. She would suspend the ring over the pregnant woman's belly. If the ring moved side to side, it was a boy. In a circle, it was a girl. It was one of many methods Granny Cline's grandmother had brought from Ireland and taught her as a young girl, and she, in turn, passed the secrets to Ellie, Polly, and Jolene.

Ellie stretched out on the bed and pulled up her dress so her bare belly was showing. Polly held the twine at the knot, with the ring hovering above Ellie's bellybutton. Polly held her hand and arm perfectly still and let the ring move on its own. At first, nothing. Then slowly, the ring started moving in a circle around Ellie's belly. They looked at each other and smiled.

"So, you were right. I'm havin' a girl!"

"It's never been wrong all these years, Ellie. Remember when you and Jolene did this on me?" Polly put her hand on Ellie's belly. Tears welled up in her eyes.

"Polly, I'm so sorry I haven't been back since your baby girl passed. You sure you want me here for this birthin'? If it's too much, I can go right back to Mommy's with Franky tomorrow."

"No! Don't be silly. Besides, your mama ain't gonna take you in. I sometimes wonder what it would be like if my little Elizabeth had lived. She'd be almost two years old now." Polly wiped her eyes. "Ye can't dwell on those kinda heartaches. It don't serve no purpose. Besides, we gotta take care of this little angel of your'n."

"As best I can estimate, she should make her entrance right 'bout the 18th of October," Ellie said.

"We'll be ready for her," Polly said.

Everyone had long ago gone to bed when Polly slipped out of Ellie's room. She crawled into bed, curled up next to Jake's warm body, and slipped her hand around his.

He stirred and rolled over onto his side to face her. "Ever'thang as it should be in there? She gonna stay here for a spell?"

"I think she is. It'll be wonderful to have a baby in the house again, Jake."

"Polly, we talked 'bout this. You know how Ellie is. She might stay for a while and then up and take the baby and leave. So, you best not get too attached to that young'n."

"I know. I won't. It'll be fine." She turned over and pulled his arm around her. "It'll be just fine."

Polly and Ellie walked to the river so Ellie could put her feet in the water. It had become their late afternoon ritual, and it was the only thing that cooled Ellie.

"What should I name her, Polly?"

The last few weeks of the pregnancy had been the worst of Ellie's life. She was miserable. Her feet were swollen; her face was swollen. She couldn't sleep. Eating gave her heartburn. The heat was unbearable, and the humidity clung to her heavy body like vines on a tree. The rainy night she had arrived was the last cool night of the summer, and it took the last gentle breeze with it. It was already September, and an Indian summer was in full swing. The temperature had hit 100 degrees every day for the past week. She didn't know how she would make it through six more weeks of this.

Polly reached over and plucked a daisy from the earth. "Maybe you could call her Daisy? That'd be a sweet name."

"I like that. Daisy. I like Deanna Day better, after Granny Cline. Call her Deannie? Should I give her Tom's last name? My last name? Walter's? Deannie Chafin? No, I don't like that. Deannie Musick? That sounds even worse. I really like Deannie Cline." Ellie mused. "We'll see." They walked back to the house and sat on the porch.

"Well, your last name's still Chafin. So I guess she'll need that name."

"I may not be a Chafin much longer. One minute Tom threatened to divorce me a'fore the baby's even born. The next he threatened to wait till he gets outa jail. That son of a bitch may never divorce me."

"Well, then is he gonna try and take this baby? If you's married to him, legally he may try just so he can hurt you."

"He don't want this baby. He may scream and act like he will only to torment me, but he'll never come near this baby girl. If he does, I'll shoot his ass."

17.

20 September 1911

Ellie went to bed with the night promising a thunderstorm. Clouds rolled in over the mountains, chased by streaks of lightning. She slept with the window open, hoping for a breeze. At midnight, Ellie woke up to a contraction. It started in her lower back, rolling around to her belly and gripping everything inside her. She was early! The little devil was four weeks early.

Ellie balled the sheets up in her fists and tried not to scream. Polly had tried to tell her what this would feel like; Ellie never dreamed it would be this bad. Polly's instructions had been to breathe quickly until it passed. The contraction was so sudden and so violent Ellie couldn't breathe at all.

The first one passed, and she let go of the sheets. She knew another would be on its way shortly. She rolled over and placed a pillow behind her back. Breathe. She needed to focus on breathing. She thought she was ready when the first twinges began. She held her breath and put the sheet in her mouth and bit hard. She needed to get Polly but doubted she would be able to walk.

The third contraction rolled around her belly. Ellie sat up, threw a book at the door, and screamed. Polly was in the room in seconds. Her oldest boy, Seth, was on her heels. Polly barked orders at him.

Polly had been preparing a basket of the things she would need to deliver the baby—extra bed sheets, scissors to cut the umbilical cord, cotton ribbon to tie off the cord, clean cotton cloths, and a jar of moonshine. Seth left the room to get the collection.

She adjusted Ellie in the bed and massaged her lower back. Polly helped Ellie breathe through the next few contractions. She flipped Ellie over and had her spread her legs. Polly inserted her fingers into Ellie's vagina to determine how far along the baby had moved down the birth canal.

"You's got a little while, Ellie. The contractions'll only get worse, so you need to breathe like we talked." Polly propped Ellie up on pillows and made her as comfortable as possible.

The next few hours were hell—for everyone in the house. Ellie screamed and cussed and screamed some more.

"Polly, get this damn thing outa me. I can't take no more. Why does this hurt so bad?" Ellie was soaked in sweat. She bit a gash into her bottom lip, and blood dried at the corner of her mouth.

Polly tipped the jar of moonshine up to Ellie's lips. "Here, have another sip of shine. Not so much. You don't want to get sick or make the baby sick."

"I don't give a damn 'bout this baby gettin' sick. I want it out of me. *Out!*"

Thunder pounded overhead, and lightning lit up the yard outside Ellie's bedroom window. The faint taste of a breeze stirred the trees. Polly's youngest son, Daniel, fanned Ellie.

The second son, Joe, was busy keeping a cold rag on Ellie's head.

Polly massaged Ellie's belly and tried to keep things moving. She coached Ellie to breathe and push with each contraction. It was five in the morning, and the baby was ready to come out. "Ellie, you're almost there. With this next contraction, you need to push with all you got. Her little head's 'bout to crown, and then we're home free."

"I can do this. I want this to be over."

The next contraction roared through her body like a locomotive, and Ellie pushed with all she had.

"Almost there. The next one should be right behind this one. Here it comes . . . push. *push*, Ellie! Push with all you got. I see her head. *Push!*"

When would this agony end? She was pushing with all her strength—what little she had left. The pain was more than she could bear. Then she felt a tearing through, and the baby came out at the break of day. Ellie fell back on the wet pillows and cried.

"There she is, Ellie. You did it. She's beautiful."

Polly lay the baby on Ellie's chest before she cut the cord. Ellie looked at the child and then looked at Polly. "Oh, Polly, she's so tiny. What am I s'posed to do?"

"Well, right now, nothin'. Just hold her. I'll cut the cord and clean her up directly, then I'll clean you up a little bit." Polly sent the boys out of the room.

Ellie looked at the baby lying on her chest. She wasn't ready for this. She had just been through hell, and now she had a crying, tiny human in her arms. Ellie wanted to sleep. She needed a long drink of whiskey and then sleep.

Polly cut the cord and cleaned up Ellie as best she could. She took Deannie to a small table the boys had brought in earlier and washed her. Ellie watched in amazement at how gentle and loving Polly was with the baby. Ellie wasn't sure she could be that loving and nurturing. Deannie stopped crying at the sound of Polly's gentle voice.

After the bath, she swaddled the baby in a cotton blanket and brought her to Ellie.

Ellie was uncomfortable holding the tiny little life that had emerged from her own body. She was uncertain about what to do. Women had babies every day and seemed perfectly happy doing so. They seemed to instinctively know what to do. Nurturing was not in Ellie's nature. She didn't necessarily feel anything for the child—other than a bit of resentment for the pain she had caused the past few hours.

Polly sat in a chair next to the bed and rubbed the baby's cheek. "Ain't she the purdiest thing you ever saw, Ellie?"

"Yes, she is. Look at all those dark curls, just like your'n. Her eyes look green, like Jolene's." Little Deannie slept contentedly on Ellie's chest.

18.

28 September 1911

The idea of motherhood overwhelmed Ellie. She had a tiny baby to care for now. A baby that was only a few weeks old and depended on her for nourishment, comfort, protection—life itself. She sat rocking this sweet, little life that came from her very own body, and she'd never felt more alone. Even worse, she felt vulnerable and powerless. Her tears dropped onto Deannie's face. The tears poured as she sobbed for all she had lost and all the dreams that had died inside her along the way. She had been striving for so long to be the person she knew she could be, but she never quite made it there. The closer she got to the edge of her dreams, the further back life would toss her to start over again and again.

She heard Polly's footsteps in the hallway. She wiped her tears on her sleeve and tried to compose herself before Polly entered.

"I've made us an apple pie, Ellie—why you cryin'?" Polly sat on the bed next to the rocking chair.

"It's all of it, Polly. Tom, Walter, the murders, now Deannie. And Jolene. I miss my sister. She left here with Deacon, and I didn't hear from her for two years. Then she came with you after Tom killed Walter, and I ain't heard a peep from her since. No letter, nothin'. Will we ever be the same?"

Polly found a handkerchief on Ellie's dresser. She handed it to Ellie and took Deannie. "Here, dry your tears, sweetheart. This'll all pass a'fore you know it. Come to the kitchen. I've baked us a pie—pie makes ever'thang better."

Ellie took the handkerchief Polly extended, wiped her face, and followed her to the kitchen.

"Jolene loves you, Ellie. You know she's in love with Deacon and always was. He's a good man, Ellie. Jake sees him on a regular basis 'bout the United Mine Workers. He and Jolene are a real good match."

"How? How does Jake see him? He goes to Paint Creek?" Ellie sat at the kitchen table.

"Sometimes. Or Deacon comes to Matewan. Sometimes they meet in Charleston. The miners are fightin' an awful fight, Ellie. The coal operators are treatin' those men like slaves. Hell, they treat the mules pulling the men in and out of the mines better. The contract up Paint Creek expires the end of March, and those men are plannin' to walk out. Strike as long as it takes."

"Whatta 'bout Jolene? What'll she do if the strike goes on for a long time? Will she come home?"

"You know that girl better'n I do. She's as tough as any three men we know. Besides, she won't leave Deacon."

"That's nonsense. They know 'bout the New River strike and how brutal the coal operators were. The United Mine

Workers couldn't stop 'em then. What makes 'em think this'll be any different?" Ellie's father, grandfather, and all their male kin had worked in the mines for as long as she could remember. They'd all been proponents of the United Mine Workers and talked about it for years around the dinner table and at all family gatherings. Tom hadn't talked much about the union one way or another. His main goal was to get back to the timber business with Devil Anse. So, Ellie wasn't aware of the latest developments in the union's push into southern West Virginia.

Jake joined them in the kitchen. "Well, that was nearly ten years ago, and we think it'll be different this time," he said.

"How'll it be any different? Those bastards are still as greedy as ever, Jake," Ellie said.

Polly placed Deannie in one of two bassinets Jake had made for her. They kept one in Ellie's room and one in the kitchen so Deannie could always be a part of the family gatherings. Polly served Ellie and Jake a piece of pie and joined them at the kitchen table.

"The union's a lot stronger than it was in 1902," Jake said. "We've got good men leadin', for the most part anyway, and a lot more members. These men know they can't keep workin' like this. Conditions are as bad as they ever were—if not worse. They've stopped payin' us with U.S. dollars, Ellie. They pay with scrip ever' chance they get. Then the only place these men can buy anythang is at the comp'ny store, where they charge 'em interest. It's criminal. The coal operators control ever'thang in the miners' lives—the schools, the stores, the doctors, their homes. All of it. They work little boys—ten, eleven years old—like they do grown men. People live in comp'ny houses and fear eviction if they even whisper the word union." Jake took a bite of his pie.

"That's why Tom refused to live in one of their shanties," Ellie said. "Said it would be the death of all who lived there. What choice do most of 'em have?"

"Tom's right. These men can't ever get out from under the bondage of the coal operators," Jake said. "Men are willin' to lay down their lives for this if need be. You can't work a man fourteen hours a day and pay him nothin' and treat him like an animal year after year." Jake jabbed his fork in the air. "Mark my words, there'll be an uprisin', and it'll be ugly." Jake finished his pie and kissed Deannie on the cheek before returning to his chores outside.

When Polly and Ellie finished dessert, Ellie took their pie plates to the sink. She washed the dishes and looked out the kitchen window. October had been dry as a bone, with no rain in weeks. The leaves had turned, waiting to make their colorful descent to the ground. How much longer would she need to stay here? How much longer before she could leave? Could she survive a winter stuck at Lynn? She doubted it. Where would she go? With a little baby, her options were limited.

Her body was still healing. She was still bleeding and sore. Polly said the bleeding should stop in three to four weeks. Ellie thought that seemed like a long time for a woman to bleed and not die. Why was something that was supposed to be so wonderful, and the crowning achievement to a woman's life, so damn painful, horrible, and downright savage? Why did so many women act like it was nothing and then turn around and do it six, seven, eight more times? She watched her own mother and aunts have babies and be out plowing a field barely a week later. How? Why? There had to be more to life than having babies and taking care of some damn man's needs.

Most every woman she knew took to motherhood as second nature. She couldn't muster up the emotions to be as nurturing to Deannie as Ellie knew she should. Polly seemed to come by it naturally for everyone. How did Polly do it?

Ellie's mind drifted to Mary. Ellie wondered how Walter's widow was taking to motherhood. Probably like all the rest, Ellie assumed, because it was expected of her. Even if Mary hated it, she'd never admit it. Polly had heard at church Mary had her baby boy a few weeks after Deannie was born. Mary hadn't been lying. She and Walter *had* been sleeping together. Probably the entire time he was visiting Ellie's bed. Her anger at Walter was growing bigger than her love for him had ever been. *Liars!* They were all liars and cheats. She could play their game better than they could, and she would win. One way or another.

19.

16 October 1911

Ellie held a small mirror and made a complete sweep of her body as best she could before she got dressed. At least her figure had snapped back within the first month, and her breasts were still high and firm. She dressed in one of her pre-pregnancy dresses. It was a little tight around her swollen chest. A baby was the last thing she needed or wanted. How was she supposed to find a man with a baby hanging around her neck?

It was her first time going to Matewan since the murders, and she was nervous. Ellie knew there would be gossip, and the reception would be less than warm.

The third Monday of the month turned out to be a pleasant, sunny day; Jake, Polly, and Ellie left early to go to Matewan. Polly sat in the middle, and Jake was on the other side of her, steering the wagon. Ellie turned her face up to the sun as the wheels lurched forward.

Jake's mother was taking care of the kids. Both women were glad to get out of the house for a few hours. Jake maneuvered the wagon through Matewan and parked it at the far end of town. He was going to talk to some men about union business; they planned to meet back at the wagon in two hours.

Ellie and Polly strolled down to the general store to get fabric and a few household supplies. They were examining a bolt of cotton when Ellie heard them. Several ladies were gathered beyond the cutting table. Polly gently placed her hand on Ellie's arm, but it was too late. The words were already gushing out of Ellie's mouth like vomit.

"I *can* hear you, you old biddies. So, you think I'm a *whore?* A *sinner?* We *all* sin. Or did you not read that part in your Bible?" Ellie leaned across the cutting table and wagged her finger in their faces. "How you think *your* sinnin's any better'n mine? You think God sees your sin of gossipin' and judgin' me as any less wrong? Judge not, less ye be judged. Is that verse not in your bibles?" The women had backed up to the wall and could go no farther.

She took a deep breath and looked at Polly.

Polly's kind eyes said, *No more.*

Ellie turned her back on the women. "Old hags ain't got nothin' better to do than judge me?" she said to Polly as she absent-mindedly examined a skein of wool yarn. The women said hello to Polly and hurried out of the store.

"Ellie, I'm so sorry. That was so uncalled for. Those women are just nasty and jealous. We knew this'd happen. You can't pay 'em no mind," Polly said.

"It still makes my blood boil. Those ole biddies ain't got no right to talk 'bout me or nobody else." Ellie slumped against the cutting table. "It don't matter what they say 'bout me and Walter. They can think what they want." She pointed to her heart. "I know what we had, and they ain't nobody can take that away from me. As for Tom, I don't care what they think or say 'bout him. He's in jail. Right where he belongs."

Polly paid for the fabric and other items, and they headed back to the wagon. As they passed the Blue Goose Saloon and Hotel, Ellie deliberately slowed her pace so she could look inside. "That's where daddy got shot. Walter said the coal operators from out of town stay there now. You think Jake's ever been in there, Polly?"

"I doubt it. He ain't got no business in a place like that. It's still a tavern, ain't it?"

"A tavern and a hotel."

"I don't think Jake has any use for the coal barons. And I'm pretty sure Jake's the last person they'd wanna see. He's fightin' hard for the union, Ellie. Well, there's Jake goin' to the wagon. We's best be hurryin' along." Polly pulled Ellie away from the Blue Goose.

20.

<u>21 October 1911</u>

Jolene was hesitant about making the trip to Polly's, but here she was on her way to Lynn. Deacon had to meet with Jake about the impending strike at Paint Creek, and he wanted her to join him. He sat quietly, guiding the wagon as it bounced along the mountain road. He had been rather insistent for the past few months that she mend things with Ellie. He was right, and Jolene knew it. It had been eating at her, and Deacon could see it. Ellie was her only sister, and they had always been so close—until she wanted to marry Deacon.

Ellie and Polly each had sent letters describing Deannie and these first few weeks of her life. Jolene was as excited to meet Deannie as she was hesitant to see Ellie. She missed her sister. She might never completely trust her again, but she did miss her.

The kids were waiting at the top of the road and came running toward them. Seth, Joe, and Daniel jumped on the back of the wagon and rode to the house with them, chattering the whole way. Polly's kids loved Deacon, even if Ellie didn't.

Deacon helped Jolene down off the bench. He took her face in his hands. "Wanda Jolene, say what you gotta say to her and make peace with it. One way or t'other." He kissed her forehead.

"I know. *I know!*" She took his hand. "I love you, Deacon."

Polly and Jake came out to greet them first. Then Ellie emerged carrying Deannie.

"Jolene, I'd like to introduce you to your niece, Deanna Day. Deannie, this is your aunt Jolene."

"Ellie, she's beautiful. I've never seen anythang so tiny and perfect. Can I hold her? Should I wash up first?"

"Don't be silly. Here, take her."

Jolene took the tiny life Ellie held out for her. Deannie looked up with the greenest eyes Jolene had ever seen, and she was in love instantly.

"I think she has your green eyes, Jolene," Ellie said. "The more I look at her, I see a lot of you in her."

"You think so? She's precious, Ellie."

"You'ns come on inside. Jake, you boys wash up. Dinner's almost ready." Polly herded the ladies into the kitchen. Jake, Deacon, and the boys stayed outside to talk about the latest developments at Paint Creek.

Jolene couldn't take her eyes off Deannie. She wasn't prepared for this rush of emotion and complete love at first sight. How could *Ellie* have something so sweet and perfect? Something conceived in adultery? Something she didn't even want? She and Deacon had wanted a baby since before they got married. Jolene had all but given up on having a child of her own. Holding Deannie made the desire for a baby come rushing at her like a flood, along with a splash of new resentment towards Ellie.

"Jolene, it looks like you and Deannie are perfect for each other." Ellie sat beside Jolene and stroked Deannie's cheek.

"Oh, Ellie. This sweet angel! Y'all must be madly in love with her."

Polly finished setting the table. "Yes, we're all in love with her. She's truly a gift from God. The boys fuss over which one'll hold her next. Jake can't stop kissing her cheeks. She certainly has changed things around here." Polly went to the door and called the men to come eat.

Ellie took the iron skillet from the oven and turned the cornbread out on a plate. Polly placed a platter of fried chicken in the center of the table.

"Jake, you wanna say grace a'fore we start?" Polly asked.

"Thank you, dear Lord for this bountiful supper and the love of family. In Jesus name, amen. Dig in."

"Boys, get you'ns a plate and go out on the back porch and eat," Polly said to her kids.

There was a moment of silence as they all dug into the feast on the table—fried chicken, mashed potatoes, green beans, and cornbread. "Polly, I swear your fried chicken's still the best I ever had." Deacon took his third chicken leg from the platter.

"Jolene, you get you'ns a few quarts of those beans to take back to Paint Creek," Polly said.

"Deacon, what you think's gonna convince Cabin Creek to join the strike, iffin it comes to that?" Jake asked between bites of chicken and mashed potatoes.

"I reckon they's gonna have to get good and fed up with how they's bein' treated. A man can only take so much. Problem is, they got men up there bossin', tellin' 'em not to join the strike—that it's gonna make things worse. Union men, mind you, tellin' 'em not to side with other miners. To side with the coal barons! It ain't right, Jake. Ain't right narry a bit," Deacon said. "Frank Keeney seems to be the only one up on Cabin Creek tryin' to rally those men to join us."

"Ain't the union tryin' to make some kinda deal with the operators?" Ellie asked.

"If you wanna call it that. I think a lot of the union leaders are tryin' to make a deal for they own damn selves, and to hell with the men workin'. I know a few of 'em that're as greedy as the operators, to tell ya the truth," Jake said.

"Well, the contract expires the end of March. That gives us five months to figure out what we're gonna do. We need to get a good solid plan and get these men ready to fight, if it comes to that," Deacon said.

They finished dinner with talk of the strike and what a fight between the miners and the coal operators would look like.

Jolene went with Ellie to help put Deannie to bed.

"Ellie, you must be so proud and happy with this little angel." Jolene pulled a white nightgown over Deannie's tiny head.

Ellie handed Jolene a small blue blanket Polly had knitted for Deannie. "She's an angel, for sure," Ellie said.

"What're you gonna do? Will you stay here?" Jolene asked.

"I don't know, Jolene. Tom's trial's next week. I'll see what happens after that, I reckon. Right now, I need to stay put till Deannie's bigger and stronger. Besides, Polly would hogtie me if I tried to leave with her now." Ellie leaned over and kissed Deannie's cheek.

Jolene finished changing Deannie's clothes and held her close. "Ellie, I s'pose we need to talk 'bout us, and what happened."

"I reckon we do." Ellie had not had a conversation with Jolene since she and Deacon had married two years earlier. Then she showed up with Polly right after Tom killed Walter, not saying a word about the incident that lay curled-up like a rattle snake between them.

"I ain't mad at you no more, Ellie. I just don't understand why you'd do such a thing. You knew how much I loved Deacon. And you knew he loved me. Why would you try to come between us and destroy that?"

"I realize now I was wrong, Jolene. I thought I's protectin' you. I thought you could do better. I thought you's crazy for marryin' Deacon. I's afraid he wouldn't treat you right. His family's 'bout the poorest, dumbest people in the county, and I wanted better for you. I see now—heck, I saw it then—Deacon ain't like his family. He's a good man. A real good man, and he does love you. I'm sorry, Jolene, and I hope you and Deacon can forgive me." Tears rolled down Ellie's face.

"I know you's concerned for me, Ellie. Deacon's family's poor 'cause they's lazy. Deacon's different—he's a hard worker and a good provider. He keeps me safe," Jolene said.

"I know. I'm still angry he took you and run off to Paint Creek two weeks after your wedding. The wedding I wasn't invited to," Ellie said. "I reckon I didn't leave you any choice after the stunt I pulled with Clara. I's convinced my plan'd work. *All* men cheat. Or so I thought. Apparently, Deacon's the one in a million who doesn't cheat. When we walked in and you commenced to beat Clara 'bout the head—that's 'bout one of the funniest things I've seen in years."

Jolene chuckled. "Between me slapping her and pulling her hair, Clara tried to spit it out that it was all your idea for her to try get Deacon to kiss her. I wouldn't stop hittin' her long enough for her to even get it out. I'm glad we can laugh 'bout it now. I was mad at you somethin' fierce, Ellie, for the longest time."

"I hope you can forgive me, Jolene. I'm truly sorry. Seems like I keep makin' a mess whenever I try to help."

"Of course I forgive you. I can't hold onto that anger. It ate away at me for months. Those horrible dreams and visions came back like I used to have when we's little. I couldn't sleep. I couldn't eat. I prayed and prayed 'bout it, but they weren't no relief from the pain." Jolene wiped the tears rolling down her cheeks. "Oh, Ellie, I've missed you somethin' terrible. I wanna put this behind us and move on. It ain't 'bout just us no more. We got this little angel now."

"I know. She's gonna need all of us, 'cause I sure don't know what to do with a little baby." Ellie wiped her tears. "I love you, Jolene."

"I love you, too."

21.

<u>25 October 1911</u>

"Jake's waitin' outside. We's best be goin' soon."

"I guess I'm as ready as I'll ever be. Let's get this over with." Ellie dreaded the day's events.

Polly hugged Ellie. "Ever'thang'll work out the way it's s'posed to. You're not the one on trial."

The three of them sat in silence on the hard wagon seat and made the trip to Matewan, where they boarded the ten o'clock train to Williamson. They arrived at the courthouse before noon and waited inside. Reporters were swarming the courtroom and wanting to interview Ellie. She refused. She didn't want to talk to anyone about that horrible day, especially reporters.

Ellie spotted Mary sitting at the front on the Prosecution's side. If anyone was the victim in this whole sordid thing, it was Ellie. Mary was still wearing her black widow's garb from head to toe and was holding her newborn baby boy. Mary played the poor widow well and was giving interviews to any reporter who found her interesting enough to talk to.

At one o'clock, the deputy escorted Tom into the courtroom. The shackles on his ankles clanged together and dragged across the wooden floor. He stood ramrod straight with his head held high. Ellie saw something in him she hadn't bothered to notice since they first married—dignity and honor. Despite the situation, he looked noble, as though he were the judge and not the defendant, as though he were the victim and not the murderer.

She flinched when his startling blue eyes bore into hers. His stare was icy and unmoved at the sight of her. She shifted nervously in her seat and turned her gaze away from him. She had nothing to be ashamed of; he was the one on trial for murder, not her. Damn him.

Tom had expected a crowd for the trial, and the courtroom was packed. Everyone was in town for the sideshow—there to get a glimpse of the man who had killed the police chief and the mayor of Matewan. He knew Ellie would be there to testify. He hadn't expected her to be the first person he saw. She was still the most beautiful woman he had ever known. But the past few months in jail had changed him. When he looked into her black eyes this time, he saw directly into her black soul as well. All the love and longing he once held for her was gone.

Tom looked over at Mary Musick, sitting there holding her infant son. Funny, Musick's wife had also had a baby about the same time as Ellie. Damn, if that wasn't a slap in Ellie's face. It gave him pleasure that Ellie must feel cheated that Musick's widow had given birth to his *legitimate* child. The fact she'd brought the baby to court was the cherry on top.

The judge entered the courtroom and asked for a plea. Not guilty, of course. The trial didn't take long. There was only one witness—Ellie. Tom sat straight in his chair as the prosecutor made his opening remarks and told what a heinous murder Tom had committed. Then it was Tom's attorney's turn to make an opening statement. He pointed out Musick had come with the pretense of arresting him. There was no warrant issued and no warrant found on Musick's dead body. Tom's attorney stated a few assumptions as to why the mayor had accompanied Musick. Tom figured that would be a mystery no one could solve. The prosecutor called to the stand the two deputies. They were witnesses after the fact, so their testimony didn't amount to much. Then came Ellie's turn.

Ellie had never been more nervous in her life. Polly and Jake had assured her the attorneys couldn't accuse her of adultery. They might, however, insinuate the relationship with Walter was more than friendly.

She placed her hand on the Bible and swore to tell the truth. She had a clear shot of Mary and her baby. Mary sat holding the child in the front row behind the prosecutor. Ellie shot her one cold glance and then looked away. She wouldn't give the old biddy the luxury of thinking she cared.

The prosecutor started the questioning. "Mrs. Chafin, can you tell the court why Chief Musick was at your house that day?"

"No. I have no idea why he was there. None a'tall."

"What kind of relationship did you have with Chief Musick?"

Ellie wanted to tell him it was none of his damn business. "Friends. That's all."

"Mrs. Chafin, were you aware your husband was planning on shooting Chief Musick and Mayor Hoskins?"

"*No!* Of course not. He hadn't planned to shoot them."

Then came Tom's attorney. The same questions about her relationship with Walter.

"Mrs. Chafin, can you tell us about the day Mrs. Musick came to your home and you accompanied her to Matewan?"

Ellie described that day's events. "She tricked me. She tried to have me arrested because she was jealous."

"Do you have any idea why the mayor accompanied Chief Musick?

"No. I don't."

"Was your husband provoked by Chief Musick?"

Ellie looked at Tom. She couldn't lie about this—not even for Walter. "Yes, he was. Walter had no business bein' there that day. There was no reason for him to arrest Tom. Tom had done nothin' wrong. Tom's a good man. A decent man. The mayor told Walter to either arrest Tom or kill him. I'm certain Walter was plannin' on doin' just that—killin' my husband."

Mary let out a gasp and cried out, "You're a lyin' tramp. How dare you?"

All eyes turned to Mary. Ellie was stunned that Mary would cry out at her testimony. Ellie had told the truth. For once in her life, she told the God's honest truth.

The courtroom exploded into chaos. The judge banged his gavel. "Order. Order in this courtroom or I will have every last one of you arrested for contempt of court. Silence!" He pointed the end of his gavel at Mary. "Mrs. Musick, one more outburst like that out of you, and I will have you escorted out by the deputy." The judge pounded his gavel again, and the crowd quieted. The attorneys gave their closing remarks and the jury filed out to deliberate.

Tom's attorney had someone escort Ellie, Polly, and Jake out of the courtroom and down the hall to a small room where they could wait for the verdict. "I'm gonna go find some coffee. Best if you girls wait here. Ain't no need to give those reporters somethin' to put in their papers," Jake said.

Polly stood at the window and watched the reporters flocking around the courthouse steps. "Jake's right. Those reporters are a bunch of vultures. Hopefully, this'll be over soon, Ellie."

"I just want this to end and put it behind me." Ellie joined Polly at the window. "I'll never understand why Walter and the mayor were there that day, Polly. I think he really wanted to kill Tom."

"What do you think he hoped would happen after that? At that point he knew you and Mary both were gonna have his baby."

"I don't know. Maybe I didn't know Walter as well as I thought I did."

Ellie spent the next two hours pacing the small room while Polly sat at the table and knitted a sweater for Deannie.

There was a flurry of activity in the hallway. Ellie and Polly jumped when the door opened. Jake entered and quietly closed the door behind him. "Jury's back. Let's get in there a'fore that swarm of reporters gets back up here," Jake said.

The jury filed into the courtroom and Tom stood as the judge entered. The jury foreman handed the verdict to the bailiff, and he in turn handed it to the judge.

The judge read the verdict and folded the paper. "Mr. Tom Chafin, the jury finds you guilty of manslaughter in the first degree. This court hereby sentences you to five years in the Moundsville State Penitentiary, minus the time served in the county jail while awaiting trial. This court is adjourned."

The trial was over in less than five hours. Tom stood, and the deputy escorted him out of the courtroom, his shackles clanging and scraping against the wooden floor once more.

Ellie, Polly, and Jake boarded the train, and Jake led them to the back of the car away from everyone who might know them. "If Mary Musick gets on this train, please shield me from the sight of her and that baby. I don't think I can take one more humiliation today," Ellie said.

Reaching for Polly's hand, Ellie leaned her head against the window and watched the boarding passengers.

22.

<u>6 November 1911</u>

Ellie woke to the baby's cries around two o'clock. She didn't move, hoping Deannie would go back to sleep. The cries got louder and more insistent. She threw the covers off and got up. "Why do you have to wake up and cry just when I get to sleepin' real good?" She gently picked up Deannie and held her close. The baby searched for her breast and quieted as soon as she found the source of her delight. Ellie was bone tired and resentful that every hour of her day was dedicated to this tiny little life. Polly insisted Ellie would be a great mother and she would bond with the baby soon enough. Ellie had her doubts. All the little thing wanted to do was feed on her breast every few hours. It was exhausting.

She couldn't stay here with Polly and Jake forever. Polly said as long as she's nursing, they should stay here, especially since Deannie came early. She had plenty of food and plenty of help. So, here she was. Stuck at Lynn in a house with a family she loved but didn't really fit in with. She needed to figure out what she was going to do—where she was going to go. Where could she go with a little baby? She had a little money from selling Tom's moonshine, but that wouldn't last forever. Her mother told her not to come back there. No man in his right mind would want her if she came with a baby in tow.

"Polly, we need to talk. Let's go for a walk, where we can be alone." Ellie handed Polly her shawl. They walked out of the kitchen and down to the river in silence. Their favorite tree was nearly bare. There hadn't been much rain for the past few weeks, and the water was low. They sat on a bed of yellow and orange leaves under the tree.

"Is somethin' wrong, Ellie?"

"No. Yes. Oh, goodness, Polly. I'm not cut out for this kinda life. You and Jake's been so good to me and Deannie, and I can't ever thank you enough. But I'm goin' stir crazy here. I want my own home. My own place. I can't live here with you forever."

"You're wantin' to leave? And take Deannie? Where? Where'll you go, Ellie?"

"I don't know, Polly. That's the problem. I ain't got nowhere to go. Especially with a little baby."

"Ellie, you can't take Deannie and leave. She's too little."

Ellie shifted uncomfortably, avoiding eye contact with Polly. A familiar restlessness had gripped Ellie. The steady routine of Polly's house was wearing on her nerves. Every day was the same as the day before . . . and the day before that one.

"Ellie, look at me. Deannie's a tiny baby, and she came early. You should at least wait till springtime. She'll be bigger and stronger then, and you'll have plenty of time to decide what you wanna do."

"Polly, I can't stay here all winter. I'll surely lose my mind. Or at least what's left of it. I feel like I'm smotherin' more and more as the days pass."

Tears welled up in Polly's eyes, and Ellie took her hand.

"Oh, no, Polly. I don't mean it toward you. You're my soul. You're the only person who's ever truly loved me. But this is *your* family, not mine. You have your husband, your kids, your home, your life. I need mine."

"Ellie, please don't take Deannie away from me. I love that baby as if she's my own."

"I've been thinkin', Polly. Maybe she should be your'n. I ain't fit to be nobody's mama. It ain't in me. I see the way you are with your boys, and I know they ain't no way I can ever be that sorta mama for Deannie."

"What are you sayin', Ellie?" Polly fought back the tears.

"I ain't rightly sure. I s'pose what I'm tryin' to say is maybe you and Jake should raise Deannie. Right here with your boys." Ellie stood up and faced the river. "You know I ain't cut out for this kinda life. Who're we kiddin'? Deannie's life would be horrible with me as her mama. I feel like I'm smotherin' plum to death, Polly." She sat back down.

"Ellie, she needs you to feed her. Please, let's get through the winter to make this decision. They ain't no need for you to make any sorta changes right now. Deannie needs you. I need you."

Ellie stared out at the river, its waters gently meandering through the mountains. As quiet and soft as the river seemed now, Ellie knew it could become a ferocious and unforgiving force, as she had seen it do most every spring. Her mind drifted back to that hot summer day she wanted to drown herself—and Deannie. She had wanted to die that day, but Deannie wanted to live. Now? Now, *she* wanted to live, just not here at Lynn with Polly and her family. And certainly not with a baby. She longed to be free to do whatever she wanted. She loved Deannie, but not the way Polly did. The last thing she wanted was a baby to care for. She saw the people in the Blue Goose Saloon when they went to Matewan. They were laughing and drinking and having fun—*that* was the life she wanted. She couldn't stay in Matewan. Since the murders, everyone pointed and whispered about her. No, she would need to leave. Maybe go to Charleston. A bigger city, more men, more money. Yes, that was what she needed to do.

"Ellie, have you heard a word I've said?"

23.

<u>Christmas 1911</u>

Ellie and Polly prepared dinner, and Jake's parents arrived to join them. His father took his hat off at the door. "Whew, boy, snow's a comin' down like nothin' I ever see'd a'fore."

"It's snowin'?" Ellie ran to the window to see for herself. The snow blanketed the back yard. The path leading out to the barn and then on down to the river was almost completely covered.

"I love a Christmas snow." Polly stood next to Ellie and peered out.

Jake's parents left immediately after dinner to make their way home safely. Ellie and Polly cleaned the kitchen, and Ellie fed Deannie.

"Ellie, you sure didn't eat much. Are you feelin' all right?" Polly asked.

"I'm fine. I hate the snow."

"Remember when we's little and we'd make snowmen and have snowball fights with our brothers and their friends? They thought they's so clever sneakin' around the barn to surprise us. *We* were the clever ones. You, me, and Jolene climbed up in that hay loft and had a perfect shot at 'em. We bombed those boys good." They both laughed at the memory. "We sure had some good times back then, Ellie."

"Yeah, we sure did have fun growin' up on this river. I want Deannie to experience ever' bit of the fun we did." Ellie teared up.

Ellie washed the final dishes and looked out the kitchen window. The Tug Valley was quiet under the Christmas snowfall.

"Well, it's time for music. Ellie, get your mandolin. Jake, you get the boys."

The family gathered around the fireplace, and Deannie lay on a quilt on the floor. Jake played the fiddle, Ellie the mandolin, and their oldest boy, Seth, the banjo.

"Aunt Ellie, that's sure a pretty mandolin you got there. You care to let me play it tonight?" Seth asked.

"You sure can. You ever played a mandolin?"

"No, ma'am."

"Well, I figure if you can play the banjo, you can play the mandolin. It looks like we got a lot of snowy days to teach you how to play." Ellie strummed the instrument and Deannie kicked her tiny legs and let out a gleeful squeal. Ellie sang, and Deannie looked at her with big green eyes and smiled.

24.

<u>Early January 1912</u>

"How much snow?" Polly asked Jake as he stomped it off his boots at the kitchen door.

"Nineteen inches."

"I think that's a record," Polly said.

"We'll be snowed in here till springtime. I sure hope that's all of it." Ellie said as she peeled potatoes at the kitchen table.

"Well, it's just January. Winter ain't got good and started yet. We might as well plan to burrow in for the next couple of months, at least," Jake said.

Polly sat down at the table with Ellie and picked up a potato.

Deannie's cries came from the bedroom. "I guess she's hungry. How can one tiny baby eat so much?" Ellie stomped off to feed Deannie.

Polly followed Ellie. "Ellie, she might not be hungry. Maybe just needin' to be held. Here, let me help you. I know you're tired."

"I'm exhausted, Polly. She's up all night fussin' over one thing or another. How did you do this so many times?" Tears filled Ellie's eyes.

"It can surely wear you down. I understand." Polly picked up Deannie and held her close. Deannie's cries faded to a whimper and then stopped altogether. "See, sometimes she just needs some attention."

"Aren't you goin' stir crazy in this house? They's so much snow, we can't even go for a walk."

"It'll melt soon enough."

The snow and ice eventually began to melt, only to be covered with more snow. January slid into February, which brought more snow and ice. Ellie's anxiety grew with each new snowfall. If she wasn't busy cleaning or helping Polly with meals, she paced the floors. She even helped shovel snow and feed the animals. Anything to keep moving and take her mind off being stuck at Lynn.

Ellie was grumpy and moody. Everyone in the house avoided her. Everyone except Deannie, who needed her for nourishment. Deannie's demands on her breasts made Ellie even more irritable. She was certain her breasts would never get used to this torture. The tenderness had eased off a bit, although it still hurt. Ellie saw it is as nothing more than an inconvenience to her. She would never understand how women dedicated their entire lives to husbands and children.

25.

<u>10 March 1912</u>

March arrived with warm rain, and the snow finally dwindled, much to Ellie's delight. It rained for three days. The Tug River spilled her banks with the rain and winter's runoff.

People living along the banks moved to higher ground. On March 10, the river crested. The sun popped out early in the afternoon and was a glorious sight. The road was a muddy, sloppy mess, but it would soon be passable.

It was another ten days before they were able to make a trip to Matewan for supplies. Ellie offered to go with Seth to get what was needed.

In town they headed to the general store and bought supplies to replenish what they had used up over the past few months—mostly flour, cornmeal, candles, and oil for the lamps. Ellie helped haul the supplies out to the wagon. It felt good to be outside moving after being cooped up for the winter.

Seth took the candles and oil from Ellie and loaded them in the back. He removed a quilt tucked in under the back bench and pulled out a bag. "Aunt Ellie, what's this?"

"Seth, I'm not goin' back to the house with you." Ellie grabbed her bag from Seth's hands. "I'm gettin' on a train to Charleston. The train leaves here in forty-five minutes. I need to get over to the depot and buy my ticket." She adjusted her hat and coat. "Tell your mama I left a letter under my pillow."

Seth took her by the arm. "Aunt Ellie, what'll I tell mama? What you gonna do 'bout Deannie? You can't just up and leave."

She placed her hand on his face. "Seth, they's things I can't explain. The letter'll help explain it to your mama, she knows how I feel, and she know'd I's gonna leave as soon as that snow melted. I love Deannie, but she's better off with your mama and daddy." She hugged him and kissed his cheek. "You take care of your mama and Deannie. Tell your mama I love her, and I'm sorry to leave like this."

Ellie reached under the wagon seat, pulled out her mandolin, and handed it to the youngster. "Seth, I want you to have this."

"Aunt Ellie, I can't take this. You love this mandolin."

"No, I want you to have it. I want you to keep it safe. You gotta promise me one thing."

"What's that?"

"You'll teach Deannie how to play. As soon as she's old enough to hold the thing, you start teachin' that baby how to play."

"I sure will, Aunt Ellie. I promise." Seth wiped the tears from his eyes.

Ellie hugged Seth and hurried down the street to the depot.

She bought a one-way ticket to Charleston and boarded the train with a mixture of dread and excitement. Mostly, a feeling of disappointment settled in the pit of her heart. Disappointment in herself for leaving. For having to leave. For not being able to be the mother Deannie needed. Not being the wife Tom had needed. She wouldn't dwell on that now. Maybe she would eventually make her way to New York. Right now, she was on the 12:10 train northbound toward Charleston. She had a few hundred dollars from the sale of the moonshine. She hoped that it would last a while. The mountains sped past the window. A whole new world awaited her.

She settled into her seat and looked around her at the other passengers for the first time. She was one of three women, and the only one traveling alone. The other passengers appeared to be businessmen—probably coal operators. One particularly handsome man stared at her. She smiled at him. He smiled back and moved over to sit in the seat directly across from her.

"What's a pretty lady like you doin' travelin' alone?"

"Well, first you should properly introduce yourself a'fore you start askin' questions."

He laughed. "John. My name is John."

"Hello, John. My name is Ellie. I'm travelin' to Charleston."

"What's your business in Charleston?"

"Now, that's a rather personal question. Goin' to visit there for a while. There's nothin' left for me in Matewan."

"Do you have family there? Where will you stay?"

"I don't have any family there, and I'm not sure where I'll stay. I figured I'd sort all that out when I get there. Where do you recommend?"

He massaged his mustache while pondering her question. "I typically stay at the Hotel Ruffner. It's a fine establishment and should meet your needs."

Ellie turned away and looked out the window. "Hmmmm . . . we'll see."

"I'd be happy to escort you there when we arrive in Charleston."

She turned and locked her black eyes into his. She knew in that moment she had him. "That's mighty kind of you."

They chatted the rest of the way. His name was John Havers, and he was a vice president with the Baldwin-Felts Detective Agency. He was from Pittsburgh and living in Charleston until the job moved him to the next city. He proudly told her he worked with Tom Felts on a daily basis, coordinating with the more important clients—all coal operators. She let him talk and brag about his job and his status within the Baldwin-Felts organization. She was skilled at feeding the male ego to get what she wanted. By the time they arrived in Charleston, John Havers didn't realize he had been hit with a meteor. He offered to pay for her room at the Hotel Ruffner. She agreed to let him, but only for two weeks, until she found a permanent place to live.

Part 2

One way in, no way out.

26.

<u>2 April 1912 (Charleston)</u>

"You've been in my bed every night since I arrived in Charleston two weeks ago." Ellie curled into John's arm.

"I'm paying for the room. I suppose I can sleep here when I want."

"Don't you care 'bout my reputation? I don't want those gossipy old Baldwin-Felts women talkin' 'bout me." She propped herself up on her elbow and stared down at him.

"What are you afraid they're gonna say about you? That you're a kept woman?"

"That's exactly what I think."

He grabbed her chin and turned her face towards him. "Well, you're my woman. That's all they need to know."

"You're hurting me." Ellie pulled her face away from his grip. "I wanna make sure they know you have your own room. So be sure they don't see you when you come in and when you leave here."

"I'm two steps ahead of you, Ellie. I've arranged for us to have connecting suites. You can enter through your door and

I will enter through mine. There are only three sets of suites that connect. We'll move into them tonight." John got up and started dressing. "Have the hotel maid help you move your things."

"I don't have much. It shouldn't take long." Ellie said.

"No, you don't have much. Actually, you don't have anything nice. You look like a country bumpkin, not a fine city lady." John tossed a wad of bills on the bed. "Go buy yourself something decent to wear and burn those rags you brought with you. We have a birthday party to go to next Friday night. It's at the Morton's house on the Kanawha River. He's a big deal coal operator, so you need to play the part of a lady. Remember, you're *my* woman, and I damn well expect you to look better than anyone there." John kissed her goodbye, leaving her alone.

Ellie couldn't believe her good luck. She would have her own suite of rooms at the fanciest hotel in the state. She locked the door and returned to her bed to count the money John had left. One hundred dollars! She could buy ten dresses.

Ellie had never owned a store-bought dress; she, Jolene, and Polly had always made their own. She had no idea where to shop for dresses in Charleston—certainly not the kind she would need for a fancy dinner party. She called for Dottie, the maid assigned to her room.

"Dottie, I'll be moving into a suite later today and I'll need your help moving my things. I don't know which room I'm moving to. Mr. Havers said you'd help me. Also, I need to buy some fancy dresses. Do you know where I should go?"

"Ms. Ellie, I can take you down to the dressmaker right away, and your suite should be ready by the time we get back. If you need a dress made, it'll take some time. She may have some you can have altered to fit you though."

"Thank you, Dottie. Let's go now, shall we?" Ellie took an instant liking to Dottie, and they chatted easily on the walk to the dressmaker. Dottie felt more like a baby sister than a hotel maid. Barely seventeen years old, she had worked at the hotel for two years.

Ellie and Dottie spent the morning with the dressmaker. Dottie was right. Anything worth having had to be made special. The dressmaker had two dresses and assured Ellie they were suitable for the party at the Morton's. She had dressed everyone on the invitation list. They would be altered and sent to the hotel Thursday morning, along with shoes, stockings, and accessories.

Ellie and Dottie strolled down to the river before returning to the hotel. "Dottie, tell me 'bout the Baldwin-Felts ladies and other people I might meet at this party."

Dottie shook her head, sending her blonde curls bouncing. "Oh, Ms. Ellie, I don't wanna talk outa turn 'bout the other ladies."

Ellie placed her hand on Dottie's shoulder. "Dottie, you can trust me. I don't want the latest gossip. I just wanna know what I'm walkin' into. I wanna be prepared."

Dot fixed her big blue eyes on Ellie and provided her with the inside scoop on the Ruffner Hotel guests. As Ellie had expected, Charleston society wasn't for the faint of heart. The wives of the coal operators and the Baldwin-Felts men were ambitious and determined to maintain their social status, either through gossip, expensive clothes and jewelry, or good old-fashioned back stabbing.

The out-of-town wives cycled in and out of the hotel on a regular basis. They came for shopping trips and special events. A few had permanent suites and would stay for weeks on end. The local ladies—mostly wives of the wealthy coal operators—came almost daily for brunches, lunches, and social gatherings. The larger and best parties were hosted at their palatial homes on the Kanawha River. Depending on their standing in the social circles, these women were intent on maintaining their status and determined to climb to the top at any cost.

Ellie had her own ambitions, and her eyes on bigger sights. John was nothing more than her entrée into a whole new world. She'd sacrificed the love of her child and her family for this new life, she'd be damned if she would settle for the first man she happened upon.

She had sent a letter to Polly her first day in Charleston. She hoped Polly could understand and forgive her. The truth was they all knew she was not the mother Deannie needed. Polly and Jake would give the child a much better life than Ellie ever could.

Her first few weeks in town, Ellie spent hours at the library reading about social etiquette and manners. She was determined not to humiliate herself by using the wrong fork or saying something improper. She started paying special attention to the way she spoke. She dropped the twang from her speech and enunciated her words.

She wanted to make the right impression on the right people, and the party at the Morton's would be her first big event to practice her new social skills. She had Dottie set up a table with a full dinner place setting in her new suite of rooms, and she spent the next four days practicing using the right utensils, with Dottie's guidance. Ellie was determined to outshine everyone at the party.

27.

<u>12 April 1912</u>

"How do I look?" Ellie asked.

"Turn." Let me see the back."

Ellie let John take in her beauty.

"Perfection," he said. "I like the green on you. It's quite bewitching."

John escorted Ellie downstairs. All eyes were on her. John's tightened grip on her elbow signaled he had noticed everyone looking at her as well. They walked out the front door of the hotel to the waiting carriage.

Ellie was nervous as the carriage pulled off the main road and passed through a large wrought-iron gate bearing an M. The horses pulled them slowly down a tree-lined driveway that circled around a fountain in front of the house. Ellie had never seen anything so grand. The place was nearly as big as the hotel. Behind the house, just beyond a well-manicured rose garden not yet in bloom, the Kanawha River flowed quietly. The carriage came to a stop, and she took a deep breath before exiting. She stood and smoothed her dress and her hair. John took her arm and led her to the front door.

Despite how well-prepared she thought she was, she was uncertain of what to do next. She decided to follow John's lead and figure it out as she went along. The Knowing was buzzing in her head, and she gave it her full attention. A butler greeted them at the door and escorted them to the parlor. The inside of the house was as impressive as the outside, with a large spiral staircase leading to the second floor. Massive paintings hung on every wall.

John introduced her to their hosts, Quinn and Mrs. Morton, and then to his boss, Tom Felts and his wife. Next was Tony Gaujot. John's jealousy seeped out when he introduced Ellie to Tony. Tony's lingering gaze on her breasts wasn't lost on Ellie or John. After the formal introductions, John pulled Ellie aside. "Stay away from that bastard Gaujot."

"Why?"

"He's a sneaky fuck, that's why. He walks around like he owns Tom Felts. My main goal is to dethrone him from his position. That job should be mine." John took a glass of champagne from one of the maids passing among the guests with trays. "Bastard was awarded the Medal of Honor last year. Of course, this was after he was court martialed and acquitted for murdering a fellow soldier. He wears the medal as a damn watch fob. No class."

"Why was he awarded the Medal of Honor?"

"He stole a canoe in the Philippines and swam across a river or something. Just stay clear of him."

After a brief cocktail hour, the butler signaled dinner would be served soon. Ellie rehearsed in her mind the placement of plates, silverware, glasses—as she had practiced all week. They gathered in the dining room, and she was thankful to be seated close to the hostess, so she could mimic her actions. Ellie was seated within earshot of the conversation between Tom Felts, John, Tony Gaujot, and Mr. Morton. She tried to keep track of Mrs. Morton's actions *and* follow the conversation. She quickly forgot about her table manners as the conversation turned to the union and the anticipated Paint Creek strike.

Quinn Morton sat at the head of the table. "Tom, what's your strategy to keep those Paint Creek miners in line?"

"As we discussed earlier this week," Tom Felts said, "basically, whatever it takes—evictions, threats, intimidation. We're also prepared to start bringing in transportation men from other states to replace the miners, if it comes to that. As you know, we have a good mix of the elected officials on our side, so I don't think a strike at Paint Creek will have any lasting impact. Just like we've done before, we'll keep those miners in check—don't you worry."

John asked, "How's the bargaining with the union coming along? Any progress there?"

The ladies at the other end of the table were babbling and giggling about something of no consequence. Ellie wished they would quiet down so she could focus on the conversation at her end of the table.

"Nothing yet. They aren't budging on their demands, and we aren't budging on our end either. Some of the coal operators are willing to make concessions to the union. I'm not one of them." Quinn Morton took a sip of his wine. "The biggest obstacle right now is getting the coal operators to stand united against this mockery of all we've done for those ignorant bastards."

"Quinn, your language. We have guests." Mrs. Morton muttered under her breath.

Quinn Morton patted his wife's hand. "I suppose you're right, dear. Gentleman, we can continue this conversation over brandy and cigars after dinner."

After dinner, John left Ellie with the ladies in the parlor while the men retired to another room to talk business. Ellie hated these social customs. In her family, the conversation included anyone who wanted to listen. The women had as much of an opinion as the men, and typically were much better at strategizing and planning.

A few of the ladies were polite and kind. The majority were nothing more than gossipy, jealous shrews. The Knowing had Ellie on guard from the moment they closed the parlor doors. A butler passed a tray of champagne. A maid of no more than fifteen years old circled and offered an alternative of tea or coffee. Most of the ladies took the champagne. Ellie held a glass herself but barely sipped it. She needed to be on her toes.

Mrs. Morton was kind and gracious. She took Ellie's hand. "Come, dear, I'll introduce you to the ladies. It's so hard to get acquainted with the men talking business all the time." Mrs. Morton made the formal introductions, offering a tidbit of information about each person.

The Knowing was Ellie's greatest weapon with these ladies. They had their guards down, if they had any, and were wide open for her to read their true intent. Ellie would use this to her advantage. If she couldn't be in the room with the men to hear about their plans, she would see what she could get out of the wives.

"So, Ellie, where are you from, dear?" Joan Wells was one of the older women. Her words were sticky sweet, and Ellie could see her true intent. She was looking for a chink in

Ellie's armor, a defect in her beauty. Hell, Ellie didn't need The Knowing to surmise this much from Joan Wells. She looked rather pinched in the face, as if she had never had a good thought about anyone in her life.

Ellie had prepared for this question. She saw no reason to lie about it, but she would certainly not divulge much information. "Mingo County. I've wanted to move to Charleston for quite some time. Charleston is now home for me."

Tom's trial had been plastered in newspapers all over the state. She hoped no one in her new circle decided to put the story together. The newspapers rarely referred to her as Ellie—she was simply "Tom's wife." If they did call her by name, it was Ella. Ellie had decided she would go by Ellie Cline, to avoid any connection to Tom. Thankfully, there were no photographs of her in the papers.

"Do you have family here?" Joan asked.

"I have a few cousins in the area," Ellie lied.

"How do you know John?"

"John and I met the day I arrived in Charleston," Ellie said.

"Hello, Ellie. I'm Myrtle Taylor. It's so nice to meet you." Ellie noticed Myrtle wasn't dressed as fashionably as the other ladies, and her speech wasn't as refined. Myrtle was short and plump, with an ample bosom and a genuine smile.

"It's nice to meet you, Myrtle. Do you live here in Charleston?"

"Oh, no. We live in Bluefield. My husband's Clyde. He's the lead attorney for Mr. Felts. We're here about every other week. Since the kids've all grown and gotten married, I travel with Clyde whenever he comes to Charleston. I just love stayin' at the Hotel Ruffner. It's so elegant. Have you been there?"

"Yes. Actually, that's where I'm stayin' for now. It's quite lovely."

"You'll need to join us for our afternoon teas and lunches. Those of us from out of town try to coordinate so we're all here at the same time." Myrtle said.

"Yes, Ellie you'll certainly need to join us for gatherings." Joan Wells joined the conversation.

"I'd enjoy that very much," Ellie said.

"Myrtle, you need to slow down on the champagne. You're getting a little uncertain on your feet again." Joan informed her.

A bright red blush creeped up Myrtle's neck and face. "Oh, my! I'm so sorry. I never seem to know when I've had too much. Joan keeps me on the straight and narrow." Myrtle giggled and placed her half-empty glass on a side table.

The ladies spent the next hour drinking champagne. They either gossiped about the women in their circle who were not in attendance or discussed their upcoming events.

Ellie was relieved when the parlor doors opened. Mrs. Morton politely announced the party was officially over and escorted them out into the foyer where her staff was waiting with their coats.

The men joined them shortly, smelling of cigars and brandy. Other than helping her on with her coat, John barely acknowledged Ellie. After the required goodbyes, John took her roughly by the elbow and escorted her to their carriage.

Before stepping into the carriage, she jerked her arm out of his grasp. "Why are you in such a pissy mood? Somethin' happen in your meetin'?" The carriage door closed behind them.

John stared at her.

Ellie shrugged her shoulders. "Fine. Don't answer me." She turned and looked out the window.

"You think you're something special, don't you?"

Ellie didn't respond. She watched the river. The Knowing roared up inside her, sending a warning to Ellie that John's rage was boiling over, but she had nowhere to run. John shifted in his seat, then Ellie felt the toe of his shoe cut into her shin.

"You whore. I asked you a question!"

Ellie grabbed her leg. "What the hell is wrong with you?"

"You! *You're* what's wrong with me. What do you think we talked about for the first twenty minutes of our meeting? *You!*" He leaned into her face and grabbed her arm. "The only thing those men could talk about was *you*. How beautiful you are. Told me I'd never be able to keep a woman like you. How do you think that makes me feel?"

"That's not my fault. You should've told them to go to hell. I didn't do anything, you crazy bastard." Ellie pulled away from him. "Let go of me."

The wagon came to a stop in front of the hotel. The carriage driver hopped down and opened the door. Ellie took his hand and stepped out.

John called after her. "Ellie, get back here."

"Go to hell." She limped into the Ruffner.

"Fine. Have it your way. I'm goin' to get a drink." John disappeared through the swinging doors to the tavern.

Ellie continued up the stairs to her room. She removed her shoes and stockings to reveal a bruised and swollen shin.

She sat at her dressing table and took the pins from her hair and contemplated her options.

John's footsteps were heavy on the stairs. Ellie held her breath, hoping he would go to his own suite and pass out. He threw open the door to her room.

He stomped over to her. "I won't tolerate you flirtin' with other men, Ellie."

Ellie firmly placed the hairbrush on her dressing table and stood to face him. She was prepared to run if she had to. "What on earth are you talkin' 'bout, John? I didn't flirt with anyone. I barely spoke to any of the men."

"Were you makin' eyes at 'em behind my back?" His gaze was unfocused.

"You aren't makin' any sense! I never left your side till I went into the parlor with the ladies. Don't be stupid."

"Oh, you think I'm stupid, do you?" He lunged at her and grabbed the top of her dress. The seam along her shoulder tore. He seized her arms, his fingers gripping her flesh. The force backed her up against the dressing table. His breath reeked of cigars and brandy.

"John, stop. Please. Stop."

"Take that damn dress off." He stepped back and started removing his own jacket and shirt.

Ellie's fingers fumbled to remove the dress.

"Here, let me help you." He spun her away from him. He grabbed the back of the dress with both hands and ripped it, sending two dozen tiny buttons bouncing across the hardwood floor. "There. That certainly makes things easier. Now get the rest of that frilly shit off."

Rattled, Ellie stumbled out of her undergarments and stood naked in front of him. John grabbed her by the arms and flung her towards the bed. She fell against it and scrambled toward the pillows. She pressed her back into the wooden headboard and pulled her knees up tight to her chest. John flung his shirt in the pile with Ellie's dress and undergarments. He wobbled as he attempted to remove his boots, eventually giving up.

Ellie wasn't sure what to expect. She had had her share of men, but none of them had been violent with her. John sat up on his knees facing her, his pants around his boots. He grabbed Ellie's ankles and pulled her toward him. She refused to cooperate, which only angered him more. He pried her legs apart. Ellie let out a cry as he fell on her bruised shin. John's full weight pressed down on her. He dug his fingers into her hips and buttocks and forced himself inside her. Ellie let out a scream.

"Does that hurt? Good. You deserve to hurt."

Fighting only fueled his anger. She closed her eyes tight and lay still, letting him continue with his sadistic self-pleasure. His breath came hot and labored with each thrust. After a few minutes, he grunted and rolled over. Ellie dared not move until she was certain he had passed out, evident by his loud snoring.

Ellie slipped quietly from the bed. She stood at her dressing table and washed his semen from her body. The smell of brandy and cigars from his breath lingered in the room and on her skin. No amount of scrubbing would remove the indignity of what she had just endured from the bastard. She looked at his reflection in the mirror and thought how easily it would be to put the pillow over his face and smother him.

28.

<u>19 April 1912</u>

Ellie stood naked in front of the full-length mirror. Her skin still warm from the bath. She traced the bruises with her fingers, from her breasts down to the soft spot between her thighs. Black, blue, green, the first one blending into the next one, like the Tug River after a summer storm.

One week had passed since the birthday party at the Morton's on the Kanawha River, and her body still ached from John's rage. Ellie reasoned the violence was a one-time event and wouldn't happen again. He'd been drinking; their relationship was new. Besides, he had apologized over and over. He'd even given her a ruby and pearl brooch, and once the bruises healed, she was going to the dressmaker to get five new dresses.

Still, she needed to get away from him, but she also needed to find out more information about the plans Baldwin-Felts had for the striking miners. John was one of Tom Felts's confidants and highest-ranking deputies. He was key in getting the information she needed. She couldn't walk away. Not yet.

John had left for Paint Creek that morning. The miners had gone out on strike the day before, and he told her not to expect him back for a few days. She was glad he was gone, but she worried about Jolene and how the strike would impact her and Deacon.

Ellie dressed and took care to make sure none of her bruises were visible. Her shin still hurt, but she could now walk without a limp. She had difficulty hiding the bruises from Dottie, who insisted on helping her get dressed. Dottie was too polite and knew her place well enough not to mention the marks, so it hung there between them, unspoken.

29.

1 May 1912

At Myrtle's invitation, Ellie agreed to attend the afternoon tea. She took a deep breath and entered the small parlor off the main hotel lobby. Myrtle was the first to greet her. "Oh, Ellie, you look lovely. That's a beautiful dress. I never seem to be able to pick out the pretty dresses. You must accompany me to the dressmaker."

"I'd be more than happy to help, Myrtle. But I think you look splendid." Myrtle could be a great source of information, and Ellie wanted to keep her close.

Ellie quickly discovered the ladies were an incessant stream of gossip. She listened but didn't partake. She had been on the receiving end of nasty lies most of her life over one thing or another. If the ladies weren't gossiping, they were bragging, either about what they had or who they knew—each determined to outdo the other. The Baldwin-Felts ladies in particular didn't know when to shut up, and they talked easily amongst themselves about Baldwin-Felts business they had heard from their husbands.

The society ladies were about as exciting as watching corn grow. Ellie would have preferred to be in the tavern on the lower level of the hotel dancing and drinking whiskey than having tea with the ladies. But, that would only lead her right back to Mingo County, or worse.

"Let's sit for a moment and chat," Myrtle said.

Ellie followed her to the small sofa near the window.

Myrtle took her second piece of apple pie from the tray held out in front of her before she sat down. "I understand John'll be spendin' a lot of time at Paint Creek with Clyde. Those damn miners are gonna be the death of us all, Ellie."

"Oh? How so?" Ellie knew if she gave Myrtle—or any of the ladies—the upper hand, they would be more likely to share what they knew.

"From what Clyde says, miners are comin' from all over—Mingo County, Lincoln County, New River—and they're bringin' in guns and ammunition to that bunch up on Paint Creek. The coal operators are afraid it'll turn ugly. So, our boys are gettin' ready for 'em. Baldwin-Felts is bringin' in hundreds more guards in the next week to keep those fools in line. An ambush of sorts is what Clyde said."

"Hopefully, the strike won't last long," Ellie said. She needed to get word to Jake that they were going to be met by hundreds of armed guards.

30.

4 May 1912 (Lynn)

The wagon bounced along the road to Lynn. Ellie looked over at her companion, his black skin a stark silhouette against the night sky. She was grateful he had agreed to come with her. Dottie had introduced her to Dayton shortly after she'd arrived in Charleston, and they had become fast friends. Dayton had a calming presence, and The Knowing had instantly told Ellie he was trustworthy and kind.

Dayton was young and worked three jobs to care for his mother and younger sisters. He delivered dried goods to the hotel and gave her the scoop on the hotel staff and who she could trust and who she needed to steer clear of. Ellie had hired him to run errands for her and escort her about town when needed. With John's money, she paid him so well he needed to work only two jobs.

In Charleston, this arrangement made perfect sense to the public. Dayton was Ellie's driver, helper, and protector. But if anyone saw her in Matewan with a strange man, the local tongues would wag. Thankfully, it was dark, and they hadn't encountered anyone she knew since they'd left Charleston. The last train to Matewan had been almost empty, and no one was around when they got the wagon in town.

She'd told John she was visiting her sick cousin. He was too busy plotting with Tom Felts to pay much attention to her. His first mistake was assuming she wasn't listening to everything discussed between him and the Felts brothers—Tom, Albert, and Lee—and Tony Gaujot. John's second mistake was thinking she was nothing more than a pretty face he could buy and use as he pleased.

She was taking a huge risk sharing Baldwin-Felts information with Jake. But she had no choice. This wasn't about her; it was about the people she loved.

Polly closed the door to Deannie's room, making sure not to wake her. The baby had finally fallen asleep around midnight. Her fever was still high, and Polly hoped it would break before morning. The night was going to be a long one—and not only because of Deannie. Jake had men coming to meet and prepare before they left for Paint Creek in the morning. The men had been arriving every few hours. Jake was expecting about twenty of them to show up before dawn.

Polly went to the kitchen to prepare a meal the men could take with them. Jake's sister and niece had arrived earlier to help. They were resting in the boys' bedroom; Polly would wake them within the hour.

Jake and several men were at the kitchen table. Polly had just put on a pot of coffee when she heard a gentle knock at the back door. She knew most of the men who would be making the trip to Paint Creek and was surprised to see a stranger standing at the door. "Hello. Are you here to see Jake?"

"No, ma'am. I's here to see you. It's Ms. Ellie ..."

"Ellie? Is she all right? Has somethin' happened to her?"

"No, ma'am. Nothin's happened to Ms. Ellie. She sent me to fetch you."

"Fetch me? To come where? Where is she?"

"She's out here in the wagon, ma'am."

Polly quietly stepped outside so as not to raise any attention from Jake and his men. Dayton led her around behind the barn to his wagon, where Ellie was waiting.

"Ellie? Is ever'thang all right? What on earth are you doin' here this time of night?"

Ellie jumped down from the wagon and ran to Polly and embraced her. "Polly, is Jake still here? Has he left for Paint Creek yet?"

"How ... how you know 'bout Paint Creek, Ellie?"

"He's walkin' into a trap, Polly. I need to talk to him. Now."

"Well, come inside. You can tell him and the rest of the men."

"No! I want to talk to Jake alone. It's best they not know it's me tellin' him. Trust me. We're all safer if they don't know it's me." Ellie pulled back and stood by the wagon. "Just Jake, Polly. And you. Nobody else."

"Ellie, what's this all 'bout? I thought you were in Charleston. I got your letters. You need to come inside and stay the night. You need to see Deannie. She's been sick for the past few days."

"What's wrong with her?" Ellie's grabbed Polly's hand.

"Fever. All the kids had it. She's the last to get sick."

"Polly, I can't let those men know I'm the one. It'll be dangerous. For all of us."

"All right. Let me get Jake."

Polly returned to the house and told Jake she needed to speak to him about Deannie. They went to Deannie's room and closed the door.

"Jake, Ellie's outside. She wants to talk to you 'bout Paint Creek. She says you're walkin' into a trap."

"Ellie? What the hell does *she* know 'bout Paint Creek?"

"I don't know. She's been livin' in Charleston. Maybe she's heard somethin'."

"Ellie, what are you doin' here and what do you know 'bout Paint Creek?" Jake didn't hide his continued distrust for Ellie. Any woman who would up and leave her infant child was no woman he could trust with anything.

"Since I've been in Charleston, I've made acquaintances with some of the Baldwin-Felts men. John Havers, especially. He works directly with Tom Felts. You know who he is?"

"Yeah. I know all 'bout Felts and his sidekick thugs Havers and Gaujot. Felts is a real scumbag who hates the union and'll side with whoever has enough money to pay his greedy ass. Havers and Gaujot do most of the dirty work for him."

"I overheard 'em talkin'—more than a few times—and they've been hired by the coal operators at Paint Creek and Cabin Creek to break the union."

"I know they're workin' for the operators. What're they plannin' to do exactly?"

"They know you're comin' with weapons. They's showin' up with hundreds of armed men to guard the mines. They have most of the politicians in their back pocket, and they'll do whatever it takes to break the union." Ellie stopped long enough to take a breath and let this news sink in. "They're gonna evict people from those shacks they call houses—by whatever means necessary."

"And you're sure 'bout this?" Jake paced in front of the wagon.

"Positive. John told me he had to leave for Paint Creek tomorrow mornin'. They're gonna be waitin' on you, Jake. Whatever you're plannin', you need to do somethin' else. You can't go marchin' in there. Those bastards are ready to ambush you as soon as you get to Paint Creek."

"And why you tellin' me this? What you wantin' for this? Money? I ain't got no money to give you, and neither does the union."

"Nothin'. I swear. You're family, no matter what. You're raisin' my little girl. You're a good man, Jake. Jolene's in the middle of that mess over there, too. I love my sister and I'll do whatever I can to keep her safe—I always have and I ain't gonna stop now." Ellie wrapped her arms around herself. "Besides, I hate those Baldwin-Felts bastards."

After Jake got all the information he could from Ellie, they agreed to have one of his men, Crowbar, come to Charleston to meet her on a regular schedule and get more information. Ellie had met Crowbar when she was living with Polly and Jake, and she agreed to meet him as often as necessary.

Jake went inside to tell his men. They spent the rest of the night rethinking their plan. They were taking guns and ammunition to the men at Paint Creek. Given the information Ellie shared, they planned a new route to get the weapons to the men and sent a messenger to Paint Creek to tell Deacon about the turn of events.

Polly stayed outside with Ellie. "Ellie, you need to come in and see Deannie. I can sneak you in the side door. Nobody'll see you."

Ellie took a deep breath and took Polly's hand. They slipped into Deannie's room and Polly lit the lantern.

Ellie took off her shawl and bonnet and sat down on the bed next to Deannie. "She's so tiny. How's she doin'? Other than the fever?" Ellie gently stroked Deannie's cheek.

"She's doin' fine. Growin' like a weed. She's usually up and runnin' things around here. We all do her biddin' most days. 'Specially Jake."

"She's more beautiful than I remember." Ellie picked up one of Deannie's black curls and wrapped it around her finger.

"Ellie, you'll never believe what happened. Mary sent for me last week."

"What on earth for?" Ellie asked.

"Her boy had the thrush. She wanted me to cure him." Polly was one of a handful of people in the area who could cure thrush. Some people thought it was just an old wives' tale that if you had never laid eyes on your father, you could cure thrush and a slew of other things. Polly's father had died two months before she was born, and she had cured nearly every kid within fifty miles.

"Old woman Cox up Thacker couldn't do it?" Ellie asked.

"No, that poor woman's in ill health herself. I thought 'bout not goin', but that baby ain't got no dog in this fight. I'm glad I went. It was 'bout the worst case I'd ever seen. Makes me wonder if she's takin' good care of him. Her house was a mess. She was a mess. She seemed tired and unhappy."

"She'll always be a bitter old hag," Ellie said.

Ellie stroked Deannie's head. "Can I sleep her with her tonight?"

"Of course, you can. I'll bring you somethin' to sleep in, and I'll fix a place for your friend out in the storehouse with a few of the other men who are stayin' the night," Polly said.

"Dayton. His name's Dayton."

"We miss you, Ellie. All of us do." Polly quietly closed the door.

Ellie took off her shoes and unpinned her hair. She couldn't believe how beautiful her child was. She had Ellie's olive skin and dark hair and Jolene's sea-green eyes. Ellie couldn't see Walter in her face at all, or Tom for that matter. Ellie was sure as Deannie got older her father's features would be apparent—whichever one it was. She sat holding Deannie's hand until Polly returned with her sleep clothes.

Polly had been worried Ellie had returned to take Deannie with her. The second she looked into her eyes, she knew she had nothing to fear. Ellie had never been the kind of woman who wanted a baby, and even less so now that she had been away. She was a free woman and wanted to continue living as one. Jake's concern that Ellie would one day return for Deannie was unfounded. Polly hoped he saw that now.

The day Ellie left for Charleston, Polly had been crushed. She knew Ellie wanted to leave, but she didn't believe she would actually do it—leave Deannie behind. She knew Ellie well enough to know she was going to put herself and her desires before anyone else—even her child. Jake had been furious at Ellie for leaving and not telling anyone she was going, and he still was. Secretly, Polly was delighted Ellie had left Deannie with her. Explaining to the boys why Ellie left had been difficult. Polly didn't want them to hate Ellie, so they simply stopped talking about her and embraced Deannie as their own.

She wondered about this man Ellie was with and why she would risk her life and the comfort of her situation for the cause of the miners. As long as Ellie did what was best and right for Deannie, it didn't matter to Polly how she lived.

Polly went to the kitchen and started making food for the men to take with them. Jake's sister and niece were already peeling potatoes.

Ellie slept with Deannie, and they both woke in a puddle of sweat when Deannie's fever broke in the early morning hours. Ellie bathed Deannie and put her in a clean sleep shirt. She changed the linens, and they returned to bed and cuddled up, sleeping until noon.

When she woke, Deannie was looking at her. Ellie smiled as two of the most brilliant green eyes stared back at her. Deannie touched Ellie's face. "Hello, beautiful baby girl."

Deannie smiled at Ellie, and it made her heart sing.

Soon after, Polly came into the room to feed Deannie. Ellie got up and dressed, trying not to watch Polly as she fed *her* baby. Jealousy and guilt slipped between them. She should be the one feeding this beautiful child. Deannie seemed so content in Polly's arms. Had Deannie already forgotten her in two months? But she couldn't be a mother to her child, not the way Polly could. Polly was born to be a mother, and since her little girl had died, Deannie was serving a purpose in Polly's life as well. Ellie ignored the heaviness in her spirit and finished dressing.

Polly walked Ellie out to the wagon and kissed her goodbye. "Please come back soon, Ellie. We miss you. Deannie misses you."

Ellie stiffened. "Polly, we both know that ain't the truth. That child don't even know who I am. I guess we should have her call me Aunt Ellie, 'cause I ain't never gonna be her mama. You're her mama now. You and Jake are wonderful parents to her, and I ain't got no business interferin' in that." Ellie tied her bonnet under chin.

"Ellie, don't say such things. Deannie's just a baby. Why, she don't recognize any of us as bein' her mommy or daddy. She goes to whichever one has the food or wants to hold her."

"No, you're wrong, Polly. I saw the way she looked at you when you's feedin' her. The love in her little eyes." Ellie took a deep breath. "No, I ain't got no business with a baby. I ain't the kinda woman you are, Polly. I can't love her the way you can. It ain't in me. I'm a free spirit, and a free spirit ain't got no business tryin' to be a mama."

Polly stepped forward and hugged Ellie. "Ellie, I want you to know Deannie's the best blessin' you could ever give me. I'll take care of her and love her enough for both of us." They both cried.

Ellie wiped the tears from her face and looked at Polly. "Don't ever tell her the truth, Polly. Tell her you're her mama and I am her auntie. Until she's old enough to understand, they ain't no reason she needs to know. And even then, it might not matter."

Polly shook her head yes, and tears ran down her face. They embraced again, and Ellie turned back to her before stepping up on the wagon.

"Polly, I truly love you. Sisters until the end . . ."

"Sisters. Until the very end."

31.

5 May 1912 (Paint Creek)

Jolene heard the footsteps on the back porch. She had been awake all night waiting on Deacon to return. She hurried to the kitchen and warmed up the dinner she'd cooked hours earlier.

Deacon entered and kissed her on the cheek before sitting at the table. He spoke in a hushed tone. "Jake sent a messenger today. He rode all night to get here. The coal operators are sendin' hundreds of those bastard Baldwin-Felts thugs to keep us in line. They should start arrivin' tomorrow or the next day. Just 'bout the time Jake and his men were plannin' to get here with the guns and ammo. So now they're plannin' on another route, and they'll let us know when they get here. He said the evictions'll start any day, so we better get prepared."

"We knew those evictions would start soon. It's pretty obvious with those Baldwin-Felts thugs policin' the creek for the past few weeks. I've been takin' a few things up to the cave ever' day—our preserved food, coffee, clothes."

Deacon handed her a mason jar half filled with ground coffee. "Here. Lois sent this, said she knew you must be runnin' low since the men've all been here drinkin' what we got most ever' day."

"Well, that's right nice of her. You want coffee now?"

"No. Save it. We'll need it tomorrow."

Jolene finished reheating the dinner, and Deacon cleaned and reloaded his gun.

"I hear Mother Jones is comin' to help organize the workers. I'll believe it when I see it," he said.

"Mother Jones is comin' here? To Paint Creek? Things must gonna get pretty bad if she's comin'. When's the union gonna do what they promised?"

"We don't rightly know," Deacon said.

After dinner they crawled into bed. Deacon wrapped his arms around her and spoke softly. "They's somethin' else we need to talk 'bout."

"What?"

"You know how you and Polly use your River Talk so me and Jake can share information?"

"Yes."

"Well, you're gonna need to start doin' that with someone else as well."

"Who? That somethin' me, Polly, and Ellie made up when we's kids. Ain't nobody knows how to write that half-Celtic, half-Cherokee gibberish but the three of us."

"Exactly." Deacon pulled away and turned her face up to his.

"What're you sayin', Deacon? You mean Ellie? What on earth for?"

Deacon explained Ellie's involvement, and Jolene couldn't believe what she was hearing. Her sister, Ellie, had taken the effort to travel to Matewan to warn Jake about the Baldwin-Felts plans. She had put herself in danger to help them.

"Does she know what kinda mess this is and how much worse it's gonna get?"

"Apparently, she does."

"And she's willin' to sacrifice her nice, comfy life in Charleston with that man? For us? Why? What's in it for her? We all know Ellie ain't gonna put herself in harm's way for nobody, especially a bunch of dirt-poor miners she don't even know. Hell, she walked off and left her own newborn baby with Polly. I can forgive her for a lot of stuff, but not that." Jolene rolled over onto her back and stared at the ceiling. "I'm not sure I completely trust her, Deacon. I know she's my sister and she'd do anythang for *me*, but she certainly never cared a rat's ass for you. Besides, we all know it ain't in her character to help nobody but herself."

"Jake says she had too much information that checked out for her to not be tellin' the truth. He's sendin' a messenger to meet with her ever' week to pass information. So, get your letter ready to send tomorrow."

Jolene had watched Ellie use The Knowing and her charm to manipulate people and situations to get her way since she could talk. She rarely did anything for someone else that didn't benefit her in some way. So why was she wanting to stick her neck out for a bunch of miners she didn't even know? What could be her motivation? Perhaps Ellie didn't realize the danger of this situation. The price to pay for helping may be not only her fancy lifestyle but her very life.

Jolene awoke in a cold sweat, breathing as hard as if she had run ten miles. The dream had been so real. But these dreams—these premonitions—always were. Ellie's hotel room was on fire, and she jumped from the fifth-floor window... she ran through the mining camp and her dress was on fire. Her throat was slit, and blood dripped from her long black hair. The Baldwin-Felts guards were shooting at her, and she cried out for Jolene to run. Jolene stood inside her doorway frozen, unable to move or speak.

The feeling of not being able to help Ellie followed her around like a ghost for days. The sight of her throat gaping open and bleeding wouldn't leave her.

Was it another premonition? Or simply a bad dream? Jolene didn't want to know, didn't want to face the truth if it was a premonition.

32.

<u>1 June 1912</u>

Before daybreak, Jolene packed up the few things they had remaining in the house—clothes, blankets, food that wouldn't perish—and slipped out the back door and up to the cave. It wasn't much, but Deacon had warned her to prepare to be without a house for a long time.

Word of the evictions spread quickly throughout the coal camp. Everyone was waiting for Baldwin-Felts to kick them out of their company houses without any chance to take the essential things they would need to survive. Along with Jolene, a few of the women had been preparing for more than a month—taking the things they could carry to a cave halfway up the mountain without attracting too much attention.

Upon her return to the house, she saw them coming up the hill. Deacon had gone to meet Jake, and she was alone. She had taken her gun to the cave the day before. She would either use it or they would take it from her; either way, it was best not to have it there.

The Baldwin-Felts thugs pounded on the door. Jolene barely opened it, and three men pushed past her. The house was nothing more than a shanty made with an open post foundation, board-and-batten siding, and a tar-paper roof. It was the only home she and Deacon had known for the past two years. There was one bedroom and a small kitchen that also served as the living room, work room—pretty much everything room. The men quickly filled the small dwelling.

"What do you think you're doin'? This is *my* house. These are *my* things, you bunch of pigs." Jolene stood her ground in the middle of the room.

"Are you Wanda Jolene Bales?"

"Yes."

"Look, sweetheart, we don't want this to be difficult, you need to get your shit and get out of this house. It ain't *your* house. It belongs to the coal company—so get out." He pushed the eviction notice into her chest.

"Where's your husband?" another one demanded.

"He's gone."

"Where? Schemin' against us?"

"It ain't none of your damn business where my husband is. And I *ain't* your sweetheart." Jolene held his gaze.

"Well, ain't you a little red-headed spitfire." He back-handed her. Jolene's head snapped sideways, and blood trickled from her nose and lip. "Now, tell me where your husband is, you mouthy little bitch."

Jolene grabbed a knife from the kitchen table and lunged at him. He side-stepped the blade, and one of the other men came up behind her and knocked the knife from her hand. She turned and kicked him in the groin and dug her dirty fingernails into his face. He grabbed her hands and spun her around away from him. He then picked her up and carried her outside and threw her off the porch. She landed in the muddy road.

They tossed out what few things were left in the house—small pieces of furniture and a few household items. Jolene picked up the items she could carry and started up the mountain with her neighbors, where she would wait for Deacon.

Jolene walked through the coal camp, watching her neighbors being tossed out onto the street like garbage. Mothers with tiny babies, grandmothers—it didn't matter. The Baldwin-Felts men were ruthless. The entire mining camp was turned upside down. Furniture, beds, clothes, food—everything—tossed into the muddy road. Women and children cried; some screamed and fought back.

The miners and their families marched out of the camp like a band of refugees to an uncertain future. With each step, Jolene's anger burned hotter. With each step, the rage inside her rose closer to the surface.

She stopped to help other families who were being tossed out. She tried to organize them and instructed them not to fight back. The Baldwin-Felts men were at the Ramsey house. They were throwing everything into the street. Jolene knew no one was there but the old man. His son was with Deacon.

She ran to help and reached the porch as they were dragging him out. "You leave him alone. Do you have no respect or decency? Can't you see he's crippled? Crippled in that damn mine you'ns are tryin' to protect?" Mr. Ramsey had lost his leg in a roof collapse at the Paint Creek mine ten years earlier.

"Now little lady, you keep on goin' and mind your own damn business."

"You go to hell. This man *is* my business. He's my neighbor and my friend, and I'll fight you tooth and nail for him."

"You think this old Negro man wants to be your friend?" one of the younger Baldwin-Felts men asked, and the others laughed.

"You damned right I'm Ms. Jolene's friend. So, you let go of me and I'll be on my way with her." The old man picked up his crutches and hobbled off the porch with Jolene's help. She instructed a few of the younger boys to collect his things and bring them to the gathering place.

"Those silly fools don't even know who they's messin' with, Ms. Jolene. This is one tough bunch of people, and we ain't goin' down without a damn good fight. They always tryin' to pit us against each other—blacks against whites, Italians against the Hungarians. They want us fightin' with each other so's we won't organize and come together with the union. What they don't understand, is inside that dark, dirty coal mine—we's all the same color—black as coal." He and Jolene laughed and continued on to the gathering place up the mountain.

Jolene had a bruised cheek and a few cuts and scrapes on her legs. She sat on a rock at the edge of the creek waiting for Deacon. She looked around at the families gathered with her. Darkness was descending, and people were trying to find places to sleep. Mothers comforted crying babies. The older children chased lightning bugs. A few of the boys played in the creek.

Night moved in, and a quietness settled around the makeshift camp. Families huddled together. Children of all ages clung to their mothers. Jolene was alone. Her friends shared their dinner with her, and then she went back to her spot by the creek and waited for Deacon.

The screams of the few remaining families fighting in the coal camp floated up the mountain as the last of them were evicted. Sporadic shots rang out. One of the older women started praying. Others joined her, softly muttering their requests to a god who seemed too far away for Jolene to have much faith he would save them from this.

Jolene wasn't sure what would happen now. Things had taken an ugly turn. The more she thought about it the angrier she became. The United Mine Workers had promised they would protect them, help them. It sure seemed simple enough at the time. The Paint Creek boys were already unionized, but they were getting two and half cents less per ton than workers in the other mines in Kanawha County. They wanted equal pay and had demanded it in their new contract, which the operators refused. It would cost them a mere fifteen cents per miner per day, but those greedy bastards wouldn't hear of it. So the miners told the operators to go to hell, and they walked out—more than three thousand men working in forty-five mines. If Cabin Creek joined, it would be well over seven thousand men total, shutting down ninety-six mines.

The coal operators had been controlling their very existence for too damn long. Told them where to live, where their kids could go to school, where they could shop. They were treated no better than indentured servants.

Jolene pondered their predicament and knew in her heart this would be a long, hard battle to win. She believed in what they were fighting for and was ready to go at it tooth and nail. She worried the strike would not end before winter. Then what would they do? How would they live? Most of the miners could barely make ends meet with a job and a roof over their heads; how on earth would they survive out here in the elements? And so many of them?

More families came up the hill. She looked around at the young mothers with babies and small children—many of them still breastfeeding. What would happen to them if this strike stretched on for months or even a year? For the first time in her life, she was happy she didn't have children. She could take care of herself and Deacon. They would take care of each other, just as they always had.

Deacon and Jake marched around the mountain with a few dozen men. More than a thousand men were spread throughout the area and armed to the teeth. Thanks to Ellie's information, Jake and his crew had been able to smuggle in the weapons and ammo needed—enough to hold off a small army. It took an extra couple of days, but they had managed to create a chain of handoffs and hiding places throughout the mountains. They used old hunting paths and Indian trails that hadn't been walked in years. Only those who had grown up in the mountains would know the routes. Deacon figured they would be using them a lot more until the strike was over. He hoped they wouldn't need to use the guns Jake had provided. But guessing by the gun fire they had heard all day, he assumed they probably would.

Deacon's main desire was to get back to Jolene. The lookouts had brought word everyone had been evicted. He hoped she was safe. Hell, he knew she was. She was tougher than any ten men he knew. And she was smart. She could read and write and strategize with the best of them. She was also a damn good shot. She was his partner, and he would never make it through this without her by his side. He wanted to hold her and look into those green eyes he loved so much. To feel her warm, slim body next to his.

She was younger than him by about ten years, and he had been warned about her family—women with Cherokee and Irish blood and hot tempers. None of that mattered to him. Against everyone's advice, he'd married her a little more than two years ago. Damn if her family didn't go crazy. Especially Ellie. Ellie always thought she's better than everybody else. Looks like she got put in her rightful place. Caused the death of two men and put another one behind bars. Yeah, she sure got set straight. Even though she was helping them, he wasn't sure what her motives were. Jolene was a different sorta woman from Ellie. From most women. She certainly was a fiery little thing. Wanda Jolene was a jewel, and he loved his red-headed vixen more than life itself. Another hour and he would be with her.

Jolene recognized him even in the dark. The tilt of his head, the outline of his broad shoulders. She stood to greet him. He dropped his gun and bag and they embraced.

He gently ran his fingers over her cheek. "Are you hurt? They told me that son of a bitch hit you in the face and then threw you down the steps."

"I'm fine. A little bruised is all. Tell me what happened. Where's Jake?"

"He's up on the ridge. Gonna stay up there tonight as a lookout." He took her hand and they walked up the creek away from everyone. "Our men brought more guns—rifles, pistols, shotguns—and the ammo to go with it. We spread it out as evenly as possible. I think every area's armed."

"Those sons of bitches are out for blood." They sat on a fallen tree and whispered. "Deacon, what happens if this ain't settled a'fore winter? It's gonna get real bad for those with little children. They's several women pregnant and due right smack in the middle of winter."

"The union's bringin' tents in a few days and settin' up down the road at Holly Grove. It seems to be the best place to get ever'body situated. We should have a tent for ever' family a'fore the week's end. It ain't much, but it's better than nothin'. They's promised to bring food and supplies as well for as long as it takes."

"I don't trust those union bastards any more than I trust the coal operators, Deacon. They all seem to be greedy and power hungry. They'll do whatever's best for them. It's startin' to feel like we's on our own out here."

Deacon pulled her close. They walked back to their spot by the cave and made a pallet on the ground at the entrance.

They fell asleep—one hand on each other and the other on their guns.

The union delivered on their word and brought tents for every family evicted from the coal camps, creating a colony at Holly Grove. Jolene stood on the ridge overlooking their new neighborhood, astonished at the number of tents. Thousands of them stood in neat rows—for the most part. They were running out of room and had erected the last few hundred wherever they could put them—by the tracks, in people's yards, wherever there was space.

Jolene had helped determine where the tents would go and which families would go where. She and Deacon got one of the smaller tents, and they were situated at the top of the hill. Most were reluctant to settle in too much, assuming this was a temporary situation. Jolene feared it would be a long while before they returned to any sense of normalcy.

33.

<u>9 June 1912 (Holly Grove)</u>

Jolene's excitement grew as she prepared to meet Mother Jones, who was due to arrive at Holly Grove on the 10:10 a.m. train. Jolene wanted to make a good impression. The night before, she had taken a bath of sorts in the creek after most everyone had turned in. Now she brushed her long red hair and braided it, then wrapped the braids together in a bun on top of her head. She put on her one clean dress; this was one time she wished she had asked Ellie for a decent dress to wear. She took a final look at herself in the small mirror. "No, this is perfect. This is who I am—the wife of a dirt-poor coal miner living in a tent at Holly Grove."

Mother Jones arrived as scheduled. In addition to ensuring Mother Jones had a safe place to sleep and food to eat, Jolene had been assigned the duty of providing details of their dilemma and acting as her assistant. They formed an instant friendship upon meeting.

"Mother Jones, they's lots of people in the camp wantin' to meet you."

"And I them, dear. Let's go meet them all."

Jolene was impressed with the old woman's energy as they toured the tent colony. "Most of the tents are up, but we still got quite a few to go."

Mother Jones offered words of encouragement to everyone they encountered. The small children followed her as if she were their long-lost grandmother. Jolene was touched by the tenderness Mother Jones showed the children. She stopped and spoke to each child with as much compassion and caring as she did the adults.

One little girl came over and handed her shoes to Mother Jones. "Hello there! Let me help you, little one." Mother Jones sat on a rickety chair with the little girl beside her. She chatted away with the child, as she slid the shoes over her dirty socks. She tied the shoelaces and gave the little girl a big hug before moving on through the tent colony.

Jolene was fascinated with Mother Jones's involvement in politics and the way she was able to navigate the political landscape. Women were still fighting for the vote, but Mother Jones was as much a part of the political scene as any man. Her fight was to create a better life for workers everywhere—not just in the Southern West Virginia coal fields. And she would do it by way of the political process or by force if she had to.

34.

<u>10 June 1912 (Charleston)</u>

John was gone to Paint Creek again. With the arrival of Mother Jones, John and the Baldwin-Felts machine were preparing for the hailstorm she would start. He'd informed Ellie he would be away more in the coming weeks.

He had left her enough money to do whatever she wanted. Problem was there wasn't anything she really wanted to do. She was restless and bored. She didn't want to shop. She didn't want to make nice with the ladies—not today. What she really wanted to do was get stinking drunk and dance all night.

The tavern in the hotel had a band through the rest of the month. She could hear them every night when she and John walked through the hotel lobby from the dining room to the stairs and up to her suite. She had caught a glimpse of the fiddle player two nights previously. Young, tall, dark curly hair. She wasn't looking to do anything other than have a good time. She deserved a good time. Dealing with the strike and sneaking out to meet Jake's messenger, Crowbar, a few times a week had taken a toll on her. She was constantly on edge wondering if John knew what she had been up to. And the ladies were so nosey, always asking where she was going and where she had been.

John would have a fit if he thought she was in the tavern, because that was certainly no place for a lady—especially his. He was trying to transform her into a proper one, and the rope of society's demands got tighter each day, threatening to crush her spirit. She wasn't John's wife. She was nothing more than his paid whore, but he paraded her around town as though she were a grand lady.

John couldn't see over his pride to realize he would never amount to everything he thought he was. He was a hired thug running with the big boys and doing their dirty work. Nothing more. And she was using him for money, clothes, and information on the strike. If it weren't for the strike, she would have traded John in for a more lucrative affair weeks ago.

His goal was to tame her and make her what he thought she should be. And she was certain that her being in the tavern drinking with the common folk was not what he thought she should be doing. Ellie didn't really care what he thought or what he wanted. As far as she was concerned, she was doing her part for the strike and the miners. She *would* go to the tavern and have a damn good time. To hell with the consequences.

She strolled around town and shopped for a new dress to dance in. She was determined to have a good time and get to know that cute fiddle player.

She slipped on her new purchase, turning to look at her reflection in the full-length mirror. The dress was pale blue with small yellow flowers. Her dark hair provided a deep contrast to the soft colors. The cut of the bodice accentuated her full breasts and tiny waist. She pulled the front and sides of her hair up and let the back hang down around her shoulders. Dinner was over, and she could hear the guests climbing up the stairs to their rooms. Another thirty minutes and they would all be tucked safely in their beds. Then she would slip down the back stairs and into the tavern.

Ellie peered over the swinging doors. The tavern was packed with lots of men and a few women. Most of the women wore low-cut dresses and had lots of cheap rouge on their cheeks and lips. Most everyone acted drunk or well on their way. Intent on observing the ladies, she didn't notice the music had stopped. The other side of the door swung open, and there stood her fiddler.

"Well, how do, pretty lady?" He gave her an exaggerated bow. "Well? You gonna come on in or stand here lookin' lost?"

"I am *not* lookin' lost. I'm just not sure I wanna cavort with the likes of them." She tossed her head toward the tavern.

"Them? Them's some damn good people in there. Maybe you're too uppity to handle it." He grinned and showed the most beautiful dimples Ellie had ever seen on a man.

"I am not. I'm not uppity. But I *am* better than most of those women. They look like whores. Are they? Whores? Paid whores?" She clasped her hands in front of her.

"Now, that ain't for me to say. Far's I can tell, a girl's gotta make a livin' somehow, and it ain't none of my business one way or t'other."

Ellie liked the way his hair curled around his face. His smile was disarming. "Well, are you gonna buy me a drink or what?"

He smiled a wicked smile and pushed open the door, bowing again with a grand gesture for Ellie to enter the tavern. He escorted her to a table right in front of the band and went to the bar to order them both a whiskey. "Here's to new friends and old whores." They clinked their glasses together, and Ellie smiled at him.

"I wanna dance. But you're playin' the fiddle all night. Who can I dance with that won't expect somethin' more at the end of the evenin'?"

"Well, there's old Coot over there. He's with the band. He's Ned's brother. Harmless enough and a purty good dancer. I'll make sure he takes good care of you. But at the end of the night, *I will* expect somethin' more."

She should have blushed, but she didn't. She maintained his gaze and returned his smile. She wanted this fiddle player in her bed. John wouldn't be back for days. Why not? The fiddler was so damn cute.

"What's your name?"

"Sammy. And you?"

"Ellie."

Ellie danced with old Coot all night. During a few breaks in the music she chatted with one of the tavern regulars, a woman named Matilda. Ellie was a little surprised they got along so well. She decided she and Matilda weren't so different under the skin. Ellie drank several more shots of whiskey and felt carefree and young, something she hadn't felt since before she married Tom.

The crowd drifted away, and the band stopped playing long after midnight. Ellie and Sammy slipped up the back stairs to her room.

"A suite? You must be a wealthy lady to be livin' in a suite at the Ruffner."

Ellie shrugged her shoulders. "You certainly don't think I pay for this, do you?"

"Oh, I didn't think so, but I don't want to assume nothin'."

"Well, you should know I have a man, so this *thing* between us will be temporary and just for fun. Nothin' serious. You understand?" Sammy placed his hands on her hips. She felt the heat of his hands through her thin dress and smelled the sweet scent of whiskey on his breath.

"I understand all I need to." He kissed the tip of her nose. "Where's this man of your'n, and when's he comin' back?"

Ellie slipped her hands up his chest and around his neck. She wrapped his curls around her fingers. "End of the week. We need to keep this between us. We can't be seen in the hotel together, and you certainly can't be seen leavin' my room."

His lips brushed her earlobe and he whispered, "I understand."

"And it'll be only this week. Understood?" She pressed her body against his.

He kissed her neck. "Understood."

He turned her around and pressed her thighs against the bed. He undid the buttons on her new dress and slid it off her shoulders. He lifted her hair and kissed the back of her neck and slipped her dress down farther. She pulled on the string of her undergarments, but he took her hands. "That's my job."

He pulled her closer to him and wrapped one arm around her, unlacing her undergarments with his free hand. He moved against her in a slow, rhythmic dance. He traced her spine with this right hand and explored her breasts with his left. She attempted to turn to face him, but he held her firm. "You sure are an impatient little thing, ain't ya?"

"I want to touch you."

"We got all night. And all night every night this week. Relax and enjoy the ride, darlin'."

Ellie's other lovers had been intent on pleasing themselves first or displaying their masculine prowess. If she happened to enjoy it as well, good for her. If not, they typically didn't notice. Even Walter, whom she thought had been the love of her life, had been more than a bit selfish in bed. The pleasing was up to her, and it was more of a performance than lovemaking. Tom had been "kind" in bed. The sex had been good, but he treated her like a China doll who had never been touched by a man. John was the worst lover she had ever had. More often than not, sex started with violence. That was, if he was sober enough to even have sex.

But Sammy... Sammy was something she had never known existed. He was slow and deliberate and wanted to explore every inch of her body with his fingers and lips. He was intent on giving her pleasure. A steady stream of pleasure was flowing through her body, warming her from head to toe, and he had done nothing more than remove her dress.

His lips floated across her back and shoulders, and she felt him hard against her. He was still dressed, intent on not letting her take control. She wasn't used to not leading this dance. She had always gotten what she wanted from men by taking the lead. Sex was her weapon. Her way to control the relationship. Sammy was different. She decided to let him lead the waltz, just this once. Let him have his way.

He removed his clothes and turned her to face him. He pulled her close and kissed her face, her eyes, her nose, her ears, her lips. He picked her up and placed her gently on the bed. He lay next to her exploring every inch of her body with his hands and mouth.

"You're the most beautiful woman I've ever known, Ellie. Your skin feels like velvet. I could spend my whole life exploring your body."

He toyed with her for an eternity, finally entering her. Their bodies melted into a rhythm that was at first gentle, then savage, then gentle again. Ellie was met with a rush of emotion and pleasure. She hadn't known making love could be this complete and satisfying.

Ellie and Sammy continued their tryst for the rest of the week. She knew she was playing with fire and waited until the day before John returned to end it. She was having too much fun to cut it short. She enjoyed the game of sneaking Sammy into her room each night after he finished playing music in the tavern.

They grew close quickly. Ellie felt comfortable and safe with him. She confided in Sammy about working with Jake and the miners. He offered to help if needed, but she refused to bring him into this war.

She hated to admit it to herself and would never admit it to Sammy—it had become something much deeper than a fling for her. Being with him was easy, and there was no pressure for her to perform. No expectations other than being together and enjoying each other. She didn't have a need to control him or the situation. He was young and fun and not so uptight and serious as Tom, Walter, or John. He was only a couple of years older than Ellie, and it showed in how he played with her. He made love to her for the sheer joy of making love to her. Not to own her, or control her, or feed his own ego. She couldn't remember when she had been this relaxed and carefree. And she would miss it.

On their last night together, Sammy leaned over and kissed her, his hand exploring her soft belly. Her body reacted despite herself. "Again? My entire body is bruised and sore. Look between my thighs. There's a bruise on each of them. My poor breasts ache to have my clothes against them."

"I'm truly sorry about that." His lips gently touched each of her breasts. "I don't recall you complaining before. I can stop?"

"Well, I didn't say it didn't feel good. However, I may have a lot of explainin' to do to John when he sees your fingerprints all over my body."

"What happens when I run into you and this jackass downstairs?" Sammy kissed her neck.

"You smile and go on like you don't know me. As if you have no clue my thighs are bruised from our lovemaking, no clue how my lips feel on your skin, no clue how my body lights up at your touch." Ellie wrapped his curls around her fingers.

"Maybe I don't want to pretend I don't know you. Pretend I don't know what you taste like."

"Well, you *will*. Or you'll never see me again." She gripped the curls and jerked his head back to look at her. "I mean it. This ain't somethin' to play around with. This is 'bout more than me bein' with him. This is 'bout a whole lotta other people, not just me and not just money. So don't go messin' this up. I mean it, Sammy. It's serious. There's a lot at stake."

"All right, all right. Don't get your hackles up. I'm lookin' forward to watchin' you be miserable with this feller and that stuck up Baldwin-Felts bunch while I'm playin' my fiddle and drinkin' whiskey and havin' a good time every night."

"When do you leave for Tennessee?"

"Not sure we are leavin' for Tennessee. We may be stayin' right here for a while. They's asked us to stay on for a couple more weeks."

Ellie was not happy to hear this. She wanted Sammy to leave. To be out of harm's reach—and out of her reach. She didn't trust herself to stay away from him. After Tom killing Walter, she had a fear of the same thing happening to Sammy, and it tore her up inside to think of anything bad happening to him.

"Look, you need to stay clear of this man. He's a ruthless son of a bitch and has killed men for a lot less than sleepin' with his woman. So don't go actin' a fool and get yourself killed—or get your hands smashed so bad you'll never play the fiddle again."

Sammy assured her he would stay clear of John and wait until she came to him.

35.

<u>22 June 1912 (Charleston)</u>

Thunder floated closer with each explosion. Lightning danced across the night sky, illuminating the entire city. The heat from the day hung heavy in the air. Ellie opened the doors to the small terrace to let the breeze in. The wind fondled her dress and cooled her skin. The storm brought a sense of freedom and power with it. Ellie longed to blow away with the storm, away from John. She needed to find a way out yet still help the miners and their mission.

For now, she was content to curl up on the chaise with a glass of whiskey and a book she found at the library earlier in the week. Sammy was gone to Huntington for a week to play music. John wasn't due back from Paint Creek until Tuesday, which gave her the night and all the next day to enjoy her time alone.

She missed Sammy already, and he hadn't been gone one day. Even though she would miss him, she was also looking forward to some quiet time. Thinking of Sammy brought a smile to her face. She refused to believe it was love, but it was certainly different from anything she had experienced before. As much as she enjoyed him and wanted him, she also knew there was no future with him. She wanted a life Sammy could never offer or provide.

Ellie tried to read but couldn't concentrate. She needed to think and determine her next move. The Knowing kept urging her to protect herself, to leave the situation. A deep dread had wrapped around her and had become a heavy shadow dragging behind her.

She sat on the chaise, her mind focused on everything except the open book in her lap. She thought of John's return, the needling dread tightening around her, sucking the oxygen out of the room. When he returned, she would put on a happy face and pretend all was well, as she always did. She wasn't sure how much longer she could keep up the charade. It was wearing on her more each day.

She could leave. Men like John were a dime a dozen. The miners would do just fine without her help. But what about Jolene? And Jake and Polly? Mostly, what about Deannie? No, she couldn't just walk away. She owed them all this much, didn't she?

The wind swirled outside and pounded into the hotel, sending rain gushing into the room. The open terrace door, no match for the strong gusts, banged hard against the wall. Ellie jumped, sending her book to the floor. She rushed to shutter it, only to be met with wind and rain in her face. She turned her head as the door to her suite opened. She was startled to see John standing there, soaked and angry.

She released the terrace door, sending it banging against the wall once again. "John? What are you doing back so early? I didn't expect you till Tuesday afternoon."

"Did I interrupt your plans, Ellie?"

She pointed to the chaise, "My plans include that book on the floor and a glass of whiskey." The wind grabbed the door again and slammed it into the wall. "What are you implyin', John?"

"Nothin'. Nothin' at all. Where's the whiskey? I need a drink." He took off his hat and walked over to the side table.

"You know where it is. It appears you've had enough whiskey." Another gust. Another bang. Ellie reached for the door.

"What did you say? I've had enough? Who do you think you are to tell *me* I've had enough to drink? You'd be livin' in the street or be back in Matewan if it weren't for me. You're bought and paid for, Ellie. Get used to it." He poured his whiskey.

Ellie stopped cold. If she turned to look at him, she would claw his eyes out or say something she would regret. Did he really think he was the best she could do? Arrogant bastard.

"I make sure you're dressed in the finest money can buy. I take you to the best parties in town. You have a suite of rooms at the fanciest hotel in the damn state." He drained his whiskey. "And you're gonna tell me I've had enough to drink?" He refilled his glass. "Fuck you."

Ellie stood at the open terrace and let the wind and rain blow in on her. She took a deep breath and pulled the door to close it. John put his booted foot against it. "John, there's no need for this. The rain's blowin' in and gettin' the rug wet."

He threw his empty glass, and it shattered on the hardwood floor. He grabbed her by the shoulders and turned her to face him. "You really think you can tell me what to do?

Do you even know who I am? How much power I have in this damn town? With those dirty, ignorant coal miners? Do you?"

"John, you're hurtin' me. Let me go." His grip tore into her shoulders, and she struggled to get free.

"Do you know?" He shook her. "*Answer* me, you tramp." He shoved her onto the terrace, the hard rain soaking her through. He shoved her hard against the railing.

"John, stop it." The iron railing cut into her lower back. He wrapped his fingers around her neck. Ellie couldn't breathe. She pulled on his knuckles, trying to pry them off, but she was no match for his strength.

He bent her backwards over the railing and her foot slipped, if he had not held tight to her throat, she would have plunged five stories to the ground. He yanked her back up to a standing position. He back-handed her across the face; she stumbled and fell to her knees. Ellie saw Dottie's horrified face across the terrace closing the door to the room next to hers. John grabbed her hair and pulled her up to her feet.

Within seconds, Dottie was knocking on the door to Ellie's suite. She used her master key to open the door. "Ms. Ellie, you in here? I wanna make sure the doors and windows are all closed so the storm don't soak ever'thang."

Ellie couldn't scream, she couldn't breathe. Startled to hear Dottie's voice, John turned. "You're one lucky bitch." He released Ellie, and she slumped to the floor of the terrace. John stormed out of the suite past Dottie as if she weren't even standing there.

Dottie ran to the terrace. Ellie was gasping for air, the rain pouring over her. Dottie picked her up, helped her inside, and closed the doors.

"Sweet baby Jesus, Ms. Ellie. What on earth's wrong with that man? He was gonna kill you. I saw you bent over that railin', and I just knew he was gonna throw you plum offa there." She helped Ellie to the chaise. "You sit here, and I'll get somethin' to dry you off and some dry clothes."

Dottie locked the door to the suite and the door to John's adjoining room. She dried Ellie's hair and helped her change.

"Ms. Ellie, your neck's awful bruised. I ain't too sure what to do for it. You wanna try some whiskey? It might warm you up and relax you a bit, if nothin' else."

Ellie nodded. Dot poured her a fresh glass and held Ellie's shaking hands as she placed the glass up to her lips.

"Dot, thank you. I'd more than likely be dead if you hadn't come to my rescue."

"Ms. Ellie, it's nothin' you would'na done for me."

Ellie took Dottie's hand and held it close to her heart. "Dot, I owe you my life. I won't forget this. Thank you." Ellie's voice came out as barely a whisper.

Dottie stayed with Ellie all night. She slept on the chaise lounge after she put Ellie to bed. Ellie awoke before dawn to find Dottie asleep. She tried to get up, moaning with each movement. Her body ached from head to toe.

Dottie arose. "Ms. Ellie, you need to stay put. Your body needs to recover from last night."

"Dottie, I'm fine. I want to sit up. Is John in his room?"

"No, ma'am. He left the hotel right after he stormed outa here," Dottie said. "I'll run to the kitchen and fetch you some hot tea."

"No! Stay here. Let's talk while we can. John could return any minute."

Dottie adjusted the pillows and helped Ellie sit.

"Dot, I need to know I can trust you. I think I can. You saved my life and you've been loyal to me so far. I don't know of anyone who would risk their life or job for someone she didn't care 'bout. You aren't like the other maids here in the hotel. You don't gossip, you're kind, and you don't take money or gifts in exchange for information or secrets."

"Ms. Ellie, I try to stay away from most of the guests here in the hotel. Those Baldwin-Felts ladies are nasty to all us maids, never even sayin' thank you. You don't treat me that-a-way. You've been kind and generous right from the first day."

"Well, I know you're as afraid of John's temper as I am."

"Ms. Ellie, I try to avoid him ever' chance I get. I don't even wanna look him in the eyes. I don't think me and him'll be friends anytime soon."

"We need to come up with a plan so you'll know if I am in trouble or not." Ellie grimaced as she shifted on the bed. "Dottie, there's more to it than John being hateful and drunk. I don't want to tell you too much. I don't want to put you in danger, but I do need your help. There's something I'm involved in that John would certainly kill me if he knew. It's somethin' that involves the Baldwin-Felts people and the coal miners."

Dottie pulled a chair close to the bed. "Ms. Ellie, I'll do anythang you need me to. Besides, I hate those Baldwin-Felts people."

Ellie and Dottie developed a system of knocks and tasks for Dottie to perform each day to confirm whether Ellie was in danger or needed her. As the days passed and they spent more time together, Ellie's trust in Dottie grew stronger. The messages from Paint Creek were getting more frequent, and

Ellie was concerned John would start having her followed if he wasn't already. Ellie decided to start using Dottie as a decoy or to pass messages to and from Crowbar and Sammy when she wasn't able to sneak away.

36.

28 June 1912 (Charleston)

Ellie checked herself in the mirror to ensure the high neck on her dress covered the purple fingerprints around her neck. She had used dandelion root and leaves in a tea to help heal them, but it was still taking longer than usual.

John had returned on Tuesday as originally planned. There was no discussion of him trying to kill her. He simply walked in, placed a box on her dressing table, and then poured himself a drink. "That's for you."

Ellie had opened the box. It was a diamond and pearl brooch. She supposed the diamonds and pearls in exchange for nearly strangling her to death was intended to be a fair trade. She would take his expensive gifts. The bastard owed her that much and more.

That had been three days ago. Now, she picked up the brooch and affixed it to the high neck of her dress. "Fitting. Diamonds and pearls sitting at the center of my bruised throat—like a crown on the prize cow at the county fair," she said.

One last look in the mirror and she left her room to join John for breakfast.

37.

<u>16 July 1912</u>

As soon as John left for Paint Creek, Ellie asked Dottie to pack a lunch. They walked out together and headed toward the river. Once they reached the park, they parted ways. Ellie took the picnic basket and met Sammy a couple of blocks away. It had been almost three weeks since she had seen him. She'd wanted to see him sooner, but the bruises on her neck from John's last beating had taken longer to heal than she had hoped.

Sammy had borrowed a wagon, and they rode out of town and headed down the crooked river road. They rode for a few miles and then headed away from the river and up a well-beaten path.

"Where in God's good name are you takin' me? This is 'bout the roughest road I've ever been on. I think you snapped a couple of ribs."

"Sorry 'bout that." Sammy took her hand and kissed it. "Almost there."

"Well, we certainly don't need to worry 'bout anybody seein' us. You're right 'bout that at least."

"You'll love it. I promise." He placed his hand on her thigh.

The wagon pulled around a bend, and Ellie was delighted. The creek had dammed up and formed a natural lagoon before it made its way to the river. The water was clear, and the swimming hole was secluded and quiet.

"So? What d'ya think?"

Ellie removed her bonnet and hopped off the wagon. "It's absolutely beautiful, Sammy. Let's get in." She took off her shoes and began unbuttoning her dress.

Sammy cocked his hat and stayed seated on the wagon, watching her.

"What are you doin' sittin' there? And why do you have that silly grin on your face? Hurry up, it's too hot to sit there. Let's get in the water." She draped her dress on a nearby tree.

She let her hair loose and stood naked with her hands on her hips. He tossed his hat beside her bonnet on the wagon seat and hopped down. He wrapped his arms around her and kissed her. "You're the most beautiful thing I've ever laid my eyes on, Ellie."

Sammy removed his clothes, and they slipped into his secret swimming hole. They swam across the pond to a rock and stretched out in the warm sunshine like two cats.

"Ellie? When you gonna leave that asshole?"

Ellie looked over at him. "Sammy, I explained this to you. I can't leave right now. My gettin' the information I can from him and passin' it to Jolene and Jake is more important and bigger than us."

"Is that your only reason for stayin'? You sure it ain't got somethin' to do with the money and the fancy clothes and the parties?" He kissed her shoulder.

She looked away. "No. Sure, I enjoy all that. But that ain't why I stay with him. I can't stand him. I can't stand that son of bitch touchin' me. I'm not sure what you expect me to do. I can't abandon the miners now. It's too important, and there's too many lives at stake."

"I know. I'll be patient. But, if he lays one finger on you and hurts you, I *will* kill him."

"You won't have to. *I'll* kill his sorry ass a'fore he even knows what's happened."

Ellie stood and dove into the pond. Sammy followed. They swam to the bank, and Sammy got the quilt and their picnic lunch from the wagon. They spread the quilt out under a tree and made love.

With their appetites worked up, they tore into the picnic basket. Dottie had provided fried chicken, tomatoes, cucumbers, fresh bread, and two slices of pie. Sammy lay back on the blanket, his hand over his full belly. "Looks like a storm's a rollin' in." Sammy pointed to the west. "You wanna head back a'fore it gets here?"

"No. I don't care if we get rained on. I don't want this day to end any sooner than it needs to."

Sammy stood and slipped on his pants. He walked over to the wagon, got a box from under the seat, and brought it over to Ellie.

She stopped buttoning her dress to take the offering from his outstretched hand. "What's this? A ribbon and ever'thang!" She removed the ribbon and gingerly opened the package. "Sammy! I don't know what to say."

"Don't say nothin'. Just play it."

Ellie lifted the most beautiful mandolin she had ever seen out of the box. It was made from flamed maple and polished to a high sheen. She thought it must have cost him everything he had.

Ellie strummed the mandolin for a few minutes to feel its tone and nuances. She played a song she and Jolene had loved growing up. Sammy sat in stunned silence and listened.

"Damn, you *are* good. You can't keep this kinda talent hidden forever."

Ellie blushed. "Sammy, I can't keep this. It's too much."

"Don't be silly. My uncle makes 'em. I picked this one out special for you. It's got softer tones and it's a bit lighter weight. I wanted it to fit your hands perfectly. And if you look inside, you'll see a special inscription just for you."

Ellie looked inside the mandolin and turned it to face the sun. The inscription read: *You are music to my soul.*

Tears filled Ellie's eyes. "Sammy, this is the most beautiful thing anyone's ever given me. Honest." Tears were streaming down her face. "Of all the dresses, the jewelry—all of it—none of it means nothin' to me. But this? I will treasure this for the rest of my life."

With one hand, he wiped her tears, and with the other, he smoothed the hair from her face. "I love you, Ellie. And that ain't gonna change, no matter what you do." He kissed her gently.

Ellie was overwhelmed with emotion. Sammy had turned on something she never imagined existed. She had never laughed so much with anyone other than Jolene and Polly. She felt safe with Sammy in a way she had never felt before.

She trusted him completely and believed him when he told her he loved her.

"Sammy? I... I want you to know I..." Thunder crashed overhead, and the rain was dancing their way. Ellie grabbed her new mandolin and put it back in its box. Sammy took it, wrapped it in the quilt, and ran to the wagon and stored it safely under the front bench. Ellie grabbed the picnic basket, their shoes, and the rest of Sammy's clothes.

They made it as far as the river road before the rain caught up with them. Tree limbs blew across their path. Then the hail came and pelted them and the horse. Ellie buried her face in Sammy's shoulder. He pulled the wagon into an abandoned barn, where they waited out the storm in what was left of the structure. It provided enough shelter to keep the hail and most of the rain off them and the horse. The wind was another matter. Ellie was certain it was going to blow the entire barn away as it pummeled the rotting wood.

In the rush to get on the wagon and moving, she hadn't had time to finish the top five buttons of her dress. She was soaked through, and the thin cotton clung to her body. Sammy pulled her close, undid the remaining buttons, and slipped the cloth over her head. He removed her undergarments and lifted her up onto the back of the wagon. The worn wood was hard against her smooth skin. The thunder crashed overhead as they made love, the fragile barn all but blowing away.

38.

<u>25 July 1912</u>

Ellie descended the stairs and entered the hotel dining room for breakfast. As much as she hated mingling with the wives of the Baldwin-Felts men, she had to gather as much information as she could on what was happening at Paint Creek. She was meeting Crowbar at 10:30.

She greeted the ladies and made a point to sit at the table with the two most gossipy ones, Myrtle Taylor and Joan Wells. "Good mornin', ladies. How are you on this fine day?"

"Well, hello there, Ellie. We sure ain't seen much of you lately," Myrtle said.

"I've been feelin' a little homesick this week, and I simply wouldn't have made very good company. With John comin' back this afternoon, I'm in much better spirits." She smiled, thinking of her time spent with Sammy.

"Oh, honey, I'm so sorry you miss your family. We miss ours too, but honestly, it's a nice little break for us to be away from the kids and the husband. We've been havin' the best time. Why, we even thought we might go to the tavern tonight. One last adventure before the men return later this week. The music sounds so good. We almost went in last night but chickened out. You should come with us. You'd be a big hit in there, Ellie," Myrtle said.

Ellie looked at her in surprise. "I thought the men were coming back tonight."

"We got word early this mornin' the men won't be back for a few more days." Joan said.

"Why are they stayin' an extra day or two?" Ellie peered over the rim of her cup as she sipped her coffee.

Myrtle leaned in and whispered to Ellie and Joan, "Well, *I* heard they's plannin' some big raid at Mucklow. They had some sort of skirmish this mornin', and the boys said that was it, they's gonna show those stupid miners who's in charge."

"That's the same information I received as well," Joan chimed in.

Ellie lowered her voice. "Oh, my. It sounds serious. I hope it's nothin' dangerous. What are they plannin'?"

Myrtle waited for the servers to refill their coffee before she continued. "Well, from what I was told, they's gonna be usin' their new Gatlin' Gun. Those boys've been itchin' to use that thing ever since it arrived up there."

"A Gatlin' Gun? What on earth they gonna be shootin' at?" Ellie tried to mimic the same triumphant and gleeful mood the other women had.

"The guards have built a fort of sorts and have it mounted and aimed right at the Mucklow camp. They's gonna fire that thing right into the camp. That'll show those ignorant strikers," Joan said triumphantly.

"At everyone or anyone in particular? I mean surely not the women and children too?" Ellie asked.

"Why not?" Joan snorted. "Those women are just as ignorant as their men and stir up as much trouble as the men. Kill 'em all's what I say."

Ellie's stomach flipped over and her heart beat so fast she thought it would explode out of her chest. She quickly regained her composure. She wanted to punch Joan in the throat to shut her up. These people were all crazy.

"Honey, are you all right?" Myrtle leaned in. "You look as pale as a ghost."

"I'm fine. A little sad John won't be returnin' tonight. I think some fresh air will do me good." Ellie couldn't finish her breakfast and excused herself from the table.

"Plan on comin' with us to the tavern tonight," Myrtle called after her.

Ellie tied her hat under her chin and calmed herself before she exited the hotel. She had written a letter for Crowbar to take to Jolene. She typically relayed the main parts of the letters for him, but there were things in the letters for Jolene only. Sisterly things Ellie hoped would bond them again. Since no one else could read the letters, Jolene was forced to correspond with her.

Ellie stepped outside into the hot July morning. She checked the time on the pocket watch she had purchased the week before. She had thirty minutes before she would meet Crowbar.

She tried to act casual as she strolled through the city. The street was busy with people bustling about. Horses and wagons stirred up the dust. One of the few cars in town motored by. The oppressive heat and the noise closed in on her. Her head pounded, and the sun seemed much brighter than it had when she first stepped out onto the street. She hadn't had much breakfast, and what she did eat threatened to come back up. She needed to get to the park but feared she would throw up before she made it there.

She took a short cut to the park to avoid the noise and people. She was unsteady on her feet, picking her way through the buildings and down a side street. She reached the back of Ms. Bea's Boarding House as the kitchen maid was emptying the scraps from breakfast. The smell was overpowering. Ellie staggered past the girl and threw up in the grass. She leaned against Ms. Bea's fence for a few minutes and threw up again.

She wiped her mouth with her handkerchief and asked the girl for some water. After rinsing out her mouth, Ellie waited a few more minutes to pull herself together before continuing to the park. Once there, she sat on the bench under the oak tree facing the river, her usual spot.

It was quiet here away from the confusion of the main street. The tree provided a cool shade, and a gentle breeze came in off the water. Ellie removed her hat and fanned herself. She wondered if she could possibly be pregnant. Why would she be so sick this early in the day? Maybe just too much whiskey? Maybe the thought of innocent people being mowed down by a Gatling Gun? She didn't have time to ponder it any longer. Crowbar quietly sat down beside her on the bench.

Ellie told him everything she had heard at breakfast.

"We knew they's up to somethin' when they built that fort. We just didn't know what. It's sure a mess up there, Ms. Ellie."

"How's Jolene? Did you give her the letter from last time and tell her I asked 'bout her? Tell her she can come here and stay with me. I'll get her a room at the hotel. She can't stay there in that damn tent in Holly Grove. It ain't safe up there."

"I told her all you said, and I give her that letter with all those crazy symbols. She said to tell you she loves you and appreciates your help in this war. But she ain't leavin'. She's as stubborn as you are. She ain't goin' nowheres. Here." He handed Ellie an envelope. "She sent you a letter back."

"If Deacon decides to ship her skinny little ass outa there, tell her to get word to me at the hotel."

He got up to leave. "Ms. Ellie, we *all* appreciate what you're a'doin' for us. We know this is as dangerous for you as it is for any of us, maybe more so. You keep yourself safe, ya hear?"

Ellie nodded and watched him walk away. The Knowing had her on guard with Crowbar. There was something in his manner when he took her letters and delivered the ones from Jolene. Clearly, he had tried to read them. She wondered if he could be trusted. Deacon trusted him, and that was good enough for her. For now.

Ellie couldn't muster the energy to return to the hotel. Besides, the last thing she wanted was to be cooped up in her room all day. Sitting here was a much better alternative. She opened Jolene's letter, and it was just as Crowbar said. Jolene wasn't about to set foot off that mountain.

Ellie's thoughts returned to her morning sickness. No, it wasn't morning sickness. It was morning and she was sick.

Not pregnant. There was no way she could be pregnant. She had used precautions—a copper penny—and he had pulled out. *Both* of them had pulled out. No, she wasn't pregnant, and she wasn't going to fret about it. There were other things, bigger things, to worry about.

39.

<u>26 July 1912 (Holly Grove and Mucklow)</u>

Deacon made sure the miners who decided to remain in the Mucklow camp were ready for a full-on battle. They were up in the hills and out on the perimeter of the camp ready to put a bullet in anything that moved. Even though they were armed with plenty of guns and ammunition, Deacon feared their shotguns and rifles were no match for the power and ferocity of the Gatling Gun.

Most of the women and children had been steadily departing since they got word about the raid. Everyone seemed to have evaporated. The sounds of the children playing and the women doing their chores had softened to a whisper.

Thanks to Ellie, most of the miners at Mucklow had moved their families out. Some had gone to the Holly Grove camp until this battle was over. A few had gotten on the train and left the area altogether to go stay with family out of the line of fire. Everyone was on edge. Mothers kept their kids close to their tents. Unless you had a damn good reason to venture far from camp, you didn't.

Deacon trekked up the mountain. The humidity, already thick, had soaked his clothes, and the sun hadn't even streaked the sky yet. He joined Jake and three dozen other miners. They'd burrowed in behind some boulders high up the mountain, almost level with the fort. Jake gathered everyone and spoke softly. "Remember, that Gatlin' is a beast and it'll cut you clean in two. It'll get hot, and they'll have to stop and let it cool after a few thousand rounds. So stay behind the rocks till it stops. That's when we go into action and start firin' at 'em. Jim'll keep an eye on the Gatlin' and signal when they's gettin' ready to fire it up again. Remember, stay close to the rocks and keep your heads down."

Barricaded behind the boulders, they watched the fort and the ground below with binoculars and waited.

The tension in the camp was wound tight. The mine guards climbed to the top of their fort. "They's gettin' ready, boys," Deacon said.

The guards opened fire with the Gatling Gun. The sun bounced off their binoculars as they homed in on their targets. They fired thousands of rounds at anything and everything that moved in and around the Mucklow Camp.

Bullets from the Gatling Gun riddled the mountain. Deacon and the others lay flat on the ground behind the rocks. Gunfire echoed through the mountains and up and down the creeks. As Jake predicted, the Gatling Gun got hot after a few thousand rounds. The guards stopped to let it cool and switched to their lever-action Winchesters.

When the Gatling Gun stopped firing, the sound of the trees splitting and falling carried up the mountain to where Deacon, Jake, and the others were hiding. They jumped into action and started firing at the guards.

"Damn, they must've fired thousands of rounds into the mountain." Deacon said as he reloaded his rifle.

"Hell, maybe this is the new way to timber. Just shoot the trees down." Jake replied.

Once the Gatling Gun had cooled, the guards fired it up again and continued to riddle Mucklow Camp with tens of thousands of bullets.

Jolene heard the shots echoing through the mountains. Everyone at Holly Grove was on edge for hours until the shooting stopped.

Jolene busied herself by checking on others, comforting them and reassuring them everything would be all right. She doubted her own words even before they left her mouth. Typically, Deacon sent a messenger to Holly Grove to let her know what was happening. No messengers had been sent since early morning. Jolene assumed it was too dangerous.

Hours later, Deacon and the men returned to the camp. Jolene ran down the path to greet him. She wrapped her arms around his neck. Then, letting go, she took one of his rifles and they walked back to their tent hand-in-hand.

She closed the flap on the tent. "You look like hell. What happened?"

Deacon sat down on the bed and took off his boots. "The Gooslin boy got killed today. Seventeen damn years old. Killed like a rat on the river bank. Those bastards killed him, Jolene."

"Who's gonna tell his mama? Should I go?"

"No. Her brother's tellin' her."

"How many dead?"

"Twelve that we counted, I fear they's a lot more we just ain't found. As far as we could count, we hit four Baldwin-Felts men—not sure if we killed 'em or wounded 'em. Jolene, those bastards aimed that Gatlin' directly into the camp for over two hours. They had binoculars and would set their sights on one of us or a tent and fire thousands of rounds directly at it. They didn't know who was in those tents and didn't care. Thank God Ellie told us this was comin' and we got most of the people outa there. It could've been a lot worse."

"Jesus Christ, Deacon. Are they all insane? What're we gonna do now? We can't compete with a Gatlin' Gun."

"Jake's bringing us machine guns next week. It might be a little too late. At least we'll have 'em for next time."

"*Next time*? How long can we keep doin' this, Deacon? This war's gettin' bloodier by the day. Many more days like today, instead of water, there'll be blood flowin' down the creek."

Part 3

Pray for the dead and fight like hell for the living

—Mother Jones

40.

<u>6 August 1912 (Holly Grove)</u>

Jake had been back in Holly Grove for two weeks. His mind was weary and his body tired. He missed sleeping in his bed with Polly tucked in safely beside him. He missed the kids. Regardless, this was his job. His responsibility. The union's support was waning and creating more tension within the camp.

The union had attempted to broker a deal with the coal operators a couple of times. When those fell through, Jake and his men had taken things into their own hands—they reached out to the Socialist Party of America and enlisted the support of Mother Jones. She was considered a radical by many of the miners, but she was a true fighter for the working men and women across the country, regardless of her political affiliation.

In preparation for Mother Jones's planned speeches at Eskdale that night and in Charleston on the 15th, she sent Jake and five others up and down the creek to rally support.

Most of Jake's men offered support without question. Others flat out refused, afraid of being blacklisted permanently. Only one of Jake's inner circle had any issues—Crowbar. Jake was surprised Crowbar would openly refuse to work with Mother Jones. Jake couldn't tolerate this sort of dissent. It maligned his authority and created tension amongst the ranks. He couldn't afford to have this poison the well.

Crowbar stated his case. "Now, Jake, you know I'm here to fight the fight as long as it takes. I've done whatever you've asked me to do. I've been carryin' messages back and forth to Charleston damn near ever' day. I've done my duty. Mother Jones is an outsider. She's a profane woman that uses worse language than any ten of us men."

Jake shook his head as Crowbar spoke. "I know. I hear what you're a'sayin'. But she's the one to deliver the message to Glasscock. She's been organizin' labor all over the country. She *is* the voice of the movement right now."

"Tell me what that old woman—who ain't even from 'round here—knows 'bout minin' or coal. What? What does she know? We don't need no woman. This is man's work. It's bad 'nuff we got a woman actin' as a spy. Women ain't got no business in this, Jake." Crowbar stood up and paced in front of Jake and the men with him.

"Crowbar, I understand your frustration—"

"No. Jake, I don't think you do. Let me tell you again." Crowbar used his fingers to count off his list of issues. "Number one: We got Ellie—a whore, no less—tellin' us what those bastards have planned for us. How we s'posed to trust a woman like that? She already got two men killed for nothin'."

"Has she been wrong yet? Answer, me Crowbar. Has she?" Jake was more concerned Crowbar had mentioned Ellie by name than the fact he had called her a whore. They had agreed to keep her name out of this.

"Not yet. I think she's either been lucky or she's just suckerin' us in. Hell, Jake, she sends letters to Jolene ain't nobody can read but the two of 'em. How we know what she's sayin'? Now let me finish. Number two: Mother Jones is an outsider who ain't got no ties to this place or coal. Number three: She's old, she's a woman, and women ain't got no place in politics, coal, or this damn war."

"Now, Crowbar, you know they call her the angel of the miners." Jake and a few of the others chuckled.

"That old battle ax ain't no angel, Jake. She waltzes in here like she's one of us. Ten years ago she goes down into the mine and moves a few rocks and acts like she's a coal miner. That old woman ain't no coal miner, Jake."

"She's on our side, Crowbar. I know you and a few of the other men don't take kindly to outsiders comin' in here and gettin' in our business—'specially a woman. But she's doin' good for us. Glasscock won't listen to us. Hell, he won't even admit we have any rights. Our best bet is to let Mother Jones come in as an outsider and let him know it's not just us. He needs to know she's gonna take our cause all the way to Washington and that others across the country are watchin' this fight and are ready to jump in. Crowbar, I need you to be in this with us. All the way. If the other men see you refusin' to join us and talkin' against Mother Jones, we could have the entire thing fall apart."

"Dammit, Jake. I don't want to, but I'll do it for you. Just don't make me work with that old woman."

Jake had no idea Crowbar felt so strongly about Ellie. Jake knew he disliked Mother Jones, but to call Ellie by name and then to call her a whore in front of the other men was out of line. Maybe it *was* time to find another messenger. The young Maples boy was hungry to help. He would address this issue with Crowbar later in private. For now, Jake and his men left Crowbar stewing in his discomfort over the old woman. They had a few thousand more men to talk to.

Deacon entered the tent. "Jolene, you ready? We got a wagon waitin' on you down at the end of the path. Mother Jones should be here soon. Take your gun and hide it in your skirts. They'll likely search the wagon, but they won't dare lay a hand on you. Jake tells me they's a few of our men not too happy 'bout Mother Jones bein' here. It's hard to tell who we can trust."

"We'll be fine. Where you gonna be?" Jolene asked.

"I'll be followin' you'ns, but not where those bastards can see me."

"How many men you think'll turn out for the meetin' at Eskdale tonight?"

"Jake's been busy all day rallyin' men to get out for it. I'd say hundreds at least."

Jolene kissed Deacon, and they headed down the path. Mother Jones was already there waiting. "Now, Jolene"—Mother Jones took Jolene's hand—"you don't have to do this. I don't want you to put yourself in any danger. You know those Baldwin-Felts bastards would just as soon kill me as look at me."

Jolene climbed up onto the wagon and took the reins. "I ain't none too worried about those bastards, Mother. Gettin' those Cabin Creek miners to join us in the strike is worth any risk. Let's go."

Jolene guided the wagon up Cabin Creek. A few dozen unarmed miners followed them on foot. They passed through the small town of Eskdale without so much as a whisper of trouble. They rounded a bend on the far end of town and were met by a dozen armed men carrying shotguns, rifles, and a machine gun.

The leader of the gunmen stepped out into the middle of the road. "Now, look here, old woman, we don't want no trouble with you. So, it's best if you turn that wagon 'round and get the hell off Cabin Creek." He pointed his gun directly at Mother Jones.

Jolene inched the wagon right up to the gunmen. Mother Jones patted her hand. "You sit tight. I'll handle this." One of the miners accompanying them helped Mother Jones step down from the wagon.

Mother Jones walked up to the machine gun and placed her hand on its muzzle. "Take your hands offa that gun, you hellcat," the gunman yelled.

"We ain't fightin' you, young man. These men are fightin' with bare fists and empty stomachs the men that rob them and deprive their children of childhood."

"I don't give a damn. I'll kill them and you."

She looked the man straight in the eye. "Listen here, you." She pointed to the hills behind her. "You fire one shot here today and there are 800 men in those hills who'll not leave one of your gang alive."

The gunman looked at the dense hills surrounding them and lowered his gun. "Search 'em for guns," he yelled back at the men with him.

After the search, he let them pass on their way to their meeting at Eskdale. "Mother, Deacon didn't say they's gonna be 800 men hidin' in the hills."

"I know dear. I bluffed the bastard." Jolene and Mother Jones chuckled.

After the meeting at Eskdale, the Cabin Creek miners decided to join the strike.

41.

15 August 1912 (Charleston)

Jolene's excitement grew as she prepared to go with Mother Jones to Charleston. Mother Jones had walked up and down Cabin Creek rallying the support of the men. Her speech at Eskdale had convinced the Cabin Creek miners to walk out and join the Paint Creek boys in the fight against the coal operators. Now here Jolene was, going to Charleston with Mother Jones where the old woman was going to make a speech on the Capitol steps inciting war.

"How many people you think'll show up, Mother?" Jolene asked.

"With the Cabin Creek boys joinin' us and the others from all over the state expected to show up, I'd say there should be thousands of miners and their families present." Mother Jones read the notes Jolene had given her. "Now, I've never given a prepared speech, Jolene. But these notes and issues you've provided are a great help to me. I wanna make sure I cover all the latest atrocities those bastards have inflicted on these people."

Mother Jones was flamboyant and fiery and strong. Qualities Jolene admired. Mother Jones was also a leader, and most of the men actually listened to her. Something not many women could command. Jolene had found a friend, mentor, and hero in Mother Jones and wanted to fight right alongside the legendary leader for as long as she could.

Jolene sent a message to Ellie informing her of the plan for the march on Charleston. It wouldn't be safe for her to be out in the streets. She could be recognized or trampled if they thought she was part of the Baldwin-Felts machine.

"Jolene, this speech'll be a turnin' point in our battle, and none of us may be safe ever again. The stakes are gettin' higher and more dangerous with each passin' day we fight these sons of bitches."

Ellie spent the day before Mother Jones's speech in Charleston walking around the Capitol area, scouting out a place from where she could watch and hear the speech. She walked around for more than an hour, finding no place where she would be safe if recognized. Starting back to the hotel, she heard the church bells across the street. The white steeple rose high into the clear blue sky. A rooftop veranda faced the Capitol Building. That would be her spot to watch Mother Jones.

Ellie sat on a park bench and re-read Jolene's letter for the second time. She'd provided details about the old woman that made Ellie even more determined to hear her speech. She had been given two opinions of Mother Jones—John's and Jolene's. Ellie wanted to form her own opinion. She already admired the old woman. It pleased Ellie to know the fiery speaker was getting under the skin of the Baldwin-Felts men and the coal operators. They were furious she was in the area and agitating the coal miners.

The miners called Mother Jones the "angel of the miners," and the coal operators called her anything and everything *but* an angel. They despised Mother Jones and everything she stood for. Ellie and John had recently attended dinner at a prominent coal operator's mansion on the Kanawha River. The dinner conversation had turned to the strike as it always did. The host commented, "That old woman Jones uses language that makes me blush. Why, that old bitch can cuss better than any sailor I ever heard." That made Ellie admire her even more.

Ellie was sick of the perfectly polite, socialite "ladies" always trying to outdo each other on manners and etiquette. It was stifling to say the least. She was certain she would enjoy having a shot of whiskey with Mother Jones and hoped she would have the opportunity when this war was over.

Mother Jones wasn't expected until early afternoon. Ellie wanted to be sure she got a seat and was prepared to wait all day and night if she had to. John had left the hotel early in the morning with instructions for Ellie to stay inside and out of the way of the miners' mob that was expected. As soon as he left, Ellie quickly dressed and met Dottie on the back steps. Dottie had packed a lunch, and they hurried through the back streets to the church. It was a hot, sticky day, and people were already gathering around the Capitol. Ellie and Dottie slipped in the side door of the church and up the back stairs to the rooftop veranda. Unfortunately, they were not the only ones with the idea of observing from that vantage point. A few other people, mostly church staff, had already staked a claim. Ellie and Dottie found a covered spot with a bird's-eye view of where Mother Jones would be speaking.

From their perch they could see the miners marching down Kanawha Boulevard toward the Capitol. They sang hymns and stepped to the beat. "Holy cats! Look at 'em, Dottie. There's so many. *Thousands*. Men, women, kids. Black, white, old, and young. All comin' here together to fight for their God-given right to a better life."

They appeared as a moving unit at first. As they got closer, Ellie could see Mother Jones leading the march. When they were on the Capitol steps, she saw Jolene marching next to Mother Jones. Ellie's eyes filled with tears at the sight of Jolene. She looked radiant, even in her rag of a dress, her red hair gleaming in the bright sunshine. Ellie wanted nothing more than to run down the steps and grab her sister. She wanted to hug her and tell her she loved her. From the rooftop, Jolene looked thin, much thinner than Ellie remembered. Ellie could not fathom what kind of life Jolene had living in the tent colony. She hoped this war would end soon and they could all get back to some sort of normal life.

Jolene had never felt prouder marching into Charleston alongside Mother Jones. She estimated three thousand people in the march, and that many more flooded the Capitol. She wondered where Ellie was. She hoped she stayed at the hotel and didn't try to blend in with this mob of angry coal miners.

Jolene stayed close to Mother Jones as the people gathered. They kept pouring in from all corners of the city. A ragtag group of dirty miners taking over the state capitol.

Jolene took her place behind Mother Jones, scouring the crowd for Ellie's face. Her eyes were drawn to a group of people on the rooftop of the church. It was too far away to make out faces clearly, but she would recognize her sister anywhere. Good, she wasn't on the streets with the crowd. A church? Of all places for Ellie to be watching this historic moment.

The crowd quieted as Mother Jones began to speak.

> *This great gathering that is here tonight signals there is a disease in the State that must be wiped out. The people have suffered from that disease patiently; they have borne insults, oppression, outrages; they appealed to their chief executive, they appealed to the courts, they appealed to the attorney general, and in every case, they were turned down. They were ignored. "The people must not be listened to; the corporations must get a hearing."*
>
> *In the name of God, what do any of those men know about your troubles up on Cabin Creek and Paint Creek? Do you see the direct insult offered by your officials to your intelligence? They look upon you as a lot of enemies instead of those who do the work.*

Damn if Ellie didn't like the old woman. She was certainly piss and vinegar. She was a powerful speaker and she told the truth. "She's sure somethin' else isn't she, Dot?"

Dottie sat on the edge of her seat. "Ms. Ellie, I didn't know a woman could be so powerful. Look at all those men down there hangin' on her ever' word. I've never seen nothin' like her."

> *I want to put it up to the citizens, up to every honest man in this audience—let me ask you here, have your public officials any thought for the citizens of this State, or their condition?*
>
> *Now, then, go with me up those creeks, and see the blood-hounds of the mine owners, approved of by your public officials. See them insulting women, see them coming up the track. I went up there and they followed me like hounds. But some day I will follow them. When I see them go to hell, I will get the coal and pile it up on them.*
>
> *I look at the little children born under such a horrible condition. I look at the little children that were thrown out here.*
>
> *Now then, let me ask you. When the miners—a miner that they have robbed him of one leg in the mines and never paid him a penny for it—when he entered a protest, they went into his house not quite a week ago, and threw out his whole earthly belongings, and he and his wife and six children slept on the roadside all night. Now, you can't contradict that. Suppose we had taken a mine owner and his wife and*

> *children and threw them out on the road and made them sleep all night, the papers would be howling "anarchy."*
>
> *When you held a meeting the other day down here at Cedar Grove, the Mail said that evening that you were drunk. I want to say to the Mail, it was a lie of the blackest dye. There was never in the State of West Virginia a more orderly, well-behaved body of men than those miners were that assembled at Cedar Grove. The Mail never told you when the mine owners and their gang of corporation pirates met at the Hotel Ruffner and filled their rotten stomachs with champagne and made you pay the bills.*

Ellie whispered, "Yes! She is *so* right, Dot. Those bastards stay drunk and indulge on the finest of everything at the hotel." Dottie hadn't moved since Mother Jones started speaking. A few feet beyond Dottie, Ellie couldn't believe what she saw. Sammy! *What's he doing here?* He winked at her. She quickly turned her head back to Mother Jones and fanned herself. She was glad it was nearly dark so Dot couldn't see her face. She longed to touch Sammy, to kiss him. He had no right to be here—looking so damn good. She dared not look at him. She wasn't sure she could resist him, and she knew her face would betray her.

> *But when they plunder from these miners, these children, my fellow citizens, countrymen, thrown out on the highways and mother insulted—do you think that they will be good citizens when they grow up? I don't. The revenge and resentment will be buried there if they*

grow into manhood, it will develop, they will kill, they will murder to get even with those who robbed them. I want the children to have the best of influence, I want the children to have good schooling, I want women to know nothing but what is good, I want to leave to this nation a nobler manhood and greater womanhood.

I can do it if you men and women will stand together, find out the seat of the disease and pull it up by the roots. Take possession of that state house, that ground is yours.

You built that state house, didn't you? You pay the public officials, don't you? You paid for that ground, didn't you?

Even though they had gone over the basic elements of her speech, Jolene wasn't prepared for the force with which Mother Jones spoke. Nor was she expecting the enthusiasm of the crowd. The miners needed a fire lit under their collective asses. Jolene was even more fascinated that a woman—an old woman at that—was the one with the flame.

Then, who does it belong to? You have been hypnotized. The trouble has been that they wanted the slave system to continue. They have had a glass for you and your wives and children to look into. They have you hypnotized. They want the ministers to tell you when you die you will have a bed in heaven.

Now, then, I will go to the tents and when those poor women—I have seen those little children—my heart bleeds for them—and I thought, "Oh, how brutish the corporations must be!" God Almighty, go down and look at those conditions! Go see those miners! They tell you about how much—they have a list of questions up here, "How much do the unions do to train the miners to clean the yards." Did you ever know of such a damned, silly insulting question?

I want to ask those fellows that put that down, "How do you suppose, when we have to fight you, we have got any time about yards?" You have got the yards. We clean them for you and you don't thank us for it. Your wife lives in style. Look down at those houses there on the river front. She dresses with the blood of children. She buys a dog and calls it "Dear little poodle, I love you."

And you stand for it! And you stand for it! And you are a lot of dirty cowards, I want to tell you the truth about it. You are a lot of cowards and you haven't got enough marrow in your backbone to grease two black cats' tails. If you were men with a bit of revolutionary blood in you, you wouldn't stand for the Baldwin guards, would you?

Ellie felt a twinge of guilt and looked down at her new summer dress, purchased with Baldwin-Felts blood money. She straightened her frock as if to smooth away the unsettling feeling. She *was* doing her part. Being the kept woman of one of Tom Felts's main men was part of that. She refused to feel guilty about living in a suite at the finest hotel in the state and wining and dining on the finest every day. Why, it wasn't her fault the miners were living in tents, was it? She didn't do this to them. She didn't do this to Jolene. What good would it do any of them if she abandoned her place and joined them up on the creek? None. Not one ounce of good would come from it. No, she would certainly not feel guilty about her lifestyle. She *was* doing her part.

They will come to you on election day. I will tell you when you can carry a bayonet and they can't meddle with you. You can carry a bayonet on November 5th, and you can go to the ballot box and put a bayonet in there and stick it to their very heart.

Now, I want to say this: Ten or twelve years ago when I came in here, you had to work eleven or twelve hours, didn't you?

They made you load coal for any price they wanted. We brought on a fight and got twice that for loading coal. We reduced the hours to nine. Up there on Paint Creek and Cabin Creek you obeyed the laws at that time. You had a good union at that time, but you have done in industrial unions as they do elsewhere, you elect the man that wants the glory instead of the man that will work for you. I am going to put a stop to that. I want to tell you we are going to organize West Virginia. I am going to stay in here until you have good officers.

That is my mission, to do what I can to raise mankind to break his chains. The miners are close to me. The steel workers are. I go among them all. Now, my brothers, don't violate the law. Let them see that you are law-abiding.

This meeting tonight indicates a milestone of progress of the miners and workers of the State of West Virginia. I will be with you, and the Baldwin guards will go. You will not be serfs, you will march, march, march on from milestone to milestone of human freedom, you will rise like men in the new day and slavery will get its death blow. It has got to die. Good night.

The crowd took more than an hour to disperse. Everyone wanted to talk to Mother Jones. Evening was upon them when Jolene and Deacon hopped on a wagon headed back to Holly Grove. "Deacon, I think we'll see a real change now. The miners sure seem fired up after Mother Jones's speech."

"Time'll tell. We sure need to settle this a'fore winter. I don't know if a lot of these families with little young'ns can survive." Deacon pulled her close and kissed the top of her head as the wagon bounced along the bumpy road.

Ellie didn't want to risk being recognized as part of the Baldwin-Felts machine, so she and Dottie waited in their seats until the miners had dispersed from the Capitol grounds. Once the crowd thinned, they began their descent down the steps to the street.

Dottie carried the picnic basket and led the way. The crowd moved slowly on the narrow staircase. Dottie was tiny and nimble and ten steps ahead of Ellie. The lack of air in the stairwell was suffocating. A hand grabbed Ellie's arm, pulling her back. She stepped aside to let the person pass her. She turned and looked up into Sammy's smiling face.

"What are you doin?" she insisted.

"I need to hold you for one second." He pulled her back through the crowd and up the stairs to the rooftop.

"Have you totally lost your pea-pickin' mind?" Ellie whispered.

They were the only ones left on the rooftop. He pulled her into a dark alcove. "I had to see you, Ellie." He kissed her and then smiled.

"*You* are insane." She wrapped her hands around his neck and returned his kiss.

"I don't think I can stay away from you. So, whatever plans you have, you need to settle it and get away from that bastard." Sammy held her close.

"I don't have a magic wand. I can't make this war go away. Did you even listen to what that old woman said? It's gonna get uglier a'fore it gets better."

"I know. We need to figure somethin' out. 'cause this not bein' able to see you when I want is killin' me."

She pulled him close. "I know. We'll figure somethin' out. Be patient."

She left him there and hurried down the steps. Dottie was waiting on the street in the dispersing crowd. They walked in silence back to the Hotel Ruffner.

42.

<u>16 August 1912 (Charleston)</u>

Ellie slipped down the back stairs of the hotel and exited out into the alley. She'd memorized the directions that Matilda, the tavern prostitute, had given to Dottie: Left at the end of the alley. Four blocks to Baker Street. Right on Culverson. One block to Pickney. Third house on the left.

With the coal miners fired up for battle at Mother Jones's presence, John planned to spend most of his days and nights at Paint Creek or in Bluefield plotting against the miners and the old woman. If Ellie waited until next week, John may return.

After she crossed over to Pickney, the neighborhood was less than desirable. She was glad she had listened to Dottie and not worn anything fancy—no jewelry—and brought only the money she needed.

Afraid and alone, she stood in front of the house at 42 Pickney Street. It appeared as all the other nondescript houses in Charleston's rundown neighborhoods—old, neglected, and in dire need of paint. The front yard was slightly overgrown, hiding most of the house.

She had no choice but to do this. How could she have let this happen again? She had slept with Sammy more than John for the past few months—still, she wasn't sure who the child belonged to. If she had to guess, it was Sammy's. John had been too drunk most of the time to complete the act.

Even if it was John's, he'd made it clear he didn't want a child. He would leave her and her child without another thought. Besides, she didn't want to have the bastard's baby. Being chained to him for the rest of her life would be a slow death in hell. As thrilled as Sammy would be to have a child with her, it wasn't what *she* wanted. She had other plans for her life—higher expectations than having a tavern musician's baby.

Yes, she *had* to do this. She took a deep breath and lifted the latch on the rusty iron gate. The gate creaked open and snapped shut behind her. With determined steps she walked up the sidewalk and rang the bell. A young black girl with caramel-colored skin and slanted yellowish eyes answered the door. "Hello, Matilda from the tavern sent me."

"Come in. I'm Sally." The girl had a lyrical accent to her voice. "You can wait over there in that room." The girl pointed to a closed door.

Inside, the house was bright and cheerful, almost whimsical with colorful art and draperies and rugs. The house was immaculate and smelled of something sweet Ellie couldn't place. Perhaps a candle or herbs. The room she entered had a chair, a table, and a small wrought iron bed. Ellie took off her bonnet, rubbed her belly, and whispered, "Sweetheart, this is best for both of us. Trust me. I'm sorry. I'm not someone you'd want for a mommy."

A petite, black women entered the room, followed by a sleek black cat. The cat reminded Ellie of Deannie with its black hair and green eyes. The woman's skin looked like sun-kissed cocoa, and her eyes were black and bright. Her unlined face belied her age, but her voice was that of an old soul. Like the young girl, she spoke with a slight accent Ellie couldn't place, but it definitely wasn't Appalachian. "Hello, I'm Eloise. The midwife. I understand Matilda sent you. How far along are you?"

"Not more than six weeks."

"You certain you wanna do this?"

"I am."

"You married?"

"No."

"You a prostitute? Like Matilda?"

"No! I am not. Why would you assume that?"

"You are friends with Matilda. Fine ladies such as yourself don't usually associate with women like Matilda."

"I got the information from her through a friend at the hotel tavern. I don't really *know* her."

Eloise looked at Ellie with a mix of contempt and suspicion. "Come with me." The cat led the way, tail erect as though leading a parade, Ellie trailing after them.

Ellie followed the woman and the cat to the back of the house to another room similar to the first one. This one had surgical utensils on a tray beside a small bed. Another small table held different colored jars and burning candles. Two rocking chairs sat in front of purple drapes drawn over a window.

"Take off your clothes and put on that gown on the bed. Pour yourself a glass of whiskey and drink it all. I'll be back in a few minutes." The cat remained with Ellie, sitting at the foot of the bed staring at her.

Ellie did as Eloise instructed. She filled the glass on the table with whiskey and drank it all. It warmed her body and relaxed her a bit.

As promised, a few minutes later the tiny lady returned. "You have two options. You can stay here all night, or I can have someone take you back to the hotel. Either way will cost you ten dollars more. You need to pay me now before we start."

"Have someone take me back to the hotel, please." Ellie took the money from her purse and handed it to Eloise.

Eloise counted the money and handed Ellie ten dollars. "Too much."

"No, keep it."

Eloise shrugged her shoulders. "As you wish."

"Does the cat have a name?"

"Boo. She was born on Halloween. The only one in her litter to survive."

"She's beautiful."

"Ah! Yes, she knows this! She is a special creature. She helps with the healin'. She will stay with you for your visit."

Eloise washed her hands. "Stand up." She felt Ellie's belly and her breasts. "Lie down." Boo jumped off the bed, moving to the small table.

Eloise pulled the gown up, placed her hands on Ellie's belly, and pressed hard. She put her ear to Ellie's stomach. "Be very still and quiet. Breathe deeply." She put a hand between Ellie's legs. "I need to feel inside. Don't be afraid. It won't hurt much." She inserted two fingers into Ellie's vagina and felt around. Ellie flinched.

"What're you doin'? It hurts. It feels like you are stickin' your fingers clean up into my womb."

"I am. I need to feel your cervix. See what the baby is doin'. How far along you really are. This will determine the method we use."

She finished her examination and washed her hands again. "As far as I can tell, you're about six to eight weeks along. Everythin' feels normal and healthy. You must understand—havin' this procedure may prevent you from ever bein' able to bear children. I can make no promises."

"I understand. Do it and let's get it over with."

"It will hurt. A lot. You will bleed. A lot. And probably for many days. If the bleedin' doesn't stop after five days, you *must* return. You cannot have relations with a man till the bleedin' completely stops. Do you understand?"

"Yes, I understand."

Sally returned to the room with a tray of tea. The tray had a pot of hot water, two cups and saucers, a small white jar, and a larger blue jar. Taking a tea bag from the white jar, Eloise poured a cup of tea for herself. She placed one of the tea bags from the blue jar in Ellie's cup of hot water and handed it to her. "Let this steep for a few minutes, then drink all of it."

"What is it?"

"An herbal mixture of pennyroyal, tansy, Queen Anne's lace, blue cohosh, cotton root, and a few other secret ingredients. You'll take the blue jar with you and drink three cups of this ever' day for three days—one in the mornin', one at noon, and one before bed. After we finish our tea, we'll wait thirty minutes. Then I'll place a special tincture inside you. This will cause a lot of crampin'. Crampin' like you've never known. Don't worry, I'm gonna give you something similar to laudanum for the pain."

Ellie sipped the hot tea and held back her tears. She knew this was necessary.

"How do you feel?"

"A little sick at my stomach."

"Good—means it's workin'. Keep drinkin' all of it." Eloise talked while they sipped. "The herbs are mostly picked around here, up in the mountains. The special ones I grow out back. My grandmother taught me all I know about herbs and medicine. She came here from Louisiana after they freed the slaves. She was a sixth-generation slave woman in Louisiana. A lot of the people 'round here called her a voodoo woman 'cause o' her skills with the herbs and medicine. She weren't no voodoo woman. She was a good woman. A fine woman who could cure about anythin' that ails ya."

"She's still livin'?" With the whiskey taking effect and the relaxed atmosphere Eloise had created, Ellie slipped seamlessly back into her Mingo dialect.

"Oh, no. She died a few months back'a this. She would've been ninety-seven years old this month. Still growin' herbs and mixin' potions and cures till the day she passed over. The tincture I'll use on you is her own recipe. She used it for years. She learned about it in Louisiana and used it on a lot of the slave girls who got pregnant—but mostly on the white women. They'd come from all over for her potions and cures. It must have been somethin' to see those lily-white women comin' back into the bayou to see my granny." Eloise chuckled. "Gimme your cup. You need'a drink one more." She filled Ellie's cup again.

"My mama was a seer," Eloise continued. "You know what that is?" She refilled her own cup.

Ellie sipped her tea. "I think so. My sister's a bit of seer. She also works with herbs—nothin' like this. Mostly ginseng and local stuff she finds in the hills to help people who're sick."

"What kinda seer is she? Dreams, visions, voices?"

"Mostly dreams and visions. No voices. She's been seein' since we's little. My cousin Polly hears voices. She gets a strange feelin' come over her and then she hears it clear as a bell. It's only happened a few times."

"How about you? You a seer?" Eloise swirled her tea.

"Me? No. Not really. Not like that. I see people as they are though. I see through 'em and their motives. Almost like I can see inside their heads and hearts— if I'm payin' attention. My aunt Ella called it 'The Knowin'.'"

"Ohhhh . . . you have the intuition. That's a good gift to have. You read people's thoughts, or you just *know*?"

"I just *know*. I know a'fore *they* know what they're gonna do or say. It's nothin' I try to do. I meet certain people and almost always know what they's thinkin' or more of what they want, how they feel. Mostly how to make 'em give me what I want. I see through their lies. Sometimes I get lazy and don't wanna know or I simply don't care all that much. That's when I usually get in a heap a trouble."

"You should practice seein' deeper inside they heart. I can show you."

"I'm not sure I wanna see deeper. Some people are scary enough on the surface."

"My mama could read your thoughts as you were thinkin' 'em. She said it made her crazy sometimes. She got tired of hearin' inside people's heads. Any others in your family like you, your sister, and cousin?" Eloise asked.

"My Aunt Ella. I'm named after her. She lives in San Antonio, Texas, now and reads Tarot cards and tells fortunes. My granddaddy went crazy when she confronted him 'bout cheatin' on my Granny Cline with Shelly Warren. She said the cards told her and the cards don't lie. Up till then, only my Granny Cline, me, my sister, and my cousin knew she even had the cards. After that, he started callin' her a witch and disowned her. So she left.

"Ella'd been teachin' us girls how to use our gifts and how to read the cards. After they called her a witch and made her leave, we girls decided to keep our *gifts* to ourselves. We developed our own language—a mixture of Celtic and Cherokee—and nonsense stuff, so nobody'd know what we's talkin' 'bout. Just the three of us. It's mostly a written language of pictures and songs and rhymes. Mostly gibberish." Ellie's mind drifted off to her sister and Polly. She missed them terribly.

"You finished with your tea?" Eloise took her cup. "Lie down on the bed."

She felt Ellie's forehead and then massaged her belly. "Try to rest. I'll be back in thirty minutes." She placed a quilt over Ellie before leaving.

Ellie pulled the quilt up around her neck. She was suddenly freezing, even though it was a hot August night and she had drunk two cups of hot tea. Boo jumped on the bed and stretched out beside her, purring contentedly. Ellie tried to fight back the tears again, but they came like a flood. She cried until Eloise returned.

"Ohhh . . . my dear. The tears are natural. The tea brings a lot of things to the surface. Things you didn't even know you had stored up inside you. Sometimes the intuition works on everyone but yourself, no?" She felt Ellie's face and head again. "You cold?"

"Yes."

"Good. It's workin'."

Sally entered the room with another tray filled with jars and a bowl of hot water. Eloise took a few herbs from each of the jars and mixed them using a small black marble mortar and pestle. She ground the herbs and then took a square of linen and soaked it in the hot water, which was infused with lavender. Once the linen was wet, she filled it with the herbs and folded it all into a pouch.

She removed the quilt from Ellie. "I know you're cold, but this'll only take a minute. I need for you to raise your legs and spread your knees apart."

Ellie was shivering. Eloise gently pulled her knees apart and placed the tincture of herbs into her vagina. Ellie was thankful it was warm. Eloise pushed the pouch as far into Ellie as possible and held it there, pressing hard into her cervix. The pain was subtle at first, and then there was a stinging cramp. Ellie wanted to curl up into a little ball, but Eloise told her she had to stay on her back with her knees apart.

Eloise held the tincture inside Ellie for ten minutes. Then she removed it and made another one. She included a few additional herbs in this one, making the pouch slightly larger. She repeated the process again and then again.

By the third pouch, the cramps were excruciating. The pain coursed through Ellie's entire body. Her heart rate slowed, and her head spun. She hoped Eloise wouldn't make her stand up anytime soon.

When she finished, Eloise allowed Ellie to curl up into a tight ball on the bed. Then Eloise took a small bundle of twigs and leaves tied with string and lit it. She blew out the flame and the smoke gently rose. Eloise walked around the room, whispering; the smoke filled the air with a pungent scent.

"What're you doin'?" Ellie managed to ask.

"This is sage. It cleanses the space of spirits and darkness. I'm clearin' the air for your little one to leave us. I'll open the window to allow the spirit to make its way home."

Ellie slipped into a deep sleep. She woke up hours later in excruciating pain. Boo was still snuggling next to her, and Sally was by her side, turning a tiny red bottle up to her lips. Ellie drifted back to sleep. When she woke the next morning, she was in her hotel bed in her nightgown. She had no recollection of returning or changing clothes. The dress she wore to Pickney Street was hanging with her other dresses. Her shoes were in their proper place. The blue jar was on her dressing table with a note "Morning, noon, night." She assumed it was Dottie who'd brought her back to the hotel.

Dottie delivered a pot of hot water and prepared tea using the mixture from the blue jar. "Ms. Ellie, you need to drink this."

Ellie took the hot cup from Dottie—the bitter truth of what she had done hanging unspoken between them.

Ellie stayed in her room. John wouldn't return for another ten days. This should all be over by the time he returned. She told Sammy she was unable to see him for another two weeks.

Eloise had said Ellie should start bleeding by early afternoon, and she did. Gently at first, but by midnight she thought she was hemorrhaging. The cramps were immense. On the fifth day, the bleeding stopped, as Eloise had predicted.

Ellie needed to get out of the hotel and feel the sunlight on her face. The past five days had taken a toll on her body and spirit. She was weak and thinner. Dottie brought the mail, and there was a letter from Jolene asking about her health.

"Crowbar came to see you a few days ago, and I told him you's sick, Ms. Ellie," Dottie said.

"I assume he's still plannin' to come today. I'll go to the park this afternoon and meet him."

Ellie had barely eaten during the ordeal and was starving. Dottie brought her a huge lunch and prepared her bath. With Dottie's help and a few stitches in the waist of her dress, Ellie got dressed and left the hotel. She took a book and walked to the river. She sat on a bench and read until it was time to meet Crowbar.

43.

21 August 1912 (Holly Grove)

Jolene heard Boyd calling her name. He had been her assistant most every day since they had been evicted. He wanted to step up and help, but Deacon had told him he was too young to go up the mountain and participate in the raids on the guards, so Deacon deputized him to be Jolene's right-hand man.

"Ms. Jolene! Ms. Jolene! Come quick! Mama says you need to come quick. The baby's comin' any minute, and Mama don't look so good."

Jolene grabbed her sack of tinctures and herbs and ran after Boyd down the hill to his tent. His dirty bare feet smacked against the damp path that had been packed down from the heavy foot traffic over the past few months.

Jolene could barely keep up with Boyd barreling down the hill to his tent. Her lungs were on fire by the time they reached the bottom.

The flap to the tent was closed, and the interior seemed nearly 105 degrees when Jolene stepped inside. Betsy was barely breathing. Her oldest daughter, no more than ten years old, wiped her brow with a dirty, wet rag. Jolene secured the flap open to let some air in and shooed the three small kids and Boyd outside. She sat on the cot next to Betsy. "How long you been in labor, Betsy? Why didn't you call on me sooner?"

Between breaths, Betsy whispered, "Ms. Jolene, I knows you got a million things you's workin' on and worryin' 'bout. Your husband's out there fightin' this battle. I didn't wanna bother you. I've had four babies and figured I could handle most of this myself." She took another deep breath as the next contraction grabbed her.

Betsy's words were true. Jolene was overwhelmed with trying to keep order in her section of the camp. She had taken a lead role in organizing things, making sure everyone had a tent and the necessary provisions to sustain life during this war. They had divided the tent colonies into sections, with leaders in each to establish a system of communication and governance. Jolene circulated amongst as many of the tents in her section as she could to make sure everyone had food and those who were sick received what medical treatment she could provide. Thousands of families were spread out all over Holly Grove and Mucklow—hell, just about anywhere they could put a tent. She could only do so much.

She was tired and hungry. Food was becoming scarce, and none of them had money or any way of buying food. The union provided some food, but it never seemed to be enough. She hoped this nightmare would be over before winter set in. How would they make it through the winter in these conditions? She daydreamed about the fancy hotel Ellie was living in—a hot bath a clean bed, a hot meal, laughing with her sister. A life of ease and comfort.

"Ms. Jolene, somethin' feels wrong with this one. It ain't feelin' like I'm used to."

"What're you talkin' 'bout, Betsy? What's it feel like?"

"Well, I ain't felt the little feller move in a few days. Didn't bother me too much. I figured he was turnin'. Gettin' ready to come outa there. Then I had a whole lotta blood yesterdee. Now, that ain't right. When I woke up this mornin' I had a pang somethin' fierce."

"Well, let's see what we can do." Jolene felt Betsy's belly and knew something wasn't right. "I'm gonna see if he's makin' his way out there. I'll need you to spread your legs." Betsy did as Jolene instructed. Jolene tried to feel the crown of the baby's head and found a foot instead.

Jolene couldn't turn the baby by herself. But the midwife had gone to the other side of the tent colony early that morning and wasn't expected back until late in the evening. The two doctors that had been visiting wouldn't be back until tomorrow. She covered Betsy and stepped outside. She sent Boyd to fetch Johnny, the camp messenger, to get the midwife.

Jolene returned to the tent. "Betsy, I'm sure ever'thangs gonna be all right. You're havin' a breech birth, but I'm gonna do all I can to get this baby outa there. We gotta get him turned. I've sent for the midwife to help me." Jolene prayed she wasn't too late.

"I don't want the kids to hear me cryin' or screamin', but the pain's somethin' fierce, Ms. Jolene." Betsy let out a long moan and tears ran down the sides of her face.

Jolene wiped Betsy's face with the dirty rag. "Betsy, I ain't got nothin' for the pain other than whiskey. I'm afraid it'll make you sick."

Jolene was determined to do all she could to get the baby turned. She looked around for a clean—or at least cleaner—quilt to put over Betsy. She found one folded on the kids' bed. Jolene pulled off the dirty blanket and froze. Betsy was lying in a river of blood. Jolene moved quickly to try to stop the hemorrhaging and realized she was fighting Mother Nature. Jolene would lose.

Betsy cried out in pain again. The pain subsided, and she grabbed Jolene's hand. "Promise me, you'll make sure my young'ns are cared for."

"Betsy, you're gonna be fine . . ."

She squeezed Jolene's hand with a strength Jolene didn't think possible for a dying woman. *"Promise me?"*

"I promise," Jolene whispered and fought back tears.

Betsy's eyelids and lips were blue. Her breath was coming in gasps and spurts. Betsy was dying, and Jolene tried to make her as comfortable as possible.

She held Betsy's hand and stayed with her until she left the cruel world in which they had been forced to live. Jolene covered Betsy with the cleaner blanket, brushed her hair from her face, closed her eyelids, and kissed her forehead.

Jolene fought back tears as she left Betsy's side. She closed the flap to the tent and looked around at the four children Betsy had left behind. Women from neighboring tents had gathered around them.

Jolene sat down between the two daughters, and the two boys stood in front of her.

"Young'ns, she didn't make it."

"The baby? The baby didn't make it? How's Mama?" Boyd asked.

"The baby nor your sweet mama made it, sweetheart. I did all I could, but that baby wasn't comin' outa there, and your mama couldn't fight any longer. They's both gone."

Boyd stood staring at Jolene. "I wanna see my mama." Tears welled up in his eyes, and he turned and went into the tent. One by one, the other children followed.

The women who had gathered told Jolene they would take care of the kids and the burial arrangements.

Jolene stood to walk back to her tent. The sky had filled with dark blue clouds, and thunder growled like an angry god demanding its next sacrifice. Jolene felt as if she had two giant river stones tied to her ankles. Large raindrops fell on her face, then turned to a steady downpour. She entered her tent soaked, tired, and angry—mostly angry.

God, why we gotta live like this? How's this an acceptable situation for any human bein'? Why're you punishin' us?

Jolene sat in her tent in her wet clothes for a long time thinking about the day's events and their plight in the damn tent colony. There were thousands of people living here. If it was this bad now, what would winter hold for them? Jolene took off her wet dress, found dry clothes, and dried her hair with a dirty towel.

The thunder and lightning moved closer, and the rain poured out of the sky harder and faster, beating against her tent. Her daddy would've called this a "frog strangler." Jolene pulled the flap back to watch the rain. Her tent sat at a higher elevation than most of the others, providing a good view of Holly Grove.

The ground was saturated, and the paths between the tents merged into one giant mud pit. The tents were sturdy enough, but most leaked. The kids played in the rain and ran through the puddles laughing and chasing each other, oblivious to the dire situation they all faced. Jolene closed the tent flap and sat on her bed. She dropped her face into her hands and cried—hard. Something she rarely did. The tears flowed. For Betsy and her unborn child. For the children she left behind. For herself, Ellie, Deannie. All of them. She cried because it felt good. It felt good to let it out, here alone in her tent, in the rain, with the mud flowing down the path.

44.

23 August (Morgantown, West Virginia State Penitentiary)

Tom counted the notches on the wall—422 days, including his time in the county jail. With any luck and continued good behavior he might get out early. His attorney was working on it. Tom took one last drag of his cigarette and stubbed it out against the stone wall behind his head.

Tom listened to the myriad of sounds on his cell block. There was a comfort in the routine of the prison. A train rumbled in the distance at 11:10 p.m. on the nose every night. He wondered where it was going. Where it had been. He often imagined he was on it and going far away from his grim reality. His mind took him out west to Colorado, then Montana; some nights he even made it all the way to California. The other sounds always brought him back to the present. Most recently it had been the new kid whimpering in the cell next to his. The kid cried most nights since they locked him up. He'd killed a man over a horse—a damn horse—and here he was locked up for the next six years.

Tom doubted the kid would make it. If he did, he'd be no good to nobody when he got out.

The guy on the other side of the whimpering kid typically yelled from his cot for the kid to shut up and go to sleep. The guards made their rounds up and down the corridor two or three times a night, their keys jangling against their thighs. The bars to the cells banged, steel-on-steel, as the guards pulled on each door to confirm none of the prisoners had gotten smart enough to jimmy the lock.

His new cellmate, a grey mouse he had named Moose, scurried around in the dark. Moose had shown up a few weeks earlier, and without any formal introduction, made himself at home. Tom welcomed the company, and they had gotten on quite well. Moose typically slept at the bottom of the bunk, tucked in under the thin blanket. Tom shared his food—if you could call it that—with the little fella, which Moose was thankful for.

Tom thought of Ellie and wondered what she had been doing with herself this past year. His brothers had visited a few months ago and told him the rumor was she dumped her newborn off on her cousin Polly and had left for Charleston with a rich man. Sounded about right. He wasn't surprised. Ellie would never change.

He thought about the baby and wondered if it *was* his. Did it look like him? Would he try to get her when he got out? He pondered these things. What on earth would he do with a kid? Especially a little girl? She was better off with Polly and Jake. Still, if she was his, he felt obligated to be a father to her. Unlike Ellie, he wouldn't abandon his child. He would know if she was his when he saw her. He decided his first stop when he got out of this place would be Polly's.

Moose climbed on the cot and under the blanket and snuggled in for the night. Tom drifted off to sleep and dreamed of Deannie and California.

45.

26 August 1912 (Charleston)

The abortion gnawed at Ellie—at her mind, her heart. It ate away a little more of her spirit each day. She lost a few more pounds and cried herself to sleep more often than not. She couldn't understand why the sadness wouldn't leave; it wasn't as though she'd ever laid eyes on the child or held it. As much as she attempted to shrug it off and put it away, it kept crawling back into her lap demanding she acknowledge it. She supposed it was grief. Grief for Deannie, the unborn child, and the children she would now never be able to give birth to.

She held a book in her hands, but she didn't want to read. Actually, she couldn't read. She stared at the pages not able to make sense of the words. Worst of all, she longed to hold Deannie and kiss her sweet face. She had to pull herself out of this dark hole before this thing gripping her spirit pulled her deeper into its clutches.

The only place she had been was to the park to meet with Crowbar. She'd returned to her room immediately afterward to sit alone. Sammy continued to send messages through

Dottie. Ellie told Dot to tell him she was sick. Even though he didn't know about the baby, she simply couldn't face him yet. She needed to grieve this tiny life she had taken. Thankfully, John was away more than he was in Charleston.

Dottie brought Ellie's lunch and sat the tray on the small dining table. "Ms. Myrtle's insistin' on comin' up here to your room and visitin' with you. Says she's worried 'bout you." Dottie set the small table with expert precision. "I told her you's fine, but she won't take no for an answer. She wants to come directly after lunch. What should I tell her?"

Ellie sat at the table and allowed Dottie to place the napkin in her lap. "I s'pose she should come. I've not had any news from her in a week or so. Tell her to come immediately after lunch. And Dottie, bring tea when you show her up." Ellie thought for a moment. "Better yet, bring whiskey."

Ellie was scheduled to meet Crowbar at nightfall. Perhaps Myrtle would share something with Ellie to make it worth his trip.

Dottie and Myrtle entered Ellie's suite promptly at one o'clock. Dottie brought a decanter of whiskey and two glasses. Ellie stood to greet them. "Myrtle! I'm so glad you came." Ellie took Myrtle's hands in hers. "I apologize for not being a better friend. I've been a little under the weather, and quite honestly, I'm so sick of this nonsense with those miners. It's simply exhaustin'. Don't you get tired of it all?"

Dottie placed the tray on the table and filled two glasses with whiskey.

Ellie took Myrtle's hand and led her across the room. "Let's sit over here on the settee and chat. I assumed you would like a little afternoon nip. I had Dottie bring us a decanter of the hotel's finest." Dottie handed them each a glass of whiskey. "I know *I* could certainly use a little pick-me-up. Thank you, Dottie," Ellie said.

Myrtle greedily took the glass from Dottie. "Ellie, you know me so well. I feel exactly the same way you do. Seems as though Clyde never has time to do anything with me. I thought on at least some of our trips to Charleston he'd have some free time. Appears Tom Felts has him busy every minute of every day."

"I know exactly how you feel, Myrtle! John's gone all the time. It gets rather borin' and lonely." Ellie sipped her whiskey. "Seems I never know what he's up to. He doesn't tell me much. I learn more from you than I do him." Ellie took a sip of her whiskey. "What are they up to this week?"

"Clyde's been busy organizin' to bring in what they call 'transportation men' or some such thing to work the mines," Myrtle said.

"Transportation men? You mean scabs? From where?" Ellie refilled Myrtle's glass.

"Clyde says they's bringin' hundreds of 'em from ever'where." The whiskey pulled Myrtle back into her country twang. "New York, Philadelphia, Chicago, Cleveland, St. Louis—all over. They'll be bringin' in 'em in pretty much ever' week."

Ellie poured Myrtle her third and final whiskey. "How long do they plan on keepin' those men here?"

"Clyde says as long as it takes." Myrtle drained her glass for a third time, and it was clear she was unable to string her words together any longer. Ellie walked her to her room and helped her to bed so she could sleep it off.

Ellie waited until dark, then dressed and exited the hotel through the back door into the alley. Leaving at night to walk the streets of Charleston wasn't fitting for a lady; besides she didn't want to encounter any of the ladies this evening. An afternoon with Myrtle was more than enough.

A warm breeze blew through the park, sending the first fallen leaves scurrying around Ellie's feet. August had not seen a drop of rain, and the first dry leaves were going straight to brown and slipping from their branches. It would be an early fall. Ellie peered through the darkness looking for Crowbar. When he approached she was startled to see it wasn't Crowbar—but Jake.

"Why'd *you* come? Is ever'thing all right?"

"I wanted to talk to you in person. I wanted to make sure you're still on our side."

"You *still* don't trust me, Jake? Knowin' I'm puttin' my life at risk? Knowin' that man would beat me to an inch of my life if he found out I was even related to you?" Ellie sat up straighter and faced him.

Jake chuckled. "I'm just messin' with you, Ellie. I do trust *you*. If I didn't, I wouldn't be here. Truth is I don't trust any messenger with what I want to talk to you 'bout. I think we have somebody in the camp workin' for the other side."

"Who?"

"Not sure yet. Somebody's talkin' though, and they ain't a lotta trust goin' 'round these days. You'll prob'ly be seein' more of me or Deacon and a lot less of Crowbar."

"You don't trust Crowbar?"

"Nope, not one damn bit. He's not completely for us. Hates Mother Jones. Apparently, he ain't too fond of you neither."

"I figured as much. He acts like he's doin' us all a big favor by passin' messages. I think he hates that he can't read the letters Jolene and I pass back and forth."

"He won't be back," Jake said. "What news do you have? Anythang we can use?"

"Jake, they's bringin' in scab workers from all over to work the mines. The first trainload'll show up tomorrow. From what Myrtle said, it'll be hundreds if not thousands as the weeks go on. They need to find bastards brave enough to come here and work first," Ellie said.

"We figured that'd happen soon enough. We'll be ready for 'em. We'll scare 'em off if we can. Any idea which train they'll be on?"

"The early train, and they'll be bringin' 'em in weekly for a while." Ellie said.

"Ellie, I have news for you. We're marchin' to Paint Creek in the next week—nearly six thousand men in addition to those in the tent colony. It's gonna be a blood bath. We got word Glasscock's on the side of the mine operators, and they're cookin' somethin' up to stop us. Anythang you hear 'bout that son of a bitch, I wanna know it."

"Other than general talk, no. John'll be back tomorrow mornin'. I'll see what I can get out of him." She didn't want to tell him she had not been paying attention to anything John or the ladies said for the past week. What had she missed?

"I'm goin' back to Lynn tonight. I won't be back till we march. If you get any news from anybody on our side other than me, Jolene, or Deacon ignore it and let Jolene know with your coded letters. Ain't nobody should be comin' to you with information or to get information but the three of us, till we tell you any different. Especially Crowbar," Jake said.

Jake made a move to leave and Ellie grabbed his arm. "Jake, how's Deannie?"

"She's fine. Growin' like a little weed."

"I'm glad to hear she's doin' so well. Give her a kiss for me." Ellie released his arm, and he got up and walked off into the darkness.

Ellie sat on the bench for a long time with the brown leaves blowing around her feet.

46.

29 August 1912 (Charleston)

Ellie and John returned from dinner. She'd spent the evening making sure his glass was never empty. She wanted him drunk so he would tell her their next plans for the miners. They staggered into her suite, and he fell into the side of the bed. Dottie had brought Ellie her mail while they had been out and placed it on her dressing table.

Ellie recognized the envelope from Polly immediately. If John saw the letter, he would be curious and insist on reading it. Ellie turned him around and proceeded to undress him.

She pulled his boots and trousers off and pushed him face down on the bed. "You stay right there while I undress." She turned from him and brushed the letter under her skirts as they hit the floor. She faced him and removed her undergarments so he could admire her naked body.

She needed to get as much information out of him as she could before he passed out. She lay beside him on the bed and slowly unbuttoned his shirt. "When do you leave again?"

"Tomorrow."

"Where you goin' this time?"

"Back to Paint Creek. It's gettin' pretty ugly up there. Those idiots think they can outsmart us. Those fools are gonna march on us in a few days. We have the governor on our side—he's gonna wait until they all get to Paint Creek and declare martial law. He's sending in the state militia to arrest every one of 'em. Damn union. If they resist, they'll be shot. We have more guards comin' from Pennsylvania, New York, New Jersey—all over. We're gonna wipe those bastards out, Ellie."

With that, he passed out. Ellie waited until he was snoring before she got out of bed. She slipped on her robe and fished Polly's letter from under her dress. She sat at her dressing table, reading the letter by the dim flicker of the oil lamp.

My Dearest—

I hope this letter finds you well. We are doing well here. The baby is more beautiful with each passing day. Her birthday is in a few weeks. It's hard to believe she's going to be one year old already.

I thought you should know her father sent a letter. He asked me to keep the letter for her until she is old enough to read and understand. He thinks he will be back in town next spring, and he wants to see her and be part of her life. We can't let this happen. You must promise me this won't happen.

I love you.

Tom was writing to Polly from prison? He would never take Deannie. If she had to kill him herself—he wouldn't take that baby from Polly. He didn't want that child. He had no reason to even assume she was his. What would he do with a child? A little girl? How would he raise her? No, she would demand Tom leave Deannie right where she was. She folded the letter, returned it to the envelope, and tucked it under the rug. She would reply to Polly's letter tomorrow after John left. She would also send a letter to Tom.

Her priority right now was to get word to Jake if it wasn't too late.

47.

30 August 1912 (Lynn)

Hours before the sun peeked over the mountain top, Jake held Polly in his arms and kissed her tenderly. "I'll be back as quick as I can. Hopefully, this'll show those bastards we're serious. We're gonna drive those guards and the scabs out. As best I can figure, we've got 'em outnumbered by a few thousand men."

"I'm scared, Jake. Scared they'll kill you, Jolene, Deacon, Ellie. All of you'ns. These people ain't got no morals. They'd kill you just as soon as look at you. Look what they did back in July with that Gatlin' Gun. You're the one responsible for bringin' Mother Jones in here, and those bastards know it was you. Then you rallied those men and marched with her to Charleston. Hell, you even declared war on the governor, and it didn't do no good. None of it. Glasscock's not for the miners—he's for the coal operators. Bought and paid for."

"Hopefully, this'll tell him we're serious. You've got enough guns and ammo here to fight off a small army, in case they get wind I'm part of this and try to come after me here. The boys know what to do. Don't go into town by yourself.

Stay here on the farm. If I'm gonna be longer than two weeks, I'll send a messenger." He held her for a long time. He brushed her dark curls from her face, kissed her again, and left.

Jake and his men traveled to Charleston to join the other miners from the area. All total, there were about six thousand men marching toward Paint Creek. They would join the Paint Creek and Cabin Creek strikers. Together, they were formidable opponents for the mine guards. They were armed to the teeth and ready for battle if it came to that.

The area was a virtual powder keg, and the tension was thick on both sides. The miners had been staging sniper attacks on the mine guards as often as possible. The guards retaliated in kind. Other than the Mucklow battle and the Gatling Gun, there had been mostly small skirmishes. As the war raged on, both sides were itching for a bigger battle.

Jake had been gone for only a few hours when Polly felt that old feeling washing over her. She knew it well. She sat down, placed her face in her hands, closed her eyes and waited. A few minutes later she heard the voice.

Prepare for a season of mourning. Be strong. Don't waver. Prepare.

It was the same voice each time and sounded like Granny Cline. It had happened several times over the years. The first time was the day Granny Cline had died. She had been on the river bank with Jolene and Ellie. The voice had told her to come quick. The girls ran all the way to Granny Cline's and got there just in time to say goodbye before she took her last breath. Then again when her mother died. And again, when her baby Elizabeth died. The voice had been silent for the past two years since then.

A season of mourning? What does that mean. Jake? Deannie?

Polly's anxiety grew as she pondered the words.

48.

1 September 1912 (Holly Grove)

The sun was still hiding behind the mountain. Jolene paced back and forth in front of their tent waiting on Deacon to make it up the hill. "Deacon, Dayton brought a message from Ellie. Glasscock's afraid we're gonna wipe out the guards, and he's gonna declare martial law tomorrow. He's sendin' in twelve hundred state militia by special trains today. They's gonna take our guns and start arrestin' people as soon as they arrive. Anybody who resists'll be shot or arrested. She says he's gonna set up a military court and start tossin' us in jail for any reason they dream up. Where's justice? What country are we livin' in? This is absolute tyranny. Those bastards'll stop at nothin'."

"Take all our guns, 'cept a couple of pistols, hide 'em in the small cave at the top of the hill. Tell ever'body else, but don't all go at once. Those guards might be prowlin' around. I'll send some men to tell Jake to turn back. I hope it ain't too late." Deacon hurried out of the tent.

Jolene gathered up their guns and ammo in a burlap feed sack and took it to the cave. It was a difficult climb up the mountain and far enough away from the tents the guards wouldn't find it. On her way, she stopped at select tents and informed the women. They headed to the cave, carrying as many weapons as they could.

Jolene returned to her tent and waited for word from Deacon. For hours, shouting voices carried up the mountain, accompanied by sporadic shots.

Jolene sat outside most of the night with a few of the other women. They took turns keeping watch. Early the next morning, Jolene was getting ready to make her rounds through the tent colony to tend to the sick.

Boyd ran toward her. "Ms. Jolene, I got word from Deacon." Boyd was out of breath when he reached Jolene's tent. "They's arrested pretty much ever' one of 'em that was in the first bunch to show up. We couldn't get the messengers out fast enough. Those state militia men jumped off the trains and started barking orders at ever' body. Those bastards took all the weapons and ammunition. I'm pretty sure Mr. Jake was one of 'em arrested. They's done set up what Deacon called 'a military court' and The Bullpen's been turned into a jail."

Jolene's heart dropped. The Bullpen had become Baldwin-Felts's idea of a torture chamber. It was a 30-foot by 30-foot pen with a wall of railroad ties about seven feet tall and a barbed-wire fence around the top. Most who went in came out maimed, broken, or near dead.

"Where's Deacon? Did they arrest him?"

"No, ma'am. He got away and is up on the mountain. They's gonna declare martial law on the whole tent colony, though. He said to tell you he'd sneak back as soon as he could."

49.

6 September 1912 (Lynn)

Jake had been gone for seven days without a word. Polly read about the declaration of martial law in the newspaper. Governor Glasscock had sent in twelve hundred state militia men to arrest every coal miner they could. At the end, they had arrested hundreds of men and collected 1,872 rifles, 556 pistols, six machine guns, 225,000 rounds of ammunition, and 480 blackjacks—pretty much every weapon Jake and his men had collected over the past six months to defend themselves against those bastard Baldwin-Felts men. The militia planned to remain at Paint Creek until Governor Glasscock lifted martial law.

Polly paced the floors. Seth returned from a trip to Matewan for supplies and handed Polly a parcel of mail containing a letter from Ellie. There was no return address or even her name, but Polly would know her handwriting anywhere. She held the letter in her hands for a few minutes, not wanting to read the contents. She sat at the kitchen table and opened the letter.

Polly—

Governor Glasscock has declared martial law on the Paint Creek and Cabin Creek miners. Most of the men who marched from Charleston to join the miners have been arrested and tried in a military court at Paint Creek.

It pains me to inform you that your husband was amongst those arrested. He has been sentenced to ten years in prison.

As soon as I have further details, I will be in touch—either in person or by mail.

Love,

Polly sat at the table staring at the Celtic cross. How could this be? Arrested? Ten years in prison? This was her worst nightmare come true. What would she do without him? Did he have an attorney? What should she do? The words from her vision came back to her:

Prepare for a season of mourning. Be strong. Don't waver. Prepare.

She quickly wrote a return letter to Ellie.

Madam—

In regard to the ten dresses you wish to purchase—are you certain you will be needing ten? I suggest we meet for a fitting next week. I can come to your hotel or you can come to the dress shop.

Please let me know which you prefer and a date and time convenient for you.

Six days later, Polly read Ellie's letter.

A room will be held at the Hotel Ruffner in your name beginning Friday, 13 September.

50.

13 September (Charleston)

Early the next morning Polly was on her way to Charleston. Her farmhand, Stanley, accompanied her. They had two rifles and two pistols with them in case there was trouble.

It was dark when she arrived at the hotel. Polly had never seen anything so fancy. And to think their little Ellie had been living here for months.

Not completely sure what to do, Polly hesitantly approached the registration desk and checked in. A bellman took her bag and showed her to her room. She barely had time to take off her bonnet before there was a knock at the door. She opened the door and Ellie hurried inside, her silk skirts rustling as she closed the door. Ellie looked like royalty. Her hair was pinned up and fastened with a ruby and emerald comb; her dress was a deep green silk.

"Polly, I've never been so happy to see anybody." Ellie hugged her tight. "I'm so sorry 'bout Jake. We'll find a way to get him out. This whole situation is completely crazy."

"Where is he now? Which jail? I wanna see him!"

"They still have him at Paint Creek in The Bullpen. They haven't released any of them, and they ain't lettin' nobody visit. I'm tryin' to find out what their plans are—if they're keepin' him there, or sendin' him to the jail here in Charleston."

"Where's that man of your'n?"

"He's still at Paint Creek. He's s'posed to be back here tomorrow. We can't let him ever see us together. So, we need to be extra careful."

"I s'pose I'll need to find an attorney. Do you know any?"

"Polly, I don't think an attorney will do you any good. It was a court martial. Fightin' it will be nearly impossible." Ellie sat on the bed next to Polly, holding her hand.

"What am I s'posed to do then? Nothin'? Just go home and live my happy life while my husband rots in a jail somewhere?" Polly wiped away the tears. "You know I can't do that, Ellie."

"For now, let's sit tight and let me see what I can get out of John 'bout their plans. Then we can make our own plan." Ellie hugged Polly. "I have a dinner with the Baldwin-Felts ladies tonight downstairs. Those old hags get a little whiskey in 'em and tell things they should never speak of. I'll try to get what I can out of 'em. I'll have Dottie bring you dinner here to your room. Whatever you need, you tell her, and she'll bring it to you. It's prob'ly best you not be out walkin' the streets." Ellie stood to leave.

"Ellie, I love you and thank you for puttin' yourself in danger for us."

"I love you." Ellie slipped out the door and down the hall.

Polly slumped into the chair by her bed after Ellie left. She wanted to wake up from this nightmare soon. She felt like a cat trapped in a rain barrel. She couldn't get her mind around the idea of Jake being locked up for ten years. Knowing there was nothing she could do infuriated her. How long could she wait here?

The fear of hopelessness rose in her throat and threatened to choke her. How would she survive without him? What would the boys do without their father? She felt ill equipped to run the farm by herself. To raise three little boys and Deannie by herself presented a rock she wasn't sure she could move alone. Ten years was a long time. Deannie wouldn't even know Jake in ten years. The boys would forget what a good father he was. *Ten years? She* couldn't live without him for ten years.

When Jake started fighting this war a year ago, when it was merely an idea he and a few of the miners whispered about, she thought nothing of it. She'd heard about the strikes of the past and assumed the coal operators didn't want another bloody battle any more than the miners did. She had woefully underestimated the power of greed.

Digging coal out of the earth was grueling work, and she understood they had to fight for a better life—for a fair and decent wage. She supported Jake in all he fought for. She understood the fight was for all of them, but it had taken away the center of her world and threatened to destroy all she held precious.

She wasn't as strong as Ellie and Jolene. They appeared to be mountains of courage and grit. She had always thought she was made of the same stuff, but now? Now she felt like a wounded bird that might never fly again. She needed to pull herself together and be strong for Jake and her children. She knew she needed to dig in deep and be ready to fight the battle of her life.

She did the only thing she knew for certain. She prayed.

"Dear God, I don't know why you're allowin' these horrible things to happen to innocent people. I don't know why you allowed Jake to be arrested. I do know you have a plan we can't see right yet. Please keep my Jake safe and alive. Show me what I need to do. Give me the courage and strength to get through this and do the right thing."

Her tears flowed down her face and she couldn't continue. She mumbled "In Jesus name, I pray. Amen." She sat on the floor by her bed and cried until there were no more tears.

Ellie made sure Myrtle's champagne glass stayed full all night. That poor woman could barely hold her tongue when she was sober—let alone with a few glasses of champagne in her. She was sure to spill her guts about the plans for the arrested miners.

"Myrtle, please do tell about those wretched men they arrested at Paint Creek. Were there really thousands of them?"

"Yes. They arrested so many of them, but only a few hundred were court-martialed. They have 'em all locked up. Some up there in The Bullpen and a few here in town. Far as I know, they ain't let out any of the names yet. Wouldn't do 'em no good anyway—they ain't gettin' out any time soon."

Myrtle snorted a mean laugh and took another sip of her champagne.

"Really? How does that work? How's it any different than a regular arrest? How can they keep 'em and not tell their families? It doesn't seem very legal—"

"Oh, sweet Ellie. You're so naïve about some things. Beautiful and young, but naïve." Joan Wells said.

Myrtle shifted uncomfortably. Ellie looked up, startled to see Joan joining them at their table. Ellie bit her lip. She understood fully what the court-martial was about and knew exactly how it worked—in a legal situation. "Hello, Joan. Please join us."

"You should certainly know by now our men don't play by the rules. They *make* the rules. Those ignorant bastards will stay in jail as long as we want them to. They don't have a choice in the matter. Regardless of what the law for *regular* folks says, our boys play by their own law." Myrtle had the waiter fill her glass for a fourth time.

"How long you think they'll keep 'em locked up?" Ellie asked.

"Damn near as long as they want." Joan slurred her words, and Ellie hoped the old hag had a miserable headache in the morning.

At the end of the evening, Ellie escorted Myrtle back to her room. "Ellie, thank you so much for accompanying me. Seems like this is a regular thing. I don't seem to know when to stop with the drinks."

"Myrtle, it's my pleasure." Ellie slipped her arm in Myrtle's to keep her steady on the stairs. "Joan sure can be snippy. She seems so angry all the time."

"Ain't you heard?" Ellie shook her head no. "She caught her husband cheatin'." Myrtle smirked.

"*No?* With who?"

"That's the best part. Her younger cousin—right in her own home. She took the girl in a few years ago. Treated her like her own child. Came home last week from visitin' her mama and caught 'em right there in *her* bed."

"*No!* And she didn't kill him?"

Myrtle giggled. "Oh, no. She likes the money and the prestige of his position too much. It means more to her than her wounded pride. She did toss the girl out on her ear, though. Rumor has it he's payin' for her a room at the boardin' house 'round the corner."

Ellie deposited Myrtle safely and continued up to the fifth floor. She continued down the hall to Polly's room and quietly knocked.

Polly opened the door and Ellie slipped in. "Did you find out anythang?"

"Not much. Sounds like they ain't lettin' nobody out or in. They're gonna keep 'em there as long as they can, Polly. No bail, no attorneys, nothin'. Good news, some of them are here in Charleston in a proper jail. They ain't releasin' names yet."

"What am I to do, Ellie? I can't leave him there. I can't go back to Lynn and act like all is well."

"I'm not sure just yet. John returns tomorrow. I'll see what I can find out from him. He'll know exactly what's goin' on, but he may not tell me much."

Ellie returned to her room and poured herself a glass of whiskey.

The closing of his door jarred Ellie awake. She had been dreaming of Sammy. A house fire was all she could remember. A dark dread settled in her chest when his bag thudded to the floor. A few seconds later, the door joining their rooms opened. She hoped he would think she was sleeping and leave her alone. She knew him well enough to know he had downed at least three whiskeys on the train back to Charleston and would be wanting another. The clinking of the whiskey decanter on the sideboard confirmed her assumptions. He filled his glass and carried the decanter over to the chair. He pulled the chair closer to the bed and sat down. Still wearing his dirty boots, he propped his feet next to her. She didn't move. He took the heel of his boot and kicked her thigh through the thin linens.

He pushed her with his boot again. "Wake up."

She stirred and opened her eyes. She attempted to sound pleasantly surprised, even though she *knew* he would return early. "John? What are you doing back so soon? I didn't expect you until mornin'." She sat up and smoothed her hair out of her face.

His growing suspicions were obvious to her. He had returned earlier than planned from his last four trips in an attempt to catch her doing something. She was much better at this game than he would ever be, and she was ten steps ahead of him. "The Knowing" was now on full alert where John was concerned.

"I didn't wanna stay there tonight." His words were slightly slurred. He must have had more than a few whiskeys on the train. "What've you been doin'? Why is your evenin' dress lyin' on the chaise? Where'd you go tonight, Ellie?"

"I had dinner with the ladies this evenin'. It was the Hunter woman's birthday. What's her name? Mabel or Mary or somethin' like that. Anyway, they decided to drink champagne and eat cake. I'm fairly certain they'll all wake up with a miserable headache in the mornin'. I only had one glass. I wanted to be bright and chipper for your return."

"I'm tired. Tired of all of this shit. Being away from you. Not knowin' what you're doin' while I'm gone is wearin' on me, Ellie."

"John, what on earth are you talkin' 'bout? I'm not doin' anything while you're gone."

"Take your gown off."

"What?"

"Stand up and take off your damn gown." He poured himself another shot. "Now! Do it."

Ellie swung her legs over the side of the bed and untied her gown. She stood and removed it and let it drop to the floor. He downed his drink in one gulp, then stood and dropped his pants. He sat back down in the chair. "You know what to do." He grabbed her and pulled her over to stand between his legs.

Ellie instinctively dropped to her knees. The smell of a week's worth of whiskey and sweat made her stomach turn, but she lowered her head. He grabbed a fistful of her hair, pushing her face into him. After a few minutes, he jerked her head up.

"What are you doin'? That hurts," she cried.

"It's supposed to. This—" he grabbed her mouth "—this is for me and me only. I don't wanna ever think you're on your knees doin' this for some other man, Ellie."

She pulled her face away from his grip. He grabbed her hair and pushed her head back down, and she continued to pleasure him. The thought of biting it off ran through her mind more than once. By the time he finished, she had identified ten different ways to kill the bastard.

51.

<u>23 September 1912</u>

Sammy lived in one of three apartments above the Black Bear Tavern on the wrong side of town, but Ellie felt safe and at ease. His place was small, comfortable, and clean. It wasn't much, just enough to contain his meager worldly possessions—a few clothes, his grandfather's pocket watch, a shotgun, a few song books, a Bible, and his fiddle—all of which he could quickly pack up at a moment's notice. His life was simple but full.

Jake was in jail, Jolene refused to leave Holly Grove, and Polly, more broken than when she arrived in Charleston, had returned home after one week. The constant battle with Baldwin-Felts and the coal operators had worn on all of them. Ellie deserved a little fun, and Sammy was the one to give it to her.

John thought Ellie was in Mingo County visiting her sick cousin for a few days. He had returned to Paint Creek and was too busy fighting the miners to control her every move. She knew it was risky, but she simply needed a break from the madness threatening to consume all of them.

Sammy kissed her neck. "You sure ya can't spend more than one night with me?"

"I'm positive. It's too risky, and there's too much goin' on for me to be away for too long. I wanna enjoy today and tonight without worryin' 'bout all the craziness." Ellie said.

"We'll have a grand time. I'm glad you ain't wearin' one of those fancy dresses you wear at the Ruffner. You're more beautiful like this."

"Polly made this for me right a'fore I left Matewan. I couldn't part with it."

Sammy carried the picnic basket to the wagon, and Ellie carried his fiddle, her mandolin, and the quilt. They headed out into the country for the afternoon. The mountains were ablaze with red, orange, and yellow leaves under a crystal blue sky. They rode for about thirty minutes, and Sammy guided the wagon down a tight path that opened up to a field of sunflowers.

"Oh, Sammy! This is beautiful. I've never seen so many sunflowers in my life! Look at their sweet faces!"

"Faces?" he asked.

Ellie laughed. "Yes! When I's little, I always thought the sunflowers looked like they were smiling at me, almost as if they have faces. And when the sun isn't shining on 'em, they bow their little heads."

"I'm glad you like it. This is one of the biggest fields 'round here and the only one that blooms this late in the year. Come on, we'll settle in." He led her up a small hill overlooking the field. They placed their quilt under a tree.

The sunflowers smiled and danced as a gentle breeze floated through the field. Sammy took his fiddle out of the case and began to play a slow classical song.

"What's that you're playin'?" Ellie asked.

"A little somethin' I learned years ago. It's called Romance by Beethoven. On a proper violin it sounds a lot better. The bridge on the violin is arched and each string can be played. Just sounds clearer. But my old fiddle does a pretty darn good job out here with the sunflowers."

"It's beautiful. Sure don't sound like somethin' you'd play in the tavern."

'No, I don't think they'd care too much for it. We play it at fancy parties and weddin's mostly."

"You never cease to amaze me, Sammy."

"Enough of my fiddle. I wanna here you play that mandolin. Sing me a song, Ellie."

"Only if you play with me."

"Let's see. How 'bout an old Scottish ballad? You know The House Carpenter?"

"I do. It was one of Granny Cline's favorites." Ellie started strumming her mandolin and the words to the song stung her heart as she thought of Deannie and the mistakes she had made.

> *'Well met, well met, my own true love,*
> *well met, well met," cried he.*
>
> *'Well, if I should forsake my house carpenter*
> *and go along with thee,*
> *What have you got to maintain me on*
> *and keep me from poverty?"*
>
> *Well, they'd not been gone but about two weeks,*
> *I know it was not three.*
> *When this fair lady began to weep,*
> *she wept most bitterly.*

> *"Ah, why do you weep, my fair young maid,*
> *weep it for your golden store?*
> *Or do you weep for your house carpenter*
> *who never you shall see anymore?"*
>
> *"I do not weep for my house carpenter*
> *or for any golden store.*
> *I do weep for my own wee babe,*
> *who never I shall see anymore."*

They spent the day playing music for the sunflowers and headed back to the Black Bear Tavern. The chaos of Ellie's days in Charleston threatened to drive her mad. But the simplicity of being with Sammy on the other side of town had calmed her mind and spirit.

They ventured down to the tavern when the music started up. The people she encountered were kind and generous with what little they had. No one was trying to impress anyone. They were all equally poor and striving to make the best life possible.

Later that night, they left the tavern and headed up the back stairs to Sammy's apartment.

Ellie was in awe of Sammy's lifestyle and how he could be so happy and carefree with so little money and no home to speak of. "How long've you lived here?"

"I wouldn't say I actually *live* here. My stuff's been here for 'bout a year. I've been moving 'round like a gypsy with one band or 'nother, playin' music and workin' odd jobs to make ends meet for a long time."

"Where's home?" Ellie asked.

"I's born and raised not far from here. I guess I call that home as much as any place. I've been movin' 'round since I's seventeen."

"Where to?"

"Roamin' to and fro from Charleston, to Louisville, to Memphis, and then over to Knoxville for a bit. I ventured even farther south to the other Charleston in South Carolina for a while. I eventually came home to West Virginia a year ago when my mama got sick. After she passed away, I figured I'd sit still and let my heart mend. Then I met you. Looks like I'll be stayin' for a bit longer than I'd planned."

Ellie wrapped her hands around his neck and kissed him. Sammy picked her up and carried her to his bed. He made love to her, the music from the tavern filling the small apartment.

Sammy fell asleep holding Ellie.

A storm was brewing, and a breeze moved the curtains. The crisp autumn night floated into the room. Sammy stirred next to her and pulled her close. She pressed into him and lay in his arms, feeling safe and uncharacteristically peaceful.

Ellie awoke early the next morning. She stood by the bed and looked out at the mountains. There had always been something haunting in the way the fog lifted slowly in a rhythmic dance with the mountain peaks and the river.

Being with Sammy in his space, she could almost see herself living his gypsy lifestyle, not staying in any one place long enough for the roots to take hold, going from city to city, playing music and experiencing life, and loving Sammy. But for how long? How long would she be happy with this simplicity?

"What'cha lookin' at?" Sammy rubbed the sleep from his eyes.

"Nothin' in particular. I love these old mountains. The best days of my life were spent traipsin' up and down the hills with Jolene and Polly." The flowers, plants, herbs, and animals had always offered a special kind of magic to Ellie. She wondered how one place could hold so much abundance within its arms.

"Get back in bed and tell me more," Sammy pulled back the quilt and Ellie crawled in next to him.

"In the summer, we'd swim in the river nearly ever' day. We'd walk up and down the mountain paths all day pickin' wildflowers and berries. Granny Cline made the best blackberry cobbler in three states. We'd help her dig for ginseng and herbs. She taught us a lot of stuff 'bout the mountains. Seems like they's always somethin' new to discover."

"Granny Cline sounds like my kinda woman."

Ellie laughed. "You'd a loved her. She'd a loved you. She was a special lady. She used to mesmerize us with tales of the Irish fairies. The fae—the magical ones. We'd imagine the fairies lived in the dead trees and the rocks in the hills behind our house. There's even a holler across the river in Kentucky called Barrenshee. According to Granny Cline, some fool tried to hunt and kill the fairies that lived there. The fae cursed the place and proclaimed it would always be barren. She warned us girls it was no place fit for an Irish lass."

"What's a shee?" Sammy asked.

"It's a hill where the fairies live."

"You still believe in fairies?"

"You don't?"

"You ever wanna leave these mountains? Go west or south or anywhere?"

"These mountains are the only life I've ever known. It's home. But, I need to break free from the shadow of this place. I wanna feel the sunshine on my face a'fore ten in the mornin'. I wanna see what's beyond the next mountain. Beyond the holler."

"You're right, Ellie. There's more to life than coal and timber. More than diggin' for your very soul underground in a mine to make some greedy fool rich," Sammy said. "We can leave whenever you want. Go out west. Go to New Orleans. I'll go wherever you want."

"I've always wanted to see the ocean. Maybe when this is all over, you can take me."

These same mountains Ellie loved so much seemed to be closing in on her. They were close, and tight, and tall. Looming over her, demanding she abide by their paths etched out over the centuries. Refusing to let her see beyond their beauty and magic.

They had shaped Ellie's view of the world and people and herself. She wondered if she would be the same person in some other place. She needed to know who she was beyond the mountains.

Running away with Sammy was full of promise and excitement. But her dreams and needs were bigger and more complicated than his tiny apartment over the Black Bear. They reached beyond playing music every night in a strange tavern along the road. It was nothing more than a romantic notion, and she pushed the idea away from her.

Ellie returned to the Ruffner with a sense of disappointment. She looked around her suite at the beautiful dresses, the jewelry—she had anything she wanted. But it felt empty. She knew Sammy could never provide her with the life she wanted, yet the night at his place had been magical. Ellie was surprised at this turn of events. Sammy had started out as a fling, something fun to do on a hot summer night. Three months later he was at the center of her life and thoughts. The more she was with Sammy, the more she detested John. As long as the miners' war raged on, she'd have to tolerate John's touch and his drunken anger.

She dreaded John's return from Paint Creek and hoped he stayed away longer. With winter approaching, she wasn't sure how much she and Sammy could see each other. They couldn't slip away for picnics and swims in his favorite swimming hole. Using her sick cousin again was also out of the question. Perhaps John would get snowed in at Paint Creek. Or better still, shot by an angry coal miner.

52.

<u>25 September 1912 (Charleston)</u>

Jake looked at the two prisoners to his left and the two to his right. The chains on his wrists rattled an objection when he raised his hand and rubbed his bruised cheek. The prisoners sitting on either side of him on the bench tried to accommodate him as best they could. They were chained together arms and feet, and when one moved, the others had to cooperate.

He was on the train to Charleston with the other striking miners who'd been arrested. They had no idea what would happen next. As best Jake could figure they wouldn't get a fair trial—if they got a trial at all. Glasscock conveniently declared martial law and had all of them arrested. At least all of them that hadn't managed to get away. Jake had been leading the march and was the first one they'd captured. He put up a fight until they knocked him out with the butt of a rifle, leaving him with a sore cheek and a black eye.

The county lock-up in Charleston would be better than The Bullpen, where they had been holding most of them. The coal barons and Baldwin-Felts didn't play fair, and justice wasn't on the menu. They seemed to make up the rules as they went along.

He thought of Polly and the kids. He was sure she was worried sick by now. He was certain Jolene or Ellie had gotten word to Polly about what had happened. He hoped she had the good sense to stay in Matewan. Making herself known as his wife could put her and the kids in danger.

As they approached the station in Charleston, the train slowed, then jerked to a stop. The guards filed them out onto the platform, placing random kicks to many of them as they stepped down off the train. Chained in groups of five, they shuffled slowly toward the waiting wagons, clumsily climbing the two steps up and into the enclosed structures. The man at the front of Jake's group stumbled up the steps, causing the other four to stumble as well. They scrambled to help him up before the guards decided to ram a rifle into his face. They were too late; Jake was bent over helping his comrade to his feet when the guard approached.

"What the hell's goin' on over here? You too stupid to climb into a wagon?"

"We're all good here. He's up," Jake said.

"Now, was I talkin' to you? You're one of the ring leaders, ain't ya?"

Jake stood still, not looking at the guard. The men chained to him started moving into the wagon.

"Stop!" The guard placed his rifle across the door. "Look at me, you filthy bastard. Answer me! You're Jake Hardin, ain't ya?"

Jake looked him in the eye. "Yes, I am."

"Well, well, well. Looky at you. All chained up and nowheres to go. How's it feel to be a prisoner?" He placed the tip of his rifle under Jake's chin and pushed his head up.

Jake stared at the guard.

The guard lowered the rifle and stepped back. "Go on. Get in there."

The men moved in tandem. The two men in front of Jake slowly made their way up the steps into the wagon. Jake placed his left foot on the lower step. The guard took the butt of his rifle and punched it into Jake's lower back. He fell face forward, the chains pulling on his wrists and ankles. He blacked out for a few seconds from the pain. The guard moved on to the next group, and Jake's fellow prisoners helped him into the wagon.

He sat on the bench, leaning into the prisoner to his left. The pain was a searing fire up his spine and down into his left leg. He closed his eyes and prayed to God to take the pain or take his life. The doors closed and the wagon pulled forward. Every bounce along the road was a hot knife twisting in his lower back.

53.

10 October 1912 (Charleston)

A hot September dissolved into October, and a blanket of yellow, red, and orange covered the mountains. From high above, things looked peaceful and gentle. But down in the hollers, along the river, and further down in the ground where the black gold waited to be dug out, there was no peace, no gentleness. The war between miners and coal operators continued like a raging fire through the mountains.

The past months had been rough on all of them. Ellie worked with Dayton to pass messages from Polly and Deacon to Jake at the county jail in Charleston.

Ellie had become anxious and fidgety. The damn miners' war, Jake being arrested—all of it—was wearing on her. Chipping away at her spirit bit by bit.

This week might be her only chance to see Sammy for quite some time.

Ellie waited until the hotel had quieted, and she slipped down the hall to the room she kept rented for Polly. John gave her enough money and he would never miss what she had spent on the room. She had kept it rented for two reasons: One—to make sure Polly had the same room when she returned. Two—so she and Sammy would have a place to meet. She didn't want to take the chance of John returning and finding Sammy in her bed. Sammy knocked on the door shortly after eleven o'clock.

"How was your night? Was it busy down there?" Ellie asked.

"Kinda slow. Shame you can't come in and listen," he said.

"You know that will never happen again."

"We may be goin' to Ohio to play for a few weeks."

"That might be best. For a while at least. Sammy, this is gettin' too risky to meet like this. It seemed to be the safest place, but John's returnin' earlier each time he goes to Paint Creek. He's tryin' to catch me doin' somethin'. It's a matter of time a'fore he figures it all out. He'll kill you and anyone else who gets in his way."

Sammy took her hands. "Ellie, I ain't afraid of him. I've gotta gun just like he does. I'm a damn good shot."

"Sammy, he has an army of crazy-ass men just like him. He's a coward and he don't fight alone—unless it's with me."

"What do you mean? Has he hit you, Ellie? I *will* kill him if he hits you."

Ellie looked away from Sammy and hoped he couldn't see the lie in her eyes. "No. No, he ain't hit me. He *is* mean and nasty, and all he talks 'bout is killin' people."

"Ellie, I can't walk away from you. From this thing between us. I won't. I love you too much. If we need to stop meetin' like this for a bit, then I understand. I'll go to Ohio for a few weeks. If he does have any idea 'bout us, that'll throw him off. But I don't wanna leave you here with that crazy bastard."

She wrapped her arms around his neck. "Sammy, I'm so sorry I dragged you into this mess. The chances I'm takin' passin' information back and forth to the miners is crazy enough. John would kill me for that alone. Who knows what he's capable of?"

"This mess could go on forever, Ellie. How much more can you help the miners? How long you gonna stay in this mess and put up with his bullshit?"

"As long as it takes. I can't leave him now. Polly's countin' on me to help her get Jake outa jail. Jolene and Deacon are livin' in a damn tent and gettin' attacked nearly every day. You expect me to walk away? *Now?*"

"No, not now. Ellie, you *do* need to figure out when enough is enough. I can't keep you dressed in the finest clothes and pay for a suite of rooms at the Ruffner. But I *can* give you a safe place to lay your head down to sleep at night. I can give you all the love you can handle. We can go anywhere you want." Sammy wrapped his arms around her and kissed her forehead.

Tears spilled down her cheeks. "Sammy, right now, all I need's a soft place to land."

"I'll be your soft place, Ellie."

They spent the next few hours in Polly's room. Just before midnight, Sammy left and hurried down the backstairs. Ellie stood by the window in the dark and watched Sammy navigate his way through the hotel's gardens and fountains. He exited onto the street through a side gate. Ellie was ready to turn and go to her own room when she saw a shadow entering the main gate to the gardens. It was John, slipping in through the back of the hotel. He would be upstairs in less than three minutes.

Ellie hurried out of the room and down the hall to her suite. It was just a few yards to her suite but felt as if it were ten miles. She slipped the key into the lock. The door at the bottom of the stairs clicked closed, and John's footsteps pounded up the stairs.

She entered her room and closed and locked her door as quietly as a mouse. She pulled her shoes off, one of them falling onto the hardwood floor. She could only hope John hadn't heard it. She grabbed a book and lay on the chaise. She pulled a small quilt over her legs and placed the opened book on her chest. She turned towards the fire and closed her eyes, pretending to be asleep. Her hands were shaking, and her heart was beating so hard and so fast she feared John would see it beating through her dress.

The door to his suite opened, and his footsteps were soft as he entered her suite. She didn't dare move. A few minutes later the door closed, his retreating footsteps faded away, and his boots pummeled the main stairs of the hotel.

She sat up, placed her head in her hands, and cried.

The next night Ellie waited until the faint sound of the band stopped. Then she hurried down the hall to Polly's room. A few minutes later, Sammy joined her.

"You quit early tonight?" she asked.

"It's dead down there." He pulled her to him.

Ellie felt safe wrapped in Sammy's arms. Safer than she had ever felt. Ending things with him would be the hardest thing she had ever done, but she knew she had to do it. It was for his own safety. His very life. And hers.

"Sammy, we need to talk. Come sit with me." She led him to the setee by the window. "Sammy, you know how I feel 'bout you. I've never had this kind of relationship with anyone. I feel so free and at peace when we're together."

"And?"

"We can't keep takin' these chances. Last night, I stood at the window and watched you leave through the garden. I was 'bout to turn, and I saw John enterin' through the main gate to the garden. I barely had time to get to my room and pretend I had fallen asleep on the chaise with a book."

"What did he say?"

"He never said anything to me. He came into the room and stood at the door for a few minutes and left. It makes me wonder how many times he's done the same thing and I didn't know he was there."

Sammy stood and paced in front of Ellie for a few minutes. "You're right, Ellie. We can't take the chance. I don't wanna take a chance of him findin' out and hurtin' you." He pulled her to him and held her. "I'm here because I wanna be here." Sammy pulled her closer.

Ellie looked up at him. "Go to Ohio and let this cool down a bit. Rumor is the governor's gonna lift martial law in the next week or so, which means John'll be back here in Charleston more. He's already suspicious, and he seems even more angry and agitated every time he returns from Paint Creek."

"I'll be in Ohio for a few weeks. Maybe a month. I don't wanna leave you here alone, Ellie," Sammy said.

"I'll be fine."

Later that night, Ellie returned to her suite. She slipped into her nightgown and sat at her dressing table. She was sad Sammy was leaving for a few weeks. But she knew it was for the best. For both of them. She brushed her hair and wondered where this would all end.

54.

15 October 1912 (Holly Grove)

Jolene and Boyd watched as the last of the state militia loaded onto the 9:30 a.m. train and left Paint Creek. "Ms. Jolene, does this mean martial law's over?" he asked.

"For now. I don't doubt that bastard Glasscock'll do it again, if he thinks it'll beat us down," Jolene said.

They headed up the mountain. "What kinda name's Glasscock, anyway?" Boyd asked.

"A fittin' one for that son of a bitch."

"Ms. Jolene, where's Mother Jones been? I ain't seen hide nor hair of her in a few weeks."

"She's gone to rally support for us throughout the country. She's meetin' in Cincinnati, Columbus, and Cleveland. Then she's goin' to Washin'ton D.C. to meet with Congressman Wilson. She might be gone for another month or so. But she'll be back."

"You think they'll help us?"

"I sure hope so, Boyd. This court martial business is un-American."

"Ms. Jolene, what's a court martial?"

"Normally, it's a military court. As far as we're concerned, it's the state's way of arrestin' us for doin' somethin' that's our constitutional right." Jolene explained what the constitution was and how their first amendment rights were being stripped from them.

They stopped halfway up the path, and Jolene sent one of the older messengers for Deacon. He and most of the able-bodied men that hadn't been arrested with Jake had been hiding out in the hills for the past six weeks.

Deacon had snuck down to see her in the early morning hours twice while he was hiding out. The first time, he'd shown up a little past midnight and snuck into the tent as quiet as a mouse. Jolene had heard him, and her hand instinctively went to her pistol. "Don't shoot. It's me." Deacon whispered.

He kissed her and crawled in the bed beside her. He lifted her gown and his hands roamed her warm, thin body. After a few hours of pleasure, Deacon slipped out of the tent. The sneaking thrilled Jolene. The illusion of a secret lover slipping into her tent for a few hours of passion made her feel like a teenager. The mere idea of making love to him, knowing it was dangerous, made her want Deacon even more.

Is this why Ellie does it?

She and Boyd continued up the hill to her tent. One of the younger kids came running up the path behind them. "Ms. Jolene, I's told to tell ye a load of 'em scabs is comin' on the ten o'clock train and we need to be ready." The boy doubled over trying to catch his breath.

"Ya don't say. You ain't got time to go get Deacon. That's almost an hour both ways. You boys go to every tent you can and tell the women to meet me down at the train as quick as they can. Tell 'em to bring their brooms, rolling pins, sticks, stones—whatever they have that'll serve as a weapon—but no guns. We's gonna beat some scabs back onto that train. Run!" Jolene went into her tent and looked around. She grabbed Granny Cline's rolling pin and headed to the train stop.

Within minutes the women from the tent colony were coming in droves. Jolene stood upon a bench.

"This battle belongs to all of us! It ain't just the men. We's all in this together," Jolene said. "As soon as those scabs try to get off that train, start pushin' 'em back and use your weapons as best you can. They's more of us than there is of them."

Within a few minutes, the ladies heard the whistle as the train came around the bend. By this time there were hundreds of women standing on the platform ready for a fight.

A handful of Baldwin-Felts men arrived on the platform as the train pulled in. The women pushed them back and off the platform, sending one of them tumbling onto the tracks. He scrambled to his feet and fell on the other side of the tracks as the train came into the station.

Jolene was out in front of the crowd. "Don't you bastards bother gettin' off that train. You ain't comin' in here and workin' these mines. We're up here fightin' for our lives and our jobs. You need to go on back to where you came from."

There were seventy-five scabs on the train and several hundred riled-up women on the platform armed with an array of household items. A few of the scabs attempted to step off the train onto the platform. They were met with sticks and brooms and hundreds of women pushing them back. Most of the men were prepared for a brawl—just not with women.

The braver of them stepped down onto the platform and pushed their way through the angry horde. One of the men punched two women in the face. He took a rolling pin to the side of his head. He fell a few feet beyond the platform, and the women dragged him to the side and rolled him down a small embankment.

One man limped back onto the train, nursing a bloody nose. One man cupped his good hand around a crooked finger after the accurate swing of a broom. Others retreated back onto the train. Thirty minutes later, the scabs had had enough. The engine fired up, and the train inched away from the platform.

The next morning, Jolene stepped out of her tent and handed Deacon a steaming cup of coffee. Deacon took it from her, wrapped his free arm around her neck, and kissed the top of her head. "When this damn mess is over, I'm gonna take you away from here. We'll go anywhere you like. Maybe the Carolinas to see the ocean, like we talked 'bout when we first got married."

"I'm gonna hold you to that, mister." She turned her face up and kissed him. "Do you think we may be near the end, Deacon?"

"Martial law may've been lifted, but this war's far from over. The mine operators ain't no closer to acceptin' our deal than they were five months ago. They think they can beat us down, 'specially with the damn governor in their pocket."

"Polly sent a letter. She's goin' back to Charleston next week. She's hopin' to get to see Jake. You think he'll get out now martial law's lifted?" Jolene asked.

"Not if they think he's one of the union leaders. They'll keep him there as long as they can. He's got a bounty on his head now. Baldwin-Felts'll be a lookin' for him as soon as he gets set free. I don't know how safe it is for Polly to go paradin' in there to see him. I don't trust those bastards to not try to hurt her."

"I'll send a letter to Ellie—tell her to keep Polly outa harms way," Jolene said. "I need to make my rounds. We gotta a couple of babies due any day now. I'll be back this afternoon." She kissed him goodbye and grabbed her sack of herbs and medicines and headed down the hill.

55.

<u>1 November 1912 (Moundsville, West Virginia State Penitentiary)</u>

The guard tossed a letter into Tom's cell. "You's got some mail, Chafin. I guess somebody on the outside still likes ye."

Tom picked up the letter. The handwriting on the envelope was certainly Ellie's, but it contained no return address. He tore it open.

> *Tom ~*
>
> *I'm not sure what your intentions are with Deannie when—or if—you get out of prison. Do not send letters to Polly telling her you will take Deannie away from her. That child belongs to Polly and Jake now. You have no business trying to raise a child that doesn't even belong to you. Leave it be. You've already destroyed enough lives.*
>
> *~ E*

Tom stared at the letter for a good long while. He sat back down on his cot, lit a match, and watched its flames dance around the page and consume Ellie's hateful words.

He had destroyed enough lives? Ellie would never change. Never acknowledge her part in anything. Sure, he shot two men—*because of her*. That woman had made a life out of destroying others.

As for Deannie, Tom wasn't sure what he would do when get out of this hell hole. He did know he would keep Ellie guessing.

56.

9 November 1912 (Charleston)

Dottie helped Ellie dress for the evening. "Which necklace, Ms. Ellie?" Dottie asked.

"I think the diamond and pearls with the ruby stone."

"Is this new?"

"Yes, a *special* gift from his highness," Ellie quipped. After getting drunk and slapping Ellie around, John always showed up a few days later with a special trinket.

Dottie chuckled and clasped the necklace. "There. You're ready to go. You look beautiful, Ms. Ellie."

"I'd much rather be goin' to the tavern tonight than to another borin' Baldwin-Felts dinner," Ellie said.

"Ms. Ellie, Sammy keeps askin' me when he can see you. He's playin' in the tavern for the next two weeks. What should I tell him?" Dottie asked.

"Tell him John's in town for the next few weeks. He needs to be patient." Ellie took Dottie's hand. "Thank you, Dot. For everything. You're a Godsend."

"It's my pleasure," Dottie said.

Ellie stood and poured herself a shot of whiskey. "Here's to another evenin' of dull conversation."

She descended the stairs and walked across the lobby to the large parlor. She heard Sammy's fiddle beckoning her through the tavern doors. She longed to touch him and run her fingers through his curls—to feel his warm skin on her skin.

John was waiting with the other men. Ellie was glad to see that most of the women hadn't arrived yet. She joined John and several others who were huddled in the corner to listen to their conversation.

"With the new governor, what're our plans?" Tony Gaujot asked.

"We plan to cause as much damage to those miners as we can before Hatfield's sworn in," Tom Felts said. "We met with him earlier this week. He's not on our side. If anything, he's neutral. He wants this strike to end as much as we do. But he's not willing to break the union for it. At least that's the impression he left us with."

"Glasscock may be our only hope to break the union then," John said. "We need to act fast. I have a few ideas. Also, winter's on our side. I think a lot of the miners will abandon their idea of a union if the weather gets too brutal."

"Don't count on it," Tom Felts said. "Those are some pretty tough people. They're used to living like animals. Let's plan to discuss our options tomorrow morning. We only have four months until Hatfield is officially the governor."

Ellie quietly sipped her champagne, taking in all the information.

After dinner, the men adjourned to a smaller room to discuss business, leaving the women in the parlor to enjoy dessert. Ellie took a few bites of the chocolate cake and excused herself. She wanted to be alone.

At the top of the stairs, she spotted Sammy at the corner of the hallway. "What are you doin? Are you *tryin'* to get us killed?"

"I made sure he wasn't comin' up the stairs with you." He took her arm and pulled her towards Polly's room. "I made Dot give me a key."

He gently closed the door behind them. "Ellie, I couldn't go another second without seein' you."

Ellie pulled away from him. "Sammy, this is not the way to do it. John is downstairs and could come up here any minute. This is insane. I cannot stay here with you."

"I'm willin' to take my chances, Ellie."

"Well, I am *not* willin' to take this kinda chance. This is simply careless and will get us both killed."

"How much longer is this gonna go on? We've got a new governor. This has to end soon."

"The new governor doesn't take office for four more months. Those crazy bastards can kill a lot of people in four months."

"You look awful pretty tonight." Sammy's hand traced the neckline of her dress skimming her breasts. "Is that a real ruby?"

"Why does it matter?"

"Just thinkin' maybe that's why you stay with him. It's a pretty fancy lifestyle, Ellie, and it's clear you're the queen of the ball down there with those people."

"No. That's not why I stay with him."

Sammy pulled her close to him and held her. Despite her anger, Ellie melted into him. He kissed her gently on the lips. "I love you, Ellie."

Ellie wanted nothing more than to stay in this room, with this man. "Sammy . . . I've got to go. If I stay here one more second, I won't leave. Do not do this again. Promise me."

"I promise."

Ellie hurried down the hall to her suite.

57.

15 November 1912 (Charleston)

The 1:10 p.m. train from Matewan pulled into the station at Charleston. Polly gathered her belongings and stepped down onto the platform. Dayton was waiting on her and took her bags. "How you doin', Ms. Polly?"

"Good as can be 'spected, Dayton. How are you?" Polly asked.

"We's all tryin' to get through this crazy mess. It's tirin', but you gotta keep puttin' one foot in front of the other, I s'pose."

Dayton escorted Polly to the Hotel Ruffner and handed her bags to the bellman at the door. "I'll see you tomorrow mornin', Ms. Polly."

"Thank you, Dayton."

Polly followed the bellman up to her room. The bellman took the key from her and opened the door. He placed her bags on a small bench and left.

A tray of food and a note had been placed on her small table.

Stay put, the donkey's still in the barn. Enjoy your lunch!

"Donkey? Surely, she means the *jackass*," Polly said to herself. Sometimes, the River Talk symbols could have different meanings.

Polly stood at the window looking out over the Hotel gardens, the array of fall colors fading. She removed her hat and sat heavily on the settee by the window. She was bone tired. What would she do here by herself all day? She looked around and spotted several books.

Tomorrow morning, Dayton would escort her to see Jake in the county jail. He'd been arrested twelve weeks ago. She wasn't sure what to expect. Had he been beaten? Was he crippled? She missed his touch, his kiss, his strong arms holding her, making the world a better, safer place.

Three dresses hung in the small closet. Obviously, gifts from Ellie. They weren't the fancy dresses she wore, but they were better than anything Polly had. They were new and clean and fashionable. She tried on each of them and chose the dark blue one. She found new shoes and a small satchel there as well. Ellie really had thought of everything.

The next morning there was a gentle knock. "Ms. Polly, I brought your breakfast. While you eat, I'll draw your bath so you can get ready to go see your husband. Ms. Ellie said for me to stay and help you get dressed and fix your hair—anythang you need."

"Dottie, that's so kind of you. I think I can manage by myself."

"No, I ain't hearin' of it. I'm here to help you. Now, you go on and eat your breakfast, and I'll take care of ever'thang else. Dayton'll be around to fetch you at ten o'clock."

Polly was unaccustomed to anyone helping her do anything. She ran the farm, took care of four kids, cooked all the meals, and cleaned up. But she ate her breakfast, which smelled delicious, and let Dottie help her.

"Did you pick out a dress, Ms. Polly?" Dottie asked.

"I did. The blue one."

"That's my favorite!"

"Where's Ellie?" Polly asked.

"She's havin' breakfast downstairs with that man."

"How is he, Dottie? What's he like? Is he good to Ellie?"

Dottie stopped filling the tub and sat down at the table with Polly. "Ms. Polly, I don't want to speak outa turn nor nothin', but he ain't good to her. I fear he might hurt her. He's a mean son of a bitch. Plain nasty. He drinks too much and he's right jealous over Ms. Ellie."

Polly sat her coffee cup on the table. "Does he strike her?"

"I've said too much. You should ask Ms. Ellie these questions." Dottie got up and continued filling the tub with hot water.

Polly assumed Dottie's reluctance to answer her question meant he did indeed hit Ellie. Even though Ellie was living in a plush hotel and had any material thing she wanted, Polly doubted she would tolerate any man hitting her in order to maintain her lifestyle. Ellie could have any man she wanted. So what was in this for Ellie? Was she really helping Jake and the miners because it was the right thing to do? Jolene and Jake were certain Ellie had ulterior motives for helping. But Polly had more faith in her cousin.

Polly bathed, and Dottie helped her dress. She pulled up Polly's dark curls in a fashionable style, securing the tendrils with a small mother-of-pearl comb.

"They's all gone from the dining room, Ms. Polly. Still, it might be best if you go down the back stairs and out into the alley. Dayton'll be there waitin'."

Polly stood and hugged Dottie. "Dottie, we're all honored to have you be a part of our circle. Your care and concern for Ellie is appreciated by all of us."

Dottie blinked back the tears. "It's my pleasure, Ms. Polly. You be safe out there, and I'll be lookin' for you to come back."

Polly quietly exited the hotel and got on the wagon with Dayton. They went across town to the county jail, where they waited for two hours. "Polly Hardin," the guard called, finally.

"Yes! I'm here. She stood and followed the guard through a series of doors. He led her into a long room. The ceilings were high, with windows around the top. The room had several long tables with chairs on either side. The guard took her to the front table and told her to have a seat.

She sat with other women waiting for the prisoners to be brought in. Several guards stood around the walls. Polly watched the door leading to the cells with great anticipation. The metal door clanked open and the prisoners filed in, the chains on their ankles clanking against the wood floor. Jake was the last one. The guard walked him over to her and told him to sit in the chair and not get up until he was told to.

Polly couldn't tell if he was limping or if the chains on his ankles made walking difficult.

"Jake!" Polly tried to hide her shock. He looked ten years older— the twinkle in his blue eyes long gone. His beard had grown out and was gray. His hair had also grown out and was nearly as gray as his beard. She placed her hands on the table and reached for him.

Jake placed his hands on the table, the chains making a thud. "Polly. I was beginnin' to wonder if I'd ever see you again." Tears filled his eyes.

"I've been tryin' to get in here to see you since you got arrested, Jake. At first, they wouldn't tell me if you were here or still in The Bullpen at Paint Creek. I've tried ever'thang to get you outa here, but they ain't budgin'. With the new governor, hopefully this'll all end soon, Jake."

"Problem is, he don't take office till March. Those bastards can do a lot of damage in four months. Have they lifted martial law?"

"Yes, last month. Some of the men've been set free. Deacon says since you're a leader of the strike they'll keep you as long as they can."

"I figured."

"Word is Glasscock's gonna declare martial law again any day now. They's been so many killin's. The men *and* women are fightin' back the scabs they keep bringin' in. They's sniper attacks almost daily now."

"How's Deannie and the boys?"

"Deannie's growin' more ever' day. The boys miss you somethin' terrible, Jake. They all said to tell you to hurry home. They's takin' care of ever'thang though. Seth's grown up a whole lot since you been gone. He's takin' his duties as man of the house to heart."

"You look awful pretty, Polly. I'd give anythang to hold you close to me."

"I love you, Jake." She leaned in and whispered, "Ellie gave me this dress. Said I needed to look extra pretty for you. She's been so good to me and the kids, Jake. I don't know what I'd a done without her through all this. She's tryin' ever'thang she can to figure a way to get you outa here."

"She still with that son of a bitch?" Jake asked.

"I'm afraid so."

"I'm not sure what her motives are, Polly."

"I know. I'm not sure what her motives are either. She could leave him whenever she wanted, Jake. You know as well as I do, Ellie can have any man in this town she desired. Bein' with that man ain't no picnic for her. I'm pretty sure he gets drunk and hits her ever' chance he gets. He's a mean person, Jake. I fear for Ellie."

"Did she have any news on this mess?"

"None that matters—she's still doin' all she can."

Jake squeezed her hands. "I love you, Polly. I want you to stay safe. Now that they's seen your face, they might try to hurt you. Keep your gun close and don't let your guard down. I'll be outa here a'fore too long and home with you and the kids. This can't go on forever."

"How're they treatin' you in here?" Polly asked.

"It ain't that bad. A few of the county police are on our side. They treat us decent. The food ain't for shit, but it's food."

"It looked like you's limpin' when you walked in."

"Those bastards put the butt of a rifle in my back when they arrested me. It'll mend eventually."

"Time's up!" the guard yelled.

"I love you, Jake. I'll be back as soon as they let me."

"I love you with my whole heart, Polly. You're my world."

The guard jerked Jake up and led him back to his cell. The other guard led Polly to the door to the outside. She would die before she let these bastards see her cry. She held her head high, walked out, and hopped on the wagon with Dayton. A cold mist filled the air. Polly pulled the cloak Ellie had provided tighter around her shoulders.

Dayton steered away from the county jail. "Ms. Polly, the governor done went and declared martial law again."

"Will this never end, Dayton?" Polly asked.

"They's been more sniper attacks, and those miners been attackin' the scabs as soon as they roll 'em into Paint Creek. They's shootin' at the trains, blockin' the tracks, whatever it takes to stop 'em."

Dayton stopped the wagon two blocks from the Ruffner. Polly hopped off and walked the remainder of the way to the hotel. She stepped into the lobby, feeling small and insignificant amongst the elegance. Polly climbed the stairs to her room, dragging the weight of the world with each step.

Dottie had started a fire in the fireplace, and the room was warm and inviting. She removed her cloak and rang for Dottie so she could let Ellie know she had returned. Polly stood by the hearth and warmed her hands.

A few minutes later, Ellie entered and joined Polly by the fire.

"How's Jake?" she asked, giving her a hug.

"He looks bad. Older, worn out. He was limpin'; said they hit his back with the butt of a rifle. Ellie, do you think he'll ever get out of there? What if they keep him locked up in that place?"

"You can't think that way, Polly. He'll get out. It might be a few more months, but we'll get him outa there."

"I'm not sure what to tell the kids 'bout Jake. I guess the truth is the best thing—I simply don't know when he'll be home."

"The governor's declared martial law again," Ellie said.

"Dayton told me. This damn war may never end."

"Are you still leavin' for Matewan in the mornin'?" Ellie asked.

"I s'pose. They ain't no reason for me to stay here any longer. I'll plan to come back a'fore Christmas."

"I've arranged for Dayton to take you home. I'm afraid those bastards might try somethin' now that they know you're Jake's wife."

"Thank you, Ellie, for ever'thang. Me and Jake and the kids appreciate all you've done for us."

"We've always had to take care of each other. That ain't ever gonna stop, Polly." Ellie said.

"What are you gonna do, Ellie? When this is over? I hope you're gonna leave that bastard."

"I've been thinkin' 'bout that. I'd like to go to New York. I've saved most of the money John gives me. I'll need all I can get to escape this hell. Hopefully, it'll be sooner rather than later." Ellie said. "I need to get back to my suite, Polly. I'd love nothin' more than to sleep right here with you."

58.

19 December 1912 (Charleston)

The Hotel Ruffner spared no expense on holiday decorations. Ellie had never seen so many Christmas trees in one place. The small parlor off the main lobby had a small tree; the dining room had a tree; even the tavern had a tree. The main lobby boasted the largest tree in the city; even bigger than the one at the Capitol. The lobby's ceilings were soaring, easily accommodating the 25-foot white pine. The staff had been decorating the monstrosity for over a week. John wanted to put a small tree in Ellie's suite, but she refused. The smell of pine throughout the hotel was overwhelming. Her suite was the only place she could escape it.

The Ruffner was alive with the excitement of the holidays and the non-stop parties. Baldwin-Felts was hosting a cocktail party in the main lobby that evening for the placing of the star on the Christmas tree. John wouldn't return from Bluefield until just before the party.

Ellie was in no mood for Christmas or celebrating. With Jake in jail, Polly and Deannie's future was at stake. Jolene was snowed in at Holly Grove. Ellie feared Jolene would probably die of pneumonia or worse.

Christmas in Lynn would be lonely without Jake, and Ellie wanted to make it as pleasant for Polly and the kids as possible. She had shopped for weeks for just the right presents for Deannie—clothes, dolls, toys, shoes—anything she might possibly need. She also bought gifts for Polly and the boys.

Ellie had the gifts delivered to the Ruffner. She and Dot met in Polly's room to wrap them.

Ellie hummed "Silent Night," tenderly wrapping each item. She wanted to send something extravagant to Jolene, but she knew it was pointless. She opted for practical things—blankets, shawls, and food. She had to keep warm and she had to eat. Knowing Jolene, she would give them away.

"Ms. Ellie how you gonna get these gifts to Matewan and Holly Grove?" Dot wrapped a tiny doll and placed the package in the basket.

"Dayton's gonna take Polly's on the train tonight. He's comin' to get 'em while we're downstairs at the party. I need you to let him in the room. He'll also take Jolene's to Holly Grove when he gets back from Matewan."

They finished wrapping the last of the gifts. Ellie placed $50 with the letter she had written for Polly. It was probably more money than Polly had ever seen at one time. Ellie hoped she accepted it. They would need food and other things. It was the least she could do.

Ellie returned to her suite and changed into a dress glimmering with green beads. John entered Ellie's suite and poured himself a whiskey. "That's a mighty pretty dress you're wearin' darlin'."

"Thank you. I hoped you'd approve."

"I think you need something else to wear, though." He stood behind her.

Ellie looked at him in the mirror of her dressing table. "What do you mean? A different dress? Why?"

"No, not a different dress. Just a little something extra." He pulled a box from his inside jacket pocket and handed it to her. "Merry Christmas, Ellie."

Ellie opened the gift. "John! Really? Why, this is simply exquisite."

He took the necklace from the box and slipped it around her neck. He fastened the latch and kissed her nape. She thought of Sammy's touch and had to make an effort not to shrink away from John's lips on her skin. John's touch was a small price to pay for such a beautiful piece of jewelry—a three-carat emerald surrounded by diamonds. She admired the necklace in the mirror. "John, this is truly beautiful. I don't know what to say."

"Don't say anything. Just show that bunch downstairs you're the most beautiful woman in this city. And you belong to me." He kissed her roughly on the mouth. "You are *mine*, Ellie."

She wasn't sure what to say. Her gut instinct was to rip the necklace off and throw it at him. She belonged to no man—especially not him.

"Be downstairs in thirty minutes. I have a meeting in the parlor. Remember, enter that room like you own the damn place."

John downed his whiskey and left for his meeting. Ellie sat staring at herself in the mirror. The emerald dangling from her neck felt more like an albatross than a fine piece of jewelry. What had she become? A paid whore like those in the tavern? Payment was payment—regardless of the amount. Did he really think he *owned* her? Did *everyone* think he owned her?

Here she was in the finest hotel in three states. She was warm, safe, and dry. She ate the best of food and wore the best of clothes—all while her sister lived like a savage in a wet tent with little food, no heat, and no hope. Polly and Deannie were looking at a life not much better than Jolene's situation—if Jake stayed in jail.

Mother Jones's words from her speech in August rang loud in Ellie's head.

She dresses with the blood of children.

No! She would *not* feel guilty. She *was* doing her part. She was risking as much as any of them. Sure, she lived in luxury and had anything she wanted, but she was putting her life in danger every single day. As much as any of the miners, if not more so. Ellie pulled herself together. She poured a shot of whiskey and threw it back, then straightened her dress and admired the necklace in the mirror one last time.

She descended the staircase like a queen and stepped into the lobby of the Ruffner. She held her head high with a confidence that belied the misery in her heart.

<u>24 December 1912 (Holly Grove)</u>

The sun had faded hours earlier. Jolene stood inside her tent watching the snow gently cover the colony of makeshift homes in the narrow valley. The sheer number of tents at Holly Grove was staggering. When the rest of the Cabin Creek miners walked out and were evicted from their company homes in late summer, they had quickly run out of tents. The union had informed them they didn't have any more funds to help them. The only option was to double up. There were two and even three families in many of the larger tents.

The gifts Ellie sent had been a godsend. Jolene kept one of the blankets and some of the food for her and Deacon. Everything else she gave to those most in need in the tent colony.

Some of the kids had decorated a small pine tree at the top of the path. They made decorations from pieces of cloth, metal, string, leaves, branches, whatever they could find. Jolene heard them coming up the path singing Christmas carols. She lifted the flap and stepped outside to greet them. They were a ragtag group of children from every ethnic background the coal camp offered—Italian, Hungarian, Polish, black, white. The kids paused at her tent and sang "Silent Night," then they moved on up the path to their Christmas tree.

Jolene admired their undying spirit. Their singing voices carried throughout the hills at Holly Grove. Perhaps a merry

Christmas *was* all in the heart and people's perception of the world around them.

24 December 1912 (Lynn)

Polly sat staring at the chest of gifts Ellie had sent. Her first instinct had been to return the gifts; she couldn't accept such extravagance—especially knowing they were bought with Baldwin-Felts blood money. The $50 Ellie included was certainly needed, but could she accept these things? Jake would have said *absolutely not*. But Jake wasn't here, and she had mouths to feed and a farm to run.

She couldn't be foolish. There was no telling how long Jake would be in jail. She'd take all the help she could get. She had to. Their Granny Cline had told them not to look a gift horse in the mouth. Damn straight she would take their money. They owed her and her family this much and more.

She opened the gifts and cried before rewrapping each one. The clothes Ellie sent for Deannie were exquisite. The toys and clothes for the boys were perfect. Polly was happy to see two dresses for herself. She would certainly wear them on her next trip to Charleston. Wearing her drab farm dress on her initial visit, she had felt more like she should be in the hotel kitchen than in one of the fancy guest rooms.

She placed the gifts under the tree and thought of the previous Christmas when Deannie was a newborn and Ellie was still with them. And Jake. Those were better times. She clung to the hope their lives would mend. Things may never be the same, but it wouldn't be this. She hummed "Silent Night" as she placed the gifts around the tree.

59.

<u>Christmas Day 1912 (Holly Grove)</u>

Christmas morning, Jolene gathered her bag of herbs, ointments, and tinctures, and quietly left Deacon sleeping in the tent. She hadn't slept well. The dreams had been strong and vivid for the past few months. Last night's dream was about the burning train again. It came careening through Holly Grove and jumped the tracks. It barreled through the tents and up the hill, the flames shooting out from all sides, torching everything. The train stopped in front of her and Deacon's tent. She breathed a sigh of relief only to turn and see Deacon on fire in their bed. It was the same dream each time and ended with either Deacon or Ellie burning as Jolene watched, unable to move.

The cold air burned her lungs, and the wind caused her eyes to water. She pulled her scarf and cloak tightly around her; she wondered if maybe she should have kept one of the cloaks Ellie had sent for herself after all.

The first stop was the Kirk tent. The youngest son was on his sixth day of fighting pneumonia. Jolene was hopeful for the kid; as long as he kept improving, he should make it.

Hundreds of families had sick children or grandparents. But only a handful of doctors, midwives, and others were available to help. And most of them came only one or two days a week from Charleston. Three kids under the age of twelve had died in the previous week.

There were thousands of people stacked on top of each other. The conditions were ripe for the quick spread of disease—tuberculosis and pneumonia crawled from tent to tent preying on the most vulnerable. Without outhouses, they were forced to dispose of their human excrement as best they could. Most people didn't have enough blankets, and nearly all the tents leaked when it rained. Many children showed signs of malnutrition. The snow had blown in weeks earlier, bringing its own set of problems with subzero temperatures.

Jolene didn't know how they would make it through this winter. It was only December, and things were already careening downhill. In preparation for the season, she had stored up herbs and ointments for months. Her supply diminished a lot quicker than she had planned. With each person she treated, especially the children, her fury at the coal operators overflowed. The union kept making promises to help with their essential needs; their assistance had fallen short in the most important areas—food and medicine. They had all underestimated the devastation the strike would bring to their lives.

The Kirk boy's mother met Jolene at the bottom of the path. "Ms. Jolene, come quick! You ain't gonna believe it. Timmy's sittin' up and talkin' and actin' like he feels a whole heap better. It's the best Christmas gift ever."

Jolene entered the tent, and sure enough, little Timmy Kirk was sitting up in bed and feeling fine. His fever had broken in the middle of the night and he'd woken up hungry. Jolene left the Kirk tent happy to have at least one child healed.

The cold wind sliced through Jolene on her way down the mountain, the warmth from her early morning hours spent wrapped up with Deacon long gone.

She had awoken just moments before the first streaks of light had broken across the sky. He'd stirred next to her, and she'd rolled over and pressed her breasts into his back. She loved the feel of him against her, and she kissed his warm skin. They rarely slept naked after relocating to the tent colony. They had to be ready to fight, run, or help someone at a moment's notice. But last night had been different. He'd returned to the camp long after midnight after he and the men had made another raid on the mine guards. With little discussion of the raid, he'd put out the flame on the lantern and taken her in his arms. He kissed her hard and removed her dress, and then his own clothes. No sweet words, no fanfare—simply a man hungry for his woman. The tents were so close together every sound could be heard in the still of the night. She moaned when he entered her, and he muffled her with another hard, wet kiss. Before falling into a deep sleep, Deacon had kissed her gently and told her he loved her. She loved that man more than life itself.

The snow crunched under her feet now as she neared her next stop at the Bowman's. The grandmother had come down with the flu a few weeks earlier and couldn't shake it. Every other day she had a fever, then vomiting, then diarrhea. Then she would have a day of sleeping, and then it would start all over. She hadn't eaten in five days. Jolene was concerned if the flu didn't kill her she would die of starvation or dehydration.

A fire burned outside the Bowman's tent. The children and grandchildren were gathered around the flames; no one spoke. The oldest daughter stepped away to greet Jolene. Her eyes were red-rimmed from an endless flow of tears. Jolene doubted she had slept or eaten in days. Jolene reached for her hand. "Ms. Jolene, Mama ain't doin' so good." She held onto Jolene as if she held the miracle they so desperately sought for the older woman. "I don't think she's gonna make it." Tears spilled over and slipped down the daughter's face.

Jolene embraced the young woman. "Let's go take a look."

They entered the tent, and Jolene sat on the cot next to Mrs. Bowman. She could barely feel her heartbeat. If not for the rattle deep in her chest, Jolene would have sworn the poor soul had already passed. Jolene assumed her time to leave this cruel world was only moments away.

"I s'pose y'all should say your goodbyes."

The daughter left the tent and told the others. One-by-one, they entered the tent and quietly said goodbye to the matriarch of the Bowman family. Jolene slipped out and let them have their moment. With a heavy heart, she went to the next family.

After hours of tending to the sick, Jolene climbed back up the hill to the tent she and Deacon called home now. It was long past supper time, and he was waiting. "Merry Christmas." He held her close. "Some of the women-folk brought food. Said they knew you'd be too tired to cook. How'd it go? I heard 'bout Mrs. Bowman. Damn shame."

"One healed, then ten minutes later, one died. Then they's twenty more near death, and fifty more startin' to get sick. Deacon, we can't keep up with it. I think it's 'bout to get a whole lot worse."

"How so?" He fixed her a plate of beans and cornbread.

"Appears most people are runnin' out of food. I can't count the families that said they didn't have enough to feed the whole family proper. Most of the mothers are goin' without so their young'ns can eat. They's a bunch of kids so skinny a good wind'd blow 'em clean away. What're we gonna do, Deacon?"

"We've been hearin' it from the men, too. We sent word, and the union said they's gonna bring more supplies and food. We just gotta wait. We may have to go get it ourselves. We run the risk of an ambush either way."

"It's only December. How's all these families gonna make it through till spring? How? This's gotta end soon, Deacon, or it's gonna be the end of us all."

60.

<u>New Year's Eve 1912</u>

Ellie sat at her dressing table listening to the strains from a violin wafting up the stairs from the lobby. The soothing melody took her thoughts to Sammy. He'd played that song for her at his tiny place over the Black Bear. It had been more than a month since he had pulled her into Polly's room. She occasionally caught glimpses of him in the tavern. Her heart ached for him. Her skin longed for his touch. She had to face the truth that a life with Sammy would never work in the long run. She was lost in her thoughts when the door to her suite opened.

"Ms. Ellie, I'm so sorry I'm late." Dottie rushed into the room. "Cook insisted I help in the kitchen with the linens and polishin' silver. Ever'body in the hotel's been tryin' to get ready for this dang party all week."

"It's fine, Dot. I'm in no particular rush to get down there."

Dottie helped Ellie into her dress and fastened the tiny buttons up the back. "Ms. Ellie, this is the prettiest dress you own. You look beautiful," Dot said.

The dress was deep purple silk velvet and accentuated her breasts and tiny waist. She wore the emerald and diamond necklace John had given her for Christmas and diamond earrings. Dot pulled the front of Ellie's hair up and slipped a diamond and emerald comb into the top.

"Ms. Ellie, you look like a princess."

"Thank you, Dot. Are you serving tonight?"

"Yes, ma'am. I'll be in the main lobby and later in the main dinin' room."

"Good. Keep an eye on me. You never know what might happen." Ellie rested her hand on Dot's shoulder. "I'm really hopin' this all ends soon, Dot. In the meantime, I have a late Christmas gift for you." Ellie handed Dottie a small package with a red bow.

"Ms. Ellie, you didn't have to get me nothin', but I'm so glad you did!" Dottie gently removed the bow and opened the tiny box. "Ms. Ellie! I don't know what to say! You sure you wanna give me this?"

"I'm absolutely positive. Let me help you put it on." Ellie took the delicate pearl necklace and latched it around Dottie's neck. She turned Dottie towards the mirror. "There. Do you like it? If not, we can trade it for somethin' else."

"Ms. Ellie, I love it." Tears welled up in Dottie's eyes. "Ms. Ellie, ain't nobody been this good to me a'fore." Dottie turned around and hugged Ellie.

Ellie wiped the tears from Dottie's eyes. "You've been a true friend to me, Dot. You best get downstairs a'fore they come lookin' for you. I'll see you down there."

Ellie poured herself a whiskey and downed it. She checked herself in the mirror one last time. She loved the dress. She loved the jewelry. She loved the parties. She mostly loved the attention. No, Sammy would never be able to give her these things.

When she stepped into the lobby, she looked toward the band. The music was so lovely and soothing. She nearly stumbled when she saw Sammy playing the violin. She hadn't expected him to be at this party. Damn him. He was dressed in a tuxedo, his curls smoothed back. A half-smile revealed his dimples when he caught her eye. Her feet refused to move, even though she knew she must.

"Ellie! There you are. What took you so long?" John asked, placing his hand on the small of her back.

"Dottie was busy in the kitchen, and I needed help with my dress." Ellie took a glass of champagne from him. "Thank you."

"Come, I want you to meet some people." John was on his best behavior. He introduced Ellie to several Baldwin-Felts attorneys, vice presidents, coal operators, and their wives that she hadn't yet met. Ellie put on her best smile and charmed them all.

Sammy's eyes seemed to follow her every step. She wanted to grab his hand and run as far away from this place as possible. But looking at him in this situation, she knew it would never work. As much as she would love to be naked with him in his tiny apartment over the Black Bear Tavern, she also knew in the long run it wouldn't make her happy. She was in her element in these types of events. She was the center of attention; she was wearing a beautiful dress and expensive jewels, and she was drinking the finest champagne. Mingling with the wealthiest people in the state brought a level of excitement to her life that Sammy would never be able to give her.

John wasn't what she wanted either, but she would tolerate him as long as she had to. Hopefully by late spring she could leave West Virginia and make a new life for herself in New York.

The band stopped playing, and Tom Felts stood in front of the crowd to speak. Ellie stood with John, but her eyes followed Sammy. He crossed the room and took a glass of champagne from Dottie. Then leaned against the doorway that led into the main dining hall and stared at her.

John leaned over and kissed Ellie's cheek. Sammy lifted his champagne glass in a mocking toast before downing its contents.

Tom Felts finished his impromptu speech and welcomed the guests to enter the main dining hall and take their seats for dinner. Ellie excused herself and headed to the powder room. Sammy followed her and pulled her into a small side parlor.

"You certainly look beautiful tonight, Ellie." Sammy picked up the emerald and held it for a moment. "Another expensive necklace. John's got good taste."

"What're you doin' here?"

"Makin' a livin', same as you apparently." Sammy shoved his hands in his pockets.

"You should've told me you'd be playin' music here tonight."

"Why? Seems like you're havin' a damn good time minglin' with the highfalutin' people of Kanawha County. You looked awfully happy out there. I'm startin' to think you ain't as miserable as you let on, Ellie. Ever' time I see you with those people—goin' to parties, teas, and dinners—you sure seem to be enjoyin' yourself."

"How dare you?"

"You and John seem to be gettin' on pretty good. He don't act much like the son of a bitch you made him out to be."

"It's all an act on my part. You know that!"

"Do I? You don't think watchin' him with his hands on you, kissin' your face, and paradin' you 'round like his prized possession don't kill me, Ellie?"

"You knew the situation when we started this relationship, Sammy. You knew! Don't go actin' all surprised and wounded now."

"You're a different person when you're with me, Ellie. A *better* person." He nodded towards the lobby. "Out there, you're one of *them*. Pompous, pretentious, and snotty. Hell, you even talk different with that bunch."

"Fuck you, Sammy!"

"There she is! *That's* the Ellie I know. Not the social climber I see out there. Is that what you really want, Ellie? Is that the life you'll be happiest with?"

Ellie hesitated and looked away from him.

"Well, I guess *no* answer *is* my answer."

Ellie straightened and looked him in the eye. "Sammy, we both know this thing between us would never work. We want different things. Yes, I enjoy wearin' fancy clothes and expensive jewelry. I enjoy fancy parties with rich people. And I will not feel guilty 'bout it. I want it all! And you can't give me any of that. You don't want those things. We've had a good time, Sammy. But it's time to end it."

"You'll learn soon enough, Ellie, this stuff you think you want so much ain't nothin' more than an empty tomb. They ain't no real joy in any of it." Sammy turned to go. "Ellie, the bitter truth you gotta live with is that *you* might've had *just* a good time. But I *loved* you. Don't forget that." Sammy walked away, closing the door gently behind him.

The Knowing reared up and screamed at her to run after him. She couldn't. She wouldn't. It would only end with her resenting him and any sort of life they made together. She wiped her eyes and pulled herself together. John would come looking for her if she didn't get back soon.

She entered the main lobby in time to see Sammy packing up his violin. He looked at her, turned away, and walked out of the Ruffner. She hurried into the main dining hall and found John.

"I was getting worried about you." John pulled her chair out for her. "You look ill, Ellie."

"I'm fine. I have a bit of headache is all. I might call it an early evenin'. Perhaps too much champagne."

Ellie struggled to eat her dinner. She forced a smile and chatted with the ladies. Inside, she was dying. Had she made the biggest mistake of her life? She loathed John, his touch, his voice, everything about him. She hated these people, but she loved the life they lived. She loved Sammy, but she would come to resent his lifestyle and him if she stayed with him. But still, her world was suddenly much darker without Sammy in it. She watched the Baldwin-Felts women at her table. Was this what she wanted to become? Boring, entitled, and rude? What had Sammy called them? *Pompous, pretentious, and snotty.* She touched the emerald necklace. It tightened around her neck, threatening to choke her soul. This is what she destroyed a life with Sammy for?

She took a drink of her champagne and prayed it was worth it.

(Holly Grove)

Jolene wrapped the blankets tighter around her shoulders and took the tin cup full of whiskey Deacon offered. He sat on their makeshift bed and crawled under the covers with her.

"Cheers, my love." He raised his own cup, and they toasted.

"Happy New Year's, Deacon." Jolene snuggled in closer to her husband. "Here's to a better year." The whiskey's warmth spread through her limbs, and the tension she held slowly faded.

"Hell, it's gotta get better. It can't get no worse," Deacon said.

"I ain't so sure 'bout that. Winter's barely gettin' started." Jolene laid her head on his shoulder.

"At least those bastards ain't been attackin' us too much durin' the holidays, other than the occasional sniper fire." He pulled her tighter and kissed her forehead. "Let's not linger on that stuff tonight. It's New Year's, and we need to celebrate as much as we can."

(Lynn)

Polly rocked Deannie to sleep in front of the fireplace. The boys were out in the yard shooting guns to celebrate the New Year. Polly's thoughts were on Jake. She planned to return to Charleston within the week to try to get him released. Ellie had offered to pay for a lawyer, even though it may very well make matters worse. Polly wasn't sure how things could get any worse.

Polly pulled Deannie closer. "Sweet baby girl, we *will* get through this. Your daddy'll be home a'fore you know it. I won't let any harm come to you. I'll protect you with my very own life."

Part 4

Then the third angel poured out his bowl on the rivers and springs of water, and they became blood.

—Revelation 16:4

61.

19 January 1913 (Holly Grove)

The church bells echoed through the mountains as Jolene packed her bag of herbs. She'd given up going to church months ago. She couldn't understand how God would let this happen to them. Besides, she was too busy tending to the sick and dying to worry about sitting in a cramped church building every Sunday. Her church was out here, with these people, trying to get through this level of hell they had been cast into.

"You looked outside yet?" she asked Deacon. "Looks like another foot of snow fell last night."

Deacon handed her a cup of coffee. "Damn, Deacon. This coffee's awful."

"Sorry 'bout that. It's a little strong." Deacon chuckled

"A little? I think it could get up outa the cup and carry me down the hill."

"It's awfully cold out there. You wanna wait a few hours and see if it warms up a bit?"

"Waitin' won't do me no good. The sick keep gettin' sicker. Since Christmas I've had over twenty new cases of tuberculosis, fourteen people with pneumonia, and too many infants to count near starvation. Twenty more people died from one thing or another. I think most of 'em's just plain givin' up. We had three more babies die yesterday, and that was right here in our section. I've heard it's just as bad in the other parts of the camp." Jolene pulled back the flap on the tent. "I love you, Deacon, even if you can't make coffee worth a damn."

Boyd was waiting for her at the bottom of the path. He had started accompanying her on her rounds through the camp; she was pleased to have his company.

"Mornin' Ms. Jolene. Where we startin' today? I heard that little baby at the Moore's ain't doin' too well. The kids were talkin' 'bout it last night."

"Well, I guess that's where we'll start."

Jolene and Boyd found the Moore's tent through the maze of new tents that had been erected in October with no rhyme or reason.

"I heard your baby ain't doin' too good. I'm here to check and see if I can help." Jolene looked at the young mother holding the child.

"I ain't too sure anythang can be done for him. He's still breathin', but he ain't made no noise a'tall since yesterdee." Tears fell down her face.

"What's his name?" Jolene held out her arms to take the infant.

"Jacob."

"When was he born?"

"Three weeks ago." The young mother twisted her dress in her hands.

"How *you* feelin?" Jolene asked. "You don't look too good yourself. You still bleedin' from the birth?"

"Yes, ma'am. I'm bleedin' a bit."

"Is he takin' the breast?" Jolene felt the baby to see if he had a fever.

"Not since yesterdee mornin'."

"Have you been eatin'? If *you* ain't eatin', you may not be makin' enough milk for the little feller."

"I eat when I can. Like ever'body else, we ain't got much food."

"Let's see if we can get a wet nurse to help out with feedin' him." Jolene handed Jacob back to the mother and stepped outside with Boyd.

"Boyd, you need to run back up the path and get Geraldine Murphy. Her baby died last week of pneumonia. Tell her we need her to come feed a baby. If she don't, he's gonna die."

Jolene examined the baby and the mama from head to toe while she waited on Boyd to return with Geraldine.

"Geraldine, I appreciate you comin' over and helpin' out. I know this is hard on you. Truth is, without your milk this little feller's gonna die of starvation. If we can keep one more alive, let's do all we can." Jolene hugged Geraldine and led her into the tent.

Little Jacob took to Geraldine as if he had not had food in days. Geraldine smiled through her tears. Jacob's mother sat on the edge of the bed and cried along with her while Jacob ate more in that one sitting than he had in the three weeks he had been on the earth.

Jolene placed her hand on Jacob's mother's shoulder. "Let's see 'bout gettin' *you* some food. I'll have Boyd or one of the others bring you somethin' to eat right away."

Jolene and Boyd left the Moore's tent. They passed by the church. The congregants were singing an old hymn Granny Cline used to sing:

Nearer My God to Thee.

Jolene felt as though God was as far away as the moon.

Though like the wanderer, the sun gone down, darkness be over me.

Jolene hummed the song as she and Boyd trudged through the tents to visit twenty-three more families. Darkness slipped between the mountains when she headed up the path to her tent. The waxing moon reflected off the snow-covered mountains, providing a gentle light as her feet crunched along the frozen path.

Deacon had a roaring fire going outside. His daily fire had become the gathering place for his men and a few others, but they had all left to return to their own tents for supper. Inside he had a small fire, just a few smoldering twigs, enough to keep their tent warm. "How'd it go?" he asked.

"As well as could be expected. Old man James died early this morning. Passed in his sleep. They's 'bout ten more babies on the way. God only knows how they'll be able to feed and care for 'em." She slipped into Deacon's arms and rested her head against his massive chest—the only place she felt safe anymore.

"The ladies brought us dinner again. Taters, beans, and cornbread. Come on and eat now." Deacon took Jolene's hand. They sat at their tiny table made of crates and ate dinner.

"When's the union bringin' more food and supplies?" Jolene spooned more potatoes onto her plate. "They promised to bring us what we need ever' week. I ain't seen hide nor hair of those bastards for three weeks, Deacon."

"It's hard to tell who's on our side and who ain't these days. Jake's been our go-between with that union bunch in Charleston. With him in jail, we don't hear things as fast as we used to."

62.

22 January 1913 (Charleston, County Jail)

Jake heard the guard's keys turn in his cell door. "Get up! You're free to go."

"How?"

"Don't ask questions, Jake. Get the hell outa here—a'fore they change their minds."

Jake limped out of his cell and down the hall, where he joined several other men he had been arrested with, and they walked together out the front door. He saw a familiar face on the outside waiting for him. "Dayton!"

Dayton embraced Jake. "I's mighty glad to you see you outa that damn place, Jake."

"Not nearly as glad as I am to be out." They walked away from the crowd and the guards towards Dayton's wagon.

"Ms. Ellie says I'm to take you back to Matewan on the next train outa town."

"That sounds like a mighty good idea, Dayton. How'd I get out? What happened?"

Dayton steered the wagon away from the jail towards the train station. "The governor lifted martial law early this mornin'. Mother Jones went to Washin'ton and met with some Congressman. I reckon she pitched such a fit they released all but two of you'ns. They said you could go, but they had your bail set so high ain't no way Ms. Polly could pay it. Ms. Ellie gave me the money and I paid your bail this mornin'."

Jake would never figure out what Ellie's motives were, and right now he didn't care. "Get me home to my family, Dayton."

"Yes, sir."

(Lynn)

Polly put the lid on the pot of stew and turned down the flame. She pulled the cornbread out of the oven and turned it out onto a plate. The kitchen door opened. "Tell your brothers to come on and eat," she said.

"I ain't got no brothers."

Polly froze. She sat the iron skillet on the stove. She hesitated to turn around, afraid her mind was playing tricks on her. Slowly she turned. And there he stood. Her husband.

"Jake? Jake!" She threw her arms around his neck. Jake dropped his cane and embraced her, pulling her closer.

"God, I've missed you, woman!"

"Jake!" She placed her hands on either side of his face. "I can't believe it's really you. How'd you get out?"

"Governor Glasscock lifted martial law this mornin'. They set my bail pretty high, but Ellie came through and paid it. Prob'ly with that bastard's money. I'm not sure if that makes it bittersweet or iffin' it's a real good joke on him."

"It don't matter. You're home. And you're stayin' home."

63.

7 February 1913 (Charleston)

Regret was the cloak Ellie had worn since her fight with Sammy. She kept it pulled tight around her heart and mind. It colored her days, her nights, her dreams, her in-between. She longed to touch him, to hear his voice, his laugh. He was the most real thing she had ever known, and she had thrown it away for what? Jewelry? Parties? Money? Would it be worth it? She wasn't sure. She was sure her spirit would never feel as free as it did with Sammy. It wasn't fair to string him along when in her heart she knew it would never work—he couldn't offer her the life she longed for. She told herself it was for the best, but was it? She could hear his fiddle most every night in the tavern, and she'd imagine walking in there and begging him to forgive her.

She descended the stairs of the hotel, intent on putting her broken heart aside and staying focused on the miners and Baldwin-Felts. She joined the ladies in the dining room for afternoon tea, which had turned into early cocktails for most of the ladies. They regarded their time in Charleston as a holiday away from the boring routine of their daily lives. Most days they were in town it was a party. Whiskey in the middle of the afternoon had become an act of rebellion or an escape from whom and what they pretended to be. The men were all gone, as usual. John had been gone for three days. She had no idea what they were up to, but she was certain the ladies would inform her. She hoped they had something worth reporting. She was meeting the messenger that night and hoped to have something useful for him to take back to Jolene and Deacon.

"Ellie, you look splendid this afternoon." Betty said. "Another new dress? John certainly keeps you in the latest fashions. It must be nice to have a man take care of you the way he does. You don't have to worry about a thing, do you? No kids, no house to keep, you float around like a butterfly. Personally, I like leaving all the hard decisions to my husband. It seems to be the only freedom a woman has."

The backhanded compliments from the ladies were a normal occurrence. Ellie smiled. "Why, thank you, Betty." Freedom? It felt more like bondage to Ellie. She really wanted to slap the smug from Betty's face. Snooty bitches. Mother Jones had referred to them as parlor parasites, and the old woman was more accurate than she knew.

Ellie took a cocktail from the server and joined a small circle where Joan and Myrtle were holding court. These gossips would know all that was going on, and a bit of liquor in their heads would loosen up their lips.

"Good afternoon, ladies. Myrtle, you look stunning in that color." Ellie had accompanied Myrtle earlier in the week to pick out some new dresses.

"Joan, is that a new hair style?" Ellie charmed the women as well as the men. Even though most of the women were jealous, they still wanted to be acknowledged by her. She was aloof enough to keep them wanting more.

"Ellie, thank you." Myrtle winked at her. "Have you heard?" Myrtle whispered.

Ellie cocked a quizzical eyebrow.

Myrtle took Ellie by the arm and led her away from the group. "The men are plannin' a delicious raid on that dreadful tent colony."

"Really? Which one?" Ellie took a sip.

"Holly Grove," Myrtle said. Ellie nearly spit out her drink.

"Holly Grove?" Ellie's heart raced, but she managed to act nonchalant. "What are those boys plannin' now?"

"Well, they sent for Clyde this morning. Apparently, there was another skirmish around daybreak, and one of our men got shot. I think he was a bookkeeper or somethin'. An innocent man in all this. Those crazy miners attacked a coal company ambulance *and* the company store at Mucklow. Our boys are tired of this bullshit, Ellie." Myrtle lowered her voice so the other ladies couldn't hear her foul language.

"So, what *is* their plan?" Ellie asked.

"Do you know about the Bull Moose Special?" Myrtle asked.

"I'm not sure. Isn't that the armored train they use to haul the transportation men to the mines?" Ellie knew perfectly well what it was. Best to play a little dumb and affirm Myrtle's superiority so she would keep talking.

"Well, the C&O railroad allowed the mine guards to outfit it with machine guns, high-powered rifles, and all the ammo they may need. That's where Clyde is now—makin' sure they load that baby up with guns and ammo. When they go through the camp tonight—this is the best part—they're gonna open fire, while those ignorant bastards are sleepin'." Myrtle snickered.

"You can't be serious! What about the women and children?"

"Them too! They's *all* trash, Ellie. You can't let that sort have the upper hand. Those wretched people need to be taught a lesson." Myrtle took another sip of her whiskey.

"I s'pose you're right, Myrtle. How are they gonna justify this?"

"Ellie, our men are so clever. They have the Kanawha County Sheriff in their pocket. He's even lettin' six of his deputies go with our men so it looks more like the law than us. They even have Quinn Morton goin' with 'em. Anyway, he's providin' a slew of his own personal mine guards, as well."

"That still doesn't legally justify what they're plannin', does it?"

"Apparently the sheriff issued a bogus warrant for *unnamed* persons."

"What's the charge?" Ellie asked.

"What did Clyde say? Somethin' 'bout a riot. Incitin'? Is that a word? Incitin' a riot. Yeah, I'm pretty sure that's what he said. It's all legal mumbo jumbo to me." Myrtle put her glass to her lips.

"It all sounds interestin', for sure. When exactly are they plannin' to do this?"

"*Tonight!*" Myrtle had a twinkle in her eye. Perhaps it was the whiskey. Ellie was convinced the entire lot of them was psychotic.

Myrtle turned her attention to another lady who was asking about her new dress. Ellie threw back her whiskey and quietly slipped out of the room.

She sent Dottie to fetch Dayton. He needed to get the message to Holly Grove immediately. Ellie couldn't wait for the messenger; he would never make it back in time to warn everyone. The Bull Moose Special's late run always arrived in Holly Grove at 10:00 P.M.

Ellie gave Dottie specific instructions for Dayton and returned to the parlor. Myrtle was on her third drink and barely able to stand up, let alone talk. Ellie saw this as a grand opportunity to help Myrtle to her room and pry more information from her.

"Myrtle, are you all right, dear? I think the whiskey may have hit a little harder than you thought."

"Oh, you may be right, Ellie. I feel a little woozy." Myrtle giggled uncontrollably.

"How about if I escort you to your room? Let it wear off a bit before dinner."

"Oh, Ellie that's a good idea. Thank you, dear."

Ellie linked her arm in Myrtle's, and they slowly navigated the steps. Ellie was happy to take her time so she could probe a bit more about the Bull Moose Special.

"So, do you think tonight's raid on Holly Grove will be successful?"

"Oh, I certainly do. Those boys of ours are so good at what they do. Those ignorant miners ain't got a clue what's comin' their way." She giggled again.

"I wonder what else they have planned. Do you have any idea?"

"No, that's all I'm aware of at the moment. You'll certainly be the first to know, Ellie. I've never had a friend like you. You've been so kind to me. Most of the ladies don't like me. They think I'm unrefined and don't dress appropriately for a woman of my status. I mean, my husband's a lieutenant to Tom Felts, and I should dress better and have better parlor manners. Dress shoppin' with you this week was the most fun I've had in years. You're always so elegant." Myrtle stumbled on the steps, and Ellie grabbed her before her face hit the railing.

Myrtle continued, "Ellie, you know the ladies don't care too much for you. When you're with us, they all want your approval of their dress or their hair. Then they turn around and call you horrible names behind your back. They say you're John's kept woman. Ellie, dammit, I don't care if you are his *kept* woman or a tramp. I like you, and you're my friend. Those old, hateful bitches are just jealous."

Ellie opened the door for her drunk companion, helped her out of her new dress, and put her to bed, promising to wake her in time for dinner. Myrtle rolled over and buried her face in the pillow. Ellie searched through the desk for anything Myrtle's husband might have left behind that would be of use. Ellie's heart nearly stopped when she found a slip of paper with the names of the union leaders and a few others listed. The list was titled "Main Instigators." Jake and Deacon were at the top of the list. She placed the piece of paper back in the drawer as she had found it and left Myrtle snoring into her pillow.

Ellie returned to her room, poured herself a whiskey, and sat by the fire.

If Dayton didn't get the message to Jolene in time, thousands could die. The entire situation was more than she could wrap her mind around. The glee in Myrtle's eyes when she spoke about the plan bordered on crazy. How could these people be so pleased that innocent people would die? She finished her whiskey and poured another.

Dayton wasn't sure if he could beat the train to Holly Grove or not. He was prepared to ride as fast as he could. Certainly, the woman who gave Ms. Ellie the information was wrong. Dayton couldn't imagine an entire group of people being that damn crazy to fire machine guns at people while they were sleeping.

He knew about the Bull Moose Special. It consisted of a locomotive, a day coach, and a baggage car. The coal barons had been using it to transport scab workers up to the Paint Creek and Cabin Creek mines. The miners had staged more than a few sniper attacks on the train, as well as sabotaging the tracks. Hell, even the women attacked those scab bastards. They tried anything and everything to stop the coal companies from bringing in replacement workers.

Dayton heard the Bull Moose Special coming up the tracks as he came around the mountain. He could see the tent colony, quiet under the crescent moon. It was late, and everybody was sleeping, with the exception of a few watchmen scattered around the narrow valley.

Dayton watched in horror as all the lights on the train went dark. Then the train slowed slightly, blasted its whistle twice, and opened fire. The sleeping strikers and their families awoke to bullets ripping through their tents. They screamed and ran for cover.

Cesco Estepp lived in one of the few houses in Holly Grove. Dayton could see him in the front of his house, running toward the back. He yelled for his wife to get their little boy and get to the cellar. Dayton watched as hundreds of rounds of ammo were shot at the house, one hitting Cesco in the face. Dayton sat on his horse, horrified at what he had witnessed.

After they shot the house and Cesco lay dead in the yard, Baldwin-Felts continued firing the machine guns at tents and anything within striking distance from the train. People ran in every direction, women and kids screaming. Dayton stayed put for fear of getting shot by either the men on the train or the coal miners shooting back at the train.

Jolene and Deacon woke to the sounds of gunfire. They threw the blankets off, jumped out of their small bed, and grabbed their weapons. They found everyone in their section already outside.

"Deacon, what the hell's goin' on down there?" asked one of the men.

"I ain't sure. Sounds like a machine gun. Get your guns. We need to go down there," Deacon said.

Deacon and thirteen others slipped through the tents to get a better look. The Bull Moose Special faded in the distance.

"Deacon!" Dayton cried. "I tried to get here sooner." He jumped off his horse. "Ms. Ellie sent me to warn you'ns, but I got here just as they opened fire. Those bastards rigged machine guns on the front of the Bull Moose Special. They turned off the lights so you'ns wouldn't see 'em. Then they opened fire right into those tents and houses by the tracks."

"They plan to come back?"

"I don't know. Looks like that train was full speed ahead gettin' outa here. I think Cesco got shot in the face, Deacon."

Deacon and the men ran to the Estepp house. Cesco lay in his yard, his face blown off. Deacon sent one of the younger boys back up the hill to get Jolene to tend to those who were hurt.

Hours later the first hints of daylight streaked the sky, and a gentle snow fell on the mountains. Exhausted, Deacon and Jolene climbed back up the hill to their tent.

"I'll get some water so we can wash up," Deacon said. "You got blood all over your hands and face."

He returned with a bucket from the creek. Jolene plunged her hands into the icy water. She splashed it onto her face. Deacon took a rag and gently washed her cheeks. Tears stung her eyes. Deacon pulled her into his arms and held her.

"Deacon, I don't know how much more I can take. They murdered that man. He was defenseless. What's Maude gonna do? She's pregnant and has a two-year-old! It's pure evil, Deacon. What they're doin' to us is pure evil. It's a thousand wonders more people weren't killed."

"Glasscock's been bought and paid for. Hopefully when the new governor takes office he'll put an end to this."

"We can only hope." Jolene rested her head on Deacon's chest.

64.

9 February 1913 (The Bullpen)

The ambush on the guard shack was scheduled for 2:00 a.m. Deacon led his men—the Dirty Eleven—over the mountain. Deacon wasn't sure where the moniker came from, and he chuckled every time he thought of it. People in the camp had started attributing the more violent acts carried out against Baldwin-Felts to the Dirty Eleven.

No one knew exactly who they were or even if there were eleven of them. Truth was, it was usually eleven, sometimes more, sometimes less. Before Jake was arrested and imprisoned, most of the time it was just Deacon and Jake.

Like a cat, Deacon felt his way through the darkness over trees, streams, and rocks. He knew these mountains like the back of his hand. His crew had stopped on the way up and retrieved guns and ammo the Italians from over in Boomer had hidden in a hollowed-out tree trunk. Deacon and his men would be joined by four dozen more men at the rendezvous point. From there they would make their descent into enemy territory.

The Baldwin-Felts men were patrolling the main roads and entrances to every holler. Those bastards weren't familiar with the mountains like Deacon and his crew. The miners had grown up in these hollers and played and hunted and walked these mountains ever since they could stand on their own two feet. They knew where every tree, every rock, every stream was situated, and they could maneuver the terrain in the pitch of night and never be detected by man or animal.

The plan was to rush the guard shack and release the men held prisoner in The Bullpen. It was little more than a torture chamber where they punished every striking miner they could capture. The ground was mostly mud, rotten food, and human excrement. Once captured, the miners were often chained to the wall or had their feet chained together so they couldn't escape.

Those who had been released had horrific tales. They were starved, beaten, kicked, and whipped—anything that could be done to them short of killing them. What food they did get was nothing more than slop not fit for a hog.

Deacon and the miners with him planned to release the prisoners in The Bullpen and burn everything in sight. If they had to kill or injure the guards, so be it. Deacon wasn't a vengeful man, but what those bastards had done at Holly Grove with the Bull Moose Special was unforgivable.

The attack at Holly Grove and the death of Cesco Estepp had to be avenged. It was out-and-out murder. Rumor was that after Cesco's burial Maude would take her babies and leave. She would go live with family someplace far away from Holly Grove. Deacon wanted nothing more than to take Jolene and run as far away from this mess as he could. But that wouldn't happen until this war was over.

The coal operators and Baldwin-Felts needed to understand who they were dealing with, and the miners wouldn't lay down their guns or walk away from this fight.

Baldwin-Felts was in the fight for money, motivated by greed. The miners were in the fight for their lives. Surrendering meant certain death—a slow, painful death of body and soul. No, they would *not* give up. They would *not* give in. The miners would fight until Baldwin-Felts and the coal barons either killed them or accepted their terms.

Deacon led his men down the slope of the mountain. He stationed a dozen men—his best shots—as snipers. He instructed them to shoot the guards in the tower on his signal. The others would attack the guard shack after the snipers opened fire.

Deacon sent two of his men closer to assess the situation. Within twenty minutes they returned with their report—four outside the gate, with more guards inside the fence and in the tower. They couldn't determine how many were inside. Three men at the entrance to the holler kept people from entering or exiting.

Baldwin-Felts had kids guarding the gate, boys who were part of the militia, most of them seventeen and eighteen years old. They gathered around the fire, smoking and sharing stories about the young girls in the camp—the ones who flirted with them—laughing about the ones who made themselves available for sex and the ones they wouldn't touch. They joked and made bets on who would get laid next.

They were relaxed, their guns casually tossed over their shoulders or leaning against the fence. Deacon smiled. The outside guards would be a piece of cake. It was what awaited them inside that gave Deacon pause.

Deacon directed eight of his men to handle the guards on the outside. The others would wait and storm the gate when they were out of the way.

With guns drawn, the eight men quietly approached the gate. A couple of the kids put up a fight. A rifle butt to the head or a fist to the nose subdued them. The miners dragged the young guards off into the bushes and tied them up.

Deacon and his team approached the gate. Five feet from the guard shack they were met with a spray of bullets—from inside and outside. Deacon wasn't sure where the other bullets were coming from. They had been ambushed. His men retreated and fought back for as long as they could. A bullet hit one of Deacon's men in the shoulder, and he stumbled off into the woods. Another was hit in the chest. He fell at Deacon's feet. He picked up the man and pulled him back into the trees, away from the line of fire. As Deacon turned to go back to the fight, something hard and heavy crashed into the back of his skull. The world went black, and the ground rushed up to meet his face.

Jolene looked at her pocket watch for the tenth time. Deacon and his crew should have returned hours ago. She knew these things didn't always go as planned and sometimes they had to take a different path home, which often took longer. A three-hour delay was a bit longer than usual. She would wait another fifteen minutes before she alerted the others. Until then she would tend to the fire outside her tent.

She placed more logs on the fire and warmed her hands near the growing flames. They had been living in this tent for nine months. Some days she wanted to run away—go to Charleston and stay with Ellie at the Ruffner Hotel, get a hot bath, eat good food, drink whiskey in the middle of the afternoon. Hell, she would probably spend her evenings in the tavern, playing music with Ellie and dancing. Running away was a fantasy in which she indulged at her lowest points—when she was exceptionally cold and hungry, like today. She wasn't running anywhere. She was hell bent on fighting this battle until its cold, bitter end.

Footsteps running up the path pulled her from her thoughts.

"Ms. Jolene, we's got word from Deacon and his crew," Boyd said. "You need to come quick to the cave."

Jolene ran to the cave, with Boyd close behind. She arrived to find seven of Deacon's crew and a few other men from the camp gathered.

"Where's Deacon? What happened?"

Jeremy Smith spoke up. "Ms. Jolene, they had the Bullpen guarded by a bunch a kids. They's warmin' by the fire and talkin', like kids do. We made sure they's nobody else 'round, and we charged at the entrance. Just as we got to the gate, those damn Baldwin-Felts men came ridin' up. They must'a been 'bout twenty of 'em. They saw us, a'fore we saw them, and they fired at us a'fore we knew they's even there. I think we's ambushed. It was almost like they knew we's comin'. They killed Donny Watts, right there. Put a bullet right in his heart."

"And Deacon?"

"They took Deacon, Ms. Jolene. He got captured, and they dragged him and three others into The Bullpen."

"Oh, dear Lord, no." Boyd ran to her side and guided her to a rock to sit down.

Deacon heard someone calling his name, as though they were calling to him from a dark cave. He struggled to stay awake. He couldn't remember where he was, thinking perhaps he was in the mine. He shook off the desire to pass out again. Once his eyes adjusted to the darkness, he quickly realized his fate. His head was pounding, and every move of his body sent a bolt of pain up his spine. He put his hand on the back of his head. It was wet with blood. He needed to get up and try to get out of there before the guards saw him. He attempted to stand but only made it to his hands and knees. The chains on his wrists and ankles tugged him back to the ground. Two others were chained next to him. "Jimbo? Is that you?"

"Yeah, it's me. They got four of us. You, me, JT, and Fred."

"How long we been here?" Deacon asked.

"A few hours. They killed Donny. Shot him."

"Damn. How? Where'd they come from? I can't remember nothin' after draggin' Roy outa there," Deacon whispered into the darkness.

"Those bastards came ridin' in and opened fire from the far end of the wall. I think they knew we's a-comin', Deacon. We's ambushed, sure as shit."

Deacon wondered if it had been Crowbar who had turned on them and told those bastards what they had planned. Jake had stopped trusting Crowbar when Mother Jones showed up. Deacon had never really cared for him to begin with.

Half a dozen guards gathered around a fire on the other side of The Bullpen next to the guard shack. Others roughed up one of the men. "Who they beatin' on over there?" Deacon asked.

"J.T. They took him right a'fore you came to. Said they's gonna teach us a lesson and start with the smallest one. They're gonna work their way up to the biggest—so I reckon' you're goin' last, big guy."

"Damn savages. We gotta figure a way outa here."

"You know as well as I do, they ain't no way out. We gotta live long enough for those bastards to get tired of us and throw us out."

Deacon rested his aching head against the wall and waited his turn.

Jolene pulled herself together. She had never been a weak woman, and she certainly wouldn't start now. Her precious Deacon was chained up in The Bullpen, and she was going to have to come up with a plan to get him out of there. Boyd brought her a tin of cold water. She sipped some of it and poured the rest into her hands and splashed it on her face. She needed her wits about her. She spent the rest of the night with the men plotting how to free Deacon and his crew from The Bullpen.

One by one, they came for Deacon's companions. He could hear the guards' fists hitting bones and flesh, noses being broken. While being beaten, the miners called the guards bastards, fuckers, sons of bitches. Pretty much every name the miners could think of. Their bones shattered, but not their spirits.

Two of the guards brought Jimbo back and chained him up once again. Deacon whispered a prayer: "Dear Lord, let this cup pass. Not my will, but thine be done." They unchained him and dragged him to the other side of The Bullpen, to the fire.

"All right, you filthy son of a bitch. Did you really think you could walk in here and do as you please? You're some kinda special stupid, ain't ya? I hear you're the ringleader of this fine band of outlaws." The guard carried a leather whip, snapping it on the ground as he circled.

"Appears to me you think you're above the law. Above our rules. We can't have your kind defyin' the order we're tryin' to keep around here. Those mines, that coal, it *all* belongs to the coal operators—not you. Ya see, Deacon Bales—oh, yeah, we know who you are—the problem is you and your kind are too stupid to win this war. You ain't got what it takes." The guard continued to circle him.

Never breaking eye contact with him, Deacon stood straight with his hands tied behind his back. "Fuck you. Without us, those bastards can't mine no coal."

He barely uttered the last syllable when the whip came tearing across his chest, through his clothes, into his cold flesh. One, two, three, four... Deacon lost count of the lashes. He stumbled but remained standing.

"You think you're pretty tough don't ya, big guy? Well, we gotta few things that'll take care of that, you filthy pig."

Another guard came over and punched Deacon in the gut. He stumbled forward, and the guard followed with an upper cut to the chin. Deacon's head jerked. He staggered but remained standing. The guard rammed him in the chest with this shoulder. Deacon staggered again and fell backward, his left wrist snapping upon impact. He refused to cry out. They were determined to subdue him. He braced himself for the beating of a lifetime.

The third guard came over and kicked Deacon in the ribs. The other guards cheered him. Deacon rolled over onto his side.

The first guard squatted down beside Deacon, his whip in his hands. "Ya still think you're a tough guy? You snivelin' little coward."

Against his better judgment, Deacon rolled over and spit in the guard's face. "Fuck... you."

The guard wiped the spit from his face and stood up. He kicked Deacon in the groin. "Chain him up," he said to the other gaurds before walking away.

They dragged Deacon by his feet back to the wall. They chained his hands and ankles as the sun's light struggled to break through the cloudy morning sky.

65.

10 February 1913

Jolene spent most of the night strategizing with the men about how to get Deacon and the other men out of The Bullpen. They ran through every possible scenario for a quick extraction. Jolene knew there were a few of the men who didn't think she had any business in the discussion. She didn't care. This was her husband, and she would do whatever it took to get him out of that hellhole.

"Well, I figure they'll be ready for us now," she said. "If they think we're brave enough or stupid enough to try to penetrate The Bullpen once, they'll be waitin' for us to try it again. They know who Deacon is, and they'll know we won't let one of our leaders stay in that hell hole."

"We need more men this time," one of the men said.

"No. We can't risk it. I'm sure they've put snipers all over that place now. They'll ambush us for the hell of it." Jolene sipped her coffee. "I've gotta better idea. You'ns might not like it, but I think it's the only option we have. Me and the wives and mothers of the men in there will go over. We'll do it in the bright light of day and plead for their release. We'll go ever' day, ten times a day, if we have to. We'll plead, we'll bitch, we'll nag till they get sick of lookin' at us."

The men all replied to her outlandish plan in unison. "No!"

"Now, hear me out," she said. "I know those bastards'll shoot anythang that moves, and they ain't got no qualms 'bout killin' a woman. But they won't shoot us with us lookin' at 'em. Besides, do any of you have a better plan?"

Around noon, Deacon heard the clanging of pots and pans and the chants of women. "Let our men go. Let our men go. Let our men go . . ."

The guards fired their rifles into the air, and the women stopped chanting. "What do you crazy-ass women think you're a'doin'?" called a guard outside the gate.

"We're here to get our men outa that Bullpen!"

Jolene?

Deacon wanted more than anything to call out to her but feared he would put her in danger if they knew she was his wife. He remained silent.

"You women have any idea what kinda danger you're in by bein' here? Now, we don't want to hurt no women, so you's best be movin' on back to your tents."

"We want you to release our men. You ain't got no right to keep 'em in there like prisoners. You ain't the law. Let 'em go."

"Now, as far's I can see, they's trespassin' on private property. This here property belongs to the coal operators, and they got caught trying to break in."

"The road I'm standin' on belongs to the state of West Virginia. Not the coal operators. And you took those men from the road. Now, turn 'em loose."

The guard spit on the ground and rested his rifle up against his shoulder. "Little lady, you sure got some guts, I'll give ya that much. Now go on back to your tent and get the hell outa here."

Deacon smiled. Damn straight she's got guts. Spunkiest little thing he ever encountered. That was his Jolene. She sure was something else.

Jolene stood her ground and resumed banging her pot with her spoon. The other ladies joined her in the chant. "Let our men go. Let our men go. Let our men go . . ." Jolene and more than two hundred women from the tent colony at Holly Grove marched back and forth in front of The Bullpen gate for two hours. Then they returned to camp.

Jolene wearily climbed the hill. She was bone tired and needed to sleep. Boyd was waiting on her with a fire blazing in front of her tent.

"You need to get some rest, Boyd."

"Ms. Jolene, I got some news. The governor declared martial law for a third time today. The militia showed up while's you down at The Bullpen."

"Damn, is that the only thing he knows how to do—declare martial law when things don't go his way? Anythang else? Any word from Mother Jones?"

"Nothin' nobody told me."

"Let's get some sleep and tackle this bear tomorrow. Thanks for the fire, Boyd."

Jolene crawled under the blankets and fell into a fitful sleep.

The next day at the same time, six hundred women joined her in the march on The Bullpen. The next day over a thousand women joined her. Their pots and pans making a mind-numbing noise.

On the third day of Deacon's capture, Jolene approached her tent to find Boyd again waiting on her with a fire. "Ms. Jolene. I got some bad news. They's arrested Mother Jones in Charleston. They's gonna court martial her. Word is they's gonna send her to Pratt and keep her holed up there so she can't do nothin' and nobody can get to her."

"What on earth did they charge her with?"

"Riotin' was one thing. Said she tried to blow up the C&O railroad. Attempted murder. Bunch a stuff."

"Damn. They're doin' ever'thang they can get away with a'fore Governor Hatfield takes office." Jolene plopped down on a log by the fire. She put her head in her hands. "What do we do now?" she asked to no one in particular.

The next day, Jolene continued her march on The Bullpen. She led the same march for the next fourteen days. Each day they added to their army. By the time the guards relented, Jolene's gang of women numbered over fifteen hundred. The noise of them banging on their pots and pans and chanting rang out through the mountains and became unbearable for the guards and nearly everyone up and down the creek.

On the night of the sixteenth day of Deacon's capture, Jolene was on her way to The Bullpen gate in a cold rain to get her man and bring him home.

66.

<u>26 February 1913</u>

The cold rain fell on Deacon's face and soaked his thin blanket. He worried about Jolene. He wondered if he had really heard her and the women outside the walls demanding they let the men go . . . or if it had been a dream. He knew she was fighting a hard fight to get him out of this hell. He smiled a frail smile as thoughts of her danced through his mind. She was strong, smart, determined, devoted. A great lover. His lover. His love. Yes, Jolene would get him out of this damn place. He drifted off to sleep with Jolene dancing through his dreams again.

He awoke hours later. It was darker and colder. He'd never been so cold. His body shivered and his teeth chattered so hard he thought his jaw would crack. Deacon never thought he would kill another person for food, but the hunger gnawed at his body and mind so deeply he was certain he would kill just about anyone for a mere piece of bread. He hadn't had water in days, and his tongue burned inside his mouth.

He started coughing and couldn't stop. He coughed into his worn, dirty handkerchief. He spit blood onto the wet ground. He figured that couldn't be good. The guards had made a weak fire for them, and he crawled over to it and tried to thaw his frozen hands and feet. He sat by the fire until it was nothing more than smoldering embers. As he drifted off to sleep again he could hear Jolene calling his name. He smiled, more inwardly than out. He loved the sound of her voice above the pouring rain.

A guard kicked him in the shin. "Wake up, Bales. You're leavin'. Get up."

Deacon jolted awake and looked up into the guard's dark face. "Jolene? Jolene's here to get me?"

"Get up. Go!" The guard jerked Deacon and dragged him toward the gate. He shoved him into Jolene's outstretched arms.

"Deacon? Oh, my Lord. Deacon? Are you all right? What've those bastards done to you? Oh, my sweet Deacon." Jolene cradled him in her arms. Two men from the camp had come with her. They carried Deacon and placed him in the back of the wagon. Jolene crawled in beside him and covered them both with a blanket.

Boyd had built a fire outside their tent, and the ladies had prepared a broth of the few things they could scrounge up. They helped Jolene get Deacon inside and brought in a pot of hot water for her to clean him. He had weeks of blood, dirt, grime, and mud caked in his hair and beard and on his skin.

One of the men held him while Jolene stripped him of his wet, dirty clothes.

Deacon felt like a burning flame when Jolene took his clothes off. Hell, they were rags at that point. It took all she had not to react when she saw the bruises and gashes on his body. She fought back the tears and the rage. She started humming to keep the tears under control.

His back had suffered the worst of it. He had gashes from beatings, and bruises and broken bones from kicks. His wounds weren't healing, and his cough was the worst she had ever heard. His lungs rattled with each breath. She prayed it wasn't pneumonia.

She washed his wounds and gently traced the gashes on his back with her fingers, praying that God would use her loving touch to heal this man she loved.

Deacon couldn't keep his eyes open. It was all going to be all right now. He was finally with Jolene, and she would get him back on his feet. As long as he was with her, he was home. He could sleep now. He closed his eyes and drifted off to sleep with Jolene humming a song as she dressed him.

At dawn he woke up soaking wet and cold. Jolene was there changing his clothes again, drying his frail body. She smiled at him and kissed his lips. That woman could make a dying man bounce back to life. He offered her a weak smile and tried to take her hand. Instead, she found his.

"Looks like your fever broke. Means you're healin'. Now, don't get all crazy and think you're gonna get up. You stay right there."

Deacon managed a bit stronger smile and winked at her. It was the best he could do.

The doctor came and confirmed her diagnosis. Pneumonia. They needed to clear his lungs, but it would be a rough road. And they still had a few weeks of winter on the horizon. She would try to help him sit up later in the day if he had the strength.

She feared his wounds would only get worse. She had herbs and a poultice to make for those, but her herbs were getting low.

(Charleston)

Dottie slipped into Ellie's room. "Ms. Ellie, you have a messenger downstairs. Says he has somethin' for you and he wouldn't let me bring it to ye. Says ye gotta come and get it yerself."

"Thank you, Dottie. Please tell him I'll be down directly."

Ellie wasn't expecting the messenger today, and he never came to the hotel. It must be something urgent or something really bad had happened. She quickly dressed and tried not to run down the steps. The last thing she needed was for John to hear about her messenger.

Maintaining her composure, she made it to the hotel lobby and looked around. A young boy stood nervously by the door. She walked over to him with an air of superiority that belied the terror in her heart. They stepped outside and walked around the block. He handed her a note from Jolene.

She read the note and maintained her calm demeanor. "What happened? How did he get so sick and wounded?"

"'Em bastards grabbed him a few weeks ago when he's on a raid." The boy looked around to see if anyone was listening. "They threw him and a few others in The Bullpen. Beat 'em and purdy much left 'em to die. Those assholes got a world a hurt comin' to 'em."

"And Jolene? How's Jolene?"

"'Good as can be 'spected I s'pose. She says you need to send ever'thang on 'at thar list. Today."

"I can't get this stuff—not today, anyway." Ellie didn't have access to a doctor—but she did have Eloise. "But, I may know someone who can. I'll meet you in the park down by the river by the boats in one hour." She grabbed the boy's shoulders and turned him to her. "Don't ever come back here. It's too dangerous. I feel like they're all watchin' every damn thing I do."

Ellie wanted to run up the stairs, but she remained calm and returned to her room. She copied the list and bundled it up with ten dollars in a silk handkerchief. She dropped the handkerchief in her satchel. The ladies were downstairs having tea and gossiping—about her, no doubt. She couldn't risk going to the lobby and out the front door. She waited thirty minutes and slipped down the back stairs and into the alley. She pulled her cloak around her and braced herself against the cold wind. She slipped through the back streets and alleys to make sure she wasn't followed. She arrived at the park and found the boy waiting for her.

"Here." She handed him the silk handkerchief with the list and ten dollars. "Take this to 42 Pickney Street." She gave him directions. "Speak to Ms. Eloise—and her only, nobody else. Understand?" She waited for the boy to nod. "Give her the handkerchief. It's got the list and money and a note. If she needs more money, she needs to send me a message, and I'll take the extra money to her myself. Once she gives you the stuff, go on back to Jolene. Tell her I kept a copy of the list and I'll send more as soon as I can."

The boy turned to leave.

"Tell Jolene I love her, and I'll be here waitin' for her."

The boy nodded and ran toward Pickney Street.

67.

<u>8 March 1913 (Holly Grove)</u>

Along with the needed herbs, Eloise had also sent a special tea for Deacon to drink. Jolene brewed and crushed and blended to create what she hoped was a concoction that would heal Deacon's lungs. She made him sit up for a few hours every day and even got him walking a bit. Only a few steps each afternoon—it was better than nothing.

His body was so weak and his cough so harsh it rattled down in his ribs. The doctor came every few days. He had nothing to offer other than what Jolene was already doing.

The ladies in the tent colony brought broth and water, and the men kept the fire going. Sleep eluded them both—Deacon with coughing and fevers and Jolene with tending to him.

The days and nights melted into one, and Jolene's concern grew by the minute. Deacon's wounds were not healing, and the pneumonia didn't seem to be clearing.

Ellie sent another parcel.

My dearest sister,

I am heartbroken to hear of your husband's declining health.

I have sent more herbs and whiskey, as well as bandages, wraps, and suture materials. I beg you to please bring him here, to Charleston. I have a doctor who can care for him, and you can stay by his side. I know it is a bit of a jaunt, I'm hoping the weather will hold out long enough for you to make the journey.

I will come to you if you won't come to me. Please send word on your decision.

Love,

Ellie's offer of a doctor was the only hope Deacon had of surviving. He needed to be in a warm, dry house—in a real bed, with a real doctor. At first, leaving the camp felt like surrendering and giving up. She couldn't leave the others. Deacon would not want that. She also didn't fully trust Ellie's intentions and didn't want to be beholden to her for anything. She believed the price Ellie would extract for her help would be more than she could ever repay. But Jolene would do whatever it took to save Deacon. No price was too high. His life was far more important than any strike. She responded to Ellie's letter.

My sweet sister,

Given the dire situation, I will accept your offer. I'm making arrangements now for the journey. Please send instructions.

Love,

68.

9 March 1913 (Holly Grove)

Jolene gave the letter to the messenger and told him to return to Ellie at the first light of day. She called on a few of the men in the camp to plan for safe passage to Charleston for her and Deacon the next night. They would be safer traveling after dark. Taking the train was too risky.

She hated to leave the battlefield, but she knew she must in order to save Deacon. The new governor had been to Ms. Carney's Boarding House in Pratt to visit Mother Jones and found her dying with pneumonia. He had her taken to the hospital in Charleston right away. Mother Jones was being cared for by qualified physicians, so why shouldn't Deacon receive the same care? Jolene spent the next few hours packing the few things they would need for the trip. She had pretty much given up on God delivering them from this hell on earth. She prayed anyway to a God who had been silent for months.

The night was long, and Deacon's fever spiked again. By early morning when the doctor came around and took

Deacon's temperature, it was at 104. Jolene had Boyd bring water from the spring.

"Bring buckets of it and make sure you get as much ice in it as you can."

"Yes, ma'am." Boyd said. He had been by Jolene's side since Deacon returned from The Bullpen. He returned twenty minutes later with four buckets of ice-cold water.

"Boyd, come here. I want to talk to you."

Boyd entered Jolene's tent and sat on the floor. "Yes, ma'am?"

"Boyd, I'm takin' Deacon to Charleston tonight to see a doctor. A real physician. I can't do nothin' more for him here. If I don't get him there right away, he may die." She took Boyd by the shoulders to face her. "I want you to stay strong and take care of your sisters and brother. We got a long battle to keep fightin' here. As soon as Deacon's able, we'll be back. You hear?"

"Yes, ma'am." He looked at the ground and then back up into Jolene's face with tears in his eyes. "Ms. Jolene, you think Deacon may die?"

Jolene cupped the boy's young face. "Not if I have anythang to say 'bout it. He's a tough old coot, and it's gonna take more than this to kill that man."

Boyd left, and Jolene sat with Deacon, applying the icy water to his face and neck, hoping against hope that his fever would break.

"Baby, this ain't the way it's s'posed to end. You promised to take me to the Carolinas when this is all over. So you need to come out of that fever and get better. We's goin' to a real doctor in Charleston tonight."

The fever remained steady for the next few hours. Deacon was in and out of hallucinations as he tossed and turned on the makeshift bed. Jolene sat by his side and rested her head on his chest, listening to his faint heartbeat. The rattle in his lungs grew louder.

"Jolene? Wanda Jolene? Where are you?" Deacon muttered between labored breaths.

Startled, Jolene sat up and placed her hand on Deacon's forehead. "I'm right here, Deacon. I'm here." She leaned over and kissed his dry, cracked lips.

He tried to speak, each breath a struggle. A coughing fit shook his entire body. He sounded like he was drowning in his phlegm. He turned his head towards her and tried to touch her face. "Jolene? You... you're the only thing." He took a shallow breath. "The only thing that's ever mattered. I'm... I'm so sorry... to leave you." His coughing became harsher. "I... I love you, Jolene. I love you, woman." With that, Deacon took his last rattled breath.

"Deacon? Deacon! Wake up! *Deacon?*" Jolene shook him.

She refused to believe he was dead. He would never die and leave her here in this hell. Alone. She held him close and listened for his heartbeat. The heart that had been beating for her since they first laid eyes on each other. This heart she had forsaken everything for was surely still beating. Those strong arms would hold her again. He would make all of this right again. He had to. She couldn't imagine a life without him.

Silence. No beating heart. No breath. Just the man she loved more than life itself, dead in her arms. She was fairly certain she screamed, but the world had gone silent and dark with Deacon's last breath. She couldn't hear or see anything. She only felt his still, lifeless body against her.

"Nooo...noooo...you can't leave me. Not like this. Please, Deacon, don't leave me. I can't live this life without you." She held his broken body with all her strength, as though she could keep him from slipping from this damnable life into the next glorious one—without her.

The women arrived at the tent to find Jolene sobbing, still holding Deacon. "No. *Leave us alone*! Jolene kept her eyes closed, rocking Deacon back and forth on the cot.

A light snow fell across the tent colony, and the temperature dropped. Jolene stayed in the same spot holding Deacon for hours. As the sun climbed up the mountains, the women convinced her to release him. They helped her clean him up and change his clothes into his Sunday best. They straightened the tent and tended to Jolene.

Three days later they buried Deacon on top of the hill at Holly Grove. For three more days Jolene stayed in their tent and cried. And screamed. And cried more.

It snowed for the entire six days, blanketing the mountains in more than a foot of snow.

Ellie had been waiting for days for Jolene and Deacon to arrive in Charleston. Eloise had promised to send a messenger as soon as they arrived at Pickney Street.

Ellie assumed it was the snow keeping them away. The roads between Charleston and Paint Creek were mountainous and could be treacherous in the snow. Under normal conditions they would have taken the train, but Deacon and Jolene had bounties on their heads. Jolene was as instrumental in organizing the strike as Deacon, and they both had a close relationship with Mother Jones.

After six days of constant snowfall, Ellie awoke to a crystal blue sky. Certainly, Jolene and Deacon would be able to start their journey tomorrow. It was already warmer, and the snow would start melting.

Another six days, and Ellie was still waiting for Jolene. Hoping Eloise had simply not had a messenger to spare, she walked over to 42 Pickney Street to confirm her worst fears.

"Ellie, I assume they're stuck at Holly Grove, due to the snow. Let's not panic yet. I heard the roads were in real bad shape a few days ago, but the snow's meltin'." Eloise took Ellie's hand and led her to the parlor where they had first met.

She poured them tea. "Their room's all ready, and I'm stocked on everythin' I'll need to mend Deacon back to health."

"I'm so worried, Eloise. I've not gone this long without hearin' from anybody. Things up there've been crazy. Those thugs would shoot their own grandmother if she crossed 'em."

Ellie stepped outside to return to the hotel. As she rounded the corner, someone called her name.

"Ms. Ellie?" Dayton walked towards her, his hat in his hands. "I just came from Holly Grove," Dayton said.

"Where is she? Where's my sister?"

"She's a'right. It's Deacon. He . . . he didn't make it, Ms. Ellie. He died a few hours a'fore they's s'posed to leave to come here."

"No! Oh, my God. No." Ellie's knees felt weak and Dayton reached out to steady her. "And Jolene? Where's she?"

"She's takin' it real hard, as you can 'spect. She ain't doin' no good, Ms. Ellie. No good a'tall. She should be here in a few days. The snow's kept the roads impossible to travel on. I had to come by horseback today. They ain't no wagon gettin' over those roads."

"Oh, sweet Jesus. She must be completely broken." Despair circled over Ellie like the buzzards that dark day in the river. She should have been there for Jolene. She had let her down, once again. But what was she supposed to do? She was here on this side of the battlefield. She had been trying to get Jolene to come to Charleston for months. No, there was nothing she could have done.

The weight of the hell they had all been through the past year pressed on her heart. With Dayton trying to comfort her, Ellie stood on the corner of Pickney Street and sobbed—for Jolene, for Deacon, for Polly and Jake. For little Deannie. She hadn't been a fan of Deacon and had done everything she could to talk Jolene out of marrying him. She knew now Jolene and Deacon were destined to be together. Jolene had loved that man with every ounce of her being. A twinge of guilt slipped around Ellie's throat as she thought of how carelessly she had tossed Sammy away. Ellie returned to Eloise's and gave her the bad news, telling her to expect Jolene in a few days.

Ellie would need to send a letter to Polly telling her of Deacon's passing. She walked around the city for another hour or so before returning to the hotel. By the time she returned to her room, her stockings were soaked through, and her feet and hands were numb.

She removed her wet clothes and warmed herself by the fire. She unpinned her hair and shook it out. It fell around her shoulders and face. John came through the door as she was about slip into dry clothes.

"Well, well, well. What have we here? A naked lady?" He walked over, took the dry dress from her hands, and tossed it onto the chair. He wrapped his hand in her long black hair. "And why are you half naked here in front of the fireplace in the middle of the day, my sweet?"

"It was so sunny and a bit warmer earlier in the day, so I took a walk. Somewhere along the way, the sun disappeared behind the clouds and the wind picked up. By the time I got back, my stockings were soaked, and my feet and hands were numb. I thought a nice hot fire and a pot of hot tea would warm me up. Dottie's bringin' up a hot pot shortly, so don't go gettin' too frisky just yet."

He looked down at her, her hair still wrapped around his hand. "Where'd ya walk to?"

"The Knowing" grabbed Ellie, and she knew he was on to her. She could read him well. She saw through to his black heart. This was an interrogation; he wanted to catch her in a lie. It was doubtful he knew exactly what she was up to, but he was suspicious. She figured she should at least put some truth into her story in case she had been seen over on Pickney. "First down by the river and then back around and somehow I ended up over on the east side of town. It's not the best place. I quickly realized my mistake and hurried to get back here."

"East side, huh? Not a place a lady like you should be walkin' to." He released her hair and tossed her dress to her just before he sat down in the chair. He removed his hat and boots. "I'm glad you made it back here safely. Be careful walkin' around this city. It's safe right around here, but don't go too far out. You could get hurt. They's all kinds of strikers makin' threats against the coal operators, the Baldwin-Felts men, and their families. Even the new governor."

"What? Someone threatened Governor Hatfield? *Already*?" She stepped into her dress and buttoned it.

"They threatened to kidnap his daughter. It wasn't clear who made the threat. Probably that bitch Jones and her gang. He promptly got more guards around his family." John propped his feet up on the ottoman to warm them by the fire.

Ellie sat down at her dressing table and put on dry stockings. "That's horrible. That poor child. Have those people no limits?"

Dottie knocked. Ellie went to the door and took the tray from her. She didn't want her in the room for fear she would deliver a message from Eloise or Jolene.

She placed the tray on the small table by the fireplace. "Would you like some tea?"

"Not really. I *would* like you out of the dress again. Not sure why you bothered."

The tea sat untouched on the table. Ellie's dry dress and stockings lay in a pile in front of the fireplace.

69.

24 March 1913 (Moundsville, West Virginia State Penitentiary)

The prisoners had finally been able to shake off winter's bite and go outside the past few weeks. The snow had melted and left behind a giant mud puddle in the prison yard. Tom would take a little mud, as long as there was sunshine. He wasn't as bothered about being locked up as he was about the boredom. And the cold. The winters had been brutal. The state penitentiary was certainly no place to stay warm. At least he had Moose to share body heat.

He'd spent each day outside sitting on a bench, thinking about his garden and his animals. He hoped his brothers had taken care of it all. He could always start over.

He wondered if they would allow him to plant some vegetables here. He made it a point to ask the guards. He sat on the stone bench with his eyes closed and his upturned face soaking up the sun planning his new garden when he got out. To the other prisoners, he hoped he looked a thousand miles away, but he was listening to every word.

The week outside had allowed the men to talk more freely. The guards were enjoying the weather as much as the prisoners, not watching them as closely. Tom felt the tension mounting by the day. Each afternoon out in the yard, the talk was more aggressive, and the rage was building.

Late that night, Tom lay on his cot listening to the train at eleven-ten, the kid in the next cell whimpering before falling to sleep, the guards making their rounds, keys jangling... something was off. What was it? He had almost dozed off and might have missed it. It was definite. He replayed the sounds back in his head. They hadn't checked the doors. No metal against metal. Why? Tom was wide awake now. Listening.

There it was. Another sound. Voices. Footsteps? He sat up and tucked Moose in his pocket. Tom moved in the darkness and peered out his cell door. He couldn't see anything or hear anyone now. A deathly silence crawled through the cellblock.

Tom heard footsteps approaching. He stepped back pressing his spine into the cold cinderblock wall, never taking his eyes off the steel bars. Five prisoners rushed past Tom's cell toward the guard station. He heard yelling, a scuffle, punches, and a chair breaking over someone's head.

Tom peered out again. The entire block was awake with yelling. Over the clamor, Tom heard the jangle of the guards' keys, then the steel bars opening... one cell, then another, then another. Tom's cell was eighth from the guard station.

More prisoners ran toward the guard station, and an inmate stopped to unlock his cell. "Run, Chafin. Get the hell outa here. Go!"

Tom didn't wait to be told twice. With Moose safe in his pocket, he stepped out of his cell and headed toward the guard station. A few guards were handcuffed together and locked up in the first cell. Others were handcuffed to cell doors and many more either unconscious or dead on the floor. Guessing by the lack of cells being checked earlier in the night, Tom supposed they had a a guard who supplied them with guns and billy clubs. The prisoners had waited for the guards to come through the doors and ambushed them.

Tom kept walking.

He stepped through the other side of the guard station. Tom heard yelling, screaming, furniture breaking, and gun shots. The prisoners had staged a full-blown riot. He didn't want any part of the mayhem. Taking this opportunity to escape was a definite temptation, and it meant one of two things—being on the run for the rest of his life and looking over his shoulder at every turn or being captured and adding another ten years onto his sentence. Neither option sounded tasty.

He put his hand in his pocket. Moose was sleeping peacefully, oblivious to the situation. Tom stood back as more prisoners ran past him with no particular destination.

They were on the second floor of a three-story building. At the end of the corridor Tom found another set of cell doors. He stepped through them and out onto the guards' catwalk. The catwalk served as an observation deck that opened up to the community floor below, where the prisoners ate their meals and spent their free time in the winter. Tom peered over the edge. Everyone was scurrying down the stairs to get to the first floor to jump into the fray or find an unlocked door to the outside.

At the other end of the catwalk was another set of doors. Tom had come through those doors when he'd first arrived.

They led to the processing center and then down to the warden's office.

The prisoners yelled for the warden to come down and show his face. Tom considered the darkened section at the end of the catwalk. Was the warden there? He gazed at the maddening mob below him. They looked crazy enough to come up and drag the warden down there. They were out for blood.

Tom slid down the catwalk, keeping his back against the wall so he wouldn't be seen by the prisoners below. More prisoners charged through the cell doors, hellbent on joining the melee below. The catwalk housed small alcoves every twenty feet or so for the guards to step into to protect themselves in these types of events. Tom stepped into one until the footsteps of the prisoners faded away as they scurried down the steps.

He reached the doors leading to the processing center and the warden's office. A single naked lightbulb burned in the small area beyond the doors. Darkness and quiet waited beyond. Hugging the wall, Tom gingerly stepped through the doors, making his way into the processing center.

The chants for the warden from below grew louder and more determined. The ring leader fired a gun to quiet the crowd. "Any of you wanna leave, leave. Remember, those guards up in the tower *will* shoot your ass. There's the door to freedom and you are free to fly. The way I see it, if we get the warden down here, he's our ticket outa this place. They won't shoot us if we have a gun to his head on our way out."

The crowd cheered.

"Let's go up there and get that son-bitch," one of the men shouted. "That bastard coward ain't gonna show his face."

"Yeah! Let's go!" the others cheered.

Another yelled, "He's prob'ly up there surrounded by guards. I heard they had a machine gun they keep up there for riots."

The ringleader spoke again. "I doubt that. The tower guards have machine guns, but not the warden's personal guards. Way I see it, we need to charge up there and get the slimy bastard."

The crowd cheered. The ringleader stirred the crazed prisoners with more talk about the unfair treatment they had received. "Let's go get him!"

Tom hurried down the hall to the warden's office. When he reached the end of the hall, the warden's door was open. One prisoner held the warden's arms behind his back; another beat his face. Tom grabbed the puncher's arm as he reared back to plow his fist into the warden's face again. Tom pulled the prisoner's arm up and behind his back and rammed his face down onto the corner of the warden's oak desk. The other prisoner pushed the warden to the floor and came for Tom. Tom met the man with a punch to the throat, then another to the gut. He fell forward, and Tom raised his knee and planted it in the man's face.

"The guard," the warden said, pointing to a man tied to the chair behind Tom.

Tom untied the guard and took his handcuffs. "You got another pair of these?"

The warden pulled a pair of handcuffs from his inside jacket pocket. Tom handcuffed the two prisoners together—

opposite hands and opposite feet. They wouldn't be going anywhere anytime soon.

Tom helped the warden to his feet. "Those crazy asses are comin' for ye, and they ain't gonna stop till either you or them's dead. I figure we got just a few minutes a'fore them crazy bastards get up here."

"What's your name?" the warden asked.

"Chafin. Look, we ain't got time for formalities. We gotta get the hell out of here. Now!"

The warden stepped over to Tom. "Chafin is it? How can we trust you? Why would you help me?"

"I ain't gonna let an innocent man get killed by a bunch of lunatics. Now, you better make up your mind right now on whether you's gonna trust me or not. I think I just showed you, you can trust me." Tom nodded toward the two unconscious prisoners on the floor.

The raging prisoners stormed the catwalk.

"All right, then. What do you propose we do?"

"First, I'll need a gun. Second, is there another way outa here besides going back that way?" Tom pointed toward the approaching mob.

The guard reluctantly handed Tom a .45. "They's stairs down that way to the main door. They got men down there. They overpowered all the guards inside, 'cept for me . . . till they got up here."

"You gotta have a secret passage outa this damn place. A tunnel? Somethin?" Tom asked.

One of the prisoners on the floor stirred. Tom took the warden's handkerchief from his breast pocket and stuffed it into the man's mouth. He wadded up a sheet of paper from the desk and crammed it into the other's mouth.

"There's an old tunnel in the administrative office, behind an old bookcase. It's close to the main door. We can sneak around so the prisoners guarding the front door won't see us, but they more than likely will hear us moving the bookcase."

"I reckon we'll have to take our chances." Tom looked at the guard. "You lead the way, and I'll take the rear. Warden, stay close."

The mob entered the processing area, screaming for the warden.

The prison guard led Tom and the warden to the end of the dark corridor. The main entrance to the prison was to the left, and the administrative office was to the right. With only one weak bulb for light, they paused to assess the situation. The prisoners at the main entrance shot at the guards in the tower. Tom motioned for the warden and his guard to make a run for it. They took the right corridor and ran to the darkened end of the hallway.

The administrative office was locked. The warden fumbled with the keys. Tom took them and opened the door.

The guard made a move to turn on the light. Tom slapped his hand. "Don't do that! Do you want 'em to find us? Warden, which bookcase is the tunnel entrance?"

The warden tapped the side of the one close to the inside wall. "This one. It's heavy and pulls out like a door, from the right."

"I'll take the side, you two take the front and pull on three." Tom whispered.

The warden was right; it was a heavy son of a bitch. They only moved it three inches on the first try. The rioting prisoners had made it through the processing center, their voices clamoring from the warden's office. They had to hurry.

"One more time, with all ya got," Tom said.

This time they moved the book case at least a foot. It scraped across the stone floor. "Go!" Tom pushed the guard and the warden into the tunnel. The bookcase had a handle on the back of it, and Tom pulled it closed behind them. It proved a lot easier to close than to open.

A blackness engulfed the tunnel. "There should be lanterns hanging here somewhere," The warden whispered.

Tom struck a match and held it up to the wall. "There," he said. The guard removed the lantern from the hook, and Tom lit it.

They descended a flight of narrow stone steps to the ground. The lantern provided some light, but mostly they walked along in the dark, feeling the wall to navigate.

After ten minutes, the warden was out of breath. "We need to stop. I need to rest."

"How long is this tunnel and where's it come out?" Tom asked.

The warden used his shirt sleeve to wipe his balding brow. "About twenty minutes to get to the end if I remember correctly. It comes out a few hundred yards beyond the fence in a field."

"Is it out of the line of fire from the guard tower? In the black of night, they won't know it's you and'll shoot at anythang that moves."

"Yes, it is out of sight of everything. From there we can go get help." The warden placed his hand on Tom's shoulder. "I understand completely if you want to run when we get out of here. Truly, I do. I can't attest to what will happen to you, but if you want to run, we shall look the other way."

Tom was taken aback by the warden's statement. "Warden, I ain't got no intention of runnin'. I'm prepared to do my time. I won't live my life on the run. So I'm with you to the end of this. Right now, I wanna get you somewhere's safe."

"All right, then. Let's continue." The warden stood up.

The three of them crawled through a mostly dry tunnel until they reached the end, where it was wet and muddy. "Shit. I hope this thing ain't bolted shut from the other side," Tom said, reaching for a wooden door.

"The plan has always been to leave it open in the event of a riot. It may be stuck from not being used, but it shouldn't be blocked or locked," the warden said.

Tom placed his ear to the door. No sound. Tom and the guard pushed with all they had. It didn't budge. "Let's rest for a minute," Tom said.

Tom sat and felt something squirming in his pocket. Moose was awake. He took him out. "Hey, little fella. How ya doing?" Tom plucked a stale morsel of bread from his other pocket and fed Moose. The guard and the warden looked on in amazement.

"Warden, this is your finest inmate, Mr. Moose."

"What's he in for? Breaking and entering or stealing cheese?" the warden asked with a chuckle.

Tom slipped Moose back into his pocket, and he and the guard tried the door once more. It cracked a tiny bit. They pushed again, and again. A rush of fresh air filled the entrance to the tunnel.

"Looks like the rain washed the dirt and mud up against the door." Tom reached his hand through and shoveled as much as he could. He rested, and the guard took over. They moved the door a little bit more. The guard rested, and Tom moved to take his turn.

The warden stood and removed his jacket. "No. It's my turn." He shoveled twice as long as either of them. They moved the door a bit more. This continued for another twenty minutes.

Tom and the guard pushed on the door with all they had, and it gave way. The three of them made their way out of the tunnel. Tom looked back and could see the lights from the guard tower. The warden had been right, it was too far away for the guards to see them. The trio ran across an open field toward the road.

When they reached the far ditch, Tom took Moose from his pocket. "Hey, little fella. No reason you need to be locked up again. Go play in the field with the other mice. You've been a good cellmate." Tom sat Moose down and joined the warden and the guard. The three of them walked toward town.

70.

27 March 1913 (Lynn)

Jake and the boys returned from Matewan, and Jake placed the mail and the newspaper on the kitchen table. "They's some stuff in the newspaper you need to read, and you got a letter from Ellie."

Polly opened the letter first.

> *My Dearest Polly* —
>
> *It pains me to tell you that Deacon has passed. As you know, he had pneumonia. Jolene did all she could to save him, but in the end, it wasn't enough.*
>
> *I'm waiting on her to come to Charleston. She will leave Holly Grove as soon as the weather breaks. I will contact you when she arrives.*

Polly wiped her tears. "Jake, Deacon's passed. Those bastards killed him."

Jake sat heavily in the chair across from Polly. "Damn. Where's Jolene?"

"Ellie says she's goin' to Charleston. I don't know what she'll do after that. I'll need to go to her, Jake."

"Polly, I ain't sure that's a good idea. Those bastards know what you look like and that you're my wife. They's likely to do just 'bout anythang to any of us."

"I won't stay at the Ruffner. I'll stay with Jolene at Eloise's. Only for a few days."

"Well, they's somethin' else you need to see. Look at the front page of the paper."

Polly picked up the paper and stared in disbelief. She read the article. "A riot? Was Tom killed?"

"Don't know. It don't give no names. One of 'em helped the warden escape. If it was Tom, there's a possibility he could get pardoned. That was the gossip this mornin' at the feed store anyway."

"He could get out? What if he comes to take Deannie? What if he does it to spite Ellie?" Polly asked.

"Tom's a reasonable man, Polly. I doubt he's gonna walk in here and grab that baby girl up and run off with her. He'll do what's right for her. But we need to be prepared 'cause he may want her to know he's her father."

"Which means she'll know Ellie's her mama."

"You're Deannie's mama, Polly—not Ellie."

"This is all too much. This war keeps draggin' on. Deacon's dead, Jolene's life's been devastated, Tom may come take Deannie, God only knows what's gonna happen to Ellie. When'll life return to normal, Jake?"

"I don't know that it ever will."

Later that night when everyone was sleeping Polly sat at the kitchen table and wrote a letter to Ellie. If she needed to go to Charleston for Jolene, Ellie would let her know. She wanted to warn Ellie about the rumors swirling through Matewan about Tom as well. If there was a chance that Tom would come take Deannie, she needed to stay close to home. She sealed the envelope and addressed it, then opened her Bible. Her tears fell onto the page and she whispered a prayer. "Dear God, where are you? I'm grateful for all your many blessin's. Please don't let Tom come take Deannie away. That child means ever'thang to us."

71.

<u>9 April 1913 (Holly Grove)</u>

Boyd finished loading the wagon with the few worldly possessions Jolene had left and returned to the tent to get her. He'd informed Jolene two days prior that he was going with her to Charleston. Ever since his mother had died in the fall, he'd clung to Jolene.

His mama was dead, and his daddy had been court martialed by Governor Glasscock. The women in the camp had taken in his brother and sisters. They were being cared for and didn't really need him to look after them.

He entered the tent and packed up the last few items for Jolene. "Ms. Jolene, I've loaded the guns and extra ammo in the wagon." They had three pistols, two shotguns, and two rifles—an old .22 pump and a single-action Winchester sniper rifle.

"Boyd, you ain't gotta do this. You can stay right here with your sisters. I'll be fine. But if you wanna come with me, I'd be happy to have you." Jolene figured he needed her as much as she needed him.

"Ms. Jolene, I wanna be with you. They ain't nothin' left here for me."

"Well, then. Let's go," Jolene said.

Jolene stopped and looked around the tent. It was empty except for a few items. This is where her love had died and her life had ended. She would go to Ellie in Charleston. The battle was nearly over. Governor Hatfield was negotiating a deal between the strikers and the coal operators. They were all hoping the negotiations would put an end to this insanity. An end to the killing. Regardless, there was nothing left for her here. She would certainly not miss the death and disease. Staying on without Deacon was impossible. She and Deacon had fought this battle side-by-side. They were warriors together and lovers until the end. They fought a good fight, but Baldwin-Felts won. Those bastards took the only thing that mattered to her. The only love she had ever known.

Who knew where she would go from there? Her issues with Ellie were insignificant now, and her sister was the only thing she had left. Mother Jones was still in the hospital in Charleston. Jolene could stay close to her mentor and, she hoped, continue on with her.

She closed the flap on the tent and turned to see nearly everyone in the camp waiting to say goodbye. Tears rushed to her eyes, but she pushed them back down. She was done crying. She had cried for nearly three weeks. It took more than an hour for the goodbyes, hugs, and well-wishes. She would miss these people. She would miss the sense of community. She would *not* miss this war, this conflict into which they had been drawn by a handful of greedy bastards who thought the miners' lives and livelihood—their dignity—didn't matter.

Jolene climbed aboard the wagon with Boyd. Two of the men from the camp accompanied them on horseback. The snow had finally melted, and the roads were still wet and muddy, but clear.

The trip to Charleston was filled with memories. She and Deacon had made this trip after they got married. It was the first time she had ever been away from her family. She would have followed him to the pits of hell. Which, in many ways, she had. The past year had been pure hell for all of them.

The mountains were alive with all the delicacies of springtime. The scent of new beginnings and a fresh start floated on the air. She would never stop loving Deacon, and she would never get over the loss of his love. Life goes on, and she needed to pick herself up, put one foot in front of the other, and move on with her life—what was left of it.

Despite their issues in the past, Ellie was still her sister, and Jolene was looking forward to seeing her. Regardless of her motivation, there would have been many more deaths if not for the information she had provided. Jolene wasn't stupid. She was certain Ellie was the kind of woman that wouldn't stray far from who she was at her core—a selfish, brazen woman whose loyalty was only to herself.

Jolene had no clue where her life would go now. Without Deacon, the future looked bleak. Going back to Mingo County was the obvious solution but not one she relished. Her mother and brother were there, but she had never had a relationship with either of them. Her brother was ensnared in their mother's anger. Jolene would rather live in a tent until her dying day than be subjected to her mother's manipulation. Joining Mother Jones in her fight was the obvious path. She could join the suffrage movement and help women finally get the vote. Right now, she needed to get to Ellie and take some time to mend her broken soul. Whatever came next would show up when it showed up.

72.

9 April 1913 (Charleston)

Ellie's anxiety over Jolene grew with each passing day. The snow had melted days before. Surely, she would be here soon. The violence between Baldwin-Felts and the miners had lessened but still continued in pockets. Governor Hatfield had visited Paint Creek and was negotiating a deal with the coal operators and the strikers. John now spent most of his time in Charleston guarding the coal operators in town for the negotiations, which limited her movements.

Dottie had been going after dinner each day and carrying messages. She had been gone for quite a long time this evening. They had devised a system. If John was present, Dottie would knock on the door and ask if Ellie would like some tea—it meant Jolene had arrived. If Dottie asked if Ellie needed her to stoke the fire, Jolene had not arrived. Each night for the past two weeks, Dottie came in and stoked the fire. Ellie was hoping she would bring tea this evening.

Dottie knocked on the door. "Come in. John's downstairs having dinner with Tom Felts."

Dottie carried a tray of tea and could barely contain her excitement. The cups rattled as Dottie sat the tray on the table. "Ms. Ellie, she's here. She got here 'bout an hour ago."

"What on earth took you so long to come tell me?"

"I couldn't come up right away. Cook needed me in the kitchen and snagged me as quick as I snuck back in the kitchen door."

Ellie grabbed Dottie and hugged her tight. "Did you see her? Did you speak to her?"

"Yes, I saw her and spoke to her. That boy that's with her was right protective of her and stayed close by the whole time I's there. I didn't feel right talkin' too much in front of him."

"A boy? From the camp? Who is he?"

"Said his name was Boyd. Just a boy. I guess 'bout fifteen or sixteen. A young man, but still a kid."

"Perhaps he brought her here and he's gonna return to Holly Grove."

"I told her you's been waitin' on her for a week now and was 'bout to jump clean outa your skin when she didn't show up. She said to tell you she loves you and hopes you can make it over there right soon."

"I don't know if that's gonna be possible, Dot. John's in town for the next week. Maybe longer. I'll need you to ferry messages back and forth between us. You must be extra careful now. John's watchin' every move I make. I'm pretty much a prisoner here. Take a different path to Pickney every time you go. If you think for one second you're being followed, turn and go in another direction or come back here. You hear?"

"Yes, ma'am. I'll be extra careful. Mr. John scares me, and I don't wanna cross paths with him for no reason at all."

"All right then, tell Jolene to lay low and wait another week until John leaves. Then we can figure out what we're gonna do." Ellie heard John's footsteps on the stairs. "Quick, start stokin' the fire like you normally do. And don't talk."

Ellie sat at her dressing table and brushed her hair. John entered and staggered to the bed. "Go, girl. Get out! We can manage by ourselves tonight."

Dottie placed the poker beside the fireplace and said goodnight.

Ellie continued to brush her hair. "Are you drunk? What kinda party are they havin' down there that you're drunk so early in the evenin'?"

"A celebration. We confirmed tonight that one of the lead strike agitators is dead and his little wife has left Holly Grove. A defeated little bitch."

Ellie wasn't certain he was talking about Jolene and Deacon. She also wasn't aware of any other husband and wife *agitators* at Holly Grove. "Oh? Where would the poor wretch go? I assume she has no money to pack up and go too far?"

"Word is the wife's here in Charleston. More than likely still plottin' with that bitch Jones. *Mother* Jones. That old hag needs to die already. She's gotta be close to a hundred."

"What on earth could they be plottin' now? Hasn't Governor Hatfield put an end to things?"

"Oh, my innocent little flower. How little you know about politics and men's business. It ain't that easy, and the coal operators'll never give in completely. Besides, this is just one battlefield. Those bastards are tryin' to unionize all over the state. This is the beginning of a long, damn war."

Ellie put her brush down and walked over to the bed. "Well, explain it to me. I want to know what you do all day and where we'll go next."

"First, I need to find this woman and get rid of her before she starts more trouble. You may not believe this, but the higher ups think she was the brains behind everything, more so than her husband, Deacon." Ellie's heart lurched and she tried not to react.

"A woman? How so?"

"Well, she can read and write and strategize. From what we know, she organized the entire tent colony and kept things running there. She also worked right alongside her husband to smuggle in all the weapons they were using. As much as I hate to admit it, it's brilliant—nobody would suspect a woman. Especially an ignorant coal miner's wife. More importantly, she and Mother Jones are thick as thieves. The last thing we need is some crazy bitch taking up Mother Jones's sword and continuing this shit when that old battle ax dies. Women ain't got no damn place in men's business."

"How did her husband die?"

"That's the best part. He staged a raid on The Bullpen one night and got captured. They nearly killed him in there. He got pneumonia, and that was what finally did his sorry ass in."

Ellie wanted to stuff a rag in his mouth. The poker Dottie had returned to the fireplace was a few steps away from the bed. She could grab it and ram it clean through his black heart. He thought she was "an innocent flower" who didn't have enough sense to know what was going on or what to do with the information? The joke was certainly on him.

"So, where do you think she is? She could be anywhere. How're you gonna find her?"

"Not sure yet. First place I'll look is with Mother Jones. She's still in the hospital here. Under arrest but allowed visitors. I'll wait around there and look for her."

"You know what she looks like? Have you met her?"

"I don't have a good description. I assume she'll look haggard and nasty—that's how they've been livin' up there at Holly Grove. And she's travelin' with a teenage boy. Some ragamuffin she picked up in the tent colony."

"What will you do to her when you find her?" Ellie asked.

"I might not kill her, but she'll probably wish I had."

John eventually passed out. Ellie sipped the tea and wondered who this boy was traveling with Jolene, and how did John know so much about Jolene's movements? Ellie needed to get word to Dottie to tell Jolene not to go near Mother Jones. She would also send her a few of her dresses to wear so she fit in with the city folks.

73.

<u>10 April 1913</u>

Ellie bathed and dressed early the next morning before John woke up. She wanted to have breakfast with him and determine what his plan was for tracking Jolene.

"Dottie's bringing you some hot water to shave. I'll meet you downstairs for breakfast."

"You sure are up early? Plans?"

"It's a beautiful spring mornin', and I'm tired of bein' cooped up in this dreary hotel all day. I wanna get out and get some sunshine and fresh air. I may walk over to the library and get some new books."

Dottie brought the hot water for John, and Ellie met her on the back stairs a few minutes later.

"You must go to Jolene immediately and tell her not to go anywhere today. She *cannot* leave that house. John's been ordered to hunt her down, and he'll likely kill her if he finds her. They want to shut her up before she conspires with Mother Jones and starts more trouble. First, you need to go back to my room as soon as John leaves. Get the three dresses I hung on the far end of the rack. Take the blue hat and the shoes, also. Take it all to Jolene and tell her that if she must go out, she *has* to wear one of those dresses. As far as I know, John isn't sure what she looks like, but he knows to look for a woman who doesn't fit in here in the city. He also knows she's traveling with a young boy. They can't be seen together. And tell her to cover that damn red hair. If he does find out what she looks like, it's the one thing he'll be lookin' for."

"Yes, ma'am. What if Cook won't let me go?"

"Tell her you are taking my dresses to the seamstress to have them altered and I insist you take them immediately. If Cook has any problems, she can come see me."

Dottie did as Ellie instructed. She held her breath the entire time she was getting the dresses. When she reached the street, she stopped and took in several deep breaths, then ran all the way to Pickney Street.

She ran into the house without even knocking. The boy who came with Jolene was descending the stairs. Dottie noted how cute he was. Young but cute. "Where's Ms. Jolene?"

"She's upstairs gettin' ready. We's gonna see Mother Jones today."

"*No!* She can't."

"I think she can pretty much do whatever she wants." The boy was certainly arrogant.

"No, you don't understand. They's gonna kill her if they find her. They's waitin' at the hospital for her. They want her dead so she can't start no more trouble!"

"Who wants me dead?" Jolene asked from the top of the stairs.

"Oh, Ms. Jolene. Ms. Ellie sent you these here dresses. She says you must wear one of 'em iffin you go out for any reason. That man of her'n. He's the one. Why, they's ordered him to kill you. 'Fraid you's gonna start more trouble with Mother Jones. They's want all y'all dead."

"Do they now? I'm not afraid of those bastards. They've already destroyed ever'thang that mattered to me."

"No! No, Ms. Jolene. You still got Ms. Ellie, and she loves you somethin' fierce. She's ready to lay down and die for you. Why, that man of her'n is mean and dangerous and he'd break her pretty little neck in a second if he knew she's your sister."

Jolene walked down the stairs and took the dresses, shoes, and hat from Dottie. "These are some right fancy dresses my sister sent." Jolene ran her calloused hands over the fine silk material.

"Ms. Ellie only wears the finest, ma'am."

"Does Ellie's man know what I look like or is he simply lookin' for a Paint Creek miner's wife who's been livin' in a tent for the past year?"

"He's lookin' for a miner's wife and a young boy. So, it'd be best if the two of you ain't seen together. Ms. Ellie says he don't know what you look like exactly. But you sure do favor Ms. Ellie a lot, even if your colorin's different. So be sure'n wear that hat and pull your hair back. They ain't too many women got long red hair like your'n, so if he does know what you look like, it'll be a dead giveaway."

"What does *he* look like? And what's his name?"

Dottie described John and helped Jolene get into one of Ellie's dresses. It was a little big, but Dottie managed to pin it in all the right places.

Jolene walked with purpose to the hospital where Mother Jones was being held—as though she visited there every day. She searched the streets for any sign of John. Keeping a safe distance behind her, Boyd followed. As elegant as Jolene looked in Ellie's clothes, Boyd still looked like a mine camp kid who had never been to the city. They decided it would be safer if he waited a few blocks away.

When Jolene rounded the corner, she spotted John standing across the street looking at every woman who wasn't dressed in the finest clothes. Dottie had described him perfectly, down to the clothes he was wearing. He was a mere one hundred feet away from her. She fondled the knife in her pocket. The element of surprise was on her side, and he certainly wouldn't be looking for a fancy city girl. All she had to do was turn left, cross the street, walk up to him, stick the knife in his gut, and keep going. Before anyone knew what had happened, she would be three blocks away.

Instead, she turned right to go up the stairs leading to the hospital, being sure not to make eye contact with John or draw any attention to herself. In time she would have the right opportunity to exact her revenge for Deacon's life on the bastard who shared her sister's bed. Today was not that day.

Mother Jones was surrounded by several people Jolene had met at Holly Grove and a few she didn't know. Mother Jones was sitting up in bed. The pneumonia had nearly killed Mother Jones and probably would have if Governor Hatfield hadn't moved her to Charleston.

Jolene removed her hat and smiled.

"Child, I didn't recognize you all gussied up. Look at you! How are you, my dear?" Mother Jones opened her arms and embraced Jolene. She patted the bed for Jolene to sit.

"I'm doin' as good as can be 'spected. I reckon you heard Deacon passed."

"Yes. A great loss to all of us. I'm so sorry for your heartbreak."

"Those bastards need to pay, Mother. They need to pay dearly for all they's took from us."

"I'm certainly gonna try to make 'em pay. We're still fightin' the good fight. I think it'll be just a matter of time before I'm officially a free woman again. But first, they're sendin' me back to Pratt to continue my house arrest as soon as I'm a bit better. But not to worry, I can raise just as much hell in jail as anywhere. I have an underground railroad of sorts that I use to get letters out to the press and a few good men in the United States Senate. As soon as the governor releases me, I'm going back to Washington. They've formed a Senate Committee, and I'll be testifyin' about all that's happened here and continues to happen. This shit'll go on forever if we don't put a stop to it."

Jolene spent the rest of the afternoon at the hospital with Mother Jones. They planned and strategized for the next wave of activity. Jolene ventured over to the window one more time before leaving. John was still there, lurking on the other corner now. He had meandered back and forth all day trying to look casual as he searched every face for Jolene. Stupid bastard. She had walked in right under his nose.

She exited the hospital the same way she entered, as though she had been doing it every day. She walked with her head erect, and again, John was oblivious to her presence. A couple of blocks away from the hospital, she spotted Boyd, and he fell in behind her and followed her back to Pickney Street.

74.

<u>19 April 1913</u>

Ellie walked down to the river and sat on the bench where she had gone weekly to pass Baldwin-Felts secrets for the past year. Now that things had reached a bit of calm, those meetings were more infrequent. John was uncertain of his future. He might be transferred to Pennsylvania or Kentucky. She wouldn't go with him. Perhaps Jolene would want to go far away. They could go to New York. They could go to New Orleans. She wanted to speak about the future with Jolene; they needed to leave this place together.

Ellie wondered where Sammy was. If he would want to leave with them. She imagined a life in New Orleans with Sammy. Playing music and being in love. Had she completely destroyed the love he had for her? She missed his touch, his gentle ways. No. This was best. For both of them. They had no future together. She needed to put any notion of a life with Sammy far out of reach.

She returned to the hotel and was relieved John was still out. Dottie came to her room and updated her on Jolene.

Ellie instructed her to return to Pickney Street and tell Jolene to meet her at the park bench by the river tomorrow at noon. Ellie changed into a dress for dinner and waited for John.

She heard his footsteps on the stairs and quickly sat at her dressing table. She brushed her hair to keep her hands busy. She had been a wreck since Jolene had planned to come to Charleston. She knew either John was watching or having someone watch her every move.

John stomped into the room in a foul mood.

"Hello, darlin'. How was your day?"

"Not good. I waited around the hospital all day. That bitch didn't show up. I wonder if the information we have is correct. Hell, she may not even be here in Charleston. I need to find out what the hell she looks like."

"I'm sure she looks like a poor wretch who's been livin' in a tent for the past year. She should stick out like a sore thumb. Who told you she was here anyway? Can you trust them?"

"I don't think I can trust anybody these days. It was someone in the governor's office—someone on the coal operators' payroll. Bribes have a way of making people tell you what you want to know. Maybe he just doesn't know what the hell he's talking about." He removed his boots. "I need to change. We need to be downstairs in thirty minutes for dinner."

Tom Felts sat at the head of the table, and Tony Gaujot to his left. John and Ellie sat across the table from Tony. The mood at the dinner table was more relaxed than it had been for the past year. Tom Felts was quiet and not his usual aggressive self. The ladies were as chatty as ever about every mundane detail of their lives. As the discussion turned to politics and the governor's proposed deal, the mood shifted to a darker tone.

Ellie knew her beauty was disarming, and she found it amusing that all men, and most women, assumed any woman with that much beauty couldn't be smart. Ellie played this game well. She asked enough of the right questions to get information and played coy to make them think she didn't fully understand the politics and dangerous business they were conducting. Her Granny Cline always told them, *Girls, you attract the right things with honey and bad things with vinegar. Use your honey to get what you want.*

It pleased Ellie to know she had been instrumental in helping sabotage the bastards' efforts to kill the striking miners.

"Governor Hatfield made a proposal to the UMW and the coal operators today. From what I can tell, neither side wants to accept it." Tom Felts spoke quietly to John and Tony.

"What do you suppose the outcome will be?" Tony asked.

"Looks like Paint Creek's considering accepting his proposal with a few exceptions. The Cabin Creek operators are not nearly as close to agreeing. They're holding out. Frank Keeney isn't wanting to cooperate. He might be trouble on down the line. I don't think this will be the last we hear from him. He could very well be the next leader of the UMW's District 17."

Ellie listened for any plans against the strikers. The men at the table talked only about the governor's proposal and what their next plan would be. Their next battleground. They talked about going south to Mingo County. She prayed not, for if so, she would feel obligated to stay with John to keep passing information. Mingo County meant Polly and Jake. And Deannie. She wasn't sure she was up to another bloody battle over coal and greed. Besides, she had grown to hate John Havers with more passion than she had ever loved any man. She was certain she would kill him if she had to stay with him much longer.

75.

<u>21 April 1913 (Charleston)</u>

There was nothing suspicious about Ellie taking a stroll through the city on a warm spring day. Within two blocks of the hotel, she recognized his footsteps from the small metal disk in the toe of his boots tapping against the cobblestones. She didn't dare turn to confirm it was him. She slowed her pace and meandered through the streets, stopping at boutiques along the way.

Ellie paused at the edge of the park to pick a few tulips and daffodils. Then she made her way to the railing and looked out over the river. Jolene was on the bench but never made eye contact. Instead Ellie turned and walked the other way.

Ellie figured she might as well make him wait and wonder what she was doing. She stopped to pick more flowers and planned her next move. For once, she was glad she had ended things with Sammy. As careless as Sammy had been, John would certainly have caught them together.

She arranged her spring bouquet and stared into it on her way out of the park. She bumped into him and used her free hand to grab her hat. "Oh, my goodness. John? What on earth are you doin' here?"

"The question is what are *you* doing here, Ellie?"

"*What?* I come here quite often. I like to sit and read, and I love the river. It's such a beautiful day, I didn't want to waste it being cooped up in the hotel. I honestly don't think I could tolerate one more tea with the ladies. They can be right triflin' at times. Come, let's sit on the bench." She slipped her arm in his.

"You sure that's all you're doing down here?"

"What do you mean? Are you accusin' me of somethin', John?"

"You're acting a little strange lately, Ellie. Like a woman who might have another man. Or a woman that's bored with the man she has." He removed his hat and looked at her. "You know I'm not the type of man to tolerate a cheating woman." He gripped her arm.

"John Havers, how dare you?" Ellie jerked her arm away from him. "Why do you insist on accusin' me of cheatin' on you? I've done nothin' but sit in that hotel for over a year, puttin' up with those shrew Baldwin-Felts bitches and snooty coal operator wives while you go gallivantin' off to God only knows where. Yes, I'm bored, but not with you. I need somethin' more to do with my time besides sippin' tea and gossipin'." She crossed her arms over her chest and attempted to look as put upon as possible while staring straight ahead at the river.

"You seem distant and secretive since I got back from Paint Creek. I assumed you were meeting some man here today."

"So you followed me to catch me with some man? Go to hell, John." She got up and walked away from him.

He ran after her. "Ellie, stop!" He spun her around to face him. "I followed you because I had to be sure where you were going. I don't trust anyone these days."

"I've done nothin' to make you not trust me."

His fingers tore into her shoulders. "I've been gone a lot, Ellie. I don't know what you've been up to."

"Where've *you* been all day?" she asked. "You could have been with me. You jumped up and tore out of the hotel as soon as the sun came up."

"I told you, I need to find this woman from Paint Creek and stop whatever it is her and that old bitch Jones might be up to."

"I thought this mess was over! I thought Governor Hatfield put a stop to it already." She pulled away from him again.

"It's not *all* over yet. There's still some of those bastards wanting a fight. My job is to find this woman and stop whatever she might be planning with old Mother Jones. We can't risk another uprising of these ignorant bastards in Mingo County. I know you're bored. I know you're tired of living in a hotel. I promise it'll all be over soon. We can go to New York as soon as this is all done. I promised I would take you, and I will. I love you, Ellie."

Ellie took a deep breath. "I love you, too." She buried her face in his shoulder, so he wouldn't see the lie in her eyes.

John pulled her close. She put her arms around him and wished for a second that she really did love him. But she didn't. She'd actually grown to despise him. She tolerated his touch. Knowing he wanted to kill her sister made her want to kill him.

They walked hand-in-hand back to the hotel.

76.

<u>22 April 1913</u>

"I gotta leave for Pittsburgh this morning on the 10:30 train," John said as they entered the dining room for breakfast.

"Today? What on earth for? For how long? I thought you were here for good." Ellie acted annoyed, even though she was quite pleased John was leaving.

"For a few days. I should be back Friday."

Ellie couldn't believe her good luck. He would be gone for three days. "Well, you better be back by Friday night. We have that dinner party at the Hardings' in honor of the new governor. I understand from the ladies everyone who is anyone in the state will be there. What time do you plan to return?"

"Should be back late afternoon."

"Why must you always be the one who goes?"

"It's a special meeting with the attorneys. Lots of stuff to discuss. Stuff you wouldn't understand, Ellie."

Ellie never knew whether she should be amused or insulted by his assumption that she wasn't smart. She smiled inwardly. The joke was certainly on him. She had outsmarted him every step of the way so far.

Tony Gaujot approached the table. "Good morning, Ellie. John. Mind if I join you?"

"Please. Have a seat," John said.

"Are you ready for the meeting with the attorneys?" Tony asked.

"Yes. One thing we need to figure out is what our next move is to squash those last few rabble rousers left up at Cabin Creek. Frank Keeney isn't going down without a fight. He's young and ambitious and wanting to make a name for himself." John paused long enough for the waiter to pour his coffee. Once he moved to the next table, John continued. "Most importantly, when Mother Jones is released, she's planning on going to Washington to testify before a Senate committee about the miners and the strike."

"We need to figure out a way to stop her and that damn loud mouth of hers," Tony said.

Ellie nibbled at her breakfast, listening.

"We'll do whatever it takes. If I had my way, I'd strangle the old bitch in her sleep." John took a sip of his coffee.

"John! You can't go 'round killin' old women." Ellie poured hot water into her teacup.

"I can *that* one."

"I wish they would hold these meetings here in Charleston. It'd be a lot easier on us," Tony said.

"Apparently, the attorneys don't think meeting here is safe and secure. Too many ears and too many damn spies. We can't trust anybody."

Ellie tried to hide her face behind her teacup.

"You really think some of our people are double-crossing us?" Tony asked.

John leaned in. "I don't know. I do know every move we've made for the past year's gotten to those damn miners before we carried out our plans. It's like they knew we were coming every single time. They were always two steps ahead of us."

"I know Felts is convinced it's someone here in our inner circle. Maybe one of the younger men—Sipple or White."

John took another drink of coffee. "I figure if we have a turncoat, so do they. We've targeted a couple of miners who might be willing to tell us what we want to know. For the right amount of money anybody'll turn. And those people are still starving and living like animals. The company's ready to pay up to $2,000 for the right information."

"That's a small fortune for a miner! So you've found someone? Can we trust what they tell us is the truth? Perhaps they want to tell us false information so we'll turn on each other." Tony motioned for the waiter to bring more coffee.

"We have a couple of men we've approached. I've not met them yet, but plan to meet at least one of them when I return from Pittsburgh. And I'll have a pocket full of money in exchange for information."

Ellie buttered her biscuit as though she was more interested in the way it spread than in their tale of intrigue. She thought she might throw up and held tightly to her knife to keep her hand from shaking.

John wolfed down his breakfast and kissed Ellie goodbye. He and Tony Gaujot left her sitting in the restaurant with her half-eaten eggs and buttered biscuit.

She left the dining room and found Dottie. "Please come to my suite when you get a moment. I need you to help get a few dresses to Ms. Delia's for alterations."

Ellie returned to her room and wrote a note to Jolene, instructing her to meet at the park at eleven, at the other end near the docks, not their usual spot. It was urgent. She gave the note to Dottie—along with three dresses, a diamond bracelet, a pair of pearl earrings, a diamond and emerald brooch, her mandolin, and a wad of cash for her to take and stash at Pickney Street.

After Dottie left, Ellie sorted through her remaining clothes to determine what she would take with her. She would take all of the jewelry. It would be worth a lot of money if they needed cash. She simply had too many dresses to take them all.

At 10:30 she heard the whistle as the train pulled away from the station. She donned her hat and gloves, slipped down the back stairs, and made her way to the park. Even though John was gone, she was concerned he may have someone following her. She took every side street and alley she could. She saw the river and let out a sigh of relief. She stepped out onto the main street and turned left toward the docks. She crossed over to the park, found a bench and waited for Jolene.

Ellie looked all around to make sure no one was watching. Jolene crossed the street on the other side of the park. She came and sat on the bench opposite Ellie. "What's so urgent?"

"John's gone to Pittsburgh for a meetin' with the Baldwin-Felts attorneys. They'll be discussing what to do 'bout Mother Jones goin' to Washington to give her testimony to the Senate. They're gonna try to stop her—at any cost. I think they'll try to kill her, Jolene. They wanna stop her from testifyin'." Ellie took a deep breath. "That ain't all, Jolene. He says they found someone from our side willin' to turn on us for money and tell him who's been sharin' their plans with the miners for the past year. He's plannin' to meet him when he returns."

"Who?"

"He doesn't know yet. Won't know until he meets him. Apparently, they have a couple of men they're talking to."

"This is bad. Who could it be? Crowbar? I never fully trusted him at the end. He gave up on the fight and asked too many questions 'bout our next moves. Jake stopped trusting him months ago. That oldest Johnson boy was always talkin' 'bout gettin' out and findin' a better way of life, movin' to the city. He likes to gamble. Rumor is he was in a heap of debt from losin' at poker. There's a few that always seemed untrustworthy to me, Ellie. When's John comin' back?"

"Friday afternoon," Ellie said.

"Well, then we need to get our plan together a'fore then. We can't leave town and not find out what Baldwin-Felts has planned for Mother Jones though. We've come too far to run now. We need to find out what they plan to do. Then we can leave," Jolene said.

77.

<u>25 April 1913 (Charleston)</u>

Early Friday morning the seamstress delivered Ellie's new dress for the Hardings' party. She had the seamstress take it in a little bit more than usual to show off her tiny waist and the curve of her hips and breasts. She wanted to turn every head in the room, and she would. Her dark skin and hair stood out against the shimmering deep lilac silk and beading.

The party at the Hardings' was the first event of the season and would set the tone for the social gatherings throughout the year. Ellie didn't want to abandon the social scene. As much as the socialite ladies annoyed her, she loved the parties, the dresses, the jewelry. Most of all, she loved being the center of attention. But that life could never continue here. John would almost certainly figure out she was the spy, and then her life wouldn't be worth a damn nickel in Charleston—or anywhere those Baldwin-Felts bastards might be. No, if she were going to continue this lifestyle, she'd have to find another man—in New York or wherever she and

Jolene escaped to. A better man than John-damn-Havers, that was for sure. A kinder man. One with more money.

With the battles at Paint Creek and Cabin Creek nearly over, the coal operators, Baldwin-Felts, and the politicians had much to celebrate. Still, they had Mother Jones, her mystery-woman accomplice, and the rabble rousers at Cabin Creek to deal with. But these matters seemed small in comparison to the battle they had been fighting for the past year.

Dottie had brought a message from John when she'd delivered the dress. He was taking the late train back to Charleston and would meet her at the party.

Ellie hoped John didn't return until much later. She would get the information she needed on Baldwin-Felts's plans for Mother Jones, leave the party early, and go to Pickney Street. They would send a message to Mother Jones, then she and Jolene would leave on the early train. If John *did* return early, she would get him drunk and leave once he passed out. Getting him drunk shouldn't be too much of a problem; he managed that all on his own most days.

"Dottie, as soon as I leave, take the rest of dresses, jewelry, and cash to Pickney Street. When you come back, do your normal job. Don't draw any attention to yourself. Wait here till ten o'clock. If I'm not back by then, go back to Pickney Street and stay there, and don't leave. I'll meet you there as soon as I can get away from John."

"Ms. Ellie, I ain't so sure 'bout leavin' you here with him. If he thinks you had anythang to do with them miners he's liable to kill you a'fore you can get away."

Ellie hugged her. "I'll be fine, Dottie. Don't you worry 'bout me."

All heads turned when Ellie entered the party. The beading on her dress caught the light and shimmered against the silk. Her first priority was to find Myrtle, who always had the inside scoop before anyone else.

"Myrtle, you look absolutely beautiful tonight. That dress is perfect."

"Ellie, I can't thank you enough for helpin' me find a dress for this party. You always pick out the best dresses for me. Look at *you*. You look regal. I don't think I've ever seen you look more beautiful." Myrtle circled Ellie to get a look at the back of the dress.

"Thank you, Myrtle. You're too kind." Ellie took a glass of champagne from the server, with no intention of drinking it. She needed to keep her wits about her this evening.

"Is John still in Pittsburgh?" Myrtle asked.

"Yes, I'm afraid so. He's supposed to show up later tonight, though."

"Well then, I suppose you haven't heard the news?" Myrtle took Ellie's hand and led her outside to the veranda overlooking the river.

"No, what?"

"They're gonna stop that old hag from goin' to Washington."

"How so?" Ellie asked.

"They have a foolproof plan, and it'll all happen the day she heads out for Washington."

"Well, that's interestin'. Seems like it'll be obvious it's them, and then she'll eventually make her way to testify. Sounds like a fool's errand to me."

"Now, now, Ellie. You know our boys are smarter than that. They've greased a lot of palms in this town and Washington."

"Well, that's certainly true. With the new governor, I don't see how they can pull it off. He took a likin' to that old lady."

"I'm not so certain she's a lady," Myrtle quipped.

"So, what *is* the plan? How are they goin' to pull this off?"

"It's quite brilliant, actually. They're gonna wait until she leaves for the train, then ... John!" Myrtle smiled broadly.

She turned to see John standing by her side. "I didn't really expect you to be here until much later, if at all. I'm so happy you made it." The Knowing raised up so strongly it made Ellie dizzy.

"Doesn't she look beautiful tonight, John?" Myrtle asked.

"Yes, she does. Ellie always looks beautiful." John took Ellie's hand and kissed it.

"Well, I'll leave you two lovebirds alone." Myrtle crossed the veranda and went inside.

"How was your trip? Do you need a drink?" Ellie knew she needed to get him drunk in a hurry and get the hell back to the hotel.

He rubbed his eyes. "Not yet. The trip was fine. I'm tired."

"Everything went as planned?"

John took her other hand and turned her to him. "Ellie, can I trust you?"

"John, are we back to that again? You show up here early and find me on the veranda with Myrtle. Certainly, if I wanted another man, I would be inside lookin' for one."

"That's not what I mean . . . entirely. Can I trust you with *everything*?"

"John, of course you can. What is this? Why do you doubt me?" Ellie fought to maintain her composure. She was certain he knew everything. She wanted to run. Her mind raced to think of a way out of this house and away from John.

Tom Felts opened the door and walked over to them. "John! There you are. Please come inside for a moment, I want to introduce you and the beautiful Ms. Ellie to the governor."

The governor? Ellie had known the governor for years. He was from Mingo County *and* he was Tom's cousin. She had planned to avoid any direct contact with Governor Hatfield and his wife tonight. She knew there was a chance she would run into them or be introduced at this party, but she didn't imagine it would be with John by her side. She certainly didn't want them bringing up Tom or the murders or Deannie in front of John or anyone else. She had neatly tucked that part of her life away.

She needed to leave the party and get back to Pickney Street and then out of Charleston. She was sure he knew she was the spy in their ranks. That look in his eyes—what was that? Hurt? Betrayal? Certainly, the man didn't really love her? No, his pride was hurt. His ego bruised. That was not love. A man like John had no clue what love was.

Tom Felts escorted them to Governor Hatfield and his wife, Carrie. "Why, *Ellie*? Is that you, dear?" Carrie Hatfield took Ellie's hands and pulled her close and hugged her.

"Hello, Carrie, Henry—it's so nice to see you both. Congratulations on the election. Our great state will be much better off with you as governor. I'm so proud of you."

John and Tom Felts were dumfounded. "You already know each other?" Tom Felts asked. "John, you never told us our beautiful Ellie had connections in the State House."

"Well, seems we *both* learned something today about our beautiful Ellie." John's rage was barely contained.

"Pray tell, how do you know each other?" Tom Felts asked.

Ellie spoke up before the governor or his wife had a chance to offer their version. "Even though the Governor and Carrie moved to McDowell County a few years ago, we're all from Mingo County. I've known them for quite some time. Matewan's a small town." Ellie looked at Carrie pleading with her not to mention Tom or Deannie or the murders. Ellie should have known they wouldn't mention it in this setting. Bad taste.

Carrie and the governor smiled. "Yes, we've known Ellie for years. I had no idea you were in Charleston. You certainly need to come see me." Carrie pulled Ellie close. "How is your sister, dear? I heard about her husband. Dreadful. I'm so sorry for your loss."

Ellie dared to look at John and was relieved to see he was engrossed in conversation with the governor and a few other men. "She's doin' fine. It was a terrible situation. Thank you. I'll let her know you asked about her."

Other people were now waiting to meet and talk to the governor and his wife. John took Ellie's hand and pulled her away from the crowd. "I think I need that drink now."

He downed a whiskey and ordered another. "So, you know the governor and his wife? *Personally*?"

"John, Matewan's a small town. Of course I know them. I wouldn't say we're best friends, but I do know them."

"Well, you know them well enough to be invited to the governor's mansion for tea. That's pretty damn well, Ellie." He downed his second whiskey and ordered a third. "What else you been hidin' from me?"

"Hidin'? I would hardly call this hidin' somethin' from you. I certainly don't know them well enough to go invitin' myself to their house. I'm certain she was simply bein' polite, given the situation."

"*Situation*? The situation, as I see it, is pretty damn peculiar." He was now ordering his fourth whiskey.

"John, you've had enough whiskey. Please, let's go."

"Oh, you want to go now, do you? Why? These are *your* people, Ellie. The governor and his lovely wife obviously love the beautiful Ellie. *Everybody* loves the beautiful Ms. Ellie."

"Please, don't do this," she whispered between clenched teeth.

"What? This is the life you've always wanted, Ellie. Well, here you are. At the top. At any cost." John made a grand gesture with his hands.

"I'm leavin'." She walked outside and motioned to a waiting carriage.

John came up behind her. "Exactly where do you think you're goin', Ellie?"

"Back to the Ruffner. I will not be humiliated by you and your drunkenness."

"You are a piece of work, Ellie. *A piece of work.*" He yanked her arm.

"Let go of me." She jerked away.

He pushed her into the carriage and sat across from her. "If you kept this from me, what else have you been hidin'? Huh? You know the president? It's apparent every man in that party wants to fuck you. I'm inclined to believe they probably have."

Ellie leaned over and slapped him. "You are disgustin'."

"Tell me that ain't why you're here? In Charleston? To find yourself a rich man?"

"You're right. I could have any man at that party I wanted. So, if that's the case, why have I been with *you* for the past year? There are men in there who could buy and sell your ass all day long, John Havers."

"You little bitch! How dare you?"

"How dare *me*? How dare you? You're the one accusin' me of cheatin' and fuckin' every man in town."

"Don't you use that language. It's not lady-like."

"You can say fuck, but I can't? *Fuck. You.*"

He struck her across the face. "You bastard." She spit blood.

The carriage came to a jerk and stopped in front of the hotel. The driver jumped down and opened the door. Ellie pushed her way out and hurried into the lobby. John stopped to pay the driver and followed.

The clock said it was 9:30. Dottie would still be there. She yelled to the front desk clerk, "Have Dottie come to my room immediately!" Ellie hurried to the back stairs and bolted up to her room.

Her hands shook getting the key in the lock. She fumbled and dropped it. John's footsteps bounded up the stairs. She slammed the door behind her and threw the deadbolt just as John reached the landing.

He tried the knob and pounded. "Ellie, open this damn door."

"Go away. You're drunk and angry. *Go away.*"

His footsteps receded down the hall toward his suite. Ellie looked at the open door that adjoined their suites. She didn't have time to lock it. She flipped the deadbolt open and stepped into the hallway. John entered her suite and crossed the room in two strides.

He grabbed her hair and pulled her back inside. She kicked and scratched him. The door banged against the wall. He dragged her across the room and pushed her down onto the chaise lounge. He stood over her. "You are really a scheming little whore, Ellie. I sure had you figured all wrong."

"What are you talkin' 'bout? You're drunk and crazy."

"That may be so, but I do know what I'm talking about. Ya see, I met a friend of yours today when I got back into town. A feller named Crowbar." Ellie slipped off the other side of chaise and stepped toward the fireplace and the poker.

John circled her like a vulture. "Turns out he had a lot of things to tell me about you. About your *husband.* I suppose you thought tellin' me you were married was a minor detail you didn't think was too important?"

"I'm not married. We . . . we divorced."

"Oh? Was that before or after he went to prison for killin' your lover and the mayor?"

Ellie backed toward the fireplace.

"He also told me about your sister. Jolene, I think is her name. She lived at Paint Creek. Now ain't that a coincidence?"

"You're crazy, John. You can't believe what some crazy old man told you."

"Well, now let's see . . . what else did he tell me? Oh, yes. That he met you in the park down by the river, almost every week for the past year to swap secrets about what we had planned for those damn miners. You sure played the dumb little kitten well, didn't you?" John stalked her like an animal. "How could you do this to *me*?" He pounded his chest with his fist. "Did you ever give a damn about *me*?"

Every cell in Ellie's body vibrated. "The Knowing" screamed inside her head—he intended to kill her. She grabbed the poker, hiding it in the folds of her dress. He came closer, and she swung it around until it made contact with his head. He stumbled back and fell to his knees. He grabbed his ear and blood seeped through his fingers and down his neck. His shirt collar was crimson. "You bitch. I *loved* you! You betrayed me. And you *will* pay."

She didn't care any longer. One of them wouldn't make it out of that room alive. "*Loved* me? You wouldn't know love if it crawled up your ass. You act all hurt and betrayed. Your pride's hurt, not your heart. And your pride's hurt because you were outsmarted—by a woman, no less. No, John, you never loved me, and I sure as hell never loved you. If you hadn't been a source of information for me to help those miners, I'd have been rid of your stupid ass after the first two weeks. Don't look so shocked. You bastards treated those poor people like animals. And for what? Money? Greed? Control? You done messed with the wrong women this time, sweetheart. We're from Mingo County, and we ain't afraid of nothin' or nobody."

John tried to stand and staggered against the table. Ellie ran toward the door. He grabbed her dress and pulled her back. He slapped her with his bloody palm. Her hair fell, and he wrapped it around his left hand and pulled her up to face him. In his other, he held his knife to her throat.

"You little bitch. I wish it *had* been another man. You workin' with that old hag?"

Ellie saw Jolene slip into the room. Ellie wanted to keep John's eyes on her. "No, but my sister is."

"Your sister? Your *sister's* the one I've been lookin' for?"

Jolene racked the shell in the rifle, and the room went silent. John jerked his head up and looked straight down the barrel. "You mean Crowbar didn't tell you that little piece of information? Let go of my sister, you bastard, a'fore I blow what little bit of brains you have right into the pits of hell."

"Fuck you *and* your sister." John pulled Ellie's head back further and held the knife tight against her skin. "You've made me the laughing stock of this town. I look like a fool. I fell for your lies. Every damn last one of 'em."

Jolene held the gun steady and aimed it right at his head. "Let her go, John. Let her go and we leave, and you never have to see us again."

"Like I'm ever gonna believe either of you bitches again?"

Ellie didn't move. The knife dug into her flesh with each breath.

"It's time to pay the devil, Ellie," John whispered in her ear.

Jolene took a step toward them. "Let. Her. Go."

"Fuck you." John sunk the knife deep into Ellie's throat and pulled it up behind her ear. She jerked her head away as the knife tore into her flesh. He lost his grip. Jolene took her shot and hit him in the shoulder.

The gunshot filled the room. Then everything went quiet. Ellie floated down and down and down. She hit the floor. Blood flowed down between her breasts, her lilac dress turning deep crimson. Jolene called her name.

Ellie tried to look up but couldn't move.

Jolene, help me, Jolene . . . all I wanted was your forgiveness.

Ellie closed her eyes.

It's time to pay the devil . . . time to pay the devil.

Dottie ran into the room.

"Dottie, find me something to wrap around her wound. A cloth, her sleepshirt, anythang," Jolene said.

Dottie rifled through Ellie's dresser drawer and returned with a long white cotton scarf. Sammy knelt beside Ellie. "What can I do?"

Jolene looked up, startled to see someone else in the room. "Who the hell are you?"

"I'm Sammy."

"Hold her head still while I put this scarf around her neck to stop the blood. We need to get her out of here." Jolene wrapped the scarf around Ellie's neck. "We'll go down the back stairs. Boyd's waitin' with a wagon in the alley."

Jolene looked at John. She had never seen so much blood. It covered the rug and most of the hardwood floor. John was barely moving. Jolene instructed Dottie to take his gun, his knife, and all the cash he had on him. She figured they would need it. "What should we do with him?"

Sammy turned to John. "Leave him."

"He knows it was us. He'll tell the police we did this," Jolene said.

"I doubt he'll be tellin' anybody two women did this to him. He'll be afraid they'll fire him if he tells that his little darlin' Ellie was the one sharin' all their secrets. I think he'll make up some fine story that won't include the two of you." Sammy looked at Jolene. "Now that don't mean *he'll* stop lookin' for you two. You need to get out of town fast."

"Well, we need to get out of this hotel first a'fore somebody comes lookin' to see what the hell's goin' on."

They wrapped Ellie in the quilt from her bed and Sammy carried her down the back stairs to the wagon. They rode the few blocks in the pitch dark to Pickney Street and Eloise.

78.

Eloise examined Ellie's neck. "She's lost a lot of blood. Sally, get the needle, thread and the herbs." Sally ran to get the items. "Boyd, you bring two bowls of hot water. Jolene, tie her hair back. Sammy, you can help me get her out of this dress."

Sammy took the scissors from Eloise and gently cut Ellie's beautiful gown from her blood-soaked body. She had on a silk chemise underneath. Her skin was cold and slightly blue. "Why's she so cold?" Sammy asked.

Eloise examined Ellie. "She's lost a lot of blood. We must get this cut stitched up or she won't be with us much longer."

Sammy winced. "You mean she could die?"

He loved Ellie, that much was clear. Memories of Deacon's last days floated in front of Jolene. She'd faced the same disbelief that the person you love the most in the world may die in your arms any minute.

Eloise soaked the three-inch cut in Ellie's throat with herbs to stop the bleeding. She cleaned the gash and then stitched it up. "It doesn't look like he severed anythin' serious. The stitches are going to be deep, and she will have a scar. John must be one crazy bastard to do this."

Sammy stayed by Ellie's side that night and most of the next day.

"Sammy, wake up." Jolene shook him.

"Is somethin' wrong? Where's Ellie?" he asked.

"She ain't woke up yet. Go on upstairs and get in the bed and get some proper sleep. I'll stay here with her."

"I don't wanna leave her, Jolene." Sammy wiped his eyes. "I want to be here when she wakes up."

"Fine. I'll sit with you for a bit." Jolene sat in the rocking chair on the other side of Ellie's bed.

"How long you been in love with her?" Jolene asked.

"Since the minute I laid eyes on her. I'd seen her in the hotel a few times, with that asshole or with those Baldwin-Felts women. Then one night she came into the tavern by herself and that was it. I was smitten'."

"How long you been seein' her?"

"Since June of last year. Then we ended things New Year's Eve. Had a big fight. Nearly killed me. Ellie made it clear she was gonna choose John and that lifestyle over me. I realized then Ellie wants things I can't give her. Jolene, they's another side to her—the Ellie I spent time with don't want those things. Maybe a woman like Ellie can't ever be happy."

"Ellie's certainly a peculiar bird, Sammy. She's always demanded more than her portion—and typically gets it," Jolene said.

Sammy stretched his long legs in front of him and leaned back in his chair. "Last night, I watched Ellie leave for the party. She looked so regal and in control of herself and her life. I's kiddin' myself to think I could have a woman like

Ellie. Back in the summer, we spent a day at the river. Her hair was down, feet were bare—she was alive that day. That's the Ellie I love, Jolene."

"How'd you know somethin' was wrong last night?"

"It'd been a slow night in the tavern. Most of the hotel guests were at that party. Dot came runnin' into the tavern as I was packin' up to leave. She'd gone up to Ellie's room and saw that John had a knife to her throat. She came to get me to help. What were you doin' there?"

"We'd planned to meet her in the alley behind the hotel. Boyd was watchin' from the front of the hotel and saw 'em go in. When she didn't come down, I got worried John was onto us, so I snuck up the back stairs to check on her. Glad I did."

"I hope that son of a bitch dies," Sammy said.

"You know you're a wanted man now. John ain't gonna let any of us get away with this."

"Jolene, I don't wanna be anywhere but here. I'll do whatever it takes to keep Ellie and you safe. I wanna kill that asshole, but keepin' Ellie safe is more important. There'll be a time and place to take care of John if he ain't already dead."

"Let's hope he is. If not, we'll need to figure what we're gonna do. First, Ellie needs to mend." Jolene stood. "I'll get us some tea."

79.

7 May 1913 (Charleston)

Jolene marveled at Eloise's skill and knowledge of medicine. Eloise had herbs Jolene had never heard of. She could now identify nearly all the plants and seeds Eloise had in her arsenal. The mixing of them was another thing entirely. She had only scratched the surface of what was possible. Eloise had several books on medicinal herbs and ancient treatments, and Jolene was soaking up all of it. She read well into the night sitting by Ellie's bed.

"Eloise, I've learned more 'bout potions than I ever thought could possibly exist." Jolene placed the tincture she'd made for Ellie on her neck.

"It's a lot of science mixed with a little magic," Eloise said.

"Ms. Jolene, you have a letter." Sally handed her an envelope.

"A letter? Who knows I'm here?"

"Dayton. He met me at the market and slipped it in my basket."

Jolene read it out loud. "He's alive. At hospital. Lost his arm. MJ released from hospital and sent back to Pratt."

"Well, if that son of a bitch is alive and lost his arm, he's gonna be hellbent on findin' you two," Sammy said.

Jolene tossed the letter into the fireplace. "If he told his boss it was us and why, the Baldwin-Felts men are more than likely lookin' for us too—and they'll eventually find us."

"I doubt he told 'em why. He don't wanna look like a fool and lose his job," Sammy said.

"All the same, I think we should all stay here and not venture out unless it's an emergency. As far as Mother Jones is concerned, they's nothin' I can do to help her now," Jolene said.

"I agree with Jolene. We have enough food to keep us until we decide what to do next," Eloise said. "Ellie has a few good hours and then slips into the abyss again, but she *is* healin'. The blood loss was extreme, and she will have a long road to get better."

Some moments it seemed Ellie was slipping away from them. Jolene refused to believe she wouldn't make it. They hadn't come this far just for her to die.

80.

<u>8 May 1913</u>

Ellie woke up in the same room where she'd ended her pregnancy the previous August—nine months earlier. Why was she here? Swallowing was difficult, and her neck hurt. That voice... so familiar, so far away. Sammy? Perhaps she was dreaming. She closed her eyes and heard his voice so clearly. She smiled.

"Hello, beautiful."

Ellie struggled to open her eyes. "Sammy? Is it really you?" Her voice was barely a whisper. "What are you doin' here? Why am I here? What's happened? Where's Jolene?"

"Whoa, slow down a minute. You sure ask a lot of questions for a girl who nearly died."

"What're you talkin' 'bout?"

Sammy told her what had happened, and she slowly remembered. "It's been two weeks? And nobody knows we're here?"

"Not as far as we can tell. We've been stayin' inside, only venturin' to the herb garden out back. You girls sure stirred up a hornet's nest."

"I wanna sit up. Can I?"

"Slow. Go slow. You don't want to rip out that fine handiwork Eloise did on your neck."

Jolene and Eloise came into the room, led by Boo. "Ellie, we've been worried sick." Jolene took Ellie's hand and kissed it.

"Well, look at our miracle lady." Eloise took Ellie's hand and helped her to the chair by the window. "You look like hell, but I think you'll be fine."

Ellie's hand went up to her hair. Two weeks without a bath or washing her hair. She must look a sight. "Can I get a bath?"

"Absolutely. I'll have Dottie get it ready for you." Eloise left to fetch Dottie.

"Dottie's here? Thank God."

Dottie came in to prepare a hot bath for Ellie. "Ms. Ellie, I'm so happy to see you up and talkin'. We's all worried sick." Tears flowed down Dottie's face.

"Dottie, I'm sorry you got dragged into this. Your family must be worried sick wonderin' where you are?"

"Ms. Ellie, I ain't got no family. It was just me and my mama, and she passed over a year ago. You and Ms. Jolene's all I got now, and I figure that's more than any girl could hope for."

Ellie tried to stand and was too weak to walk on her own.

"I'll bathe her," Sammy said.

"Be sure not to get the wound wet. And be gentle," Eloise said.

Sammy shooed everyone except Boo out of the room. Sammy removed Ellie's gown, then his own clothes. They climbed into the big tub together. Boo sat on the edge of the bed keeping watch over Ellie.

Sammy sat behind Ellie in the tub and held her for a moment. "I love you, Ellie. You scared the hell out of me. These past two weeks have been the scariest I've ever lived through."

She leaned into him. "I'm sorry for the mean things I said, Sammy. Sorry for draggin' you into this mess. None of this is fair to you."

"Shhhhh . . ." He gently washed her from top to toe and kissed her body as he went. He washed her long hair, careful not to get the bandage wet. Once out, he gently dried her, kissing her again. He pulled a yellow cotton dress over her head.

She sat at the dressing table while Sammy combed out her hair and braided it. "I look horrible. I'm so thin and pale."

"Eloise says you lost a lot of blood. Her and Jolene's been doctorin' you with herbs to build up your blood. You've been in and out of it. Barely eatin', and you ain't been outa bed much at all."

She stood on wobbly feet and grabbed a handful of her dress in her hand. It was at least one size too big. But she was alive, clean, and safe. For now. She would take it.

Sammy helped her out to the herb garden, where Dottie, Jolene, and Eloise were having tea. Boyd and Sally joined them—Ellie noticed Dottie tense up when the two appeared.

The fence was high, and no one could see in from the street, but they spoke softly to not arouse attention. The sunshine felt good on her face. The smell of spring filled her fragile lungs.

"Eloise, this is a tiny bit of heaven right here." She sipped her tea and nibbled at a biscuit. "I can't thank y'all enough for savin' my life. I'm grateful for each of you." Tears slipped down her cheeks.

Jolene took her hand and kissed the tears. Sammie took her other hand and kissed it. Boo jumped up in Ellie's lap.

"You are welcome, dear," Eloise said.

"We need to plan how we're gonna get outa here. Where we'll go. I sent a letter to Aunt Ella in San Antonio. She says we can come there. It's prob'ly the last place John'll think to look for us. I think we should go as soon as you're able to travel, Ellie." Jolene said.

"All of us?" Ellie looked around at the group.

"You want me and Sally to go?" Eloise asked.

"Yes, of course. We're all in this together. I fear John'll find out we were here and come for you. And hurt you. He's ruthless."

"I'm not afraid."

"This is a small town, Eloise. The hotel staff, they all talk. They'll figure it out. It's a matter of time a'fore John puts it all together."

"Well, we know he didn't die. Accordin' to Dayton's letter, they had to cut off his arm. I guess I shot him right at the shoulder and it couldn't be saved," Jolene said. "He's still in the hospital. Apparently, he lost a lot of blood as well."

"Eloise, how long before I can travel?" Ellie asked.

"One more week, at least. Depends on how well you take care of yourself. You need to eat and drink the tea and potions I give you. Then we'll see."

"What must you do to leave?" Jolene asked her.

"I don't want to leave my herbs, but I realize we can't take them all on the train. I have seeds, but we will need time—at least a week to pack things."

They spent the next week packing trunks. Ellie's dresses and Eloise's herbs and potions took up a lot of space. They needed the dresses to sell and the herbs for Eloise to set up shop in San Antonio. Sammy had only a few clothes and a fiddle. Jolene and Boyd had guns and a few clothes. Dottie and Sally had five dresses between them. By the end of the week they were ready to go.

"Jolene, we need to send a letter to Polly and let her know where we're goin'," Ellie said. "I've written it. You need to add what you want, and we can both sign it."

Jolene took the letter from Ellie.

Dearest Polly,

The war still rages here. We must leave as soon as possible. We're going to visit Auntie for a while. John attempted to kill me, and Jolene shot him. He lost an arm, and I nearly lost my life. He will be looking for us and we can't take the chance of returning to you and bringing this nightmare to your door.

Please tell Deannie I love her. I'm sorry to abandon you completely. But know that we will return as soon as it is safe.

"Give me the pen." Jolene said.

Sisters until the end—to protect, love, defend.

No man or child shall come between. On each other, we will lean.

We will kill for each other if we must. Bone to bone, dust to dust.

Toward each other we will bend. Sisters until the end.

81.

17 May 1913 (Moundsville, West Virginia State Penitentiary)

Tom sat by himself in the prison yard, smoking a cigarette. Since the riot, they only let one cell block outside at a time to keep the inmates from scheming. The warden had allowed Tom to start a small garden in the corner of the yard—tomatoes, onions, and lettuce. There wasn't much room for anything else.

Tom sat with his eyes closed, his face upturned toward the sun. A shake on his shoulder startled him out of his daydream.

"Chafin, come with me," the guard said.

Tom ground out his cigarette with his foot and followed the man inside. They walked up the stairs to the warden's office.

The warden stood when Tom entered. "That will be all," the warden said to the guard.

Once the door was closed, the warden came out from behind his desk and shook Tom's hand. "How are you, Tom? It's good to see you."

"It's good to see you, warden."

"Tom, it's taken some time, but I've been able to grant you a full pardon for your help during the riot."

"Ya don't say?"

"*Full* pardon. All charges will be erased from your record. You are a free man, Tom."

"I can leave? Now?"

"Yes. I've arranged for a wagon to fetch you at two. The guard will take you down to the gate. The wagon should be there now. I also have a train ticket for you and $10 cash." The warden handed Tom an envelope.

"A train ticket to where?"

"Anywhere you want to go."

"Warden, I'm not sure what to say other than thank you."

"No, Tom. I thank you. Without your help, I would surely have been killed during the riot. You saved my life, and for that I will be eternally grateful. If there's ever anything I can do for you, please don't hesitate to contact me."

Tom shook the warden's hand again and walked out of the Moundsville State Penitentiary a free man.

The wagon took him to the train station. He had a free ticket to anywhere he wanted to go. California was his first choice. He figured this might be his only chance to get there.

He wondered if Ellie was still in Charleston or if she had moved on to greener pastures. He thought of Deannie. What if she was his child? More than likely, Musick was the father. Either way, she was Polly's daughter now.

Tom weighed his options, then stepped up to the ticket counter.

82.

18 May 1913 (Charleston)

On a quiet Sunday morning while the city still slept, Sally went ahead to the train station and purchased the tickets. The others followed with the trunks.

Ellie put on a simple, dark blue dress. "Well, I certainly never expected to wear anything so drab and plain again."

"You look fine. Besides, we need to blend in as much as we can." Jolene tied Ellie's bonnet under her chin to cover the bandage.

"What's gonna happen to us, Jolene? Will we ever see Polly and Deannie again?"

"Yes, we will. We'll stay in San Antonio long enough to let this die down, and then we'll figure out what to do next. Let's just get outa here for now. They'll be plenty of time to decide what we wanna do after this."

Sammy knocked on the door. "Y'all 'bout ready?"

"Yes, we're ready," Ellie said.

"You look beautiful, Ellie."

"What if I have big ol' ugly scar under this bandage?" she asked.

"You'll still be the most beautiful woman in the world, Ellie. A scar ain't gonna change that." Sammy pulled her into his arms and held her. "Come on, we gotta go. The train leaves at 8:10."

They took every back street they could to the station. The trunks were loaded on the train. Sammy carried his fiddle and Ellie's mandolin, and they took their seats in the last car. Boyd and Sammy sat at the window and searched the platform for any sign of John or Baldwin-Felts men. Boo crawled out of his basket and curled up on Ellie's lap.

Jolene took Ellie's hand. Ellie held her breath until the train lurched forward and pulled away from Charleston. Their journey to a new life in San Antonio began.

Acknowledgements

So many people helped me find my way along the path that led to *Blood Creek*.

First, I want to thank my sweet, beautiful mother, Deanna Collins, for passing along the love of a good story and for being a warrior full of grace. You inspire me every day.

My baby sister, Dionne, and her husband, Thomas Copley. You provided so many details about Poppy Tom, moonshine, guns, coal, mountains. You are my rocks. Also, thank you for being part of the photo shoot for the cover. It's not everyone who will dodge a train for me.

My niece Natalie Harmon Caple-Shaw for being my muse for Ellie and letting me photograph you in the river, on the railroad tracks, in the creek, pretty much wherever I wanted, for the cover photo.

My nieces Morgan Maples and Alexis Fluty for putting up with my insanity (again), making me laugh (every day), letting me bounce my ideas (and other things) off you, and helping me work out the plot knots when I would get stuck. And thanks for those dramatic readings. (Those will be outtakes someday.)

My sister Susan for demonstrating the power of good storytelling from a young age. *Big Witch* will live in my heart (and nightmares) forever.

My niece Amy for understanding that writing is a solitary endeavor. As much as I want to come out and play, the story calls me daily. I promise I'll come hug you more often now.

My early readers: My mother, Bryant Bales, Dionne, and Morgan. Your feedback was invaluable.

Barb and Roby Chafin for the use of your beautiful farm on Mate Creek for the book cover photo shoot.

Brandon Kirk for providing me with a cache of historical documents and articles on the mine wars.

Drollene Brown, a native West Virginian, thank you for my first edits and keeping my dialect and story structure on point.

A world of gratitude to Wandering in the Words Press—Jennifer Chesak, what a force you are! Thank you for making me a better writer. I couldn't do this without you. Michael Mann for your thorough edits and suggested rewrites, confirming my historical references, and for just knowing about the movie *Matewan*.

A special thanks to Tommy Copley for regaling me with stories of Poppy Tom, Mingo County strikes, and coal. You are a wealth of information. Alvin and Sam Harmon for the information on Poppy Tom and Ellie and delicious stories of the mountains.

Thank you JKS Communications and Hannah Robertson for helping me get news of this jewel out to the world!

Also by Kimberly Collins:
Simple Choices

And the upcoming books of the series:
"Mingo Chronicles"

CPSIA information can be obtained
at www.ICGtesting.com
Printed in the USA
LVHW111405230919
631940LV00002B/142/P